THE
TIN HOUSE

ELIZABETH OWEN

The Derwent Press
Derbyshire, England

www.derwentpress.com

The Tin House
by
Elizabeth Owen

ISBN 10: 1-84667-031-4
ISBN 13: 978-1-84667-031-2

Book design by:
Pam Marin-Kingsley, www.far-angel.com

Published in 2008
by
The Derwent Press
Derbyshire, England
www.derwentpress.com

To my wonderful parents,
Tilly and Jim,
with much love
and graditude.

CHAPTER 1

March 4, 1912

Three-year-old Billy slept on one of two chairs that stood in a dingy room. His father, Sam, walked in circles as he nervously paced the floor.

To pass the time, Sam decided to make a cup of char. He put two scoops of loose tea in a teapot. Then, he folded a piece of cloth to protect his hand before he reached for the handle of the kettle that hung above a glowing fire in a black, leaded grate. Flames licked the bottom of the kettle and made the water boil rapidly. Scalding steam rattled the lid, moving it up and down, as it clicked out a merry tune. The fire hissed as water from the full kettle sputtered onto the hot coals.

Sam poured the water into the teapot and waited for the brew to steep. He shivered as he walked across the yard to the brew house to refill the kettle. Knowing the nurse would need hot water later, Sam returned the full kettle to the hook over the fire. He poured his tea from the teapot into a cup that he held with both hands, warming them against the nighttime chill. It remained cold outside even though spring was around the corner.

His wife Elizabeth had been in labour upstairs for hours. Sam worried, remembering that she had a difficult time giving birth to Billy, too. Pacing again, the young husband stopped long enough to listen intently at the foot of the stairs. He heard the midwife directing his wife.

"Come on, Elizabeth, one last push," the midwife said. "Then it will all be over."

"It's a girl," she called down to Sam five minutes later.

"Are they both all right?" Sam called back to her.

"Fine," she replied, "You can come up now."

"Isn't she lovely," sighed Elizabeth in a whisper. Her eyes were ringed with dark circles, and small lines creased her forehead. Still,

Sam thought, his wife never looked more beautiful. Elizabeth began to relax after her long ordeal and closed her eyes.

"I'm going to name her Matilda after my sister, but we will call her Tilly," she told Sam in a breathless, very soft voice just before she sank into sleep.

Sam and his family lived in Bilston, which was a part of Wolverhampton, the largest city in Black Country. Part of the English west midlands, the county produced coal, iron and steel and was named for the rich, dark earth of coal country.

Like most of the town's young men, Sam worked in the iron foundry. The work was heavy and constant. As they loaded iron bars into the furnace in intense heat, sweat dripped from their faces and soaked the coarse fabric of their work shirts. Stretched over bulging muscles in their shoulders, arms and back, the wet shirts outlined their strong builds. It was not unusual for family members to work together in the foundry. There were many father-son teams, and Sam's two brothers and stepbrother worked along with him like most of the workers, they grew up in the village.

After a full week in the foundry, Sam looked forward to Saturday. Then, he worked a part-time job as a coal deliveryman, and spent as much time as possible tending his vegetable garden in a plot provided or allotted with the house.

Two magnificent shire horses pulled the coal cart used for Sam's coal deliveries. The proud black horses had shaggy white hair around each hoof as well as long, white manes. Their foreheads were marked--one with a blaze and the other with a star. Sam brushed the horses until their coats glistened, admiring them as he worked. His extra job as well as growing their vegetables helped his young family make ends meet since Elizabeth no longer worked outside the home. Before the children were born, she worked as a shoe machinist.

Sam, Elizabeth and the three children lived in a tiny back-to-back house in a row of twenty homes. Each of the houses had a small, dingy room downstairs and an equally small bedroom upstairs. The bedroom ran off a tiny landing that was just large enough to hold Billy's horsehair mattress. Baby Tilly slept in a makeshift crib in the drawer of her parents' dressing table. Sam considered himself lucky to have the dressing table. A customer on his route gave it to him when Sam delivered the family's coal.

Elizabeth adored her two children. She called them her "perfect family"—a boy and a girl. She felt proud as she pushed Tilly in her Dunkley pram while Billy toddled along at her side. They took frequent walks and often greeted their neighbours. Elizabeth brought them to nearby buildings, shops and gardens. She liked to take them places, making sure that they did not feel imprisoned in the yard.

It seemed no time at all until Billy started school. Elizabeth was proud as she walked her little boy to school while pushing a curious Tilly sitting up in the pram. Billy wore new clothes, and his hair was slicked back. It seemed to Elizabeth that the years since Billy was born flew by. *"My God, how time flies."* she thought as Billy joined the line of first year children entering the school. While she walked home with Tilly, Elizabeth considered her good fortune. *I am blessed to have two beautiful, healthy children and a hard-working husband.*

The next three years passed swiftly as Billy learned to read, write and do simple mathematics, and Tilly grew more independent. It was time for Tilly to join her brother at school. Billy was old enough to walk to school on his own, and Elizabeth trusted him to watch out for Tilly. Each day she watched them from the top of the entry way as they skipped down the road hand in hand.

After school, they hurried to play in the yard with the other children. Elizabeth often watched from the window as they played hopscotch and hide and seek. She also sometimes heard them singing simple songs and skipping ropes that they cut from the ends of the washing lines. The yard stretched the whole length of the twenty houses, and the children were safe with their many playmates there.

The brew house, shared by all the families, stood in the centre of the yard. None of the rows of houses had running water, so the brew house housed a community water pump, the only source of running water. Each of the women carried water in buckets for use in their houses. The main room of the brew house held a number of deep dolly tubs where the women worked "dollying" and boiling their whites in the big boiler. They stoked up the fire beneath the boiler, and the room grew stifling hot from all the steam created by the boiling tubs of laundry. Elizabeth enjoyed laundry days when she scrubbed and rubbed her clothing on a rough washboard to clean them. She enjoyed "nattering" with the other women, all of them scrubbing and rubbing up and down on washboards.

All of the families shared the eight toilets that ran along the back wall of the yard. Men came once a week around midnight to empty them. They were known as "midi men" because of the time they worked. No one else worked in the brew house, officially, but the women took turns keeping the brew house and toilets clean.

Some Saturdays when Sam finished delivering coal, he came home to delight his children with a ride in the cart before he took the horses and rig back to the stable. He would put clean sacking down before he called the children. He lifted each child easily and then swung them into the cart, making sure they sat and remained sitting neat the front to be safe. Other children in the yard often climbed into the wagon with them, or a few of the older boys hung onto the back of it. Sam led the horses and took care to made walk them slowly so no one would get hurt.

"Hold tight," Sam called to the children as he took the reins in his hands. "Walk on," he quietly commanded the horses, who tossed their heads as they pushed forward and their muscles took the weight of the cart. The children always giggled and sang as they went along, and that added to the festive feel of the ride. Elizabeth smiled as she watched them. She noted that Tilly, who was usually very shy, tossed her shiny, ebony hair from side to side and sang along with the others. She wore a huge grin on her face.

On Saturday nights, Sam usually went to the local pub for a pint of ale with the other men on the street. They got on well together. They had to be considerate of one another since they lived so close together.

One of the children became ill. In the next few days, the illness spread to several more children in different families, but the doctor was not sure what the illness was. He knew, though, that it was serious since the children had high fevers and remained ill for many days. The doctor ordered local officials to post a notice in the yard of the row house:

DANGER:

CONTAGIOUS ILLNESS.
HEALTH MINISTERS REQUIRE THE FOLLOWING:
STAY HOME AS MUCH AS POSSIBLE.
WASH HANDS FREQUENTLY WITH
SOAP AND HOT WATER.

CHILDREN MAY NOT ATTEND SCHOOL
UNTIL FURTHER NOTICE

One toilet was designated for use by the families with sick children. However, Elizabeth made sure Tilly and Billy used a bucket in the cottage instead. When Elizabeth also fetched water for the family she took precautions to make sure her treasured children remained healthy. She followed the posted rules, and she also wiped the tap in the brew house with a cloth and disinfectant before she used it. Elizabeth did not take chances with her children's health.

Sam's allotment was only a half mile away from their house. He grew all their vegetables, and Elizabeth made the family's bread several times a week. They did not use much store bought food. Therefore, the only source of infection she and Sam worried about was the toilets and the water tap in the brew house.

After several days, the children grew bored with the quarantine, and complained about being "cooped up in the pokey house."

"Can we go to the allotment with you," they begged when they saw Sam getting ready to go out.

"Okay," Sam replied, warning, "If other children are there, you must stay away from them." Looking towards Elizabeth, he added, "They can do with the fresh air."

Over the next few weeks, four children from their row house died. The disease was never named, but the neighbourhood mothers thought it was dysentery, a disease of the intestines. Eventually, the illness ran its course and finally went away. When the children were allowed to return to school, they were eager to see their friends and delighted to play outside again.

"We have missed you all," Tilly's teacher said, welcoming them back. There were two empty chairs in her classroom where two of the dead children used to sit. The teacher asked the children to pray for their friends, and they all felt sad about their lost classmates

When the weather grew warm, school closed for the summer recess. Elizabeth packed camping teapots, pans, tin cups, plates, and clothing into sack bags. The children were excited because it was harvest time.

Every summer, Elizabeth and her children joined other working-class people to help migrant farm workers bring in the hops harvest. Women, school-aged children and a few older men made up the group from Bilston. Most of the men stayed home because they were unable to leave their jobs.

Squealing with delight, the children scrambled up onto the horse-drawn cart, and settled in for the long ride. They started out laughing and singing, but by the time they arrived at the hops fields, the rocking motion of the cart had lulled them to sleep.

The children slept together in the barn or in a long shed while some of the migrant workers lived in portable huts made from corrugated tin. Each night, the children laughed, tittered and told stories until they fell asleep.

They woke early in the mornings to the sound of the magnificent cockerel crowing. After eating breakfast and drinking their mugs of tea, they set about hop picking, the dust off the hops flew everywhere. It was hard work, for the money they received, but they loved the open-air living and work until dusk.

"Cock-a-doodle-do!" a magnificent cockerel crowed loudly, awaking them each morning. They ate breakfast and drank mugs of tea before they started picking hops each day. The hops plants were fragile, with lacy foliage that crumbled and blew everywhere like dust. Picking was hard work for the money they received, but the families enjoyed being in the open air and camping out for the weeks that they worked the crop.

The parents worked each day until dusk, but the children ran off to play when they got bored. The adults encouraged their children to enjoy the holiday. Since hops plants grew eight to ten feet high, picking them was back breaking work. The adults toiled long hours, stretching their backs and arms as they reached up for the bundle of pods on top of the plants. The children spent the afternoons playing in grassy meadows and exploring the barns and fields, All of the families enjoyed eating sitting around camp fires. They brewed their night time tea, sang songs and had what Elizabeth described as "good, long natters."

Elizabeth wanted to pick lots of daisies, said. So, the little girls sat for hours making the chains, and then they put them around their necks, pretending they were pearls.

"When I'm grown up I will have a real pearl necklace," said Tilly.

Then, the children chased the beautiful butterflies that flitted from plant to plant in the fields of long, sweet grass.

"Shall we play hide 'n' seek," Tilly asked her friends. There were hundreds of hiding places, but Tilly always hid in the long grass. The others left her until almost last, since they always knew where to find her.

"Why do you always hide in the grass?" they asked her.

"Because I love the way it smells—it's so fresh." Tilly also loved the scent of the wild flowers that grew in the long grass.

All too soon, the hops season ended. The children were reluctant to leave the countryside and their new-found friends. Most of the families had husbands and fathers waiting for them at home, but they still cried as they said goodbye to their friends to whom they grew close in a few short weeks.

"See you next year," they called out as the carts pulled away.

"It's going to be a long journey back home," Tilly said as she seated herself next to Elizabeth and began to cry.

"You will see them again next year," Elizabeth said, soothing Tilly with a hug. She noted that her daughter made a few close friends despite her shyness.

Sam was overjoyed to have his family home. He grabbed Tilly and then Billy in his strong arms. They all laughed as he swung each child around. Then, he hugged Elizabeth. He didn't usually show so much emotion, but his family had been gone for a long time.

After the visit to the healthy country, Sam and Elizabeth sat talking for hours, after the children were tucked up for the night. Elizabeth told him about the people they met there, the campfires at night and the fun the children shared while they were away.

"Life was very much the same for me here," Sam said. "I followed the usual weekly routine work, gardening and a drink or two at the pub on the weekend." They talked late into the night, but neither of them told the other they were lonely when they were apart. They seldom talked about the love they shared.

Back at school, Tilly was dying to tell her teacher about the holiday. She ran up to her and chatted about the friends she made while hop picking with her mother.

"I can't wait for next year," she said, excitedly.

"I'm glad you had a good time," the teacher answered.

When Tilly stood in the shaft of light that came through the classroom window, the teacher saw red highlights in her long, ebony hair and couldn't help touching it. As the child took her seat, her teacher noticed her beautiful, dark blue eyes that were fringed with thick black lashes. She tried hard not to show that Tilly was one of her favourites.

Every Sunday morning, Sam and Elizabeth, who were devout Catholics, took the children to church. Elizabeth held Billy's hand and Tilly clung to Sam. The parents hoped their children would remember these peaceful and joyous Sundays together. They wanted to provide Billy and Tilly with a deep faith that offered joy and comfort throughout their lives

Time passed swiftly as Sam worked; Elizabeth cared for the family. The children studied at school, and the family enjoyed weekends and holidays together. Elizabeth found it hard to believe that Tilly was ten years old. But, she had another birth on her mind as she absent-mindedly ran her hand over her abdomen.

Pregnant with their third child, she wore a long, back skirt that hid her bulging abdomen. Elizabeth didn't want another child, but her church forbade the use of birth control, and abortion was unthinkable.

Elizabeth put Tilly's and Billy's breakfast on the table before them, and sat down to speak with them. "I have something to tell you," she began, a bit hesitantly. She cleared her throat before adding, "Imagine! When you come home from school this afternoon you will probably have a new brother or sister."

Billy wasn't impressed. He was nearly fourteen and would leave school soon. He was already learning to be a cobbler, and his uncle had promised him a job when he finished school. Tilly, though, was delighted and could hardly contain her excitement.

"I will help you to look after the new baby," she promised her mother.

Tilly would have trouble concentrating on her school work because she was so happy about the baby. She wanted to stay home, but her mother insisted that she go to school. As she set off with Billy, Elizabeth stood at the top of the entry, waving to them just as she always did.

"My mother will have a baby today," Tilly told her teacher, who looked at her dubiously.

The teacher knew Tilly was one of two children, but she doubted that Elizabeth would have more.

Later that day, the teacher left the classroom to retrieve a message. When he returned, she took Tilly aside and told her that her aunt had come to take her home. She led Tilly into the hallway where Billy waited with their aunt.

"You have to come and stay at my house," said her aunt. "But, your father will be round for you later." She told them they had a baby sister, but their mother wasn't feeling very well.

"Come on, Tilly. Dry those crocks for me," her aunt said, throwing a soft dishcloth to her after they had the tea.

It was difficult for Tilly and Billy to fall asleep on the hard, cold floor. Eventually, though, they slept huddled together to keep warm. When their uncle shook them awake the next morning, they were startled, and it took them a few minutes to remember where they were.

"Come on, wake up, you two, there's no room to move in here, with you on the floor," their uncle said, in a gentle tone. He had his morning tea and left for work a half-hour later.

"How long do you think we will be here, Aunty," Billy asked. .

"Until your father comes for you," she replied.

Tilly and Billy hoped it wouldn't be long because they knew their aunt to be stricter and less even-tempered than their mother. As the children ate breakfast, there was a tap at the door, and their father arrived. Tilly ran to him and hugged him tightly.

"Can we come home now?" she asked. "I am dying to see the new baby."

"Go outside with Billy for a few moments," Sam replied because he wanted to talk privately with his sister-in-law. Tilly was worried because her father looked sad, and his eyes were red as if he had been crying. It seemed like an eternity before he called them back in.

"Sit down, you two," Sam began as Tilly climbed onto his lap. "I don't know how to tell you this," he said as tears rolled down his cheeks.

Billy and Tilly look scared.

"What is it, dad, is it the baby?" asked Billy

"No," he replied. "Far worse! It's your mother. Something went terribly wrong and she died in the middle of the night."

Both Billy and Tilly started sobbing. They couldn't believe they would never see their mother again. Tilly pictured Elizabeth's smiling face as she stood at the top of the entry, waving them off to school. Was it just yesterday?

Gulping for air between sobs, Tilly asked her father when they could come home and where the baby was.

"The woman next door is looking after her until I can make other arrangements," he replied.

Sam didn't want Tilly in the house, because Elizabeth's body was still lying in their bed. He had spent the night next to her, reluctant to leave her alone. Over and over again, he remembered that Elizabeth had been all right until a few minutes after the birth. He never found out exactly what went wrong.

Tilly knew the woman her father enlisted to care for the baby. She had a toddler about two years. However, she did not know that her neighbour still nursed her two-year-old, and that she was able to serve as a wet nurse for the baby

Sam, who blamed the baby for Elizabeth's death, wanted nothing to do with the child. He did, however, allow Tilly to visit. "You can come to see the baby, but you must not go into our house," he said. "I will ask Aunty to take you, and you cannot come home yet." Sam had a lot of arrangements to make.

Billy did not want to see the baby. Indeed, he had not wanted a baby sister in the first place.

"Isn't she lovely," cooed Tilly as she gazed at the baby named Mary as she nestled in her neighbour's arms. "Can I hold her?"

"Of course, you can," the woman replied, placing Mary in Tilly's arms. She watched Tilly sway gently back and forth, cuddling the baby against her chest. Tilly had no way of knowing she would never see her sister again. All the way back to her aunt's house, Tilly talked nonstop about the baby. She visualized herself helping her father to look after Mary. Her aunt remained silent, but Tilly couldn't wait to make up for the baby's lack of a mother by loving her in a special way.

Meanwhile, Sam allowed Billy to return to home. He was much less certain of his ability to care for Tilly. At nearly fourteen, Sam reasoned that the boy was almost capable of caring for himself. He was scheduled to leave school and begin working at the end of the term.

A few days later, Billy went round to see Tilly. "I've just come from Mother's funeral," he told his sister. "I never saw father so upset." He told Tilly that they gave him permission to leave school now rather than waiting for the end of the term,

Tilly's aunt had softened a bit towards her. She allowed her niece to sleep in the bed with her and her husband even though it was a tight squeeze. "It won't be for much longer," the aunt told her husband.

17

Tilly climbed the stairs on her way to bed that night with a heavy heart. She missed her mother so much that she thought she'd be unable to sleep. Tilly tossed and turned and then cried her heart out until, finally she was exhausted, she fell asleep. The heartbroken child thought of her mother in Heaven with the angels and wished she was with her.

"Come on Tilly, let's have you," said her aunt, shaking her awake a few days later. "You have to get up early this morning. I have your breakfast ready for you."

Tilly rubbed her eyes, washed quickly, and combed her long hair. She sat down to breakfast unaware that she would never forget this day. Tilly wondered if she had upset her aunt in some way because the woman was unusually quiet. Tilly shrugged her aunt's mood off, though, because she knew she was childless and not used to having young people in the house.

"Come here, Tilly," her aunt said, getting a pair of scissors out of the drawer. She approached Tilly with the scissors in one hand and a basin in the other.

"What are you going to do with those?" asked Tilly with fear in her heart.

"I have to cut your hair short because your father's coming to fetch you today," she replied, putting the basin over Tilly's head. "You won't be able to keep your long hair clear of lice, now that your mother is no longer here."

"Oh, please, don't cut my hair. My mother would never do that," Tilly pleaded, running her fingers through her long thick hair.

"Your mother's gone!" replied her aunt, ignoring the child's distress. "You have to pack your things up after I've finished this."

Tilly looked sad as her hair fell round her feet, but she obediently held her head up and listened to the "snip, snip, snip" of her aunt's scissors. Her face was damp with tears that she repeatedly wiped at with the back of her hand, attempting to dry them.

Suddenly, Tilly began to think of going home. She grew excited, and forgot about her hair. Hadn't she prayed that God would help to go home every day for the two long weeks she had stayed with her aunt? Now, at last, her father was coming for her. At least she would be able to see the baby and help look after her. *I will let my hair grow again*, she vowed, silently.

As she sat at the window watching and waiting for her father, Tilly ran her fingers through her cropped hair, attempting to get used to the new length. Finally, she saw him coming up the path.

CHAPTER 2

Tilly watched as Sam started up the path. Someone was with him, and she was dressed in unfamiliar clothing. He introduced her as Sister Mary, noting that she was a nun. "You are going with her to live in a convent because I can't take care of you anymore."

"I don't want to live in a convent. I want to come home with you," Tilly cried. "I will help you to look after the baby and do all the housework!" But Tilly's pleading was not acknowledged.

"No, Tilly, it is all arranged. Your aunt in Yorkshire will bring up the baby, and you must go to the convent," Sam said sternly. "Billy will stay home with me because he is old enough to look after himself."

Tilly has heard about this aunt who lived in Yorkshire, but she had never met her. She simply could not believe what she heard her father say. *"Is this a joke?" My father idolizes me, doesn't he?*

Searching Sam's face, Tilly realized he meant what he said. The shocked child cried and pleaded with Sam as she clung to his waist. "Please, don't send me away, I will be good, I promise. I won't do anything wrong," she said through her tears.

The nun took Tilly firmly by the hand and pulled—actually, almost dragged her—to the car waiting on the road. Tilly was almost hysterical by this time, but Sam made no move to help her as she struggled with the nun. The nun's vice-like grip on Tilly's wrist allowed her to practically throw Tilly into the back seat of the car. The distraught girl continued to plead with her father as the nun got into the back seat beside her.

A second nun, who waited in the driver's seat, immediately started the car and drove off. Only after they started moving did Sister Mary release her grip on Tilly's wrist. Sam waved goodbye as the car drove away, but if Tilly saw him, she did not wave back. She turned her face towards the car seat and sobbed. Tilly was so confused. She was being sent away and none of it was her fault. At that moment,

Tilly hated her father. *What is going to happen to me next?*

Life at the convent was hard. Tilly and the other girls got up very early to begin each day with prayer. Sometimes they lost count of the Hail Marys they said. All of the girls spent every morning cleaning. Tilly scrubbed floors on her hands and knees, rubbing up and down in unison with the girl next to her until her knuckles bled. She worried that the nun who inspected their work would not think it was good enough. Tilly and the others took many a clout to the head from the nuns.

Tilly spent some time studying, but as the years passed she was working more and studying less. Laundry duties, which took several hours a day, were added to her house keeping chores. She was exhausted by the time she crawled into bed at night. When Tilly had a little spare time, she crocheted small items. The needlework reminded Tilly of her mother, who taught her to crochet. She used to love to sit with Elizabeth and watch her as she crocheted.

A few of the other girls in the convent planned to be nuns when they grew up, but not Tilly. She prayed for the day she would be able to leave. She had no idea where she would go, but she knew she did not ever want to go back to her father.

One day the abbess sent for her. "Sit down, I have some bad news." Tilly had heard that before, and she was a bit afraid. But this time, it was her father who had died. Tilly wasn't too bothered, because as he hadn't wanted her. *Why should I care about him?* He came to see her a few times at the convent, but he refused to change his mind about taking her home.

Tilly, who was nearly fourteen now, could not wait to get out of the convent. But she had no home and wondered where she could go. She knew she could only leave with the permission of the abbess. Her brother Billy roomed in lodgings at his girlfriend's house. He had a cobbler's shop in a shed at the bottom of the family's garden and was doing well. However, Tilly had no contact with him.

"How much longer do I have to stay here?" Tilly asked one of the nuns, who agreed to find out.

A few days later, the abbess sent for Tilly. "I hear you want to leave us."

Tilly was frightened because the abbess seldom talked to her charges. Her knees trembled and she shook, but she nodded, answering the nun's unspoken question honestly. "I found a place in service for you, but you will have to work hard or they will get rid of you."

Tilly didn't know what "in service" meant, so she shyly asked for an explanation. The abbess told her she would live with a couple or a family and be part of the staff that keeps the house running well. "Go pack your things together, and one of the sisters will take you part of the way."

It had been nearly four years since Tilly arrived at the convent. She went there as a child and had become a beautiful young teen. She put her few clothes and comb in a sack and thought they looked lost at the bottom of the large bag. Waiting, Tilly sat deep in thought. *I hope they don't get rid of me. I don't want to die.*

The abbess did not intentionally scare Tilly when she said the family could "get rid of her." She meant that the family could return her to the convent or ask the abbess to place her elsewhere else if they were unhappy with her work. The abbess was not aware that Tilly misunderstood her.

In truth, Tilly was a bit scared at the thought of moving, and she hoped she was doing the right thing, There were a few tears as she said good-bye to the other girls in the convent. They were like sisters to her, and she would miss them.

Thinking of her mother, Tilly settled down in the car. She wished Elizabeth was still alive. On this ride, though, Tilly did not cry. When they drove away from the convent and into the country, she became quite excited, but she was still apprehensive. *Surely, it will be better than the last four years.* She smiled to herself as they passed small cottages dotted about the lanes and rode through several villages. *It would be wonderful to live in one of these cottages.*

The nun turned the car into a car park at the side of an inn. "Come on, Tilly, follow me," she said, getting out of the car and walking across the car park, Tilly meekly followed behind her, They entered a small room where a man and woman were sitting. The tall and elegant woman stood up and moved towards them, holding her hand out. She shook hands with the nun, and then offered her hand to Tilly, who shyly looked down but grasped the woman's hand.

"Hello, Tilly. I am Mrs Palmer and this is my husband, Mr Palmer. We hope you will be happy working for us." Those were the kindest words Tilly had heard since her mother died.

As they pulled out of the car park, she waved to the nun and settled into the backseat of the car that Mr Palmer drove while Mrs Palmer sat by his side. Tilly was happier than she had been in years. They drove through a few small villages and continued through rural country for about an hour. Finally, they pulled up at a gate on a road that led through a field of grazing cows.

Mr Palmer got out of the car and opened the gate, and then got back in. He drove down the road and around the bend. Tilly held her breath in awe the first time she saw the Palmers' beautiful black and white farmhouse. It was surrounded by a courtyard and several outbuildings.

"This is it, Tilly," said Mrs Palmer, "This is your new home."

Tilly gasped at the size of the place as she walked inside; totally amazed that she would live in such a nice place. She liked the bright farmhouse kitchen with its grey slab floor and admired the large wooden table in the centre of the room. She noticed that the fire in the cooking range made the house feel homey.

"Follow me, Tilly, bring your bag," said Mrs Palmer. "I want to show you to your room." She led Tilly up two flights of stairs into a large room with oak beams.

There was a double bed, a dressing table and wardrobe. *Is this my room?* Tilly was excited. *A whole room of my own at last!*

"Come down after you put your clothes away, and we'll have a cup of tea and a bite to eat," Mrs Palmer said. "I bet you are starving, aren't you?"

It didn't take long for to put her things away. So she took a few minutes to look out the window. She saw trees and meadows with cattle grazing. *What beautiful scenery!* Tilly had never in her life been in such a lovely place. She poured water out of a pretty, decorated jug that stood in a matching bowl on her dressing table. The new in-service girl washed her hands and face, and then made her way to the kitchen. "I got lost," she said shyly.

"There are many doors and rooms, but you will soon get used to them," replied Mrs Palmer. She served a tea of sandwiches and beverage and told Tilly she would work with two women from the village. "You must be up early, ready to work," she said.

"I'm used to that."

Mrs Palmer said her husband would rap on Tilly's door at five a.m. until she got into a routine, but the cockerel might wake her first. She was to report the woman from the village who would be there in the morning.

"Ruby is very pleasant," Mrs Palmer said. "You will get on fine with her, but she won't let you slack."

Tilly was awake for hours before she fell into a deep sleep. In the morning, she woke with a start to the sound of the cockerel crowing; and for a few seconds, wondered where she was. She dreamed she was hops picking, and then she remembered the farm, and jumped out of bed. It was still dark, but she could just make out the outline of the barns and cow sheds from the window. *I am not dreaming after all!*

Tilly washed quickly and then dressed in the clothes Mrs Palmer gave her the night before. She would have to ask for a pin to put in her belt because the clothes were far too large for her small frame. Then, with butterflies in her stomach, Tilly went down the stairs. The delicious smell of bacon and eggs cooking enveloped her before she even reached the kitchen.

"Good morning," said the woman who stood cooking breakfast. "My name is Ruby." She was younger than Tilly expected—in her early twenties. Tilly noted that Ruby wore a pleasant smile on her pretty face.

"Good morning," replied Tilly shyly. She knew instantly that she would like Ruby.

"The cutlery's in the drawer in the table." Ruby said. "Lay it for five, please." She explained that Mr Palmer and the two cowhands ate first, before she and Tilly would eat their meals.

"What about Mrs Palmer's breakfast?" Tilly asked. .

"She will be down later. She usually eats on her own in the

parlor," replied Ruby. With breakfast was over and the washing up finished, it was time to clean. Ruby told Tilly to start by scrubbing the kitchen floor, and she showed her where to get the cleaning supplies.

"You made a good job of that," Ruby remarked when Tilly finished.

"I have scrubbed bigger floors than this, in the convent," Tilly said.

Next, Tilly followed Ruby upstairs to learn the daily routine. They made the beds, and then cleaned the bedrooms, landing and stairs.

"We have to polish the landing and stairs every two weeks," said Ruby, pointing to beautifully polished oak floors and stairs.

Noticing a shaft of sunlight on the floorboards that seemed to enrich the wood, Tilly admired the highly polished and spotless floor. "It is so richly colored."

"It's called elbow grease and polish," laughed Ruby, running her duster along the dark, wooden banister, as they made their way back downstairs.

It only took Tilly a couple of weeks to learn the daily routine. By then, she was making ploughman's lunches for everyone. It was her job to take the lunches and a jug of tea to the men at their work in the fields outside. Tilly shivered as she crossed the courtyard, as it was still a bit nippy outside. She blushed as she handed the food to the men. It was a long time since she had been in the company of men. In fact, she had not know any man since she left her father.

"I shall be off now," said Ruby. "It's time I went home. By the time you have cleared up, Cook will be here. She's starting back today." She warned Tilly to make sure she cleaned up properly, but she also told her not to worry too much about Cook. "Her bark is worse than her bite," she said when she was leaving. "I'll see you in the morning."

Tilly cleaned until everything was as shiny as a new pin and then sat down at the kitchen table to daydream.

"You haven't got time to sit there!" a voice boomed, startling her. .

Tilly quickly jumped up and although she was quite scared, she managed to speak.

"You must be Cook," she said, hoping the woman did not notice her shaky voice or her trembling hands.

"I am, and that's what you will call me, "Cook said in a stern voice. "Now get cracking. You must start preparing the veg to be ready for tea. It must be ready at six on the dot, no earlier, no later, unless otherwise specified."

Tilly selected a knife and started to prepare what Cook referred to as "the veg."

Meanwhile, Cook mixed ingredients for pastry and bread.

"Have you ever made dough?" asked Cook.

"No, but I've cleaned and did laundry most of the time."

"Well you had better keep your eyes on me, while you carry on doing that, because you might have to do it if I am off or can't get here for some reason," said Cook.

As Tilly started to cut the cabbage up, her knife slipped. It nicked her finger and caused blood to drip on her skirt. Tilly thought the accident happened because she tried to watch Cook and cut the veg at the same time.

Raising her voice, Cook took Tilly to task. "Watch it you stupid girl. Those knives are very sharp."

Despite an occasional reprimand, Tilly loved living at the farm. The work was hard, but not as hard as the work at the convent. As the weather grew warmer, she carried cold drinks to the farm hands in a large enamel pitcher. The men were hay making, and that made her think of hops picking. She knew her mother and brother would have loved the farm.

"Come on, Tilly," one of the men called out to her. "Stop daydreaming, we're dying of thirst!"

Startled, Tilly jumped. She was dreaming so intently that she did not even realize she had reached the men. "Sorry," she said, handing them the jug of cider. Turning swiftly, she skipped back through the long grass to the farm, her lovely dark hair blowing in the breeze.

Tilly let hair grow long again over the months she lived at the farm. She tied it back, tucking it under the cap she had to wear while she carried out her duties. As soon as her work was finished each day, though, she allowed her hair to flow free.

Ruby was right all those weeks ago, Tilly thought. *Cook's bark is worse than her bite.* Tilly quite liked the woman after getting to know her better.

"It's best we all get on together," Cook had said to her. "As long as you know this is my kitchen and what I say goes."

At last, Tilly had a day off, and it happened on the day that Mr and Mrs Palmer were getting ready to go to church.

"Would you like to come with us?" asked Mrs Palmer. "It's a Church of England, though."

"I would love to," replied Tilly. She was brought up in the Catholic faith, but she believed any church was better than none. It didn't take her long to get ready. She untied her hair, and then put a clip at her side parting.

Mr Palmer had already started the car, when his wife got in beside him, and Tilly quickly clambered into the back. They drove up the lane, passed another farm on the other side of the road and then a cottage. These were the only two dwellings beside their farm on the entire lane. They soon reached the fork in the road at the top of the steep hill.

"It is known as Botters Hill," Mrs Palmer said, pointing out a number of large, well-maintained homes on the left. She said the villagers called them "posh houses."

"A few yards farther on to the right is the road that leads to the village," Mrs Palmer added. "It takes about fifteen minutes if ever you walk up here. However, if you do, make sure you tell us first."

The church was smaller than the one Tilly went to during her years at the convent, but she thought it was beautiful, surrounded by majestic trees.

"It's beautiful," said Tilly gazing at the grounds before she went inside. Tilly tried to concentrate on the service, but she sensed someone looking at her. Turning her head slightly, she spotted two good-looking young men staring at her. Tilly quickly looked away. She blushed and felt so hot. *I hope I'm not going to pass out.*

"It looks as if you have a couple of admirers," remarked Mrs Palmer as they left the church. "Be very careful because both of those two young men are about four years older than you." She noted that Tilly might be gullible since her life was sheltered until now. "If you need advice, ask me," she finished.

The next day Tilly described the two young men to Ruby and asked who they were. Ruby said their names were Jim and Bill and that they lived down the lane on the left just before the church. "I wouldn't take much notice of them. All the girls are after them."

When Tilly had lived here for several months, Mrs Palmer took her to Redditch, a nearby town, for groceries. Tilly became excited when she was getting ready. She hadn't been to town and she looked forward to the trip.

Tilly saw one of the young men who admired her in church when they drove through the village. He was pushing his bike, with a bucket and ladder tied to it. He nodded as they passed, touching the peak of his cap and winking. Tilly blushed again. Since there were few families with cars, Jim knew each of the village cars and to whom they belonged.

Mrs Palmer parked near the market to shop for groceries first. Tilly noted that Redditch was larger than she thought it would be. When she got out of the car, Tilly noticed the church that stood in its beautiful Triangle grounds. It included a bandstand and fountain, and people sat on benches reading newspapers.

"What a lovely town," Tilly said.

She meekly followed her employer into the market where they purchased a few items. After that, they went off to Perks Shop for more required things. Tilly loved the hustle and bustle of the marketplace as well as the church and grounds in the centre of town.

On the way home, Mrs Palmer pointed out the bus route. "You will want to go on your own one day," she told Tilly, "but the buses don't run down by us." She explained that Tilly would have to walk up to the village first because that was as far as the buses ran before they turned and went back to Redditch.

One of the farm dogs always followed Tilly as she walked in the fields on her days off. With the dog at her heels, Tilly pretended she was his mistress. *If ever I get married, I will have a dog of my own.*

By her eighteenth birthday, Tilly had been living at the farm four years. Mrs Palmer gave her the day off, and the girl decided to go into town. Just as she reached the top of Botters Hill, she heard the bus drive off. *Drat! I've missed it.* She knew there would not be another bus on this run for hours. However, if she walked up towards the main road, she might just be able to catch the bus that ran from Bromsgrove. Tilly began to walk faster because she knew she had ten minutes to catch the second bus.

Halfway up the road she noticed a young woman coming from a house on the opposite side of the road. She heard her calling, "Hello there."

"Hey," Tilly called back. She had seen the girl, who was about her age, on several occasions before when she walked through the village. The girl crossed over the road, and fell in step with Tilly.

"We don't see much of you this end of the village," the stranger said. "Are you off somewhere nice?"

"I'm going down town, but I just missed the bus at hill top," replied Tilly. "It's my birthday today, and I have the day off."

"What a coincidence, that's where I'm heading," the girl said. "If we step on it a bit we will just catch the one from Bromsgrove." Touching Tilly's arm, she introduced herself as Doll, and Tilly reciprocated.

"I knew your name," said Doll, "Ruby told us about you." Still hanging onto Tilly s arm, she added, "Quick, I can hear the bus coming up the hill." They ran across the road together, laughing. Doll lost Tilly's arm as they climbed the steps onto the bus then sit down together. They talked easily together.

By the time they got to town. Doll had invited Tilly to the village dance on Saturday night and promised to introduce her to other young people there. Tilly felt as if she had known her new friend all her life.

"Hope to see you Saturday," said Doll, as they got off the bus in the village on the return trip.

Tilly was a bit worried about her clothes. She did not have many—just the few things she bought for her birthday, plus a couple of dresses she acquired over the four years at the farm. *I hope Mrs Palmer will let me go to the dance on Saturday.*

Tilly walked out the door on the night of the dance with Mrs Palmer's words of warning ringing in her ears. "Watch what you do, and don't be late coming back." She guessed it was good advice.

Tilly stood outside Doll's gate for ages, then, holding her breath, she quickly walked down the path, trying to get some Dutch courage to knock on the door. *What if Doll has forgotten she had asked me?* But Tilly needn't have worried.

"Come in," said Doll, opening the door to her. "Meet my family."

What a happy family, thought Tilly after meeting Doll's mother and two sisters.

Then, there was a rap at the door.

"Yoo-hoo," called out a pleasant voice as the door opened and Lou walked in. Doll explained that she and Lou worked together, and that all three girls would go to the dance together. Tilly said Lou was a "lovely, bubbly girl," whom she was happy to have as a friend.

"Come on girls, let's get cracking or we shall be late," Lou laughed after they talked for a while.

At the village hall, Tilly spotted the two men who stared at her every Sunday in church. *One of them seems a bit more interested in me than the other,* Tilly thought. She noticed that he seldom took his eyes from her during the services. Her heart began to beat faster, and she started blushing as the two men young came towards them.

"This is my brother Jim and his mate Bill," said Lou.

So, Jim is Lou's brother!. Tilly's heart started beating faster as he shook her hand. He was about five feet eight tall, just about two inches taller than she, with deep blue eyes and dark hair.

Tilly listened as Lou told her about her mother, Jane, who had only one arm. She had lost the other one in a fire, when she was a little girl. Lou explained that the accident happened when Jane and her elder sister Liza had been given half an orange each by their mother. But her sister had a tantrum. She screamed that Jane's half was bigger than hers, and then threw her half of the orange into the fire.

Lou said her mother tried to retrieve the orange, but she slipped and fell into the fire. Her jumper caught fire, and her hand and arm were so badly burned that they had to be amputated just above the elbow. Even though Jane had only one arm, her house was spotless. Lou said her mother took pains to live a normal life.

Both Jim and his friend Bill were painters and decorators, but they also did odd jobs,. Bill lived over the road opposite Jim. He also took his ladders on his bike, but he had a small cart with two shafts attached to each side of the back wheels on his bike to carry his paint. Bill and Jim had been friends since they were small boys. .Bill fancied Jim's sister Lou's friend, Edna, lived near town met Lou and Doll at the factory where they worked.

Tilly had really started to enjoy life now that she had brilliant friends. She enjoyed the village dances for a few months, but just as she learned to dance well—winter came and shut the village down.

The sky was so full of snow one morning that Tilly thought it would never stop. Snowdrifts were six feet high in places.

"We won't be going anywhere for a while," said Mrs Palmer. She looked out of the kitchen window and turned to Tilly. "We need to get cracking. We'll need your help clearing the snow. We all have to muck in because it is vital that we get our milk to the customers."

Mr Palmer and the farmer up and over the road knew they would be frantically clearing snow if they each worked alone. So, they had an agreement. Each of them would begin at his own property and continue up the lane until they met in the middle. From there, they would work together, clearing the lane as far as Botter's Hill. The lane got less measurable snow than the farm areas because it was lined with trees on both sides. The branches formed a protective shield where they arched over the road.

"I don't think we will be seeing Ruby or Cook today," said Mrs Palmer.

Tilly and both Palmers worked hard to shovel a path to the shed. Tilly felt sweaty, but her feet were freezing. Her hands were warm since they were protected by gloves lined with rabbit fur—a gift from Mrs Palmer. At last, they reached the shed where Mr Palmer kept a contraption that hooked onto the back and sides of the trailer. He harnessed the shire horses to it, and the team slowly dragged and pushed the deep piles of snow to the sides of the road.

"Come on, Tilly," Mrs Palmer said. "After they've finished hooking up the horses, we will change out of our wet clothes."

Tilly felt important cooking breakfast. *I bet Cook will have a go at me for using her range.* She just finished cooking when Mr Palmer returned. Tilly passed him a plate heaped with eggs, and bacon as well as a large mug of steaming hot tea.

"That looks and smells good, Tilly. I hope it tastes as good as it smells."

"How are you getting on out there with the snow?" Mrs Palmer asked on entering the kitchen. "We are clearing it bit by bit."

Mrs Palmer sat down at the table. Today she would eat in the kitchen with her husband. She would also help milk the cows, but it was not the first time she took over some of the chores. The cows were already mooing insistently. Their udders were full since they would normally have been milked three hours earlier. The Palmers depended on the cows for their livelihood, and they treated their animals well, keeping them inside in bad weather. The storm lasted three days so they were inside for quite a while.

Eventually, a couple of the farm hands managed to get there. "We got lost in the snow drifts a couple of times," said the one worker.

There's hardly any snow up the top half of Botters Hill," added another. Botters Hill got significantly less snow during every storm because of the arch made by the trees. By the end of the day, Tilly was absolutely exhausted. Her arms, legs, and back really hurt from all the shoveling. She was glad to get into bed, and she fell asleep right away.

The next morning, she could hardly move her arms because her muscles were so sore. It seemed to Tilly that winter would last forever, especially since she worked long hours and missed her friends.

CHAPTER 3

S uddenly it was spring; On a Saturday afternoon, Tilly made her way to the village. She hadn't been there for ages, and she hoped to see one of her friends. Tilly walked to the shop on the hill, slipping and sliding on the last patches of snow and ice that remained in scattered shady spots. But, she knew no one there.

She turned at the top of the road and walked back down again. Nearing Doll's gate, she wanted to call on her friend, but she wasn't sure if she should knock on the door. *Will they think I'm cheeky?*

Tilly gingerly made her way down the path and then stood at the back door for what seemed like an eternity. Then, holding her breath, she quietly rapped on it.

"Come in," a voice called out, but Tilly just stood there until someone inside opened the door.

'Why, it's Tilly. Come in," said Doll's mother, "Doll, look who's here!"

"'How lovely to see you," said Doll, hugging Tilly.

"I can't stay too long," blurted Tilly. "I have to be back to help with the tea."

"At least have a 'cuppa' with us. It will warm you up a bit."

Sometime later, Tilly reached for her coat, preparing to leave. "Bye everybody, "she called as she headed towards the door.

"Hang on," said Doll, pulling her coat and scarf off the nail near the kitchen door. "I'll walk part way down the lane with you." She put on her overshoes and they went out, chatting and catching up on the news as they walked down the hill. Before they parted at the half way point, Doll asked Tilly to try to come back next weekend. Tilly ran the rest of the way home, glad that it was all downhill.

The next week seemed to go by faster since had plans to meet Doll's on Saturday. By the time she started out for village, she decided the day was beautiful even though it was still quite chilly.

Snowdrops, crocuses and daffodils peeked out of the grassy area along the sides of the road. The trees were still bare, but they showed small signs of life again. *How lucky I am to be living in such a beautiful place!*

Tilly spotted Jim riding his bike directly towards her as she reached the corner of the village. Her heart immediately started beating so hard that she was sure someone else could hear it. Jim and Percy, who was with him, were going to patch a roof for a customer. Tilly learned that it was actually Percy's job, but you wouldn't catch him on a ladder since he feared heights.

Percy was ten years older than Jim and lived on the same lane. Known to be a "mother's boy" and a bit spoiled, the older man owned a few houses near town. He was good to Jim, since he often paid him to do odd jobs to keep up his houses and their yards. Doll told Tilly that Percy was "well off.."

"Hi, Tilly, It has been a long time," Jim said in greeting. "How are you? I haven't seen you for ages."

"I know," she answered. "We were snowbound for much of the winter."

"That's the trouble down there, it's all open, you always get it worse than us," he added.

"How is you sister, Lou?'" asked Tilly.

"Fine," he said, and quickly added something that had been on his mind. "The dances are starting again in two weeks time. How would you like to come with me?"

Tilly blushed and felt herself going hot from her throat past her ears as she quickly answerd, "Yes."

The next two weeks seemed to go very slowly, but she could see patches of brilliant blue sky among the trees and hedgerows, and that the bluebells were just beginning to poke their out of the dirt on the roadside near the earlier blooming spring flowers. *What a magnificent sight they will make when they flower! This has to be the prettiest time of the year!*

By Saturday, Tilly was a bit worried about the dance because she was not sure that Jim would remember he invited her. She knew that a couple of girls in the village liked him because Doll told her about them, and she didn't want to upset anyone. Tilly got panicky as she prepared for her first date, wondering if he would turn up.

Tilly set off for the village, but Jim surprised her. He waited just out of sight of the farmhouse at the first bend in the drive. Sitting on the gate, the young man wore his best clothes, a trilby hat in one hand and a cigarette in the other. Tilly's heart beat nineteen to the dozen again. *What on earth will I say to him?* At that moment, she almost wished she had said no when he asked her out. She was that shy.

Jim jumped off the gate, nodded at her with a smile of approval, and looped his arm through hers as they fell into step together. Tilly needn't have worried because Jim soon put her at ease. He broke the ice by asking how she came to live at the Palmer Farm.

"It's a long story."

"That's all right. I'm a good listener."

Tilly started to tell him about her life, but they arrived in the village before she finished. Both Lou and Edna waited just inside the door of the hall. They greeted her, grinned and teased her about Jim.

"Don't get too smitten with him, Tilly, all the girls fancy him," said Doll.

"I shall not," replied Tilly. However, even as she spoke, she knew she had already fallen for him. Edna went out with Bill, and Lou dated a lad named Ted, whom she met at work. The group was complete when Doll arrived with her date, a young man Tilly had never seen before. She introduced him as Bert, a fellow she met at work.

A girl standing on the opposite end of the room kept staring at Tilly. Since that made her uncomfortable, she asked Doll to show her to the loo. Tilly wanted to ask Doll about the staring girl, but just as she spoke the girl came in.

Tilly nudged Doll, who looked up, "Hi, Jessie," she said. "Meet Tilly."

After greeting the girl, Tilly was about to follow Doll out the door when Jessie caught hold of her arm. "Just a second, I want to talk to you," she said. " I saw you come in with Jim, and I had been out with him a couple of times. I hoped to be his girlfriend."

Tilly thought Jessie looked young—about thirteen. "It's the first time I have been out with him," Tilly told her. "He might not ask me again."

After that conversation, Tilly didn't stand as close to Jim as she had before. She didn't want to upset anyone. She enjoyed the group for the rest of the night, wondering why Bill and Jim came to dances since neither of them knew how to dance. Neither did she for that matter.

When Jim walked Tilly back home, she asked him about Jessie. He admitted that he had walked her home a few times because it was his way. "But, there's no romance or anything like that. She's only a kid of fifteen."

They reached the farm gate, and Jim asked Tilly if she would go to the next dance with him. He gave her a quick peck on the cheek, and then she was gone, running down the drive. Tilly was over the moon, as she slipped quietly into the house, and up to bed. She contentedly fell asleep as soon as her head touched the pillow.

The Palmers were very strict with Tilly and kept a tight rein on her. They made sure that she knew her place. Mrs Palmer often told her to, "Never forget where you come from."

"No way will I forget that," was always Tilly's reply.

A few weeks after the dance, Tilly and Jim became an item. So, Tilly was happier than she had been since her mother died. Sometimes she still wondered about her brother and sister, but her life on the farm was good.

Whenever Tilly went to the village, she would get excited, hoping she would see Jim. Once she went to the village shop for a few groceries for Mrs Palmer and saw Jim cycling towards her

"Lou told Mother I've been seeing you," he said, jumping off his bike. "She wants to know if you will come to tea after church on Sunday."

"I will have to ask permission of Mrs Palmer first."

Tilly got permission, but she was a bag of nerves by the time she walked out of the church that Sunday. She had seen Jim's mother in church many times, but they had never spoken. His mother always sat at the back and was first out and gone before anyone else.

"See that you return in a decent time," warned Mrs Palmer as she said goodbye.

Jim looped his arm through Tilly's, but she still worried about meeting his mother. This was the first time she would walk down the lane where Jim lived, but she did glance down there every time they passed it on the way to or from church .

Jim's house was only a few yards down the lane where there was a farm and about eight small cottages. Jim's house was the first of two on the righthand side. As he took the three wide steps to the door, Tilly became more nervous with each step, cringed, and tried to hide behind him.

"Come in, our wench," said Jim's mother "Let's be 'avin a good look at ya." She eyed Tilly up and down. "I expect you know my name is Jane, and that's what I want you to call me," she said. "I don't like being called Missus—it makes me feel old. Now sit down and have your tea."

Tilly's legs were trembling and she was glad to sit down. After glancing around the room, she decided it was a much nicer house than the one in which she grew up, but her childhood seemed like a distant memory now.

The house had windows on both sides of the room, so it had plenty of light. Jane served steaming tea with homemade cakes, bread and jam. Tilly wondered how Jim's mother did all the cooking, cleaning, washing with just one arm.

On the walk back to the farm, Jim told Tilly about his relatives, especially his favourite—Uncle Jack, who was his mother's brother. "You will like him," Jim promised.

Jack lived in the village in a tiny cottage with his wife, Eve, and their four children. In one of eight in a row of terraced houses, it was so tiny that the furniture seemed crammed in, and the pieces often touched one another. In the living room, the sofa was flush against a wall, but it was also jammed against a table on one side. The table was pushed against the wall opposite the sofa and a chair was pushed against that. When Tilly heard there were several children, she shook her head and asked how they all had room to sleep.

"We have been wondering that for years," Jim replied laughing. "They always seem to manage and to be happy."

The terraced houses were very close to the road just opposite the bus stop. All the tenants had running water, but the toilets were outside round the back of them. Often people who waited for the bus used the toilets, but Uncle Jack and his neighbours didn't mind. Village people who had spare newspapers dropped them there so Eve, or another of the women, could cut them up into small squares; hung them on a nail, and use them for toilet paper

Jim and Tilly continued to talk as they neared the Palmer Farm after the tea with his mother. He explained that he and Uncle Jack sometimes took Lilly and her sister May to the woods across the street from their house. Jim invited Tilly to come along on Saturday afternoon. Jacks other daughter and son were older and didn't go with them.

After assuring Mrs Palmer that she had no plans to go to the woods alone with Jim, Tilly got permission to join Jim and his family. When Saturday finally arrived, Jim was a bit late meeting her at the shop. She looked in the shop window, a bit worried that the passers by would think she was loitering.

"Sorry I'm a bit late," panted Jim, out of breath. "I found a puncture in a tyre when I went to get on my bike, so I had to mend it." Tilly waited as Jim secured his bike at his uncle's house.

"Come on," Uncle Jack called. "The children are waiting."

They crossed the road with Uncle Jack and the three children and moved into the woods. The two children kept running ahead, hiding behind the trees, and then jumping out and shouting, "Boo."

The girls giggled as they ran off, their long dresses blowing in the breeze. Tilly could see why Jim loved his Uncle Jack so much. He was kind and easy to talk with. Tilly didn't mind when he called her "Deary,' even though Lou told her he used that name for everyone he liked. Although Tilly was usually shy, she was comfortable with Uncle Jack and called him 'Deary' right back.

Jim and Tilly were together whenever they had time away from their jobs. They continued to enjoy the village dances. Jane invited Tilly to dinner often and the pair spent some time almost every weekend in the woods with Uncle Jack and his children.

On one jaunt into the woods, Jack stopped and sat down on a fallen tree that had been felled in an earlier storm. May took one of Tilly's hands and Lilly grabbed the other. Jim sat down beside his uncle, and they watched Tilly and the girls running ahead.

"This is the best time of your life, watching your children playing," Uncle Jack told Jim. "When your turn comes, cherish it." Looking at Jim to gauge his reaction, Uncle Jack said, "You know, Tilly is a very lovely girl." He pointed to her playing with the two girls and added, "She is so great with the girls that you would think they had always known her."

"I know. That's the girl I'm going to marry. I have been thinking about it for a while."

"Have you asked her yet?"

"Not yet, but I think she will say yes. However, it is no good asking her at the moment because we wouldn't have anywhere to live."

"Does Percy have any empty properties? You've worked on enough of his houses to know he owns several."

"I have been thinking about asking him, but I don't want him teasing me, I always said I would never get married."

A few days later Jim answered the door to Percy, who came to talk about a job on one of his properties. "The tenants are complaining about water gushing down the walls, so there is some guttering to do," he said. "The house is quite big, though. Do you think you can do it?"

"No trouble at all." Jim assured him.

"Come on then," said Percy. "Get your bike, and I'll show you the house."

Until then, Jim did only small jobs for Percy, but this was a major undertaking. Percy also promised "a lot more work" if Jim did the big job well. Percy said he would also ask Mr White, the letting agent, who collected his rents and those of other property owners, to keep Jim in mind when they needed work done on their properties.

Jim took this opportunity to ask Percy if he had any empty houses.

"Not at the moment, but, I will ask Mr White to put you on his list. I can see you are smitten with young Tilly."

Jim was grateful to Percy, whom he considered to be a shrewd businessman. Indeed, Percy often found jobs for both Jim and himself. He knew that Percy lived quietly with his mother; he never smoked, went to dances or had pints at the pub. His one love was bowling. It was ironic that the only Bowling Green in the village was at the back of the local pub.

Jim was repairing the guttering when Mr White came to see him. He knew he had to get this job right even though as it was the first time he tackled anything that big.

"I'm just checking the job," said Mr White. "By the way, Jim, I heard you're after a house, and I have one coming empty in a couple of weeks' time up the Cross. It's not very big but it will be a start."

Jim decided not to tell anyone about the house in case it didn't come off. His mother often repeated the wise, old words: "Don't count your chickens before they're hatched, son."

Two weeks later, Mr White called up to see Jim where he was working. "I have more work for you," he said. "And, here's the key to that cottage I told you about."

Jim waited until Mr White was out of sight, then jumped on his bike and cycled down to the Palmer Farm. He needed to see Tilly. Instead of pedalling down the hill, he just let the pedals go and put his foot on the back wheel, using his foot as a brake.

"What are you doing here?" asked Cook, as she opened the door to him. "You will be getting Tilly into trouble coming here."

"Please let me speak to her, just for one minute."

"What on earth's the matter?" asked Tilly, coming to the door.

"It's very important for me to see you tonight. Meet me at the top of the hill at six."

Tilly wondered what was going on; Mrs Palmer wouldn't be pleased about this. She wasn't usually allowed out in the week.

"What's so important it can't wait until the weekend?" asked Mrs Palmer But, Tilly couldn't answer her question. Mrs Palmer allowed her to go, but she told her not to let it happen again.

Tilly ran as fast as she could. It was no joke trying to run up Botters Hill, especially wearing a long skirt. She looked 'round, making sure no one else was about.

Then, picking the folds of her long skirt up in her arms, she hurried on. Halfway up the hill, she stopped to catch her breath and to ease the stitch in her side as well. At last, she could see Jim waiting at the top of the hill.

"What happened?" asked Tilly, still panting and out of breath, "Botters Hill seems to get steeper every day."

"Here, sit on my bike and get your breath back! I will push you on my bike. I have something to show you," he said. Jack told her they would leave the bike at Uncle Jack's since they must catch the bus.

"There's the bus coming," said Tilly, just as Jim came back from putting his bike in a safe place.

"Two to the Cross, please," said Jim, settling in the seat of the bus.

They rode for three stops, and got off the bus. "This must be it," Jim said, opening the gate to the walkway of a small terraced cottage.

"Who lives here?" Tilly asked, but Jim just felt for the key in his coat pocket and held it up so she could see it. He unlocked the door and they stepped inside.

Tilly noted that it was a lot smaller and darker than Jim's mother's house. In addition, it smelled quite frowzy!

"Have you got to do some work here," she asked.

"No, this is where you and I are going to live," Jim said. He hesitated a moment and then blurted out, "I want to marry you, Tilly. If you say yes, we can live here."

Tilly was astounded! Jim had never told her he loved her or even hinted at marriage before. His proposal was totally unexpected. Without waiting for her response, Jim wrapped his arms around her and began kissing her—slowly at first and then, passionately.

"Please say, 'Yes.'"

But Tilly was stunned and stuck for words. She had not realised that Jim was that keen on her. She wondered what Jessie would say now, since the younger girl often said Tilly's relationship with Jim would not last. But it had already been two years since their first date at the village dance.

"A penny for your thought or thoughts," said Jim, a bit unnerved that Tilly had not yet responded. "You haven't answered yet."

"I was thinking" she replied and grinned. Finally she said the words Jim waited to hear. "Yes. Oh, yes, Jim! I will marry you if Mr and Mrs Palmer say its okay."

They walked back to Uncle Jack's house with their arms around each other. After knocking, they made what Uncle Jack later called a "grand entrance." Jim kept one arm on Tilly's shoulder and pulled her close to him as he excitedly made an announcement.

"Uncle, Aunt, Children" he called out. "Tilly said yes! We are going to get married, and you're the first to know."

That night Tilly could hardly sleep. She was awake for a long time remembering Jim's kisses, thinking about a wedding and moving to a cottage of their own. She also rehearsed what she would say to Mrs Palmer the next morning. .

"It will be all right, won't it," she asked Mrs Palmer the next morning after she told her about Jim's proposal. .

"I will discuss it with Mr Palmer," her employer said. "We can't stop you! You are twenty-one now, but make sure you are doing the right thing," she reminded Tilly that she had no family to turn to if anything went wrong.

"Oh, I am sure," replied Tilly, who had never been surer of anything in her whole life.

She was busy polishing the oak wood landing at the top of the stairs with Ruby, when Mr Palmer called her into his study. Tilly followed him into the room, a bit nervous at being alone with him.

"Will you ask Jim's parents if we can call in on them after church on Sunday to discuss the wedding?"

Jim's mother, Jane, was delighted when Jim and Tilly told her they would get married. She had grown fond of Tilly and loved her like another daughter. "You are nearly twenty-five now, and its time you settled down," she said to Jim, after congratulating them heartily.

"Can I be a bridesmaid?" asked Jim's younger sister, Sally.

"Of course you can," replied Tilly. "You will look lovely with your flaming red hair." Sally's beautiful hair was the same colour as Jane's hair.

Jim's other sister, Lou, who already loved Tilly, was glad for them, "Ted and I are getting engaged soon, too," she said, as they talked about the coming wedding.

As Tilly expected, Jane gladly welcomed the Palmers to tea after church. She served homemade cake along with the perfectly brewed tea. They all exchanged pleasantries for a few minutes.

"You know Tilly was brought up a Catholic," said Mrs Palmer, "So, there might be a problem with getting married in the village church." She noted that the Catholic Church would not recognize a marriage blessed in the Church of England, a civil marriage performed at the registry office either. Mrs Palmer was pleasant, kind and polite; but when she looked around Jane's family home, she wondered how families with more than two people managed to live in such small cottages.

She needn't have worried abut the church, though, because Tilly was adamant about getting married at St. Phillip's, the local church she had grown to love even if it meant changing her religion. "I haven't been to a Catholic church since moving here," she said. "I love the village church."

After tea with the Palmers, Jim went to see the vicar who lived just around the corner at the rectory across from the church. The vicar promised to sort out any problems connected with the wedding. He liked Jim, especially because he knew Jim did most of the work when he hired Jim and Percy to do odd jobs at the church or dig graves at the Mother Church at Tardebigge. The vicar often noticed Percy standing around or leaning on his shovel. Before Jim left the rectory, they set a date for the wedding in two month's time.

Finally the day of the wedding arrived. Jim merely walked up the lane and across the road to the church, but the Palmers brought Tilly to her wedding in a horse-drawn carriage. The beautiful church, where Jim worshipped all his life, was radiant with candlelight and fresh flowers. The pews held the members of a loving family that would welcome the bride as one of their own. Indeed, one of the older members, Uncle Alf, shepherded Tilly down the aisle.

Although she wore a simple black suit instead of a traditional gown, everyone thought Tilly was breathtaking. She wore flowers in her glossy, black hair as she walked down the aisle.

"This is the best day of my life,'" the elated bride said, walking back up the aisle on Jim's arm. The family was so big that it almost filled the church, and Tilly noted that it might take a while for her to remember each person by name. They were her family now, and she was pleased. Their friends Bill and Edna and Doll and Bert were also at the wedding. *I have family and friends. What else could I ask for?*

Prior to the wedding, Tilly had only met Jim's grandmother Sarah, briefly. She knew, though, that Sarah was known to be a hard worker. Tilly thought she had a friendly face—a face Tilly saw repeated in Jim's sister Sally, her granddaughter. The resemblance between the two was unmistakable. *Sally looks just like Sarah when she smiles*, thought Tilly.

After the wedding, they celebrated at the Fox Inn. They ate good food, danced, told family stories and celebrated into the evening hours. Many times during her special day, Tilly cried tears of joy. She didn't want the day to end.

The next morning, Tilly awoke in the cottage at the Cross that the family helped them to furnish before the wedding. She glanced around the small bedroom while Jim slept beside her. Trying not to disturb him, she quietly got out of bed and tiptoed down the rickety stairs. She put the kettle on and washed up while it boiled. Tilly started their first full day together by carrying a cup of tea up to Jim.

The cottage was a couple of miles from the village, so Jim looked for a bicycle for Tilly to ride to work at the Palmers. "It is too far for you to walk every day," he said, before heading to Uncle Jack's shed to see what he could "sort out" for her.

A few hours later, Jim returned pushing a rusty bike.

"Let's see you ride it, Tilly," he said, holding the saddle while she climbed astride it.

"It's a man's bike!"

"I know," he replied, holding the bike steady. "It's the only frame I could get 'hold of."

"That's it, push the pedals 'round," he encouraged, but Tilly started laughing as she wobbled and then fell to the side.

"You will be fine with a bit of practice," he said, smiling at his bride. "

"But, where's the brake?" asked Tilly

"Well, you have to use your foot," Jim said, climbing on the bike and showing her how to put her foot against the back wheel. Tilly looked doubtful as he added, "Don't try this down Botters Hill. Walk down there or you will break your neck."

Later when Tilly arrived home from work, Jim dished up their tea. "Uncle Jack gave me some pig meat and fresh vegetables from his allotment; I thought I would surprise you," he said.

"I didn't know you could cook like this," replied Tilly, sitting down at the small table given to them by one of their relatives. "It smells good," she said, picking up a forkful of food. "Mm, tastes delicious."

"How did your day go?" Jim asked, seating himself at the opposite end of the table.

"That hill's a killer, there's no chance of riding a bike up there," she said. "And the muscles in the back of my legs are really aching."

"They will probably hurt even more when you wake up in the morning."

A few weeks later Tilly approached Mrs Palmer to ask if she could have Saturdays off. "I haven't been feeling well," she explained. "I feel tired out."

Mrs Palmer said she would ask Ruby to look around the village for Saturday help, but she worried about Tilly because she had never complained of being tired before.

A few days later, Tilly was hard at work when all of a sudden she retched all over the kitchen floor. She'd been feeling a bit queasy on and off for days.

"Sit down, Tilly," said Ruby, gently leading her to a nearby chair. "Don't worry about the mess, I will clean it up."

At that moment Mrs Palmer walked in. "I think you ought to go to the doctor's," she said softly. "Do you think you could be pregnant?"

"I don't really know," replied Tilly. "I am sorry for the mess."

The next morning Tilly was in a dream as she walked down the steps from the surgery. She couldn't believe that she was really going to have a baby. It delighted, but worried her at the same time.

Jim was over the moon about the baby, but also a bit worried as well, worried in case he can't earn enough money to look after them. He got on his bike, and rode down to tell his mother, Jack, Eve, May and Lilly. They were all delighted since they loved Tilly, and were always popping in to see her.

"What did the doctor say, Tilly?" asked Mrs Palmer the next day.

"You were right," she said with a smile on her face, "I am pregnant."

"I'm delighted for you both," said Mrs Palmer. "I will have to get someone ready to do your job when it gets too much for you."

Tilly was glad Mrs Palmer had brought the subject up since she felt it was time to leave the Palmers employment, and had been shy about asking to leave.

"We will be sorry to see you go! You have been here a long time and you are a great worker! We will miss you. I'm sure we will see you about. Ask Jim to let us know what you have after the baby's born. And Tilly, take this envelope and open it when you get home."

Tilly couldn't wait to get home. She's free at last—to start her own life. Reaching home, she wiped the tears off her cheeks, and walked up the little path. Then she saw Jim's bike, leaning against the cottage. Unable to control the flow of emotion any more, she burst out crying and ran into Jim's outstretched arms.

"What's the tears for?" he asked, stroking her hair.

"I'm free at last!" she said.

Tilly had forgotten about the envelope tucked away in her pocket.

"At last I'm free after twelve years of scrubbing floors!"

Tilly hardly slept a wink that night and when she eventually dozed off her dreams are of her childhood days with her mother and brother in the hop fields.

Tilly lay in bed next morning, thinking about the last twelve years of her life. She vowed that what happened to her will never happen to any child she might have.

Tilly slowly made her way downstairs, where Jim was at the table, smoking and drinking a cup of tea. He always loved his cups of tea.

"Jim, I want you to promise—if anything ever happens to me, you will always look after any children we might have. Swear to me on the Bible."

"Of course I would! I would never let any child of mine go through what you went through, but nothing's going to happen to you," replied Jim. "Come on, Tilly, cheer up! This is the first day of your new life. Let's have our breakfast, then get on the bus to Astwood Bank to Granny's house, you haven't been there yet."

"Just a piece of toast for me," she replied, watching Jim cut the bread in slices as big as doorstoppers.

As they approached the gate that led to Jim's granny, Tilly was amazed at the size of her garden. It was bigger than the allotment her father had when she had been a young girl. The full washing line stretched all the way down the garden, the clothes on it gently blowing in the breeze. The cottage was similar to the one they lived in, but was very dark at the one end. Tilly blinked at the darkness as they walked inside. She could just make out the huge pile of clothes lying on a sofa bed. She wondered where all the clothes come from since there are only two people living there.

"Who's that?" Sarah called out from a little doorway the other end of the room.

"It's us," said Jim. "It's Tilly's first day as a free woman and we are celebrating."

As her eyes slowly get used to the dimness, Tilly can just about make out the doorway at the end of the room.

"I'm in the scullery!" Gran said. Tilly knows Jim's Aunty Rose lived in the cottage attached to this one; all her three children have left home. "Hi there," the pleasant voice called out again as Jim and Tilly peep round the door,

Jim's granny was standing there ironing. The neat pile of laundry smelled lovely and fresh. Sarah wasn't very tall, about five feet and quite plump. She had a smile that lights up her whole face.

That's where Sally, Jim's sister, gets her smile from, thought Tilly. She remembered that smile from her wedding.

"Will one of you make a pot of tea?" she asked. "The kettle's on the hob. I could just drink a nice cuppa and we can celebrate."

Jim set about making the tea since he knew where everything is kept. He had lived here the first few years of his life and Sarah hadn't changed anything. Tilly poured milk into the cups.

"You can sit in John's chair," said Gran. "He's gone round to do some gardening for Alf and Ethel, they live in Forgate Street. Alf doesn't have much time to do it himself, so John offered to help him. My daughter Liza lives not far from you and Jim."

"Yes, I know," replied Tilly. "I've met so many I can barely remember who's who. How many of you are there altogether?"

"I have had twenty-one children all together, but sadly I lost twelve of them—some during child birth, one aged three, one at six, three sets of twins stillborn," Sarah's eyes brimmed with tears." Then there were the elder twins, they were in their twenties when they caught polio. That's enough of that…" She wiped the tears away with the cuff of her sleeve. "It will take you ages before you remember them all.

"I know," replied Tilly. "I'm confused now! I only really know Uncle Jack and his family."

"My Jack," says Granny. "He's a wonderful son and so good. Everyone loves my Jack. By the way, Tilly, my name's Sarah so that's what I want you to call me."

Jim had been silent all this time. He had never heard Tilly talk this much before. She and his grandmother were getting on like a house on fire.

"I think I will walk round to see John at Aunt Ethel's house. Tilly, are you coming with me?" he said.

Tilly was deep in thought, hoping her baby would be all right after hearing all of Sarah's problems.

"A penny for them," said Jim, touching her arm.

Tilly looked at him. "Sorry, I'm miles away."

"Are you coming round to Aunt Ethel's?" he repeated.

"'You carry on round. I will stop and help your granny. I can come round to Ethel's another day."

"I'm sure your baby will be okay," said Sarah as Jim left for Alf's house.

"How did you know what I was thinking?"

"By the look on your face," says Sarah.

"Who's John?" asks Tilly.

"He's my husband," replied Sarah.

"How come Jim doesn't call him granddad?"

"Jim's granddad died years ago. I have been married twice since then."

"Who does all this washing belong to if there are only two of you?" asked Tilly, and pointed to the pile of washing stacked neatly on the sofa.

"'I do washing and ironing for the better-off people. I fetch it in the Dunkley pram. I take the middle piece compartment off the bottom of the pram and put the washing in there. It's surprising the amount you can get in," said Sarah. "I used to do the Earl of Plymouth's washing and ironing as well, but I can't walk that far any more—it's way too far."

"You used to walk all that way?" asked Tilly in a surprised voice.

"'I did. You have to do these things if you need the money. You don't get now't, for now't, you know."

"'It must be at least fourteen miles there and back."

"And quite hilly in places, might I add. My husband John used to be a gardener for the Earl of Plymouth, that's how I got the washing job. It had to be spot on, though. Look at the time!" said Sarah. "We have been babbling for ages."

At that point, Jim walked back in with Aunt Ethel in tow behind him.

"I was expecting to see you with Jim, when he came round," says Ethel sharply.

Tilly felt uneasy, and blushed. Ethel had been one of the witnesses at her and Jim's wedding, and she was a lot sharper tongued than the rest of Jim's family.

"Don't be too hard on her," Sarah said. "Tilly and I have been getting on like a house on fire."

"Make another pot of tea, Tilly, will you please? We will all have a cuppa' and a piece of that cake I made yesterday."

"We will be making our way back home now," said Jim, handing Tilly her coat.

"Make sure you come again," Sarah called, waving them off.

"You made a good impression there," said Jim.

"I think your Granny's a marvellous woman," Tilly said. "She made me feel so welcome. I felt as if I had known her for years."

"Did you open the envelope Mrs Palmer gave you?" asked Jim.

"I forgot about it, but we will open it in a minute,'" replied Tilly, sitting down on one of the two wooden chairs in their kitchen.

Jim put the kettle on for more tea as Tilly opened the envelope! She gasped. "Look at this Jim!" she squealed, waving a five-pound note in the air!

"Flipping heck!" said Jim." Where did that come from? I've never seen one of those before."

"Hang on, there's a note as well," added Tilly. "It's from my father; it simply says 'Sorry, love, dad.' He must have given this to the nuns all those years ago. Tilly knew her father had been a shrewd man, but never imagined he had money like this. She still couldn't forgive him for all the hard years she had endured. The love for her father had gone the day he had sent her to the convent.

Tilly was pouring the tea, when she heard a tap on the door.

"Who is it? Come in, we're having tea," she said.

"It's only me," said Lou, poking her head round the door. "Mmm, smells lovely, our wench. Got any to spare?"

"Sure I have," said Tilly. She always prepared plenty so they can always use it in the morning for breakfast.

"Guess what?" said Lou in her cheeky laughing voice. She started eating from the plate Tilly sat in front of her "Ted has asked me to marry him, and I've said yes!"

Tilly was pleased for both of them as they were a lovely couple. The pair was always so jolly and smiling.

"You know his parents are better off than us, so they said I can stay at their house until we get married—if I want to."

"And are you going to?" asked Tilly.

"We could save more money like that, and we wouldn't be paying bus fares up and down to work. They live within walking distance of where we both work. After I am through here, I'm off home to tell Mother and Father the good news."

CHAPTER 4

The warm liquid ran down Tilly's legs, as she stood by the bed shaking Jim.

"Wake up, Jim, I think my water broke," she said. "I just had a pee and couldn't stop. It's good I didn't wet the bed, we would never have got it dried out in this weather."

It was winter and snow covered every inch of the village.

"'I have a few niggling pains as well, and the midwife said to fetch her when my water broke." Jim took a match and lit the candle. Then, he lit a cigarette as the clock tolled six—it was six o'clock in the morning. "Okay, I will go in a minute."

Tilly wished Jim wouldn't smoke in bed. No one else in the family smoked except Jim's Uncle Jack. Tilly often thought Jim smoked because he tried to be like the uncle he admired so much.

"The nurse said not to fetch her until the pain was quite bad, didn't she?" asked Jim.

"Yes I know," said Tilly. "Will you check that the fire's okay first and leave the stair door open to let a bit of heat up here? It's freezing!" She looked at the pretty patterns Jack Frost made on the bedroom windows and shivered. "Oh, and Jim, make sure the kettle's full and on the hob."

"The fire should be all right, I stacked it up with wet slack before coming up to bed last night," he replied, dropping his fag end in the piss pot, also called a jerry. He pulled his trousers up, put his cigarettes in his pocket, and lit another candle. Then, picking the jerry up, and he gingerly made his way downstairs, hoping he didn't spill any on the way.

Jim emptied the jerry down the sink, and stoked the fire with the poker, watching the flames spring back to life from under the dried out slack. He made the tea, and then took a cup up to Tilly, who by this time had more pain.

"Here, drink this up while it's nice and hot I just poked my head outside, and it's freezing like the clappers," he said. "It's a good job the midwife only lives round the corner." He said he would "pop

52

in" and tell her Tilly was in labour before she started her rounds.

"You won't have it yet," Nurse Brown said after examining Tilly. "I will just give you an enema and you hold it in as long as possible."

"What's an enema?" asked Tilly, watching as the nurse took a container with a tube attached out of her black bag.

Then she shouted at Jim to bring some hot water up. "I have to put it up your bottom to flush out the muck that's up there, it doesn't hurt," she said, cooling the water down.

"I don't fancy that at all."

"It makes the birth easier for you," the nurse said, continuing with the procedure. When she was finished, she told Tilly that she would stop in to see her several times in the next few hours to check on her, and she advised her to "Keep as busy as possible to keep your mind off the pain."

Tilly tried to keep busy, but she couldn't concentrate—she had never felt such pain. She looked over to where Jim sat in his chair with his cuppa in one hand and his cigarette in the other. *No wonder we are always running out of milk!*

"Come on," Nurse Brown said to Tilly when she returned for the third time. "Lie on the bed and let's see what the little bugger's up to."

She told Tilly the baby would come in "no time at all" if she did exactly what she was told. The nurse also instructed Jim to "make sure you have the kettle on the hob" because "I will need some boiled water in a while!" Jim had remained downstairs and the nurse called his instructions down to him.

What the bloody hell's happening? Jim was worried because he thought he heard Tilly calling for her mother. Meanwhile upstairs, Tilly has thoughts of her own. *If this is childbirth, I don't want any more babies!* She couldn't help but think of the fact that her mother died in childbirth.

Just when Jim thought he couldn't bear to hear Tilly's cries any longer, Granny Sarah walked in.

"I could hear Tilly up by the gate,"' she said. "I will go up and give her some support." Sarah washed her hands in the small bowl before making her way up the creaking stairs." "It won't be much longer," She said as she took Tilly's hand.

"I think this is a big bugger," the nurse said.

She told Sarah that Tilly thought she was going to die the way her mother did and asked her to help calm Tilly down.

Sarah talked soothingly to Tilly while the nurse checked on her progress.

"I'm going to stretch her cervix a bit to try and ease the baby's head out," she told Sarah. With that accomplished, Tilly finally felt the urge to push.

"That's it push! Keep pushing—the baby's coming—it's coming, and it's here," she said offering a running commentary as the birth proceeded.

"It's a boy, guys. What a plonker he is!" she said, proudly as if she, herself, had given birth. "I knew he was a big 'un." Nurse Brown weighed him. "Wow! Ten pounds, nine ounces! "

"Where were you hiding him," asked Sarah. "I didn't think you were that big carrying him."

"You have done him proud, Tilly," added Nurse Brown, finally giving Tilly some credit for her part in the birth.

"I will fetch the water up for you," said Sarah, "and I will get Jim to make a pot of tea for us."

The nurse washed Tilly first, and then the baby. When he was washed and swaddled, she placed Tilly's sweet-smelling, new son next to her in the bed. She finished just before Jim entered the room with the tea tray.

Tilly's face was flushed as she lay back on the pillow. Jim thought she never looked more beautiful than she did at that moment. Looking at the baby, Jim could understand why Tilly had been shouting. He could hardly take his eyes off the baby and he was amazed at the size of him, especially because Tilly had been so slim before she became pregnant. It was hard to believe such a big baby came from so small a woman,

Nurse Brown called in twice a day for the first week and once a day for the second week. Every time she came, she called the baby Plonk, until that name stuck with him. Tilly and Jim named him Ray, but everyone else called him Plonk.

"Hi, our wench," Lou said to Tilly when she came to see her new nephew. "How's little, or should I say, "big" Plonk getting on? Oh, he's lovely!" she cooed. By the time Ray was born, Lou and Ted had been married for a month, and Lou easily confided in Tilly. "Ted and I are trying for a baby as well, but I hope I don't have one that big."

Tilly was ecstatic each time she put the baby on her breast to feed him. At last, she had someone of her own flesh and blood, and she was content to hold him in her arms. "No one will ever put you in a home, my little one," she said to the baby.

Jim's mother adored little Ray, who was her first grandchild. "I can't wait till he's older, to give him a good munch," she says. "Well done, our wench."

Jim and Tilly were the first of their group of friends to have a baby. But Lou and Ted were trying to get pregnant and Edna was already pregnant not long after her wedding to Bill. Doll and Bert's wedding was next. Like Tilly, Doll quickly became pregnant.

"Seems like you started the ball rolling, Tilly," said her mother-in-law, Jane, who was very fond of Tilly and treated her like a third daughter. Tilly felt bad that her own mother didn't live to see her child, but she was grateful for Jane, whom she considered her new mother.

"I don't know what I would do without you," Tilly told Jane.

Because of their family and friends, Jim and Tilly were never lonely. In addition to Jim's mother and sisters, his cousins May and Lilly, Uncle Jack's girls, popped in frequently to do odd little jobs for Tilly. Their elder sister Evelyn was working. They adored the baby and liked to take turns holding and playing with him. .

Lou and Ted now lived in a small terraced house at the other end of town, and Doll and Bert, now married, lived with Doll's mother, a widow. Her house was quite modern with three bedrooms and a bathroom off the kitchen, so there was plenty of room for all of them.

Edna and Bill lived across the street from Jane with Bill's mother, where Bill had lived all his life. He decided to bring his bride home since his mother lived alone. For the most part, they all got on well. However, Edna didn't see eye-to-eye with Bill's mother on some things. The problem was that Edna wanted to care for Bill, but his mother resented anything she did for him. His mother had taken care of him for many years and it was hard for her to change.

Tilly loved being a mother. Perhaps her father had done the right thing for her, if going to the convent and then to the Palmers was the way she met Jim. She would sometime think back to her years in the convent and in service. Although she loved her new life, she still could not forgive her father for all the hard work she was forced to do at the convent. She hated it—hated the heartache she suffered when she lost her mother and her family. She found it especially hard to forgive her father for making her face that heartache alone.

Tilly's work in the convent and at the farm did, however, put her in a good place as far as housework was concerned because she found looking after Jim and their baby a doddle. Most days, she walked up to Jane's house—about five miles there and back. After her cuppa with Jane, she usually popped over the road to see Edna, who now had a little girl named Jan, whom Tilly described as "pretty as a picture."

Other times Tilly called on Doll or their friends called in on her. "Fancy a walk downtown?" they'd say. On other occasions, Tilly walked down town to do a bit of shopping on her own, carrying her bundles home in the compartment of the Dunkley pram. When she went downtown, she usually walked further to Lou's house on Beoley Road. Lou, too, had a baby within a year of her marriage.

"Where do you get your energy, Tilly, that's what I'd like to know," Lou asked, passing a cup of tea to her.

"It's because I had to get up early for so long my body is used to it," Tilly answered. After visiting for a while and having her tea and a sandwich, Tilly said she had to get home to get tea ready for Jim. "It's a long walk home—uphill all the way from here." She noted that Jim seemed to be getting a bit restless because he had been spending more and more time away from home lately.

"What's the matter?" asked Tilly one Sunday morning as Jim opened the door to go out.

"It's this bloody house!" he replied. "I can't get my head 'round it." He went on to say that the small size bothered him most. "You couldn't swing a cat round in it if you tried," he said, adding, "I'm going to look 'round for a place nearer to mother's house, I hate living this close to town."

Tilly felt for him as she preferred where Jane lived as well. Jim had nearly always lived in the country with his mother in the little cottage down the lane. The lane went on for miles and was hardly used at all. About a mile down, there was a water splash where the stream ran over the road. It was quite deep at times. There was also a little narrow wooden walk at the side of the lane across the water. Jim and Bill spent hours there in their younger days sitting on the little wooden bridge, their legs dangling over the water. They tried to catch sticklebacks and other fish, with their homemade fishing nets. It was at the fishing hole that Jim learned to whistle like the birds. He could name them all, and when he whistled, you couldn't tell any difference between him and the birds.

I think I am pregnant again," said Tilly as Jim walked back into the house that night.

"That's all I need at the moment!" he replied." How will we manage in this pokey hole?"

"Others manage okay. Just look at the house that Uncle Jack and Aunt Eve live in, that has to be the smallest of all, and they have three teenagers living with them now that Evelyn had married."

Baby Ray was a year old and walking. He was such a good baby that everyone wanted to pick him up and munch him. He was as big as a three-year-old, had blonde curls and big deep blue eyes—the little boy was everyone's darling. Tilly knew she ought to have his hair cut, but she kept putting it off. People who didn't know them often said he was a lovely little girl.

Granny Sarah Stopped in to see Tilly once or twice a week. When she did, Tilly would walk two and a half miles back to Jane's house with her. With her routine of visits and family events, Tilly's second pregnancy passed pleasantly. She enjoyed keeping house and making meals for Jim and the baby. She also loved being part of Jim's loving family and their circle of friends. Everything but the size of their house was perfect. And, truthfully, Jim was more bothered than she by the smallness of their house and its location.

"Jim, fetch the nurse for me, please," asked Tilly, announcing that the time for the birth of their second child had come. She had made arrangements with Doll to look after Ray during her confinement, and she asked Jim to take the toddler there. While he was gone, Tilly saw a shadow pass the window, and she called out, "Come in."

"It's me, Nurse Wooldridge," the woman said. "You will have to put up with me because Nurse Brown is off duty." She urged Tilly to "come on" upstairs. "Let's be 'avin a look to see what's happening."

Tilly got up on the bed. She had heard all about Nurse Wooldridge from talk in the village. People said she was "a character and a wonderful person all rolled into one." While the nurse examined Tilly, Jim returned from Doll's house.

That didn't take you long, did it?" said the nurse, going back downstairs. "Now get off your arse and get me some hot water, then keep out of my bloody way unless I call you."

Jim smiled to himself as he got the water ready for the nurse, and then he put the kettle back on the hob ready to make the tea later

"Okay, bring the water up, Jim, and make it snappy. Don't come in, put it on the top stair," shouted the nurse. "It's another boy, a beefy little bugger he is like his brother," she added, putting him in a napkin.

She pulled the four corners together, puts the hook through it and then hung it up from scales. The baby was curled up inside the napkin made of terry-toweling.

"Nine pounds," she said. "You have some big buggers for someone so slim, don't you, Tilly?" Jim and Tilly named him Ken, but the name 'Beef' stuck with him for years.

On the nurse's last day of visiting in the second week of the baby's life, Jim gave her some newly laid eggs, which his mother, who kept a few hens, gave him. Nurse Wooldridge was pleased. She brought them home and presented them to Nurse Brown, with whom she lived, like a prized gift.

I like Jim," she confided to her housemate. "He seems a decent chap, and we will enjoy these eggs, won't we?" She wondered how Jim managed to get hold of fresh eggs

Jim was doing a job for one of Mr White's clients when Mr White stopped up to see how the job was going. "Hi there, Jim," he called out, looking up the ladder to him. "How's it going?"

"Fine," replied Jim, coming down the ladder to speak to him.

The rental agent had another reason for visiting Jim. "I have a couple of empty houses so if you're still interested come down to my office before five tonight."

"I will be there with my boots blacked," replied Jim.

By four thirty, Jim finished his work, jumped on his bike and pedaled like mad. It only took him fifteen minutes to get to Mr White's office. After they greeted each other, Mr White offered Jim two keys. One for the old school that would no longer be used as a school and had what he called "a lot of potential," and one a bungalow on the same drive as the school.

Jim cycled home as fast as he could with a big grin on his face. "Come on, Tilly, put the boys in the Dunkley, we are going for a walk." In no time, they were heading for the village where Jim grew up. As they walked past Uncle Jack and Aunt Eve's house, Tilly asked if they were going to stop. "On the way home," Jim answered and kept walking.

"Are we going to your mother's?" Tilly asked, puzzled.

"Wait and see," he replied as they proceeded around the corner.

Maybe we're going to see Doll, Tilly thought, as they neared the Plek, opposite the place where Uncle Jack had a stable.

"We have to go down this drive by the air raid shelter," said Jim, turning to walk down the road.

"How come we're going down here?" asked Tilly." It looks like it leads to fields."

"It does but there's something else here as well," he said as she spotted a huge shed with a little gate at the side of it. Jim walked in front and opened the gate for Tilly. There behind the big shed was a handsome, prefabricated bungalow. As Jim unlocked the door and they stepped inside, the evening sun poured into the room through large windows. "Oh Jim, this is heaven!" said Tilly.

The small kitchen even had running water, and there was a large larder, an ample lounge, two big bedrooms and beautiful gardens. "This is like paradise," she said.

"How would you like to live here?"

"Like it! I would be over the moon if I could live here. This is the best house I've ever seen, and it's right off the road."

Jim scooped Ray, who was playing happily in a bit of grass outside, up in his arms. "Come on, son, we have another place to look at." But Tilly did not want to leave the bungalow because she fell in love with it the moment she set her eyes on it.

"We might as well see the other one while we are here," said

THE TIN HOUSE

Jim, keeping his fingers crossed. He was hoping Tilly would like the other house better since it had lots of ground with it. He knew the place because it was where he went to school as a boy. Jim had been trying to get back to the village for two years. Now he couldn't believe his luck. In his opinion they had the choice of two of the best places in the village.

CHAPTER 5

The Tin House

Reluctantly, Tilly pushed the pram back out through the gate, looking back, and not believing her luck. Jim followed her carrying Ray. "Come on, it's only 'round the corner."

"Wow, look at that view!" said Tilly as they rounded the bend. "It's fabulous, you can see for miles." There at the end of the drive stood a tin house. Tilly had not known that either house existed before today. Fields surrounded the whole of the tin house. And a huge railway carriage lay adjacent to the side and front of it. *How did that get there?*

Around the back of the house was a small orchard of apple trees, with well over an acre of land, and a little tin building in the middle of the ground. Tilly guessed it was the toilet. Jim unlocked the door of the house and they stepped inside.

The size of the rooms amazed Tilly. "This must be the central room," she said, looking around. The room had cracked red quarry tiles on the floor, and a smooth, black-leaded grate with two hobs and two ovens. The one they had at home only had one small hob and oven.

What a wonderfully large room it was! There were six doors leading from it, and Tilly started exploring by walking through the nearest one. It led to the next room, which also had an old cracked, red quarry floor, and measured about ten feet by twelve feet at one end. With a tap coming through a hole in the outside wall, the old, flat sink was shallow at six inches deep, but it was three feet long and two feet wide. There was a furnace for boiling water at the side of the sink, and the other end of the room had steps leading down to an open coal hole with a pile of slack still in the corner.

"I could do something with this," remarked Jim. "I could fill that hole in and level it off. It would make a brilliant kitchen and it would enlarge the room to about twenty-four feet. Just think about that, Tilly!"

Tilly didn't answer because her mind was still on the bungalow.

The next room was narrow, about five-feet wide, but it was twelve feet long. "I wonder what they used this room for?" said Tilly

"The children used to hang their coats in here."

The next room had a boarded floor and great, big windows spreading across the whole front of the room. It was about twelve by eighteen feet and bright with the evening sunlight.

"The view is fantastic," said Tilly, opening the window to let some air in. "It's about twelve feet higher on the outside," she said, hanging her head out of the window.

"Yes, I know. It's because it's built on a slope."

The next doorway led to a huge larder with lots of shelves. "Plenty of room in here for hanging pig meat," said Jim. "It's got the gas in as well," he added, spotting the gas meter standing at the other end of the larder. "You could get a single bed in here easy," he said, shutting the door as they came out of the room. "It's just upstairs we need to look at now."

Tilly followed Jim upstairs. She noticed a large landing and considered it a waste of space. They moved on into the front bedroom. It was a twelve feet square with a roof that sloped down almost to the floor at one end. The room was bright with two huge windows. They proceeded through the door to the other bedroom.

What a sight! Two large window frames filled nearly all the back wall.

"It's just like a picture," said Tilly, looking out. She could see for miles. The tops of the houses look like small dots in the distance—at least three fields away.

Jim joined her at the window and they noticed a farm house about three miles away as well as the forest beyond that. "I had a lovely view from my bedroom window at the farm, but this house is so high up, it's an amazing sight," Tilly exclaimed. "There's easily enough room in here for four double beds."

They walked back downstairs and outside and waited while Jim locked the door behind them. As they started to walk back up the drive, Tilly looked at Jim's face. She loved the bungalow but, she knew in her heart that Jim would be happier living in the tin house. She could visualise him digging the garden, and she began to plan on keeping some hens in the railway carriage.

"I wonder how they got that railway carriage there," she mused.

"Christ knows!" he replied." It must weigh tons and tons unless it was dismantled first."

Tilly looked over as they passed the bungalow, but her thoughts were of the floors in the front room of the tin house. *I will soon have those boards in the front room shining like new pins, just like those at the farm.*

"Well what's the verdict?" asked Jim, as they made their way back up the road.

"Although my heart says the bungalow, my head says the tin house…" But before she could finish, Jim picked her up and swung her around.

"Whoopee!" he shouted. "I'm so glad. I can build a pigsty up at the top of the garden, and a furnace, to cook the pig swill in, and you can have some chickens."

"Can I have a dog?"

"You can have two, if you like," he said, grinning from ear to ear. He asked her to "carry on home" while he called in on Aunt Eve and Uncle Jack. He wanted to tell them about the house and to ask their help with the move on Saturday. Jim also wanted to tell Bill about the bungalow, since Edna wasn't happy living with his mother.

"Great," replied Tilly thinking it would be good to have Edna living that close to her and Doll just down the road. Jim didn't want to say anything in front of Bill's mother, so he was glad to see Bill outside doing a bit of gardening. "What brings you down here this time of day?" asked Bill, putting his hands up to his eyes, shielding them from the brightness of the setting sun.

"I have a super surprise for you, Bill,." Jim said. He told him about the bungalow and the tin house.

"That's brilliant! Edna will be over the moon. She and mother don't get on at all."

"If you want it, Bill, you will have to be outside Mr White's office first thing in the morning, when I take the keys back. Believe me, you and Edna will love the place."

Jim and Bill were waiting outside Mr White's office, before he arrived. "I don't mind who has the properties as long as the rent's paid," he said when they told him.

"I shall build a greenhouse and put a grapevine in it in that garden you went on about," said Bill as they cycled back.

Uncle Jack arrived bright and early on Saturday, with his horse and cart. "Come on, Jim, leave that bloody teapot alone, and get cracking." He urged Jim to start getting the bed and the small amount of furniture he and Tilly owned into the cart. Uncle Jack told Tilly to put the children's clothes and her own into the Dunkley pram and to start towards the tin house. "Call in on Eve on the way, since she and the girls are coming to help you put the things away." He further instructed her.

Tilly knew the move would not take long because there really wasn't much to put away. All of the children's clothing and hers, too, would fit in the bottom of the pram. The children had mainly nappies and one outfit each. Like most of her friends, Tilly washed clothes every day because none of them had more than one change of clothing. She hoped to get a part-time job when she found someone to take care of the children, but she knew it would be a long time until she and Jim had much more clothing and enough furniture to fill the tin house.

Everything was in the house by midday.

"That didn't take long, did it?" said Uncle Jack, who by this time was sitting on the bottom stair that protruded into the living room. He ate a sandwich the women prepared for the moving crew.

"There wasn't a lot to move," replied Jim, sipping his third cuppa tea.

"Come on, Jim, leave the teapot alone," Uncle Jack said for the second time that day. He loved his tea, but Jim seemed addicted to it. He reminded Jim that it was time to "get cracking" on moving Bill and Edna. "I just hope he told his mother he's moving," Uncle Jack said.

Edna was all smiles as she came to the tin house to be with Tilly.

"I came early because I don't want to be there when Bill says goodbye to his mother. He never told her we were moving until this morning," Edna said. "She was not a happy person."

"It's not as if she won't see him again," replied Tilly.

That evening, Edna, Bill, Doll and her husband, Tilly, Jim and Uncle Jack sat outside The Tin House sharing a large bottle of brown ale.

"It's so peaceful down here," said Jim.

Uncle Jack said. "You're so lucky to have this place." The older man told Jim earlier that he wished he had as fine a place to live. He also promised to come back to help Jim with the garden.

Tilly and Jim slept like logs that night. The next morning, they were awakened by the birds singing outside, instead of the traffic and clip clop of the milkman's horse. Tilly decided living there was "absolute bliss." The house seemed to have its own personality, and Tilly always thought of it as an entity rather than a thing. Whenever she wrote its name on paper she capitalized it, so from then on, the tin house became 'The Tin House,' a home with a name.

Jim liked to look out the window at the numerous cows and two shire horses that grazed in the field that belonged to the farmer down the road. Jim noticed them earlier in the week when he rode his bike past the farm. He called Tilly to the window to see wild rabbits playing amongst the moon daisies in the meadow just beyond the field.

"I love it, Jim." she sighed. "It's like living on our own on an island." Tilly had no desire to go anywhere else. She had what she wanted—a good husband and two healthy boys. *We could isolate ourselves here if we wanted to.*

Edna felt just as happy in her bungalow with Bill. She asked Bill to make a hole in the hedge by their house so that Edna could see The Tin House and walk across Jim's garden to see Tilly. Later Edna and Bill also made the hedge lower so that they could see more of the view across the fields and up to the woods.

"The soil's not bad, needs a bit of soot and ashes on it, though," said Uncle Jack, as he dug by Jim's side. He noted that the digging was hard work after they had put in a full day at their jobs.

"It's hard for me, and I'm twenty years younger than you," said Jim. "We will do a couple more rows then call it a day. Are you going to have a cuppa with me after?"

"I sure am."

Jim knew that Uncle Jack wouldn't go home until after dark, as he, like the rest of the family, fell in love with The Tin House and everything that surrounded it. In fact, he spent more and more time there as the weeks went on. Uncle Jack always sat on the bottom stair, his cup in one hand, a rolled up cigarette in the other, smoking his ciggie right down. He even stuck a pin in the last bit, and smoked it until it fell off the pin, letting the tiny pieces of 'backy' that were left fall in his 'backy' tin. He never wasted a grain of tobacco.

The garden was finished at last, planted with all sorts of vegetables. Jim left the two beautiful lilacs and gooseberry bushes alone. He also left a small plot of garden for Tilly, who wanted to plant some gladioli, her favourite flowers. Tilly thoroughly enjoyed the scent of lilacs that wafted into the house on the breeze while they were in bloom.

By the time a few months passed. Tilly and Edna deepened their friendship until they felt like sisters. Tilly was always making pastry or some sort of pies—apple or gooseberry. She also made jam tarts, and Edna, who enjoyed the desserts, was often a guest at The Tin House.

One day Edna announced her second pregnancy. Her first child, Jan, played everyday with Ray and they got on well together. Doll, whom Tilly loved, was still Tilly's best friend, and she was always happy when Doll came to visit.

"Every time I come down here you're on your hands and knees scrubbing the floors, surely they don't need doing every day," Doll scolded. "Do they?"

"I have to keep them clean Ken has started crawling now," replied Tilly.

Jim's veggies were coming up well so he and Uncle Jack hoed in between the rows every night and on the weekends, digging the garden of all the weeds and banking the potatoes up as they worked.

But the garden wasn't the only thing that kept Jim busy. He still worked long hours as a handy man, and he had dreams of starting a small farm. He arrived home from market one day with a crate of day-old chicks tied to the back of his saddle.

"We will put them in a bigger box, and keep them by the fire," he told Tilly, taking them into the house. "Then, when they're a month old, they can go in the little side room to keep warm." After they were a few months old, Jim planned to put the chickens in the railway carriage just as Tilly envisioned months ago when they first saw The Tin House.

"There are fifty," Jim continued. "I don't know how many will be pullets or cocks, but it doesn't matter the pullets will lay and I can sell the cockerels at Christmas." He looked forward to having all the veggies and eggs they needed, and he planned to sell any surplus.

Uncle Jack had his pick as well, because he worked as hard as Jim did in the garden. However, a great deal of space still remained in the front of "The Tin House.' Jim already planted four large garden plots—more than enough for him, Uncle Jack, and their friends with surplus to sell.

The tin toilet was about forty feet away from the front of the house and about eighty feet of spare land ran past that. Uncle Jack proposed that they build a couple of pig sties there. "I will pay for the materials if you will build the sties," he said, "But don't tell Aunt Eve I gave you the money.' They decided to build the sties up at the top, and the furnace between the sty's and the toilet.

When the materials arrived, Jim started building at once, using every bit of his spare time until at last it was finished. Jim was quite pleased with the sties. This was the biggest project he had ever tackled, and Uncle Jack was impressed as well.

"You did well there, Jim," he said. "You know, the next move is to buy the sows, so we must go to pig auction at Bromsgrove."

"Those two will do," said Uncle Jack, days later in Bromsgrove, as he pointed at two young sows and put in his bid. Jim knew his uncle had done this many times before.

He had always kept a pig in his stable, but now he bought another horse, so he'd no longer has room for a pig.

After doing the deal and arranging to get the sows to The Tin House, Jack looked 'round for Jim. He smiled to himself thinking that Jim had been gone for half an hour now. He knew just where to look and made his way to the beer tent.

"I thought I would find you here," he said.

"Only having an 'arf," replied Jim.

Some people in the village used to keep their potato peelings, stale bread, and other leftovers for Uncle Jack, who used to boil it up in galvanised buckets on the hob in the tiny cottage where he lived. But, now they had a first-class operation. They had the furnace at The Tin House.'

Jim and Jack fetched scraps from people in the village in sack bags. They slung the bags on their bikes and took them to The Tin House and threw it into the furnace. The aroma of the pig slop cooking was quite good. They allowed it to cool a bit and then scooped it out with a big ladle into buckets and mixed in some meal. Tilly thought it looked and smelled surprisingly good—almost good enough for people to eat.

It wasn't long before both sows were in pig and due to produce farrows, or litters of pigs. "Keep your eyes on the sows for me, will you please, Tilly," Jim called out, jumping on his bike. "Jack and I are putting a farrowing rail up tonight, to stop them from rolling on the piglets."

Tilly went up to the sties a few days later, Ray and Ken toddling behind her, and the chickens behind them. Tilly picked her two children up. One pig came out of the sty into the run, grunting.

"Shush," said Tilly, to her two boys. "I think the other one had her piglets I can hear squealing' going on. We will go and find Dad he's only working down the road."

She put both boys in the pram. Ray was a bit big for a pram, but it was quicker than allowing him to walk. Tilly was in a hurry. She wanted Jim to check the piglets as soon as possible.

She had ten, but two of them are dead," said Jim, going into the house. "She must have rolled over on them but there are eight left—not bad for her first time." Jim warned Tilly not to go near the sow even though he made sure she was positioned so that her teats were under the rail. "I don't want her disturbed."

A few days later, the other sow's piglets were born as well. She had eleven but lay on two, so that left Jim and Jack with seventeen piglets two of them for fattening and killing, the rest to be sold at market.

The piglets grew quickly and they were soon ready for market. Uncle Jack and Jim agreed that they would split the money they made on the pigs. "Come on, Jim, leave that bloody teapot alone," said Uncle Jack, poking his head in the kitchen door. "The truck's coming." Tilly held her two children while the truck backed its way towards the pigsty.

"We are going to have a job separating the pigs, keep the children out of the way," Jack warned.

"I'm taking them inside," she replied, knowing there would be some bad language flying about. At last, the pigs and their owners were off.

Mr Tomlinson was scheduled to come the next day, a day Tilly had been dreading, to kill the remaining two pigs, Tilly was so attached to the pigs that she cried at the thought of killing "her pigs." She wiped a tear from her eye, while Jim shrugged his shoulders.

"That's what we bred them for, you knew that," Jim said. "I don't think I will be able to eat any of it," she replied.

"You ate it before when we have had it from Uncle Jack."

"I know, but I never saw them when they were alive."

"That's the way it goes, Tilly it's the best way to get on and survive."

When Tilly heard the sound of the motorcar she knew it was Mr Tomlinson coming to slaughter the two pigs. She cringed as she heard the sharp click of the stun gun, and next minute the straw was ablaze, burning the hairs off the pigs. Tilly could smell burning, then, she heard hissing as water was thrown on the fire to douse it. They didn't want the meat to start cooking.

Tilly heard a repetitive noise as they scrubbed the pigs clean. After a few more minutes, Jim came into house with a bucket of chitlings, small intestines of pigs that were cooked and eaten as food, and some trotters, cooked pigs feet, for the children to suck on.

"Come on, Tilly, pull yourself together, we still have a lot to do, and we need you to clean these chitlings. Must I wash and plait them, too?"

Tilly sat staring at the bucket in front of her and another clean bucket half full of water by her side. She prayed that she wouldn't be sick as she started to wash them. They felt slimy when she tipped them into the water, and she shuddered.

If that wasn't enough to turn Tilly's stomach, the sight of her husband, his uncle and Mr Tomlinson struggling into the kitchen carrying the dead pigs could have been.

"Leave that a minute, there's a good girl," said Mr Tomlinson. "I will show you how to plait them after we have hung these pigs up."

Tilly had scrubbed the red quarry tiles until they were spotless and strewed sawdust over them earlier on in the day. Jim was putting hooks up through the ceiling, getting ready to hang the pigs. They would have to hang for a few days before Mr Tomlinson returned to cut the meat up.

"This is how it's done," he said, sitting beside Tilly, showing her how to plait the chitlings. "Here, you try." Tilly soon got the hang of it.

"Who's going to eat these?" she asked Jim.

"Not us, I wouldn't eat them to save my life. I know mother will have some, she loves chitlings, and so do a lot of other people."

"I'm off now. I will show you how to make the lard when I come back," said Mr Tomlinson. "You have plenty of rosemary in the garden, don't you? We will need plenty of that."

Mr Tomlinson came back in a couple of days to show Tilly how to make the lard, which smelled delicious as it was melting over the heat on the hob, the aroma of rosemary twirling all through the house. "We will have some on toast when it's set. You can't beat toast done by the fire with homemade lard on, it's gorgeous," the butcher said.

The hired butcher started to cure the hams and sides of bacon before he wrapped muslin all 'round them. Mr Tomlinson finally left them to hang up in the pantry where Jim would be able to slice some off for breakfast every day. Uncle Jack, too, would come to The Tin House to fetch his share because he had no room to store it at home. The chops and joints were cut up.

Uncle Jack and Jim planned to share a lot of their meat with the people in the village who saved pigswill for them. Elsie and Sam lived at the top of the drive on the right hand side of the road. They never seemed to laugh or smile and they looked as if they were getting on a bit. Tilly reckoned Elsie couldn't be any more than fifty, even though she looked years older. She was a little thin woman, who always looked worried. Jim felt sorry for Elsie, he reckoned she had a bit of a rough time with Sam.

"'Av you any spare pig meat, please?" she asked as Jim opened the door. Jim knew it was Elsie he has seen her walk past the window.

"Come in a minute, Elsie," replied Jim, "I will get you some."

Tilly smiled to herself Jim was such a soft touch. Elsie and Sam had geese in a pen up in their garden, which they fed their scraps to, so she wasn't really entitled to any pig meat. Sam's geese were kept in a tiny run and were absolutely filthy. You couldn't see what colour they were for mud.

Tilly and Jim had geese, too. But their geese were allowed to roam on the land. They were as good as guard dogs, cackling like mad if anyone came down the drive. Tilly always knew if someone was about. The postman, however, feared them and left the post at Edna and Bill's—not that Jim and Tilly never had much post anyway—all they seemed to get were bills. "Do you want these chitlings, Mother?" asked Jim.

"Yes, please, we would love them I will take some for my mother as well."

"I know Sarah loves them, she told me," said Tilly.

Jane took the chitlings from the pail, popped them into a covered dish and promised to bring the dish back the next day.

Tilly had named one of her hens Henrietta and the hen followed Tilly just about everywhere she went when she was outside in the yard. Henrietta didn't lay her eggs in the hen house with the others either. She laid them on the back porch as if they were presents for Tilly.

Tilly was hanging the washing on the line with the two boys hanging on her skirt and Henrietta pecking at her feet. She heard someone calling and looked up to see Edna waving from across the yard.

"Quick, Tilly!" she cried out. Tilly picked up the boys and ran across the garden to the bungalow. "I need the nurse quick!" said Edna. "Leave the children here and run to the phone box, and ring the nurse."

Tilly was back in no time instructing Edna to get into bed while she put the kettle on the hob. The nurse arrived just in time to take over as Tilly waited in the kitchen where the boys and Edna's Jan played. In less than a half hour, Nurse Woodridge came out of the bedroom. "You two should do a swap," she said, laughing. "It's a girl."

Bill was shocked when he came home to a new baby. He had only been gone a couple of hours. "Bloody hell, Edna! You didn't hang about, did you?"

They named the baby Jill, and eight months later Tilly gave birth to her first little girl, whom she immediately named Elizabeth after her mother. Soon, though, the baby's name was shortened to Eliza. Tilly was chuffed with two boys and a girl, she really felt she had the perfect family, and she did not want more children. *That's it —now I am content!*

Tilly dressed the children and then put her new baby and Ken into the Dunkley pram. She was off for a walk to see Jane, but she would stop at Edna's house on her way up the drive.

"I am going to Jim's mother's house for a walk do you fancy coming with me?" Tilly knew Edna liked Jane.

"Hang on a minute," replied Edna. "I will have to call in at Bill's mother's house first and show my face," she said as they start walking. "We could walk all the way 'round the village after we leave Jane's, it's such a lovely day."

Both Ray and Jan were only four years old so they took turns sitting on the bottom of Edna's pram. With Eliza and Ken in Tilly's pram, there was no more room.

Edna didn't stay very long at Bill's mother's house and she was soon over to Jane's where Tilly visited for a longer time with Jane. When Edna came in, Jane welcomed her and poured them all another cuppa tea. Finally Tilly stood up. "We should be off now," she said after thanking Jane for the tea and cake. Tilly reached for her jacket and Jane helped her get the children back into their coats, and they were ready to go. "It's such a lovely day we are going to walk all the way round past the church. It is so pretty in the yard there."

"Hang on," said Jane, donning her jacket, too. "I think I will come with you, the fresh air will do me good." They passed the vicar as they walk by the church

"Afternoon, Vicar," said Jane, then they carried on round down by the little stream with the little bridge over it. The three of them stopped to show the little ones over the bridge picking the little ones up to see the water rippling over the pebbles, which lay on the bed of the stream. They just stood there looking and listening to the sound of the running water and the birds singing. Tilly wondered if Jim used to stand here when he was a boy. She would remember to ask him when she got home

They continued down the little hill to the end of the lane opposite the site where The Old Fox and Goose Inn, used to stand before it was knocked down. Their walk took them up the main road to the final hill where the posh houses stood. Tilly remembered that the other half of the moneyed people lived there. They took a right turn and were on the home stretch—Heathfield Road, where the bungalow and The Tin House stood. The two women parted as they came to Edna's gate, and Tilly continued down the drive home with Jane and her three tired, but happy children. When they got into the kitchen, Tilly sat down to nurse the baby while Jane made tea.

"I really enjoyed that walk," said Tilly.

"So did I. I've always enjoyed walking that way."

Both Ray and Ken, who climbed onto the old tatty settee, were asleep, so the women had time to talk. As they talked Jane peeled potatoes for dinner, but she didn't stay to eat. "I will do these for you and then I'll be off," she said.

Tilly was still amazed at how fast Jane could peel potatoes and do all sorts of things with her one arm. She often thanked God for her mother-in-law, whom she now considered to be almost like a true mother to her.

The next day, Tilly called for Edna and they walked to St Luke's School at the Cross to put Jan and Ray's names on the register. "His name is John," Tilly stated, even surprising herself. She could not think why she said that, but she decided it just sounded better than Ray. John was his middle name, and his grandmother always called him little Johnnie.

When the children started school Tilly and Edna took turns taking them to school, and a few months later Doll's son started school, too. Then, all three mothers took turns bringing the children to and from school.

One night Jim came home and made a confession to Tilly, "I have been borrowing money from my mother, and she needs it back."

"Why did you have to borrow? You have had plenty of work," Tilly replied, but she knew the answer to her own question. Jim was a soft touch and he allowed people to pay him later for pig meat and farm produce. How often had she heard someone say, "Can you do me a favor? Can I pay you later?"

"I'm thinking about going to Bromsgrove tonight," he told Tilly, explaining that he had an idea. He outlined his plan of approaching the owners of the pubs to see if he could entertain people with his whistling. "No one knows me there. They don't know what I can do."

That night Jim dressed up in his best suit and cap. Tilly thought he looked quite handsome. "Wish me luck," he called out to her as she stood outside the door with the children, waving him off.

"Okay, let's hear you," said the owner of the first pub.

Jim started whistling, and the man couldn't believe his ears. Jim sounded just like Ronnie Renaldo, a well-known entertainer of the time.

"You can start tonight," he said.

It was Saturday night and the pub was packed, but Jim was a complete bag of nerves. However, he needn't have worried. They loved him! He was a huge success. When he came in that night he had placed his cap on a table, and people began putting money in it. Jim did not expect the pub owner to pay him, too, but the did pay him, saying. "You were great. Don't forget to come again next Saturday."

Jim was chuffed, for when he picked his cap up there was lots of money in it. Running for the last bus, he just managed to jump on as it left the station. Tilly was fast asleep when he got back, so he quietly crept into bed.

The next morning Tilly was up early as usual, and the baby wanted feeding and changing. Making herself a cup of tea, she sat down to feed Eliza. Tilly sat, quietly humming to herself, idly looking 'round the room, until she suddenly spotted the money on the table. *Where on earth did all that come from? I hope Jim didn't do anything daft.*

Jim came into the kitchen carrying the bucket. A jerry was no good for him when he's been drinking. When he saw Tilly, though, a smile lit his face from ear to ear.

"How about that for a night's whistling?" he asked, adding, "I want you to go down town Monday to treat yourself to something new to wear."

"Wow, thanks, Jim. I've never seen so much money. You can pay your mother back now." Not one to dwell on any situation, Tilly moved on. She asked him to help her clean up because she expected his sister and brother-in-law Lou and Ted and their little ones.

First, he had his pot of tea and a rasher of bacon on his toast. Then, Jim picked the broom up and started sweeping. He quite liked housework. He and Tilly looked forward to a pleasant afternoon, and Lou and her family soon arrived with a hamper full of goodies as usual.

Lou, Ted, and their little one all came up on Ted's motorbike and sidecar. Tilly wished Jim would get a job like Ted had since he and Lou always seemed to have money.

"Come on, let's all go to the field," said Tilly, getting a couple of old coats for them to sit on. They would enjoy the scenery while the children played tag and made daisy chains.

"Do you like butter?" Tilly asked her little child, holding a buttercup under her chin. She watched the golden glow reflected back as the brilliant sunshine shines on it.

"Yes you do," she said, cuddling the baby to her breast.

The two men took the older children over to the forest, three fields away.

"Pick some mushrooms from under the rook trees on the way back, will you,"

Tilly called out to them. Tilly and Lou watched until they became little specks in the distance. Later, as they made their way back, the smaller children ran down the hill to meet them.

Jim and Ted held their arms out to them, scooping the toddlers up and twirling them 'round.

Another day, Tilly and Doll were taking their children for a walk when two women, who were walking the opposite way, stopped and started talking to Doll. The two women were village people, and they completely ignored Tilly, as if she wasn't there. This had happened on occasion before.

"What's up with them?" asked Tilly. Surely, people have accepted her by now she's been living on the village twelve years.

"Take no notice," said Doll. "They just think they are better than anybody else."

Tilly knew it must be some other reason, but she didn't know what! She thought it might be because she lived in The Tin House. Anyway, they could please themselves she was all right with the friends she had. And as long as she had them and Jim's family, she didn't give a hoot.

Jessie got married at last, and she and her husband Pete started coming down to The Tin House along with the others. Tilly was still a bit dubious about Jessie's husband. *Gosh, where did she get him from. He talks so posh?*

Tilly thought he would have been too posh to talk to them she still had a broad Black Country accent. Pete turned out to be a kind and polite man. Tilly worried though a bit about Jessie when Jim was around. She could not help believing that Jessie might still be a flirt who would let a bloke know if she fancied him. She realized that Pete seemed secure with Jessie, but she still wasn't entirely comfortable with her earlier rival. Eventually, though, Tilly began to like Jessie—she turned out to be funny and kind, and she provided them with many a good laugh.

"Another bloody boy!" said Nurse Wooldridge, coming out of the bedroom. It was the nurse's last day of calling in on Tilly.

Today, Jim passed her the new-laid eggs that were his gift to her on such occasions.

"Do you want to book me up for next year, Jim? Or are you going to tie a knot in it?" asked the nurse, putting her black bag on the back of her bike.

Jim smiled. They had named the new baby "Derek"

"It's a good thing we chose The Tin House to live in, isn't it? Otherwise we'd be out of room by now," said Jim.

CHAPTER 6

Tilly and Jim were eating their tea when Aunt Ethel walked in. "I'm here to do a deal with you," she said in her matter-of-fact voice. "I don't really know how to say this, but Alf and I have a lot more money than you two."

"Spit it out!" said Jim. "'We're not mind readers."

"Alf and I have been thinking a lot about this. We can't have children so we are wondering if you will let us have either Eliza or the new baby. It seems that you two can breed like rabbits."

"Over my dead body!" screamed Tilly, standing up. "Piss off and get out of my house!"

This was the first time Tilly ever swore in her whole life. Aunt Ethel was shocked. She actually thought Tilly and Jim would let her have one of their babies. After all Tilly had gone through in her childhood, there was no way she would allow anyone to have one of her babies.

"We will pay you," added Ethel, thinking Tilly had not understood her bargain.

"Just go home and leave us alone," Tilly replied. She wanted nothing more to do with Aunt Ethel even though she loved most of the members of Jim's family as if they were her own flesh and blood. Until now, all of them were always welcome at The Tin House.

Uncle Jack's daughter May, for example, often came 'round. She pitched right in, helping with whatever needed doing. She would wash or dry dishes, fold or iron laundry, soothe a cranky child, read stories or play with her young cousins.

"Everybody says you were born with a round arse, May," said Tilly, meaning that May was always up and doing things—often for others—rather than sitting.

May didn't know what they were talking about, and she didn't care either. She just liked working. Her sister Lilly had finished school and was working, but she still came to see Tilly and the children most nights. Of course, Uncle Jack, who continued to be Jim's partner, also came every night to help with the pigs and gardening.

When little Derek was three years old, Tilly was ready to deliver her fifth child. But, this labour was not like the others. This child didn't want to be born. After several hours of labour, Nurse Wooldridge was worried. "Jim, go fetch the doctor quick as you can. I need help with this one," she said with a note of urgency in her voice. Jim was off like a shot.

Later, Tilly struggled mightily to give birth as both the doctor and nurse worked to help her. She screamed each time she felt the urge to push and gasped and panted between pains to gain strength for the next push. Finally, she delivered a baby boy weighing ten pounds, eight ounces. Tilly was utterly spent. Every inch of her body ached, and she longed for deep, healing sleep.

"I thought we were going to lose you," the doctor said, advising Tilly and Jim not to have more children.

"It had to be bloody boy, didn't it," added Nurse Wooldridge.

"This is definitely going to be the last," Tilly said softly as if she did not have the strength to raise her voice. "I was afraid I would die like my mother did—I am totally exhausted."

Jane, Granny Sarah and Aunt Ethel had been there all day caring for the children, calming Jim and assisting Nurse Wooldridge. It was Aunt Ethel's first visit since the row over the babies three years earlier.

"Right," said the nurse. "Tilly needs complete rest and quiet because she has worked hard and is tired out." She asked the women to take the older children for a couple of days.

"I will take Eliza," said Aunt Ethel, beginning to put things into a bag. Jim decided to ask Edna to care for Derek, and his mother took the two older boys.

"They will have to have a few days off school," Jane said. "I can't take them all that way to their school." Ray no longer went to the neighbourhood school, so Jane would have had to walk more than three miles.

At the end of three weeks, Tilly was back to normal, taking everything in stride. All of the boys were back at home, but Eliza was still staying with Aunt Ethel and Uncle Alf. "Jim, go and get Eliza," she said. "I want her back today."

As Jim opened Aunt Ethel's door, Eliza jumped up and put her arms 'round his neck. He swung her 'round and Eliza clung to him and wouldn't let go.

"Has she been all right?" asked Jim.

"Fine," replied Ethel. "We loved having her. Can we have her again some time?" She then told Eliza to show her father her new shoes.

"Smashing," Jim said, admiring them. "I can see she has new clothes on as well, thank you very much."

"Shall we walk round to your grandmother's so she can see Eliza before you take her home?" asked Aunt Ethel.

"Okay."

Before they left, Aunt Ethel started undressing Eliza. "I'm changing her clothes," she said. "She can't take them home, but she can wear them when she comes to stay again." She then proceeded to dress Eliza in her old clothes. Jim knew what she was up to. He knew Aunt Ethel was thinking that Eliza would want to go there all the time if she could have better clothes.

"Can I take my new doll with me?" asked Eliza.

"That's not a very good idea, is it?" replied her aunt. "The boys might break it."

Jim was fuming! *Fancy Ethel taking the doll off her!*

The three of them walked round to Sarah's in silence. Eliza enjoyed going 'round to her great gran's every day. She also enjoyed playing with Dorothy, the little girl next door to her aunt's house. Dorothy was an only child and her parents thought she could do no wrong. If she and Eliza had a tiff, it was always Eliza's fault.

Jim glanced at Eliza, as they sat on the bus on the way home. "Why the glum face?" he asked her.

"I wanted to bring my doll home with me," she replied.

"I will buy you one for Christmas even though money's tight." Jim was determined. *Eliza will have a doll for Christmas!*.

The little girl soon forgot about her doll when she saw her mother and brothers and the new baby Joseph. "Did you like it at Aunt Ethel's?" Tilly asked her.

"Yes, I did like it, but I was there too long. I wanted to come home to you and dad!" She told Tilly she "got told off" because she wouldn't sleep on her own, and they wanted her "to sleep in the bogey room."

Eliza called it "the bogey room" because when she was there, she could hear a lot of noise from the pub next door. It wasn't exactly next door, though. It was at the back, almost touching Aunt Ethel's house.

"I missed you and dad so much," Eliza continued. "I also missed playing with Ken, Derek and Jill." She worried that Jill, Edna's daughter, had found new friends to play with while she was away.

Ken, Eliza, and Jill went to a different school from Ray and Jan. The school was three miles away and they had to walk up a long lane to reach it. It was perched high on the top of a hill, near the church and cemetery where Jim and Percy dug graves. The scenery was beautiful. Granny Sarah told them the Earl of Plymouth and some of his family were buried in the cemetery.

Jim was under a lot of pressure now to earn enough money to care for his large family. He and Tilly didn't worry much about food, but clothing and everyday expenses like bus fare and dinner money added up.

"I will get a job to help you out, Mother" Ray said.

"You can't do that. You're only ten years old, far too young to be thinking of work," Tilly replied. "Don't worry, we will be all right." Tilly smiled to herself as she put her arm 'round her eldest son, who was growing so rapidly that he was as big as a boy of fourteen. *What a lovely boy!*

Ray and Ken had lots of school friends who came to The Tin House and loved playing there. Tilly served them pies or cakes when she has the ingredients to make them.

If she lacked the materials to make pies and cakes, though, they ate bread with anything for toppings—condensed milk, lard, syrup, even sugar. The children loved her snacks.

When Christmas arrived Jim remembered his promise to Eliza. The child could see that her pillowcase, which usually had a few nuts and fruit in it, was quite bulgy. She scrambled off the bed, all excited.

As she pulled a beautiful chocolate-coloured doll from the pillow case, Eliza he squealed with delight.

"Oh Mom," the child said, struggling to get the little tin pram out. She was over the moon, hugging and kissing her mother and father. Eliza never had presents like this before. Father Christmas must have thought she has been really good this year.

All of Tilly's and Jim's friends visited 'The Tin House" during the Christmas season. Jessie brought the baby daughter she had a few days before Joseph was born in a red velvet dress, looking beautiful. All of Tilly's children enjoyed their gifts, and Tilly and Jim were grateful for the blessings of friendship during another Christmas season.

"Come on children, it's six o'clock—Time to go to the gasworks for the coke."

The children hated Saturdays in the winter. They all had to go to get the coke because coke was rationed one bag per person, and even little children counted. Tilly and Jim needed to get as much coke as possible because they had a large house to heat.

"Eat your porridge up first, it will keep you warm," Tilly instructed.

The smaller children sat in the pram on the way down to the gasworks, but that was the easy part. When there was not too much snow, they cut through. the woods on the wide path, which was used pretty well all year, and shaved a half mile off their journey. When the path was blocked, they had to use Muskets Pathway, the longer way 'round.

The gasworks was about three and a half miles away—all downhill. The queue was usually about half a mile long, and they were freezing cold by the time their turn came. They made the trek to the gasworks every Saturday all winter long. The trip back home was physically taxing. After their sacks were full, they had to walk uphill, slipping and sliding as they pushed the heavy load on the pram. Even though coke was lighter than coal, it seemed to take forever because five bags was a lot to fit in a pram. The bags kept slipping in the pram so that they hung off the edges, and the children had to hump them back on.

Hours later they arrived home, their feet and hands freezing. The children would cry because they stung and ached as the feeling came back into them. Tilly hated to see them distressed, but it was the only way they could keep The Tin House warm, it was so big. The children knew they were in for a treat tonight! Ray heard his parents talking with Edna and Bill about going sledging at six o'clock in the field by the side of The Tin House, and he spread the word to the other children. So they grew excited as darkness fell. A sledge was a sled with runners that was usually pulled by dogs to transport a heavy load.

Jim and Bill made holes in a tin dustbin they were going to put three buckets of coke each for the fire. Dead on five thirty, Jim carried a shovelful of fire from the fire in the house and took it outside into the field. He put it in the bin, placed some coke on top, and wrapped some newspaper around the higher holes to draw it. The fire was soon blazing, and green grass began to peep out as the heat of the fire thawed the snow around the bin.

The children were dressed up warm. Jim had been busy all morning making a sledge, while Tilly had put lots of potatoes in the three ovens. People from up the road joined them, after they heard the children having squeal in delight as they sledged down the hillside. Jim took the jacket potatoes out of the ovens, replacing them with house bricks to warm them later. Bill made a big jug of cocoa for the children, who were having a wonderful time. It was almost like daylight because the moon shone so brightly, casting shadows over the snow.

Tilly went into the house before the others, checking the children's clothes that she left on the end of the fireguard to keep warm. She then checked that Jim put bricks in the oven so they would be ready when everyone returned, knowing they would be freezing cold.

Tilly got some old coats and wrapped the hot bricks in them. She then placed them in the children's beds. As the children came in one by one Tilly took their clothes off, briskly rubbed them down in front of the blazing fire and then told them to they run upstairs to snuggle in their warm beds.

Tilly had told Lou that she would like to get a job to ease the pressure on Jim, and it wasn't long before Lou heard about one at the B.S.A. motor bike factory where Ted worked. She told Tilly about a vacancy in the canteen, on the early shift, making tea and cooking breakfast.

"That would do you, Tilly, wouldn't it?" asked Lou, as she told Tilly the details. When Tilly called to check on it, the manager asked her to start the next morning. So, Tilly got on the first bus in the morning and worked until nine a.m. Then, she went home so Jim could go to work. This arrangement continued and the job worked out fine.

On Saturdays, Tilly took Eliza with her. The child loved going to the factory with her, and some of the men made a fuss over her. One man always gave her a penny, which she spent in Perks' shop, getting broken biscuits, which she shared with her brothers when she got home.

The summer holidays arrived, and Uncle Alf came to visit, asking if Eliza could come to visit him and Aunt Ethel.

"For how long?" asked Tilly.

"Just a couple of weeks."

"No longer than that," said Tilly, remembering the last time Eliza stayed there.

Aunt Ethel was really pleased to see her, and Eliza soon got the button tin out to play with the buttons. There were hundreds of them. She loved the different colours and shapes, and she played contentedly until bedtime arrived.

"Come on, Eliza, up to bed," said her aunty. "This time you have to sleep in your own room."

"I don't want to sleep in there," replied Eliza. "It's the bogey hole."

"Don't be so silly!" said her aunt. "You will do as you're told while you're here."

The bedroom was about four foot wide, with a really low roof that sloped down to the floor. There were no windows, just two open-air grids in the wall that was adjacent to the pub yard.

Eliza lay there cringing. She could hear the men in the bar, getting louder and louder. She cried as she heard the men swearing and taking their snuff, then sneezing and spitting on the floor. She lay awake, her tears turning into quiet sobs. Then, as the pub emptied, she fell asleep.

Eliza awoke the next morning to the call of her name as her aunt shouted upstairs. Rubbing the sleep out of her eyes, she went downstairs, making sure she didn't trip on her long cotton nightdress.

"Get washed then put these clothes on," said her aunt. They were the same clothes that her aunt had taken off her the last time she stayed here. But the clothes were too small. Eliza had grown a lot since then. The little girl put her own clothes on, and Aunt Ethel gave the others to Dorothy. The girl next door was a bit smaller than Eliza.

Aunt Ethel then took Eliza 'round to see Great Gran Sarah, who was having a lot of trouble getting about like she used to. She had a terrible bad back, was in great pain all the time and sort of shuffled 'round the furniture. Grand Dad's chair, which he usually occupied at this time of day, was empty.

"Where's Grand Dad?" asks Eliza.

"He's dead," replied Great Gran.

"I'm sorry, I didn't know," said Eliza.

"Little girls should be seen and not heard," Aunt Ethel piped up. "Come on, Eliza, time to go," she said, after doing a bit of cleaning for her mother Sarah. "When we get back, you can play with Dorothy from next door. Don't get into any mischief!" said Ethel, as Eliza skipped outside.

"No Aunty," replieds Eliza, knocking on Dorothy's door.

"Can you come out to play?" she asked Dorothy.

The two of them were playing hopscotch on the path when, "Quick, come on!" called Dorothy, running towards the Brew house as it started raining. Eliza ran after her. Two boys from next door on the other side of Aunt Ethel's house were there doing a bike up.

"I know," one of them said. "Let's climb on the mangle and see who can jump the farthest." Taking turns, the two boys jumped first, marking the spot where they landed. "Because you girls are smaller, you can jump off the draining board," the older one said.

Dorothy jumped first while Eliza stood on the end, then, she took her turn. Crack! To her horror, the board snapped in half! Eliza was beside herself her aunt was so very strict. *What will Aunt Ethel say?*

"Don't worry," one of the boys said to her. "It's our mother's mangle. We will explain and tell her it was our fault, she knows what your aunt's like."

That night Eliza was counting buttons when Dorothy's mother came in. "Has Eliza told you she broke the mangle?" Eliza cringed. Dorothy told her mother!

As soon as Dorothy's mother was gone Ethel flew into a rage, grabbing Eliza. She twisted her 'round, put her over her knee and pulled Eliza's pants down.

"You little cow!" she screamed, reaching for the ruler Eliza was using earlier, and beat her on her bottom with it.

Eliza was screaming so much that Uncle Alf came running 'round from the pub. Alf was appalled by the sight he had never seen his wife in such frenzy before. He grabbed Eliza and cuddled her to him. Her uncle held her until her sobs subside. She pretended to be asleep, petrified in case her uncle went back to the pub, but he carried her upstairs, and put her gently to bed in that horrible bogey room.

Eliza didn't murmur after being put in bed. She hated her aunt for what she has done, but she hates little Dorothy and her mother even more. Eliza never wanted to see them or her aunt again as she lay in bed, hardly able to breathe.

At last, she heard her aunt and uncle snoring. *Now's the time to make my move!*

Her heart was thumping so loud that she thought it might wake them, as she crept downstairs, put her coat on, grabbed her shoes, quietly unlocked the door, and stepped outside. She left the door ajar as she went out, because she feared it would make a noise if she shut it properly.

The street lamp outside was dimly lit, casting eerie shadows that made it easier for her to see. Eliza had never been so scared in all her life. She was going home, running as fast as she could, her little legs shaking. She was scared stiff. Her bottom hurt her so much, it felt as if it was on fire. She just had to get away and get home to her mother and father, even though it was a four-mile distance. She dodged a couple of car lights and got scratched as she hid in the hedges, and then stumbled, grazing her knees.

Tilly awoke with a start.

"Jim, wake up, I'm sure I hear Eliza calling and crying!"

Jim, snoring, woke. "Go back to sleep, you've been dreaming, woman!"

"There it is again."

Jim jumped out of bed, and ran downstairs. Tilly was right behind him. They didn't normally lock the door but the latch was loose and the door kept flying open. Jim unlocked and then opened the door. There stood Eliza, all dirty and bleeding, her clothes torn from hiding in the brambles.

"What has happened to you?" cried Tilly. "What are you doing here in the middle of the night?"

Eliza was crying so much that she wasn't making much sense at all.

"Stoke the fire up, Jim." Even though it was summer, it had been raining all afternoon and evening so Jim had lit the fire.

"Then get me a bowl of warm water, I will wash her," said Tilly, taking Eliza's clothes off. Then, turning her 'round, she saw her bottom!

"Oh, my God!" she wailed. "Look at this, Jim."

"Who's done this to you?" he asked Eliza.

In between sobs, she proceeded to tell her mother and father about the mangle and the beating. Jim wanted to go straight up to see his uncle and aunt, as they'd always been a very close family. How could his aunt have done this to his little girl?

"I will kill them before the day is out!" said Jim.

Tilly didn't know whom she hated more, Ethel or the woman who told Ethel. Unable to sleep, Jim was up at seven a.m., and he hardly touched the pot of tea he made. Jumping on his bike, he was on his way to see Aunt Ethel.

Just as he was riding past his Uncle Jack's house, the door opened and Uncle Jack, who was just going round to the toilet, came out.

"Where 'yer going this time on Saturday morning?" he asked Jim.

Jim was shaking as he told him about the hiding Aunt Ethel gave Eliza.

"Hang on a minute, go inside," replied Uncle Jack. "You put the kettle on while I nip to the lav. I'm peeing myself, and the piss pot's full. Be quiet, the others are in bed."

Jim made the tea but he was shaking so much in anger that he had a job holding his cup. Uncle Jack came back in as Jim's lit a cigarette up.

"Now, what's the matter, Jim? I've never seen you in this state before."

"It's that bloody sister of yours!" replied Jim. "I'm going to kill her!" Jim carried on telling him all about Eliza's bottom and her running home in the middle of the night. Uncle Jack was horrified. "Look, Jim, you go home. Here's a tanner, get Tilly to take Eliza down town to buy a toy or something. And, Jim, don't tell Aunt Eve I gave it to you. I will borrow your bike and I will go to see them."

Uncle Jack knew if Jim went up in that state, he might hit Aunt Ethel for doing that to Eliza. The trouble with Ethel was she was so prim and proper, she never had children of her own, and she had a quick temper.

"What's this I hear about you giving Eliza a thrashing, Ethel? It's a good job I stopped Jim from coming, he would have had your guts for garters."

Ethel admitted she had gotten carried away with beating Eliza with the ruler.

"You know Tilly and Jim won't let her come here again, don't you! The poor kid wouldn't want to come anyway," Uncle Jack said, noting that a sad thing that would come from the beating was that Alf, who loved Eliza to bits, would be heartbroken—but Eliza certainly wouldn't be going there again.

Jim was looking after their other children while Tilly took Eliza downtown, holding her hand as they walked down the main street. Suddenly Eliza tightened her grip and tried to hide behind Tilly.

"What's the matter!" she asked Eliza, then she spotted little Dorothy smirking at her while Dorothy's mother looked in a shop window!

"I would love to knock that smirk off your Dorothy's face, the sneaky little bleeder, and you're no better! Have a look at Eliza's bottom," said Tilly.

"I know! I heard her through the wall."

"Why didn't you go 'round and stop it?" said Tilly.

"I didn't want to interfere," replied Dorothy's mother.

"Well, you won't be twitting on her again, that's a certain fact. Eliza won't be going there anymore." With that, Tilly and Eliza turned and walked the other way. Eliza bought some marbles and some broken biscuits for herself and her brothers then gave her mother the change. They headed off, to wait in a long queue in the market to buy some bananas. Jim might moan about them being a long time but he would be pleased for the children to have bananas they were a luxury they don't have very often.

Jim was having trouble with the kitchen roof, it was leaking again. There was a downpour of rain, and there were holes everywhere, so there was a lot of' patching to do. He would have to get some corrugated tin.

"Where on earth am I going to get that from?" he asked Tilly.

"No good asking me, I have no idea."

There were buckets, pots, and pans all 'round the kitchen floor, catching the rainwater when Percy came by to see Jim. "I have some work for you."

"Just the person I want," replied Jim. "I need some corrugated tin for the kitchen roof. Where can I get it?"

"Don't worry, Jim, I will sort it out for you," answered Percy, and a few days later five sheets of corrugated tin arrived. Jim would now have to get someone to help him, but since he couldn't afford to pay anyone he got the two eldest boys to help. "Thanks for your help," he said, praising his two sons. "We did a lovely job. If you stand up the garden you can see the patches on the roof."

Ray and Ken were sliding down the top half of the roof, and

both Eliza and Derek wanted a go as well, but they would have to wait until their dad wasn't about. He would "do his nut" if he knew they had been up there.

The next day Eliza cautiously climbed the ladder with Derek close on her heels, following her to the flat part of the roof. They crawled up the slope to the top and slid down, petrified. They climbed back down the ladder, and they put it back where they got it from. They wouldn't be doing that again, they decided. They were scared stiff up there.

Ray had been going down to the farm at the bottom of the road, doing odd jobs. The farmer loved him. When he left the farm on Saturdays just before six, Ray called into the shop on his way home. The shop had its own bakery out the back where they made bread and cream cakes.

"Do you have any stale cakes left I can have?" asked Ray.

Mrs Sheppard, who owned the shop, had already put the cakes in a bag for him before he got there. He was usually the last customer of the day, and they never close the shop until he has been in for his cakes.

"How much do I owe you?" he asked.

"Six pence, please, the same as last week."

Ray arrived home with his bag of cakes. He put them on the table, and then he sat scoffing them with his arm bent 'round them. His sister and brothers were watching him, their mouths watering.

"Can we have a bite?" they asked, their mouths drooling.

"Wait, you can have some when I am full up." Ray had a sweet tooth, always did. He cut up what was left. "Who's going to polish my shoes?" he asked, rubbing his tummy.

"I will," they chorused, putting their hands up. Ray found them all a little job to do, and then, he shared the remaining bits of cake between them.

CHAPTER 7

E very other Sunday, a man, who was a distant relative, came to visit at The Tin House. Eliza looked forward to seeing him arrive on his motor-bike because he always brought her a big box of chocolates. He liked to be alone with Eliza so he probably planned his visits late in the morning when Jim was working in the garden and Tilly was preparing dinner.

"Come on, give uncle a kiss," he would say. He always scooped her up in his arms and sat her down on his lap, making sure she was facing him. "I want a bigger kiss than that," he would say, insisting that she kiss him full on his mouth. Although he called himself "uncle," Eliza knew he was a distant cousin.

His lips were wet and sloppy, and Eliza would wipe her mouth on her sleeve.

"That's not very nice," he told her one Sunday, bouncing her up and down on his lap.

"Why is your lap so hard?" asked Eliza.

"Is it hard?" he asked. "I will tell you a story about a little girl I know I give her chocolates and money, and she lets me put my hand in her knickers."

"What ever for?" asked Eliza.

"We play mothers and fathers," he replied.

"Well, I'm not allowed to play that!" said Eliza. "My mom always says not to play that game with boys or men."

"Okay," he replied, "but don't tell anyone about what I said. That's our little secret." Eliza wondered if she should tell Tilly, but she had a vague feeling that she would get in trouble, so she remained silent but avoided her visitor. Eventually she realized he was a pervert.

Both Ken and Eliza were allowed to play up the long drive now that they were a bit older, though Ray had been playing up there for ages.

"Keep away from Mr Weaver's house and mind the traffic," said Tilly.

There wasn't a lot of traffic using the road, just a handful of cars and the bus, which went to the bottom of the road four times a day, turning at the bottom, then back to town.

Ray worried about his brothers and sister and their friends playing in the road he kept telling them to clear off, shouting, "You should be playing in the fields or up the woods."

"If I make a swing will you promise to play on it?" he asked the younger ones. Ray asked the farmer if he could have some of the thick towing rope out of the barn. When the farmer found out that Ray wanted to make a swing for the kids, he told him to take all the rope he needed.

Ray wanted to put the swing in the shade. "I know. I will hang the rope from the giant oak tree that stands so majestically in the field by The Tin House'." About a dozen children were there, watching him, waiting for a go on the swing.

The children also used the Plek to play in. The main entrance was for lorries, which were kept 'round the back. They belonged to Ernie Cater, whose wife was a friend of Jim and Tilly's. The two Cater boys also played with the others at The Tin House. A copse with numerous kinds of trees was adjacent to the side entrance. A large felled tree lay on the edge, the same tree that Tilly and Jim used to sit on when they were courting.

Now, the children all sat there and played 'I spy' or just talked for hours. There were children from up and down the road. If Eliza ever went to ask any of them call to play, their mothers always said no, they couldn't come out. However, if Jill called for the same friends, she always came back with him or her. Eliza wondered why some people were hostile towards her and her brothers—she had tried asking the other children why they couldn't come out with her, but they said they didn't know.

On a Sunday afternoon, Tilly, Jim and the children were outside enjoying the sunshine, just sitting, talking together with Lou and Ted, who had come to see them.

"Shush, listen. I think I hear a car coming down the drive," said Tilly. Sure enough, they saw a car coming 'round the corner of the drive towards them. "Who can that be?" they said together.

The car stopped, and out stepped a man, two women, and two children. Tilly and Jim stood up as the man approached them. Then, Tilly had a flicker of recognition. *It can't be. Yes, it is. It's my brother Billy!*

He ran to Tilly, and they threw their arms round each other, crying as they embraced. Jim wondered what was going on. He had never met Billy and didn't have a clue what he looked like. Tilly was now thirty-five years old now, and she hadn't seen her brother for twenty-five years—she still knew him, though, he hadn't changed much at all.

"How did you find me?" she asked him as they hugged again. Tilly didn't want to let him go.

"I wrote to the convent, and they sent us to Palmer's Farm. When we got there, they directed us here," Billy said, adding, "I never forgot you, Tilly. A mate of mine lent me his car, and here we are."

The two other women were still standing by the car with the two children. The boy and girl held one woman's hands. "Come and meet your sister Mary and my wife Olive."

Tilly had only seen Mary once—the time when she was a couple of days old, but now the two sisters embraced. Mary, who served in the WAFFS, looked smart in her uniform, but by the time Tilly let go of her, she seemed a bit overwhelmed. She explained that she knew about Billy from the aunt who raised her. When she was stationed close to his home town, she had looked him up. Jim observed that Mary looked a lot like Billy, but completely different from Tilly. She was fair and shorter than her sister.

Tilly then hugged Olive and remarked on the beautiful children. They were shy at first, but after a short time they were playing with the others and enjoying themselves. Tilly noticed that her sister talked a bit posh, and she also felt that Mary thought she was better than them. However, Billy and Olive had broad Black Country accents, and Tilly and Jim felt at ease with them. They had a good time catching up on all that had happened since they last lived together, Billy and the others stayed until seven o'clock and left after evening tea.

"We will keep in touch with you, Tilly, I won't let you go again," said her brother.

After they left, Tilly and Jim had another cuppa at the table together. Tilly asked Jim what he made of her family.

"Bill and his wife are great, I'm not so sure about your sister she seemed a bit stuck up."

"I had the same feeling. Mind you, she was been brought up an only child so she was probably spoiled."

Soon after the visit, Tilly learned she was pregnant again. She gave birth to another baby boy, her fifth son. This one was named Michael, and he weighed in at ten pounds. Jane, whom Tilly said was a wonderful grandmother, came to help look after the other children. May, too, came to help with the housework and the children even though Jim had time off to care for them. She was always helpful and never complained. Jim had high praise for May, whom he described as 'wholesome and attractive.' He said, "May's marvellous she will make someone a good wife, and she'll be a fabulous mother, too."

Uncle Jack was sitting in his favourite place on the bottom stair with a hand-rolled cigarette, so thin it kept going out, hanging from his mouth. The smoke curled up and turned his moustache ginger. He was fixing the children's shoes so they would be ready for school. "Jim, these kids have been walking with no soles in their shoes," he said, cutting pieces of leather with the jack knife he always hung from his belt to hold his trousers up.

"I gut hell," said Jim, polishing the shoes after Jack gave them new soles and heels. The old English expression "gut hell" meant appalled or I am appalled.

Every Monday morning, Tilly did her big washing. She was dollying some washing when Edna knocked at the door and poked her head inside.

"Can I borrow your water and boiler when you have finished, please, Tilly? There's a hole in my boiler."

"Okay," replied Tilly, brushing a strand of wet hair from her brow. The steam was so thick in the kitchen that it felt like a sauna. When Edna saw Tilly hanging her third line of washing out and getting the first few batched that were already dry off the line, she knew her friend was finished washing and ready to do her ironing.

Edna put her washing in her pram and crossed the garden to Tilly's house. "Here I am," she said, pulling some clothing out of the pram. "Can I use your line as well? Your garden is a lovely spot for drying clothes."

"I know, I am lucky to live here," Tilly said as she stopped ironing and placed the iron back on the hob to reheat. While she was waiting, she made them each a cuppa tea. "Tell me, Edna, how come you don't keep getting pregnant like me?"

"I guess I'm just not as fertile as you or luckier perhaps," Edna said. She hesitated and then added, "Why don't you try the cap?" She offered to go to the clinic with Tilly since she had been thinking of going too. The two women carried on with their washing and ironing. By the time they finished, the children started arriving home from school.

Tilly was busy getting the tea ready. She was starting a new job, cleaning offices at the Alloys Factory with her neighbour Mrs Harris, at five. She left her other job during the late stages of her last pregnancy. She would have liked to return to the canteen at the motor-bike factory, but there were no openings there.

Tilly did a good job of saving water. She had used her washing water to boil laundry for eight people, and Edna used it for five people. Now Tilly's six children were going to bath in it. She quickly added more water to cool it down for bathing because she wanted Eliza to take her bath before she left for work. That way Tilly could ensure that her daughter would have privacy. The boys could bathe on their own or with Jim as supervisor.

95

Jim managed to get hold of a darts board from one of the pubs where he sang or whistled, and Doll and her husband were there when Tilly returned from work for a game of darts and a bottle of stout. Tilly's bus stop was near The Rose and Crown, so she volunteered to pick up the stout on her way home. Jim would stick the red-hot poker into the stout to liven it up a bit.

Tilly threw her dart! Sss.ss.sst! They heard the hissing sound of escaping gas as the dart pierced the thin lead gas pipe that ran around the top of the room that was painted a cream colour. The bottom half of the wood was painted green, and a rail ran between the two colours. Ted took his chewing gum out of his mouth and stuck it on the tiny hole while standing on a chair. He wrapped the softened gum 'round the pipe and Jim eventually painted over it.

Are you ready, Tilly?" asked Edna next day. Off they went to the clinic to be fitted for one of the caps. What a laugh they had! The caps were large and round and each one was kept in its own tin.

"Let's fit you up and show you how to use it," said the clinic nurse.

"Do you have to measure us?" asked Edna

"Of course I do, there are all different sizes," the nurse said, explaining how to wash it, put the cream on, and then fit it.

By the time Tilly was done that night, Jim was asleep. *That's the best form of contraception I know.* The next morning she had to wash the cap, dry it, dust with powder, and then put it back in the tin.

"It's just like looking after another child, isn't it?" she said to Edna later that day. "There's one thing in its favour, though, it don't eat."

Jim's highlight of the week was listening to Dick Barton and Paul Temple on the wireless. When his programs were on, everyone had to be silent. That wasn't difficult because Tilly and the children enjoyed listening as well. The large acid battery that ran the wireless had to be charged up twice a week at Hopkins Garage up the Cross. Ray or Ken would take it on the handlebars of their bikes. "Mind you don't spill acid on yourself," Tilly always reminded whoever left the house with the battery.

"Mom, the gas man's on the way down," said Derek as he came in from school.

"Good," replied Tilly. "We might get a good rebate the meters choc-a-block. It's been ages since it was last emptied."

The meter allowed people to pay for their gas as they used it. It took shillings, sixpence pieces, and pennies. Sometimes, they paid too much and got money back. The Gas Board always set the tariff higher than the actual cost of the gas used because so many people put washers in the meter when they were low on cash. By setting the tariff higher, the board insured that there would be adequate money for the gas used. Any surplus was returned to the customer. Tilly thought of it as a small savings account and was happy when the board's workers came to empty the meter.

"How much rebate do I have?" asked Tilly.

"Three shillings and eight washers," he replied. "The washers were equal to a penny." Tilly put the shillings in her purse and the washers back in the cupboard, ready for the next time they ran out of money.

It was seven a.m. a few days later, and Jim had a big day ahead of him because someone would be buried later in the morning. It rained all night so he had to make sure the grave did not have too much water in the bottom of it. Using a bucket on a long piece of thick towing rope, he ladled as much of the water as he could, but then he put the small ladder in the hole. He shuddered as he climbed into the hole to get the last of the water. *There is something creepy about climbing into a grave.* During the burial, Jim sat in a little hut on the cemetery grounds. He had to wait until the mourners left before he shovelled the soil back into the grave on top of the casket.

"I'm knackered," he said to Tilly when he arrived home from work.

Eliza, Derek, Jill and other friends clamoured aboard the school bus that was packed as usual. Derek went to the back of the bus, and Eliza sat at the front. Neither of them had bus fare The conductor held his hand out for Jill's fare. "My brother's got mine, he's down the back of the bus somewhere," Eliza said.

By the time the conductor got to the back, Derek said, "My sister's got mine at the front." The conductor was too busy trying to keep children quiet to realise what was going on.

Eliza was friendly with a girl named Beryl. She was adopted as a baby and seemed great to Eliza, but Beryl's parents were very strict with her. Eliza noticed that her friend seemed to be afraid of her parents—especially her mother.

Beryl had beautiful bright red, curly hair that shone like pure copper. She came to The Tin House to play, but she didn't dare to let her parents know she had been there.

"You have lovely parents," she said to Eliza. "I wish I could live with you."

Eliza, too, had a wish. Every time she combed Beryl's beautiful hair, she longed for beautiful curly ringlets like her friend had.

"Isn't Beryl's hair lovely, Mom?" Eliza asked.

"Would you like some ringlets in your hair?" asked Tilly, guessing Eliza's secret wish.

"Oh, please, can you?"

Eliza sat ripping strips of rag up that night while her mother proceeded to wind her hair round the strips. Eliza didn't get much sleep because she couldn't get her head comfy. The next day when the rags were taken out, she had a mass of ringlets.

"You look lovely," said Tilly, combing the curls.

"Does it look as nice as Beryl's?" asks Eliza, looking in the mirror.

"It surely does!"

Beryl was chewing her gum, doing handstands in the school playground with Eliza and Jill when an older, bossy girl approached them. "When we go back to the classroom, Beryl, put your chewing gum on the headmaster's chair," she said.

"I can't do that." said a shocked Beryl.

"Just do it or else," the girl repeated.

Back inside, the headmaster sat down and started the lessons. Then, he stood up and walked toward the black board. He stopped in mid stride, putting his hand behind him and feeling his bottom. All at once, his face turned bright red. He turned around, looked at his fingers in disgust and stormed out of the classroom. Ten minutes later, he was back wearing different trousers. He was such a kind headmaster, normally, that the children had never seen him looking so furious before.

"Right," he said, moving the chair back. "Before we resume lessons I want the name of the person responsible for this sick joke, if that's what it supposed to be."

"It was Eliza," a voice from the back of the class called out.

"Was it you, Eliza?" he asked.

"No, sir."

"Well, until the person who did it owns up Beryl won't be going to the Festival of Britain."

Everyone was silent how did he know Beryl had done it?

Beryl cried all the way home, while Jill and Eliza tried hard to console her. "I don't know how I am going to tell my parents," she said.

"I wonder what happened to Beryl this morning, she didn't call for me," said Eliza the next day, as she and Jill waited for the school bus.

"Here she is," said Jill, nudging Eliza, as Beryl and her mother came 'round the corner. Beryl looked scared stiff as she got on the school bus. Her mother clambered up the steps behind her, prodding Beryl towards the back of the bus.

At school, Beryl's mother went into the classroom to see the "Head." She blamed the incident on the "company Beryl kept lately" and gave him money to buy a new pair of trousers. After school, she was still angry and gave Beryl a "good telling off."

"If ever you play with that lot up there again, you will be in deep trouble," said her mother. "Stick to the children from this end of the road. You won't be going to play outside for two weeks, and you're only going on the trip because the headmaster talked me into it. He said it wouldn't be fair after you had owned up!"

"It was nothing to do with Eliza!" said Beryl, upset that everyone wanted to blame Eliza.

"Don't backchat me, now get upstairs, and don't show your face again until morning!"

The day of the trip was getting closer but Eliza still didn't have any decent clothes to go in.

"What am I going to wear, Mom?"

"I don't know. There's no spare money at all."

"I can't go then!" cried Eliza.

"What's she crying for?" asked Ray's friend, who had just walked through the front door.

"Eliza needs new clothes for her trip," Ray answered, "but, we just can't afford it, at the moment."

"I will ask my sister if she has anything you can borrow. She's younger than Eliza but about the same size."

The next day he was back as he promised with a dress, cardigan, socks and shoes. "Doesn't your mother mind lending them out," asked a grateful Tilly. "After all, she doesn't know us."

"Don't worry about it."

"Look at me!" said Eliza, putting the clothes on.

"You look lovely," replied her mother. The dress was pale, lilac check gingham with a belt that tied at the back. *I wish I could afford to dress Eliza like that.*

The day at the festival was brilliant! Eliza had never seen anything like it in her life before, nor had any of the other children. They had a fabulous day—an unforgettable first outing for Eliza.

Tilly washed and ironed the clothes that Eliza wore, and put them back in the bag. "Thank your mother very much," she said to Ray's friend, handing him the bag back.

"That's okay, I just borrowed them. I never asked her," he admitted.

One of the other girls at school wanted to come to The Tin House to play. She lived in one of the posh houses on the top of the road and had heard about all the fun they had there.

"Come after school if you want, my mom won't mind," said Eliza.

Less than a half hour after she got off the school bus, the girl was down at The Tin House.

"This is Una," Eliza said, introducing her to her mother.

"Would you like a lard sandwich?" asked Tilly. "It's homemade with rosemary."

Tilly knew that most children were hungry after school, and she always offered them something to eat.

"I haven't had one of these before," Una replied.

"You don't know what you've been missing," Tilly said.

"That's delicious, thanks," says Una after eating the sandwich.

What a nice girl she is. Tilly, who knew of Una's father, liked most of the children's friends. Una's dad was one of the builders from the top road who worked in partnership with his two brothers. They had a big lorry and were quite well off.

But the next day, Una avoided Eliza at school. Every time Eliza looked at her, she looked the other way, so Eliza went up to her in the playground.

"Do you want to come to The Tin House again after school?"

"I can't," Una replied. "My dad says your dad's a bastard. I mustn't play with you anymore."

"What's one of those?"

"I don't know, but my dad says your dad's one, he didn't say what it was."

Back at home, Tilly and the children were eating their tea of home-produced bacon and eggs, when Jim walked in. "You're late today," said Tilly.

"Yes, I had to finish a job," he replied.

"I hope they're going to pay this week," said Tilly.

"What's a bastard, Dad?" asked Eliza. "Una's dad told her you are one."

Jim went deathly pale and rushed outside with a look of horror on his face. Tilly ran after him.

Is this why a lot of people don't speak to us? What harm had she, Jim or the children done to deserve this? Jim was always doing jobs for his neighbours and the people in town—half of them for peanuts, and they soon spoke to him then.

Apparently, a local chap raped Jim's mother, Jane, whose parents were quite wealthy! Jane was left with the baby, and she had no help from the father. Lots of babies are born out of wedlock these days, most of them hidden or adopted, but it was considered a major scandal when Jane was young.

Tilly realized that was the reason Jim was so close to Uncle Jack. He had been in the same household as him until he was eight, and his mother married Josh. It all fell into place now. That was why Jim married Tilly in a different name to the one everybody called him. It had been quite confusing at first. Tilly and her children had one name—Jim's legal name, but he was also known around town by his stepfather's name. This was not all that unusual since Jim was still a young child when Jane married.

Jim and Tilly had another policy due to mature, and Bill and Edna had a similar one, so the two couples decided to bring the electric line to the bungalow and The Tin House. Wow, what a difference it made. They said goodbye to the gas mantles that were so delicate they couldn't touch them or they disintegrated into fine white ash. A mantle was a reflective device consisting of multiple threads used with a gas lamp. When the mantle was heated, it gave off brilliant illumination by reflecting light from a gas flame.

Many times Tilly and her family sat with just the gas lit with no mantle attached. It was just like the jet flame on a cooking stove, and it gave off hardly gave any light at all.

Ray now worked on the farm full time and he loved it. He brought "boistins," the first milk a cow made after she gave birth, home for his mother to make a pudding with. It made extremely tasty pudding since it had the consistency of egg custard—it was considered a delicacy.

Ray and Ken wanted to hunt rabbits so he could sell the meat and his mother could make gloves from the pelts so he bought ferrets, a practice that some hunters frowned upon, to use in the hunt. He and Ken rounded up the ferrets and put them in a box. They were ready to start to the woods. "Do a bit of wooding while you're in the fields, will you, please," asked Tilly.

Off they went down to the fields carrying their sack bags, one for the rabbits and one for the wood. Ken stood behind the hedge in the next field, where Ray had found a rabbit warren with two or more entrances. Ray was just about to put the ferret down into the warren, when a voice called out, "What are you doing, Ray?"

He jumped! It was the farmer for whom he worked.

"Ken was hiding on the other side of the hedge, when Ray picked up a few pieces of wood and put them in his bag, "Just doing a bit of wooding," he replied.

"Okay," said the farmer. "Make sure you don't break any of the new wood, will you?"

"I will make sure of that"

"Phew, that was close," said Ken, as the farmer moved out of hearing distance. With that, the brothers went back to the rabbit warren and trapped seven rabbits. Ray wrung their necks to kill them, then, slinging the sacks over their shoulders, they made their way home.

Tilly easily gutted and skinned them—something she learned to do when she lived on the Palmer Farm. The boys already had customers lined up for the rabbit meat. Also, Tilly made beautiful, soft rabbit fur gloves from the pelts for her children. The gloves kept their hands warm and toasty just as Tilly's rabbit fur lined gloves kept her warm when she was in service on the farm. *That seems like a million years ago.*

"Tilly, do you think you could make some gloves for my children, too?" asked Edna, admiring the gloves Eliza wore when she came inside while Edna visited at The Tin House.

"Sure. I will be glad to make some for Jan and Jill when the boys go hunting again," Tilly said. Everyone knew Tilly to be exceedingly generous, so no one was surprised when she finished and delivered gloves for Edna's whole family.

After summer arrived, about twelve children played rounders in one of the fields. A British ball game similar to American baseball, the term "rounders" referred to rounding the bases after hitting a ball. The children cheered each other on and were having a great time.

Ray and a new friend lay in the grass talking. Eliza, who had been caught out and was out of the game for a while, sat nearby. She sat idly making daisy chains on the warm grass, when she overheard Ray's friend tell him a joke. Eliza didn't understand the joke, but Ray had a good laugh over it. Tilly was at work, so she couldn't ask her, but when she glanced up, she saw her father down the drive putting something in the dustbin.

She shouted to him and then ran down there. Her father looked up, saw her and waited for her. He caught hold of her hand as she skipped into the house with him. "Dad, I have a joke for you," she said, laughing as her father sat in a chair. But, Eliza only got to the end of the sixth word when Jim jumped up out of his chair.

"Where the bucking hell did you hear that from?"

His face looked like a raging storm and his voice was like thunder. Eliza had never seen her father in such a rage. Before she could move he started hitting her with a stick he picked up from by the fireplace. Knowing she wouldn't make it past him to the outside door, she ran upstairs, but caught the last blow on the back of her leg, and the stick broke in half.

Eliza climbed up on the beam as quickly as she could. She knew better than to show her face again that night. She didn't even know why she deserved a hiding, but she would ask her mother the next day. Eliza never forgot that hiding she never forgot the joke either!

Jim and Tilly already had plans for another policy that would soon mature. Jim would buy an accordion so he could play in the pubs again. He intended to keep whistling as well. He also wanted to improve the kitchen, which he would start by filling in the coal hole.

"The coal can go outside," he said, noting that he would ask Uncle Jack and his son Lally, whose given name was Leslie, to help him fill the hole in with loads of rubble and soil. He planned to tackle the fill and allow it to settle for a few weeks. Jim would then seal the area with concrete, but that, too, needed about a week to dry.

When that was done, Jim laid red quarry tile on the floor. He also put large windows on the side and back of the room, dramatically changing the amount of light there. Finally, he put a new sink and cooker at the new end. Jim was proud of the new kitchen. A short time after it was completed, he was delighted to find a long kitchen table at a house sale that fit nicely along the side window.

Now, they sat at the table and looked out over spectacular scenery. They could see their garden and fields as well as the forest beyond. It was beautiful in every season. Now, Tilly could easily keep her eye on the smaller children as they played in the fields too.

With the kitchen finished, Jim decided to tackle the biggest job of his life—he wanted to make the side room into a bathroom. He needed a place for the sewage to go, though, so his first task had to be the cesspit. Jim was used to digging graves so digging a cesspit wouldn't be too much of a challenge. Concreting and sealing it, though, could be a huge chore.

Six weeks later it was finished—they had an inside toilet and bath. Wow, what luxury! They had cold running water in the bath but no hot water, so Tilly put plenty of water on to boil and carried it in. She was delighted that she only had to pull the plug to empty the bath water. *And it is sheer bliss not having to go outside to the tin toilet any more!*

Jim was working more for Percy, and one of the children had to go up to Percy's house on Friday nights to get his pay envelope. All three of the older kids wanted to go, because Percy's mother usually gave goodies to whomever went.

"Ray, you went last time," said Jim. "Ken and Eliza can go this time."

"Okay."

Derek and some of his friends were playing on the footpath over the road by the turkey farm. They risked angering Mr Weaver and being yelled at when they played there. Their grumpy neighbour didn't like children at all. Ray was riding down the road on his bike when he spotted Derek.

He meant to get Derek away from the turkey farm as he rode quickly down to him. Bang! Ray's brakes failed and Derek's went flying. He lay on the ground screaming, one leg twisted under him and rapidly swelling up on the front.

Ray gently picked him up and carried him home to The Tin House. Someone saw it happen, and within ten minutes Lilly came running into the house.

"I hear Derek's hurt his leg," she said.

"I think it's broken," replied Tilly.

"Ray, run to the phone box and ring for a taxi. I will take him to hospital," said Lilly.

"I don't know how we would manage without your family," said Tilly.

The doctor confirmed Tilly's diagnosis of a break, and he placed a cast on Derek's ankle and lower leg. Four hours later, poor Derek was still crying. The cast the doctor put on only covered his ankle and lower leg, but the boy had pain up to his knee and higher. "I can feel the bone grinding together!" he wailed.

"I'm taking him back to hospital," said Lilly. "He shouldn't be crying like this."

"I agree," replied the doctor back at the hospital. "This bit of plaster's no good at all."

He removed the first plaster cast and replaced it with one that went from the top of Derek's leg to his toes. A couple of weeks later the boy was hopping all over the place, and he was soon on his feet again.

A few weeks after Derek's accident, Michael walked out from behind a bus and got hit by a car. The chap who ran into him took him to the hospital, but he called into The Tin House to get Tilly on the way. She had to leave the smaller children with Ken.

Michael was unconscious with a fractured skull. Tilly sat with him and held his hand even though she wasn't sure he knew she was there. May, who heard about the accident from neighbours, was soon off to look after the other children so that Jim could join Tilly at the hospital.

"Go home, Tilly, I will stay with Michael," said Jim.

"I can't," she replied. "I can't leave my baby like this."

Just then a nurse walked in with a razor.

"What are you going to do?" asked Tilly.

"I have to shave his head in case the swelling doesn't go down," she said. "It may be necessary to operate on him."

Tilly was praying and crying at the same time. *Why was he in the drive anyway, when he wasn't allowed up the road?* She fell asleep with her head resting on the bed, but she woke with a start to the sound of Michael whimpering.

"Nurse, come quick!" said Tilly.

"That's a good sign," said the nurse. "It shows he's coming round. Go to the kitchen, Tilly, and make yourself a cup of tea. You look shattered."

Tilly sipped the boiling hot tea, nearly scalding her throat. Then, carefully carrying her tea, she returned to the ward. Michael was fully awake and smiling at her. She felt like an enormous weight had fallen away from her heart because she now knew he would be all right. Two weeks later he was home.

"Just keep him a bit quiet for a few days any problems, bring him back," said the doctor when he discharged Michael.

Eliza, Derek and Jill were walking down the lane from school with other children, making their way to the bus stop. School was finished for the day, and the boy in front was poking the hedge with a stick. Suddenly, as he poked, he disturbed a wasps' nest. All of a sudden Eliza was covered from head to toe in wasps. She had walked straight into the swarm, and the angry wasps were all over her, but Jill and Derek also had a couple of stings, too.

At last they reached the bus stop. Everyone was screaming even the bus conductor, who tried to brush the wasps off Eliza and also got stung. The other children didn't want Eliza on the bus, but the driver wouldn't leave her there. Some wasps flew around the bus scaring everyone, but most of them remained on Eliza—in her hair and down her clothes—and they kept stinging her..

At last they reached the bus stop where Eliza, Derek, Jill, Beryl and a few others got off. As Eliza came down the steps of the bus, she saw her mother waiting with a note. Tilly wanted Eliza to go back on the bus to Perk's shop, a chore Eliza often did to help her mother, especially when they were short on groceries.

"Please, don't make me go down to Perks, Mom," cried Eliza, brushing a wasp from the side of her eye. "I've been stung all over."

"If you don't go, Eliza, there won't be any tea tonight. I don't have any money and that's the only place we can have stuff on tick."

Nearly all the children living in the area were off the bus and heading home, but Eliza obediently got back on the bus, wondering if her mother realized how badly she was stung. She was still crying as she reached Perks' shop, but she tried to stem her tears as she stepped inside.

At last Eliza arrived home.

"I'm so sorry," said her mother. "I had no idea you were stung so badly."

Derek, who went home right after school, told Tilly that Eliza was really hurt.

"Let's get those clothes off you," said Tilly, pulling her daughter's clothing over her head. There were still lots of dead wasps in her vest and pants, and a few still moved in her hair.

Tilly washed Eliza and dried her off. Then she took a cube of laundry blueing and put it in a muslin bag. She soaked it in water for a few minutes, so the cube would dissolve, and she wrung it. Then, she rubbed the blueing all over Eliza's wasp stings. Tilly wasn't sure how it helped, but she knew people had been using laundry blueing to soothe insect stings for years.

"I had no idea, Eliza. I am so sorry," she said again. "You know what your father's like though—if there's no tea or sugar in the house."

One day during the summer holidays, Derek got the idea to go picking black currants. "We can make good money doing that," he told the others, encouraging them to come along. They walked the five miles there. Every time they filled a bucket the farmer who owned the fields weighed it. They received a coin for each bucket picked that they could cash in at the end of the day, By then, they were hungry and tired.

"I've had enough for today," said Derek, and his friends agreed. After having their last lot of blackcurrants weighed, they cashed the coins in for money. It was about four o' clock when they started home. The battered band of weary pickers stopped at the railway lines to see 'Big Bertha', the train, that was due any minute.

They sat on the embankment, and waved at the driver, who waved back, as the train went rumbling past them. They wearily walked the mile and a half to the bus stop in Tardebigge.

"Been black currant picking?" the bus conductor asked as they got on the bus, their faces stained with black currant juice.

"How did you know?" said Derek.

"Just guessed," he smiled.

They loved fruit picking, they always took some home to their mothers to make jam, and they shared their money with their mothers, too.

"You are good children," said Tilly, taking the squashed berries from them. "I can make some pies with these."

Derek and his friends did the same thing during strawberry season, but picking from the low plants was back breaking, bending over all day. They ate as many as they put in their punnets, small baskets made of thin, interwoven strips of wood, that were commonly used for berries.

Later on in the year, when the local farmer ploughed his potatoes, they went spud-bashing. They filled their buckets, then the sacks that were scattered along each row. This was hard toil! At the end of the day they went home caked in mud. Tilly heard them scraping their boots on the iron bar that Jim rigged up. He wanted the red quarry floor to stay clean—he would get the floor cloth out as soon as he saw a speck of dirt about.

The children loved to see their mother's face when they handed her half of their money, but they would have to wait this day until she got home from work. Their Uncle Jack helped Jim clean their shoes, as usual, to have them ready for school the next day.

The two men were relaxing after what Jim referred to as "a bad day." He finished the job he had been working and knocked on the door for the money.

"I can't pay," the man said—a reply Jim hated to hear. "Will you take something out of the house instead of payment?"

"The story of my bloody life," said Jim.

"What does he have that's any good?" asked Uncle Jack.

"He has a nice piano," replied Jim. "I wonder if he will let me have that."

"Just ask him, he can only say yes or no!"

"If he lets me have the piano, I'll be able to have a go at playing it. I can't see it being much different than an accordion."

Later, the same night, the children were getting rowdy.

"I wish those bloody kids would calm down a bit!" said Jim. "They're getting on my nerves tonight."

The children had been running in and out all night, arguing and bickering among themselves.

"I'm not telling the lot of you again! Get up to bed, bed, bed, bed! Get them off down here, down here, down here, and shut that stairby door!"

The children know they should get upstairs quickly and out of his way when their father said that. They had felt his hands on their backsides more than once.

Uncle Jack was sitting in his usual place at the bottom of the stairs, smoking his roll-up, and taking no notice of the commotion around him. He and Jim were still cleaning the kids' shoes, but he stood up and out of the way, as the children ran upstairs. Then he got back to work.

Half-an-hour later there was a scream and a thud. "What the bloody hell are 'yer' doing?" Jim shouted up the stairs.

"Sounds as if the scream came from the back of the house," said Uncle Jack.

He and Jim ran outside just in time to see Eliza come limping 'round the corner.

"Oh, my God, she must have fallen out of the bloody window!" said Jim, picking her up.

The other children were scared stiff. "Quick!" Ken shouted.

"Climb on the beam. Dad will never reach us there." They were always climbing on the beams and then jumping off on to their beds, so they quickly scrambled upwards.

Jim was still holding Eliza in his arms when Tilly arrived home.

"What's going on?" she asked, seeing Eliza's tear-stained face.

"Eliza fell out of the back bedroom window and through the wheelbarrow," he began. "You know there was glass in it from that broken pane in the front room that I replaced the other day, and she fell right through the bottom. I don't know how she wasn't cut or killed!"

"I asked you to get rid of that broken glass the other day!" replied Tilly, taking Eliza from him. "How could she fall all that way? The back bedroom window is at least twenty feet from the ground."

"It's twenty feet from the ground in the front room due to the slope outside. Where do you hurt?" said Jim.

"My knee," replied Eliza, sliding off Tilly's lap and gingerly walking round the room.

"I'll keep her home from school tomorrow," Tilly said. "For tonight, she can come in our bed tonight so we can keep an eye on her."

"If I had gotten hold of the other kids earlier on, I would have killed the little buggers!" Jim told her.

When Eliza got up the next morning they were all amazed that she had only a small mark on her knee. If Uncle Jack hadn't been there to witness the situation, no one would have known she had gone through the window and had a twenty foot drop.

Tilly sat the children down and asked them what happened the night before. Apparently, they had been looking out the window at a field of horses that belonged to a band of gypsies. They herded more than one hundred cob horses into the back field earlier in the day. That night, the children stood at the window gazing at them. Eliza had been leaning out of the window, admiring the beautiful horses.

Derek was next to Eliza and Ken was holding Michael, when all of a sudden Ken stumbled. He dropped Michael, and then knocked into Eliza, who went flying out the window. Ken grabbed Michael off the floor and just managed to hold on to him to prevent from falling out the window as well. "You must never open that window again," said Tilly, "or I shall be very angry. It's a wonder Eliza wasn't killed last night."

Jim and Uncle Jack now owned a horse and trap that they bought at the horse fair since Uncle Jack's last horse had been gone for a few years. One lovely Saturday afternoon, Tilly told the kids to get ready to go out in the trap that night. "Get some blankets because it will go colder later on," Jim added.

He took them to Dodril Common Woods, where the children ran in and out of the trees as they explored the grounds. On the way home, they went into The Country Girl, a pub near the woods, and shared a glass of pop. Then, they got back in to the trap and went to a pub closer to home.

It was a new pub that stood across the road from where The Fox and Goose, which was knocked down a few years earlier, had been. The children loved it. There were swings and a roundabout, surrounded by beautiful rhododendron bushes. They each had a glass of pop there.

"Home time!" their father said, coming out of the pub with a smile on his face. He was half sloshed again. It was not that he drank a lot. He only had to have a couple of pints to feel the effects because alcohol went straight to his head, but he was usually in a good mood after a drink.

They all shivered as they climbed back in the float. "We will be home in a few minutes," said Tilly, covering them up with the blankets.

Ray went out regularly with his friends. He was sixteen now and thought he was too old to go out with his parents. In fact, he started smoking now. He no longer considered himself a child. He said he was a man, and he certainly worked like one.

The next day, Tilly was outside with the children. They noticed Jim and Uncle Jack leading a horsedrawn cart down the road towards them. "What do yer have in the float?" asked Tilly. Jack backed the horse to the front door. He pulled the old sheeting off his cargo revealing a piano, and he, Uncle Jack and the boys slid it into the living room.

"Where did that come from?"

"From that chap who owed me money for the job I did ages ago."

The children loved it. Jim was as good at playing the piano as he was at the accordion. It only took him a little while to figure out how to play it. Eliza adored it. Her friend Jill has a piano in her house and her sister Jan played. Jan took piano lessons every week and played well.

"Sit here," said Jan, showing Eliza the scales. "I will give you an idea how to play a tune."

Eliza was chuffed, and she managed to teach herself a few tunes. *Maybe dad will get rich and I can take lessons like Jan.*

The smaller children had a go playing on it, but they soon got bored. As far as Eliza was concerned, though, the piano was the best thing they ever had. She practised until she could play a tune all the way through, but she could only play with one hand. *Never mind, if I keep practising, perhaps I will be a famous pianist one day.*

A couple of nights later they were all awakened in the middle of the night by someone trying to play the piano. Jim got up, and silently crept downstairs. The room was lit up by moonlight shining brightly through the window.

"Is anyone there?" called Jim, switching the light on. A mouse ran out from the back of the piano.

"There's the culprit!" laughed Jim. He decided to put a mousetrap behind there tomorrow night, and hurried back to bed. The next day Tilly told him she wasn't surprised they had mice since she had found tiny footprints in the chip pan earlier in the week.

Derek wanted to go to the bluebell woods, but Tilly wouldn't let him go on his own. "Jill and I are going with him, Mom," said Eliza, immediately gaining Tilly's permission. "Make sure you are back before I go to work, "Tilly said.

The children loved the bluebells—they were so beautiful! After playing and tracking in the woods, the three of them picked a huge bunch of the beautiful bluebells. Laying them in their arms, they carried them back home for their mothers, placing them in the jam jars.

As soon as Tilly woke Sunday morning, she realised that Jim's half of the bed hadn't been slept in. She thought he might be asleep downstairs because he had been doing his Saturday night stint at the pubs at Bromsgrove and was sure to have had a few drinks. She went downstairs, expecting to find him slumped on the old sofa, but he wasn't there. Tilly looked in the other two rooms but no Jim. It was not like him to stay out all night, Tilly worried. She sent Ken to get Uncle Jack. "Tell him it's urgent! "

Ken jumped on his bike and pedalled like the clappers up the road to Uncle Jack's house.

"Mom wants you she says it's very important. I don't think dad come home last night."

Uncle Jack got his bike from round the back of the cottages and rode back with Ken. "What's up, Tilly?" he asked, walking into The Tin House.

"It's Jim. He didn't come home from Bromsgrove last night."

"I will see if I can find out where he is. Come on, Ken, hop on your bike. Let's see if we can find him." Once before, Jim missed the last bus home. However, he walked home on that occasion and arrived in the early hours of Sunday morning.

Ken and Uncle Jack cycled slowly, one on each side of the road. Uncle Jack knew there was more than a possibility that Jim had gotten drunk. It wouldn't be the first time. If that was the case, though, he could have fallen anywhere.

When they passed the canal at Tardebigge, Jack thought he heard someone coughing. "Hang on," he called across the road to Ken. "I need to take a look down the towpath."

Putting his bike to one side, Jack gingerly walked down the towpath. There, under the hedge, was Jim, his feet sticking out. He was deathly white. His clothes were soaking wet, and his accordion was by his side—soaking wet and ruined. Jim said he had been was so drunk that he missed the last bus home. He started to walk, but the rain poured down in torrents, so he tried to get shelter under the hedge.   However, he was so confused that he forgot where he was and landed at the edge of the canal. A few more feet and he would have fallen into the murky water.

Uncle Jack could see that Jim was ill. He was semi-conscious and delirious. "You see that big house over there, Ken?," he said after scanning the neighbourhood. "They're sure to have a phone. Give them this penny and ask them if they would kindly ring for an ambulance."

The ambulance soon arrived and took Jim to the hospital. Uncle Jack and Ken raced back to The Tin House to tell Tilly. "I will get you a lift to hospital," Uncle Jack said.

Jim had problem breathing that was soon diagnosed as pneumonia. He was lucky, though. After two weeks of treatment, he was discharged from hospital.

The doctor told Jim that he must cut down on his drinking and smoking. "You had a lucky escape this time."

CHAPTER 8

Jane was ill. Her son and daughter, Jim and Lou, as well as Tilly, the daughter she gained through marriage, were taking turns sitting with her, but their children—Jane's grandchildren—were not allowed to see her. Jim and the others answered, "Poorly," whenever anyone asked how Jane was doing. She was, in fact, dying from throat cancer, and her family was devastated. Jim spent nearly every night sitting with her.

One day during her illness Jill, Eliza and Derek were sledging down the drive. It was only a small slope, but all of a sudden the sledge tipped up on the bend, spilling them out. Eliza screamed and the others landed on top of her. She lay with her arm twisted underneath her.

"Get off me!" she screamed at them.

"I'm afraid her arm's broken," said the doctor at the hospital after looking at the X-ray. "We will have to put it in plaster of Paris, but it won't hurt as much once the plaster cast is on."

After she spent several hours tending to Eliza's arm and making sure her daughter was comfortable once they got home again, Tilly wearily made her way upstairs to bed. She was thinking about Jane—upset that the only mother she had known since she was ten wouldn't be with them much longer. She also worried about Jim, who was with Jane again tonight. Eliza called out, breaking into her thoughts, "Can I sleep in your bed with you, please, Mom?"

"Okay."

"Where's Dad?" Eliza asked, getting into Tilly's bed, oblivious to her mother's worries.

"He's up with Granny Jane. She's not very well."

In the middle of the night, Eliza woke abruptly and heard her father sobbing. She had never seen or heard him cry before.

"Mother's gone," he told Tilly, who started crying as well.

116

"What are we going to do without your mother?" Tilly asked. "She was like a mother to me, too."

The next week, tears trickled down Jim's cheeks as he put his foot on the spade, and pushed down as hard as he could. *This is one thing I never thought would happen—I never expected to dig my own mother's grave.*

"I don't know if I can face this ordeal," Jim said on the day of his mother's funeral. He threaded new laces through the holes in his best shoes. Then, he brushed them until he could see his face in them— his mother always insisted that his shoes were perfectly shined when he was a child. It was a small thing. But he did it lovingly as a tribute to Jane.

"You know you have to face it," said Tilly, putting her arm around his shoulder and looking into his eyes. "It will be hard for all of us," she added gently. "The Tin House just won't be the same without Jane popping in and out."

The log pile was low, and the weather was freezing. It was not a good situation since Jim had been out of work since the snow came. Outside work was always slack in the winter months, so there was not much money about. Tilly managed to keep the house going with her wages, but the money she earned wasn't enough to pay for all the fuel they needed to keep their large house warm. It was a certain fact that Jim could no longer ask Jane for help, and he wouldn't dream of asking his stepfather.

"What about Uncle Jack?" suggested Tilly.

"I can't ask him again. Don't worry, I will think of something."

The next morning Tilly woke to the sound of sawing. What on earth was Jim sawing this time? She hoped it was not another chair. Soon there wouldn't be any left to sit on. And they burned too quickly anyway. Shivering, she got out of bed and walked over to the window. She had to blow her breath on the windowpane to clear a space in the pretty pattern Jack Frost left on the glass so she could see out.

She didn't see Jim outside the front, so she went to the back bedroom where the children were still fast asleep. Tilly blew her breath on the window in there, too, and looked out. There was Jim sawing the apple trees down. He didn't stop working until all five trees were down. *Goodbye to apple pies later in the year.*

When Tilly looked out some time later, Jim was absolutely soaked. She knew he must have been freezing because it was beginning to snow. Tilly wished she had a camera to capture the scene of Jim sawing rhythmically as snow swirled 'round him. By the end of the day, he had neatly stacked a huge pile of logs in the porch.

"That will help the coke and coal last a bit longer," said Jim, scraping snow off his boots. Tilly put the kettle on to boil as he came in. "I'd love a cuppa, Tilly," he said, "I'm bloody frozen. This is a big house to keep warm."

Another policy matured, and Jim knew exactly what he wanted to do with the money. "Here you are, Tilly. The children need coats and shoes." Ray bought his own clothes now that he earned money, and Ken shopped on his own. Tilly would take the other four children shopping after school.

Eliza definitely needed something new. She was going to Lilly's wedding soon in Jim's place. He decided to give his invitation to Eliza because he didn't like weddings or socialising in large groups. When he told Tilly he would stay home to care for the other children, she knew it was an excuse, but she looked forward to spending a day with Eliza among family and friends.

Tilly took Joseph and Michael to meet Eliza and Derek as they got off the school bus. "Jump back on," she said. "We're going to town." The boys ran to the back of the bus quite excited since they usually bought all their clothes from jumble sales held in the village hall.

Eliza spotted a beautiful coat hanging in a shop window. "Oh, Mom, can I have that one?" she asked, gazing longingly at the coat.

"I'm sorry, it's not practical."

Taking them into the shop, Tilly asked the clerk to show them coats that fit Eliza. "Not too expensive," Tilly said, feeling important.

It wasn't often that she had a sum of money to spend.

"Here you are," said the shopkeeper, delivering a couple of coats from the back of the shop. Eliza tried them on.

"Can I just try the one in the window please, Mom?"

"All right," Tilly said. *It won't hurt to try it on.*

Eliza admired the lilac coat with deep purple, velvet trim 'round the cuffs, collar and pockets. She stroked the velvet cuffs after she put the coat on, and looked up at her mother, pleading with her eyes. Tilly looked at Eliza, who was beautiful in the coat. She hesitated only a minute. *Bugger it! If Jim goes mad it's tough.*

"Okay, we will take that one," she said. Eliza was over the moon! She had never had a new coat before, and this one was a dream. She remembered that she had new clothes at Aunt Ethel's but they were never really hers. Tilly's thoughts were a bit different, *Christ knows what Jim will say when he sees it—he will probably do his nut.*

Tilly didn't have long to wait. Eliza couldn't wait to get the coat out of the bag to show her father, even though Tilly wanted to break it to him gently and was holding her breath. *Well, here goes!*

"What the bloody hell have you bought her that bloody thing for? It won't last five minutes! Take it back tomorrow and get something a bit more practicable. I gut hell, Tilly!" he said, raising his voice. "I thought you had more bloody sense than that!"

That night Jim met Tilly as she got off the bus after the evening shift. "I thought we could have a drink at the local," he said. If Tilly could keep Jim in a good mood she might be able to talk him into letting Eliza keep the coat. She practically held Jim up as he staggered back home. He only had a couple of drinks, and he was still half pissed.

Tilly hoped the children had been good. She warned them before she went to work. *At least he's in a good mood.*

"Please be extra good tonight," she said to he children before she left for work. She desperately wanted Jim to let Eliza keep that coat. Tilly had never seen Eliza's eyes light up the way they did when she agreed to buy the coat. The house was quiet when Jim and Tilly got home. Tilly immediately spotted the coat hanging up on the front room door. A note attached to it said simply, "Please Dad." The two youngest children were asleep in bed, the others sat talking.

Jim looked at the children. "Bugger it, she can have the bloody coat it isn't very often they have anything new."

Eliza kissed him. "You're the best dad in the world."

The next morning Tilly woke Eliza early. They were going shopping downtown, but they planned to stop in at Aunt Lou's house first.

"Can I put my new coat on?" asked Eliza.

"Okay," her mother said. "But you can't wear it all the time. It's for the wedding, remember."

They went off up the road, making a quick stop to see Aunt Eve. None of them ever went past Uncle Jack and Aunt Eve's house without calling in. Eve was standing in her favourite place, holding her long skirt up at the back as she leaned back, warming her arse on the fireguard. She was always doing that.

"Just warming Jack's supper!" she said, giggling. Everyone agreed that Aunt Eve was quite a character—cheerful and often giggling.

Next, they went over the road to catch the bus. When Tilly and Eliza reached town, Tilly did a bit of shopping. Then the two started walking to Lou's house. They had just reached the top of Beoley Road when a lorry passed them and churned the slush up all over Eliza's new coat!

"What will Dad say? He'll go bloody barmy!"

Aunt Lou got a damp cloth and tried to clean the coat, but the more she wiped the worse it looked.

When Jim found out later in the day, he was not pleased, "I told you it wasn't practicable!"

Edna's daughter, Jan, worked at the laundry, and saved the day. She offered to take the coat to be dry-cleaned. She said she could get it done free. "Thank you, Jan, you are a lifesaver." Tilly said.

Ken, too, started working at the laundry. He wanted to be a mechanic, and he was keen to learn a trade. He was determined he would not be poor like his parents. Luckily, the laundry wanted a young trainee, so he started working with Reg, who took care of the laundry's vans.

"We have six vans, Ken, and it's up to us to keep them in good running order," Reg said. Ken learned quickly, and he loved his job at which he earned two pounds a week. His pay was significantly more than Ray's one pound, ten shilling for his work on the farm "I'm going to look out for another job," said Ray. "If you can earn that much, so can I."

Jill and Eliza played up on the links a lot. They went there to meet some boys including two brothers who lived on an estate near town. Jill's youngest sister Val and Derek were with them as they played tracking right up until dusk. One of the boys looked like a Greek god he was tall with blonde wavy hair, and Eliza considered him to be "really handsome." *What a cracker!*

Eliza's heart fluttered every time she was near him. Sometimes she and her friends sat on the brow of the hill that overlooked the estate below, talking hours. At other times, they climbed the conker and chestnut trees. Depending on what time of the year it was, they would shake the trees until the nuts or conkers fell off. They would take some home for the young children.

"Who wants to earn some money?" asked Jim one morning before he left for work.

"I do, Dad," they all replied at once. They knew the job was picking caterpillars off the young cabbage seedlings he planted a few days ago.

"I will give each of you a half penny, but the one with the most caterpillars can have one penny."

The children knew they would be able to use some coupons for sweets from the ration book, if their mother hadn't swapped them all for tea and sugar coupons. Edna and her family had a sweet tooth, and Jim liked his cups of tea.

It was early in the morning, and there was no milk at The Tin House, which was nothing unusual. "Go over to Mrs Hunt's house and ask if we can borrow a pint of milk," Jim said to whoever happened to be up. "Just take it off the window sill if she isn't up. She will know we have it." Mrs Hunt was a widow with five children, and Jim did a lot of odd jobs for her.

Tilly was now pregnant again so she had to put her jobs outside the home on hold. That meant that Jim had to try to earn more money somehow. He decided to buy cocks to fatten up so they would

121

be ready to sell at Christmas time. He went off to the market to buy the cocks.

Jim bought a hundred cockerels—so cute, all yellow and fluffy—that came in an old orange crate. He put a stick over the box and then attached two light bulbs to the stick, plugged them in and switched them on. The heat from the bulbs kept the chicks warm, and he eventually managed to rear eighty of them. He took orders for a couple of weeks, and by the time they were grown, all of them were taken.

When the children arrived home from school Eliza wanted to play the piano, but when she entered the lining room, her beloved piano was gone!

"I'm sorry, Eliza, your father chopped it up for firewood."

"Oh, no!" she cried. "I can't believe he did that to the piano that I loved." Eliza cried herself to sleep that night, saddened that now she would never learn to play well.

Jill asked Eliza and Derek to go to the pictures on Saturday, but Eliza knew her mother didn't have money to buy the tickets. Jill felt sorry for Eliza. She was her best friend and she asked her to go every week. Eliza promised to ask her mother.

"Can we go to the pictures in the morning, Mom?" asked Eliza.

"I'm broke. Ask Ray if he can pay for you."

"Sorry," said Ray. "I gave Dad some money last night. I've only enough left to last me the week."

"We can't come!" Eliza told Jill.

"I have an idea,' replied Jill. "What if we walk down Muskets Path to town? I will let you and Derek through the back door of the cinema, and with the bus fare we save by walking down, we can pay your fare back home."

There was quite a queue outside the back door of the cinema. It was no wonder the manager never cottoned on. Jill paid for her and her sister at the door, and chose seats near the emergency exit. She, then, headed to the toilets where the back door was located. She pulled the latch up and opened the door, so Eliza and Derek could scurry inside. They ducked down as they came in and quickly sat down next to Jill and her sister. "Don't ever tell Mom," Jill threatened her sister.

Eliza and Derek were about to leave the house to go to school, when Eliza, turned to say bye to her mother. She hesitated because her mother looked pale, and then asked, "Are you all right, Mom? Shall I stay home to help?"

"No, you pop off to school. I will be all right."

Eliza worried about her mother all day, knowing that Tilly was pregnant. "I hope she's all right," Eliza said to her friend. Jill said she was sure Tilly would be fine.

Eliza was standing at the front of the bus going home, impatiently waiting to get off first. She wanted to get home because she had worried about her mother. She jumped from the bus steps just as soon as it stopped, and almost knocked down her cousin May, who was standing there.

"I have been waiting for you," said May with a big grin on her face! "Guess what! You have a baby sister at last."

Eliza shrieked with delight. So that was why her mother had looked so pale and tired this morning! Eliza and Derek ran down home to see the new baby.

She was beautiful with a mass of black hair, and Tilly looked radiant with a big smile on her face. "That's it now," she said. "This is definitely the last one."

They named the baby 'Mollie' and called her 'Mo.' Jessie sat by Tilly's bed, she had her son on her lap and was breastfeeding him. She has just fetched him from school—he was six years old and still being breastfed! Jessie was still sitting by Tilly when Ray came home from work. He had a friend with him. Jessie got her boob out and started feeding her son again.

"Good grief! Those are bigger than some of them cows' udders down the farm!" Ray said. Jessie laughed, and "squibbed" him with milk. She didn't give a bugger who saw her boobs. She was the dead opposite to Tilly, but they got on like a house on fire.

Jim had some money left from selling the cockerels at Christmas, so he bought a maroon, Tansad pram for the baby. Ray went to town and bought his new sister napkins of terry towelling, and a lady from Bromsgrove sent a new pink satin cover and pillow case to go on it. Jim met the woman, a widow who was quite wealthy at the pub where he whistled. When Tilly saw that gift, she reckoned that Jim and the widow were up to mischief. *I will put a stop to that as soon as I'm back on my feet.*

Ray often brought his friends to The Tin House to eat or hang out. One friend had a sister named Daisy, who delivered milk on weekends. She needed help so she asked her brother to see if Eliza wanted to help on the milk round on Saturday and Sunday mornings. However, it meant that Eliza would have to sleep at Daisy's house because they had to be at the farm at six a. m.

The house Daisy lived in was enormous. It had nine bedrooms and a giant bathroom, a massive hallway, a huge pantry and cellar as well as five large rooms downstairs. Four different doors led outside. Daisy's father was tall, quite frightening, and very strict. It was "a good job" the house was big because Daisy had to sneak Eliza in to sleep.

The milk round was pleasant in the summer and freezing in the winter, and unfortunately it was winter. They had to harness the horse, named Dolly, and load large churns of milk as well as two crates of bottled milk onto the cart. Both Daisy and Eliza wore gloves, but the cold seemed to go straight through them. Most of the customers left clean, empty jugs outside along with the exact amount of money to pay for the milk right next to it. The girls ladled milk out of a large churn and into the jugs. A few people bought bottled milk, which was just beginning to become popular.

By the time they finished the route and arrived back on the farm, the milkmaids were freezing. Daisy cashed up and did the books, while Eliza washed empty bottles from the bottled-milk customers so they would be ready the next day.

At least once, Eliza needed to pee and couldn't hold it any longer. She felt the warm liquid trickle down her legs. Soon her legs, too, were icy cold as her wet pants froze. By the time she got home the tops of her legs and her calves were chaffed and raw from the wet, freezing trousers she borrowed from her brother. She had to tie the waist and bottoms of the legs with pieces of string to make them fit better.

Late on a spring evening about six o'clock, a whole throng of children assembled over at the Plek. Most of them were thirteen or a few years older, but there were a few seventeen and eighteen year old youths, too. They decided to play hide and seek. Two people were designated as seekers. They started to count to one hundred, and everyone else quickly scampered to find hiding places.

There were lots of hiding places. Daisy and Jill hid behind the laurel bushes in Weaver's garden, when, all of a sudden the door opened. Jill "legged it" out of there, but before Daisy could move, Mr Weaver grabbed her by the scruff of her neck and pulled her into the hallway. She was standing on the mat, shaking and absolutely terrified—so scared that she wet herself and soon stood in a pool of urine.

Mr Weaver didn't say a word, he just stood looking at her, smirking, enjoying the look of terror on her face. A knock on the door broke the silence. As Mr Weaver opened it Daisy ran past him and ran as fast as she can. Right behind her was Ken, the one who knocked on the door.

"I shan't be hiding there again," said Daisy. "I was shit-scared and I'm soaking wet."

"I don't think any of us will," replied Ken.

Ray was ecstatic. He had finally saved enough money to buy a radiogram and records. He purchased recorded songs by Mario Lanza, Johnnie Ray and Frankie Lane. He liked to sing and was always trying to sing "Because You're Mine" just the way Mario Lanza did. He also liked instrumental music and bought a recording of Winifred Attwell on piano. The younger children teased him. "You think you'll be a famous singer one day," they would say and giggle.

Ray didn't care if they teased him—he loved his music, and he didn't want anyone else to touch his radiogram or records. "Not even you or Dad," he told Tilly, emphatically.

Jim walked around the house, eyeing it from all angles and came to this verdict. "It's time to do the house up." He threw out the grates and even the boiler in the kitchen had to go. He installed new grates and got a new stove.

"I shall miss those hobs," said Tilly.

"We have to keep up with the times."

Tilly walked into the house carrying the two heavy bags of shopping she got from Perks' shop downtown. She called in after leaving her early morning shift at work. She plonked the shopping on the table, wondering what was inside the huge box in the kitchen. She lit the gas under the teakettle and wondered. *What can it be? I haven't ordered anything.*

"Haven't you opened it yet?" said Jim, walking into the kitchen. He reached for a knife to cut the string, then proceeded to unwrap it. Tilly couldn't believe her eyes. It was a brand new washing machine. That meant no more scrubbing and dollying, and it boiled the water as well as doing the washing.

Jim made a small round hole in the wall in the kitchen adjacent to the bathroom He wanted to be able to boil water in the washing machine, put the hose through the hole in the wall and pump it straight into the bath. Tilly thought that was sheer bliss. *Clean hot water and mo more carrying it from the kitchen to the bathroom.* She said she felt like a princess.

It was Eliza's job to scrub the living room floor and get the tea after she came home from school, because Tilly had her cleaning job to do. Eliza got half a crown a week for scrubbing the floor every night, but one night, she got really annoyed. She finished the floor and was cutting bread for tea. The younger children kept running in and out, pinching the slices as fast as she could cut them.

"The next one to do that is going to get a good slap with the flat of the knife," she said. Eliza was just cutting another slice, when

Joseph ran in and grabbed a piece of bread. As he did it, Eliza hit him with the flat end of the knife, like her father did.

"Got you!" she said, giving him a glancing blow on his back. Joseph ran upstairs, screaming his head off. *Why is he screaming like that? I didn't hit him that hard!* Five minutes later, Joseph was still crying, so Eliza went to him upstairs.

"What's all this noise? I didn't hit you that hard," she said, walking through the open doorway into the bedroom. She stopped dead in her tracks—a look of horror on her face. Joseph was covered in blood. She ran to him. His white school shirt was bright red from all the blood.

Oh God! What have I done to him? When Eliza pulled his shirt off there was a gaping gash about an inch and half long. Shaking, she ran to get a clean napkin, and she frantically tried to stem the flow of blood.

"Come on, I have to get you to hospital," she said to him. Eliza put her arm round Joseph as they walked up the drive together. She was crying as well. She hadn't meant to hurt him. She begged him not to tell their parents. "If you say you were walking down the drive backwards and fell on some glass, I will give you my half crown on Fridays."

"Okay," replied Joseph.

As they left, they spotted Mr Wall, who was putting his car away in the Plek. When Eliza called him he could see all the blood on Joseph. "I will take you to the hospital, just hang on. I will get my car back out."

The doctor who saw Joseph was concerned about the cut. "It must have been a sharp piece glass to do that to you," he said after stitching the wound. "Be more careful in the future."

Joseph and Eliza had to walk home. They cut through Muskets Path, since they had no money for bus fares. It was late by the time they got home. Tilly had already seen the trail of blood, and she wondered what happened and where her children had gone.

Eliza gave her half a crown to Joseph for weeks until one day she had enough. "Joseph, I'm not giving you any more money. I have to work so hard for it," she said.

"I will tell Mom you cut my back if you don't."

"Go on, then," replied Eliza. "See if I care."

When Joseph ran to tell his mother, she did not believe him. "Don't be daft," she said. "Why would she do that?"

"Another bloody boy!" said Nurse Wooldridge. "I thought you had finished having babies!"

"So did I," replied Tilly. "I hope this is the last, I'm forty now and I don't want any more."

"You bin saying that since young Ken was born. You had two babies then, now you have eight."

The latest addition was called Biron, and he was the apple of Jim's eye He could do nothing wrong in Jim's eyes. By the time he was a toddler, Biron was quiet and clingy, and he followed his mother and father whenever he could.

Eliza left school and joined Jan, Jill and Ken at work in the laundry. "You will work in the sorting department, that's the only vacancy available," said the supervisor named Enid. "It is where all the dirty washing is divided into the different categories, whites with whites, darks with darks—you'll get used to the categories—oh, and keep all smelly socks in their own pile." The women who worked in sorting were often bitten by fleas as some of the dirty laundry was rife with them.

Eliza retched as the stench of stale piss on the sheets hit her nostrils. I hate it!" she said to her supervisor.

"Put your name down to be a floater," Enid replied. "It's one way to get a transfer.

"Come on, get up, Eliza!" her brother shouted one morning as Eliza lay in bed. "If you're not up in one minute I'm going without you. You will make us both late for work."

She jumped out of bed, still half-asleep, and rubbed her eyes against the brightness of the early morning sun shining in the bedroom. She had been in a deep sleep probably because she and Jill spent the night skating at the rink. "I'm knackered this morning."

"Jump on the crossbar," said Ken as they reached the top of the drive. They rode together on one bike many times before. "Don't go as fast as you usually do!" begged Eliza, but Ken ignored her and pedalled as fast as he could. Taking the shortcut down the links, Ken picked his feet up, free-wheeling. They whizzed down the hill so fast that Ken had a hard time stopping the bike at the bottom of the hill, but he cut a half mile off their trek to work. "It's a wonder we were not killed, at the speed you go," Eliza fussed.

Ken pulled up in the laundry yard just as the "hooter" went off. They knew it was eight o'clock when Eliza slid off Ken's handlebars and entered the laundry. As she clocked in, she noticed one of her workmates coming up behind her coming from the opposite direction.

The woman caught up with her as they clocked in—right on time. "I don't know," the woman said, shaking her head. "Here you are, Eliza, with your hair all over the place from riding on your brother's crossbar. I just passed Harry walking up the road in his uniform, looking like a Greek god." Harry was the boy Eliza was hooked on—one of the lads she used to play with on the links.

Ken was called up to enter the Royal Air Force. His orders said he would be stationed in Cyprus, where there was trouble. Tilly and Jim didn't have a clue where Cyprus was nor did anyone else they knew. They eventually learned that Cyprus was an Eastern Mediterranean island near Turkey where the people were fighting to gain independence from Great Britain, a feat they accomplished in 1960. Ray, who was older than Ken, was exempt from the service because he worked on a farm.

When Ken had been gone a few weeks, Eliza's realised how much she missed him, especially because she now had to get up earlier to walk to work with Jill. When she was late, she had to walk the shortcut through the links on her own. That frightened her because she remembered that a man had exposed himself there one day as they played.

As the year went on, Jill and Eliza started going to local dances. They were both good dancers and had plenty of partners. If they lacked a partner, though, they danced together with Jill in the lead. They took part in barn dances, and they liked jiving and ballroom dancing, too.

Ray never went to town. He was happy just going to the Brook Pub down the lane. It was a quiet little inn for a quiet chap. Ray had no interest in dancing or skating, but he loved to sing a good song. The pub he used was three miles away, but Ray walked the six-mile trek every night. He wasn't interested in girls. He said he was too young for that.

"I've been thinking about going into the services, Mother," he said one day, shocking her. .

Tilly tried to talk him out of it. She already had Ken in the forces stationed in Cyprus, and she worried because she hadn't heard from him in ages. But Ray was adamant. He said he had enough of working on a farm, and his mind was made up. That same week he joined the Colstream Guards.

Jim made a proposal to Eliza. "How about packing your job in, Eliza?" He explained that Tilly, who was pregnant again, needed help with the washing and ironing as well as cleaning The Tin House. Jim also wanted Eliza to help watch the younger children so that Tilly could go back to work when the baby came.

"She can earn more money than you get at the laundry," Jim reasoned. He also pointed out that May had two children of her own now and that she, like her sisters, was married. She could no longer help Tilly as she had in the past.

Eliza didn't want to be tied down that much because there were a couple of fellows she was keen on. One fellow, whom she sometimes dated, had such a fabulous voice that he won numerous talent competitions at carnival time. When Eliza brought him home, Jim always asked him to sing "Green Door" since the doors to The Tin House were painted green. Jim always applauded when "the singer," as Jim called him, finished his song.

Eliza met Sam, who she thought was absolutely gorgeous, on a blind date. He was tall and had jet black hair, but he wasn't always around. She said he was here one minute and gone the next. Eliza also noticed that all the other girls fancied Sam as well. He usually came to pick Eliza up from The Tin House on his motor-bike.

One night, Sam borrowed a mate's car since he was taking Eliza to Alcester Mop, a local street fair, with another couple—a friend of his and one of Eliza's. Sam wasn't a very good dancer, and he kept Eliza laughing. He picked her up and swung her onto his shoulders, and he then walked proudly around the Mop. Eliza thought the night flew by. *What a wonderful night this was.*

Jill and Eliza leisurely strolled down Muskets Walk, making their way to the local cafe at the bus station in town. There they met other friends on Saturday afternoons.

"Can I join you?" said a girl, who appeared to be crying, as they sipped their coffee.

"Help yourself," Jill said, gesturing to the empty chair. "What's up?" she asked as the girl sat down. This girl was a total stranger to both Jill and Eliza.

"My boyfriend hasn't turned up!" she sobbed, getting a photo from her bag. "Here he is," she said, passing the photo to Jill.

"Christ!" said Jill, who looked at the photo before handing it to Eliza.

When Eliza looked at it, her jaw dropped because it was photo of Sam. *We both have the same boyfriend!*

Later, Eliza asked Sam about the other girl. "She's just a friend," he replied, and Eliza stupidly believed him.

Tilly gave birth to another little boy, who weighed eight pounds and was her seventh boy. Nurse Wooldridge remarked on the changes Jim made over the years in The Tin House. She would not have predicted that Jim would work as hard as he did to keep his large family going, but that was a long time ago. Now, she readily admitted that he did a fine job.

"Yes," said Tilly. "Despite all the hard work I wouldn't change a thing since the day I met Jim."

They named the new baby 'Sam,' and Tilly was soon on her feet and back at work. Eliza was still at home, looking after the children. She often pretended she was little Sam's mother.

Tilly was on the early and late shift again. She usually came home from her morning job, ate something, and took a nap with the two youngest, Biron and Sam, in the afternoons. When she awoke, she had a sandwich and cup of tea before she went off to work again.

It was Thursday—Tilly's pay night—she planned to meet Jim at the bus stop and have a drink at The Rose and Crown. That meant that Eliza couldn't go out. She was stuck with the children and finding it very hard work.

Another evening, Tilly and Eliza were sitting by the fire pegging a new rug, when a shadow passed by the window. There was a quiet tap before the door opened. "It's Ray!" squealed Tilly, standing up, holding her arms out to him. He had been away for six months.

"I've been discharged because my hearing isn't a hundred per cent."

"Good grief, Ray. How you have grown!" remarked Tilly, giving him another big hug. "How tall are you?"

"Six foot two," he said. "It's because I learned to stand upright."

"Hi son," said Jim, embracing Ray, after he came in from work. "Am I glad to see you! Why are you back?"

Ray repeated that he has been discharged.

"I suppose you will be going back to the farm to work, won't you, son?"

"I don't think so, the money isn't much good. I was based with a chap who used to work in a car-making factory he said the money's really good there," Ray said. The factory was about nine miles away, so if Ray wanted to work there, he needed to buy a car first. "I learned to drive on the tractor when I worked on the farm," he said, noting that he always wanted a car, but he could not afford one. He had enough money now, because he received a sum of money when he was discharged from the service.

A few days later Ray came home, driving an old car, and grinning from ear to ear. The car was beige and black. One window didn't wind up properly, but he was the first of his friends and relatives to have a car, and he was "chuffed to buggery" with it.

Ray got the job at the car factory, but he complained about the plant. "I hate it. The noise is deafening even to me, but I am determined to stay because the money is so good." Now, instead of walking down to the pub, he drove down in his car. That night, Ray walked into the house with two young men following behind him.

"Meet my drinking partners," he said. The two brothers lived on their father's farm. Eliza considered them "a real good laugh" and "very good looking."

Ken also finished his time in the forces, and he brought a beautiful watch for Eliza back from Cyprus. She was thrilled to bits when he handed it to her. "I love it. I've never had a watch before—it's just lovely, Ken," .she cried as he strapped it on her wrist.

Ken invited Eliza to take a weekend trip. He and one of his colleagues in the service became friends when they were in Cyprus and discovered they only lived forty miles apart. Ken decided to visit on the weekend, and Eliza was delighted to accompany him.

"We can stay there for the weekend and come back home Sunday night," he said. The brother and sister put a few things in their bags, and then they were off. It seemed to take them forever in Ken's old banger, but at last they reached Pete's house.

"Hurry up," he said. "We were waiting to go to the clubhouse." The club was massive. "This is my cousin Jean," Pete said, introducing them to a pretty girl.

Phew she's nice! Ken thought as he said hello to her, and by the end of the night he really had "the hots" for Jean. He asked if he could see her the next week.

"Okay," she replied. "I will look forward to seeing you again."

"Can I have that watch back that I bought you, Eliza? I want to give to Jean."

"Get stuffed!" said Eliza angrily.

"This week passed really quickly to me," said Ken, as he and Eliza got in the car to visit with Pete and Jean the next weekend.

The band in the pub they went to asked people to" have a go" and sing on stage.

"Go on, Eliza," urged Ken. "You know you can sing."

Eliza was shaking as she nervously belted out her favourite song,

Old Fashioned Girl, by Teresa Brewer, and she got great applause. She had sung before on several occasions, but never to an audience this big.

They had fun and the time passed too quickly. Sunday night, when they had to return home, came all too soon.

"It's ten o' clock, we will have to be going," said Ken. As they drove, Eliza nodded off. After a while, though, she woke startled.

"What's that sound?" she asked just before they heard a bang. The tyre burst, and they didn't have a spare. Ken kept on driving until the tyre shredded. He drove on the rim with sparks flying off.

"I think there's a garage 'round the next bend," he said. "Ah, there it is, but it's closed."

"We haven't got any money anyway," Eliza reminded him.

"I will have to knock on the door and get the man up, and see if he can help us out."

The chap was not happy about being roused from bed at such a late hour, but Ken gave him bullshit about being on emergency leave. The chap kindly sorted out a good tyre and tube for them. Then came the crunch, no money He scrutinized them for some time before speaking. "I will have that watch you're wearing," he finally said to Eliza after eyeing them up and down. "You can have it back when you give me the money you owe me."

Ken got his old job as a mechanic back at the laundry because he had learned a lot in the forces. He told Reg, whom he worked with, "I shan't be stopping here long. I've learned a lot about cars and lorries in the forces." He had some saving to do, however, before he could leave.

Ken still went to Pete's on the weekends. He and Jean had grown close, and it was hard for him to wait out the week between his visits to her.

When Derek left school, Ken managed to get him a job at the laundry as well. They were expanding quickly, but Ken has other plans for his own future that did not involve the laundry. Still, he did not want to let them down since Mr Cellar, the owner, was good to him.

"Ken, will you call in to pay that garage man for that tyre next time you go to see Jean? I want my watch back, please?" Eliza asked him.

Meanwhile, Ray brought the two farm boys back for supper again. Jim winked at Eliza before addressing her in front of the boys, "Why don't you make them a nice sandwich?"

Eliza knew what her father meant. The family liked to played tricks on the children's friends by making sandwiches of things that usually were not served together. This time, Eliza made a few selections. cheese and jam, cheese and condensed milk, jam and lard. The lads ate the lot and never batted an eyelid. Tilly, Jim and Eliza laughed, and the two lads just laughed with them.

"I quite like that one," said Eliza after they had gone

"I will get you fixed up," said Ray, and that was the start of her seeing Joseph. Eliza liked the fact that he had the same name as on of her brothers, and her Joseph seemed quite nice. When she started seeing him, they went to the pubs and listened to music. Eliza was a bit dismayed that he didn't dance, because she was a good dancer who loved it.

Eliza was smitten with Joseph. He was quite handsome and whenever she was near him her heart raced. As they grew closer, they took long walks in the fields and woods. Eliza was amazed that he knew so much about wild life and plants. She was proud to be seen with him at the pubs, the cinema and at parties in friends' homes and at their weddings.

They went to Jill's wedding when she married her "smashing chap," Graham, and visited with other friends who were married. May already had two children, and Jill's sister Jan had married a few years earlier. Eliza thought Ken would probably marry Jean.

After Joseph and Eliza dated for several months, they decided to get married. It was a quiet wedding in the village church with refreshments at The Tin House. The couple moved into several rooms over the diary farm where Joseph's parents lived. The rooms looked out over the farm that lay in a valley, and Eliza thought the view was breathtaking

Eliza recalled her first few meetings with Joseph's parents. It was on Pancake Day or Shrove Tuesday, the day before Lent started, several months ago. Eliza would never forget it because she thought she made a fool of herself. The four of them—Eliza, Joseph and his parents—sat down to a dinner of fish and chips. Eliza shook what she thought was salt all over her meal only to discover that she had sugared her fish and chips. She had never seen a sugar shaker before and hoped no one noticed. She had to eat the fish and chips that way—talk about odd combinations! Maybe it was payback for the odd sandwiches she served her friends. She had a hard time finishing them because they tasted so sweet.

At the same meal, Joseph's mother also served the milk in a jug and used proper salt and pepper cellars. Eliza had seen similar cellars at Aunt Ethel's house years before, but she never had used a milk jug. The entire bottle of milk always stood on Tilly and Jim's table, although they did use a sugar bowl. The youngest children very often had their milk in sauce bottles, with a teat or rubber nipple forced on the top of it.

At first, Eliza found it very difficult to live at the farm. It was so quiet. The farm was wonderful, and the rooms in the house absolutely enormous. It was very much like the Palmer Farm where Tilly worked. It was actually on the same route, too—about two miles past the farm where her mother went from the convent more than twenty years ago.

Eliza needed to see her mother as she hadn't seen her for weeks. "Can you give me a lift to Mom's before you go to work in the morning, please?" Eliza asked Joseph.

"No," he replied. "You're not going anywhere on your own." *If he thinks that, he doesn't know me very well. I won't stand for that.*

Because she didn't want any "aggro," she decided to walk up to her mother's and then get back before her husband arrived from work at night. That way no one would get hurt and there wouldn't be any rows. Joseph had become jealous and possessive since their marriage.

Eliza crept out the dairy way, hoping her mother-in-law was not about. It was quite windy as she walked 'round the winding lanes, enjoying the birds' songs and the rusty red and orange coloured autumn leaves. Some of them were gently falling, while those that were already on the ground made a rustling noise as the wind made them dance along the lane. Eliza walked faster once she neared Botters Hill. She couldn't wait to see her family.

Tilly was so pleased to see Eliza that she hugged her for a full two minutes before she let her go. She wondered why Eliza had not come to see her and was a little worried about her daughter. She was uneasy about Eliza walking the four miles from the dairy farm alone.

"I want you to stay until after school so that Joseph can walk home with you," she told Eliza, adding, "He can take his bike with him and then ride back."

"I don't think he will ride up Bottor's Hill," replied Eliza, knowing that she almost always walked her own bicycle up the hill, She knew she would be cutting it fine if she stayed until after school, but she would feel safer walking with another person.

Tilly and Eliza sat and chatted, had sandwiches and tea, and played for a while with Biron and Sam. The boys were still babies and they missed their big sister or other mother. They cried when she and Joseph waved to them as they started back to the farm—they thought Joseph would go away for a long time, too "I wish I could take you both with me," Eliza said as she left. "But it's not possible."

After they walked two and a half miles, Eliza sent Joseph back home. She stood and watched as he jumped on his bike and cycled off, disappearing 'round the bend in the lane.

Hurrying down the next lane, she crept through the dairy. *Good, there's no one about!* Her heart pounded inside her chest as she climbed the stairs, missing the one that creaked, and then stepped into the room, breathing a sigh of relief! She quickly got the evening tea. *This worked out fine.*

"I'm pregnant, Mom," said Eliza on her next visit about two weeks later.

"Oh, Eliza, don't have a rook of children like me. It's so hard and you know what Joseph is like with you."

"I will be all right, Mom."

"I hope so!"

The winter snow prevented Eliza from walking all that way to her mom's house, and she was due to give birth to her baby, in a couple of months. Eliza's mother-in-law started taking her into town every Friday when she did the main shopping so Eliza arranged to meet her mother in the café down town. At least she could see her once a week.

"Ray's courting," said Tilly.

"Really?" I didn't know he had a girlfriend."

"Yes, he does, and her name is Marge—what a looker she is too! They're getting married next week."

After a few months, Ray and Marge rented a tiny cottage, just up the road from Uncle Jack's and Aunt Eve's house, and 'round the corner from The Tin House.

The days were slowly getting longer, and even though it was still cold, Eliza looked forward to spring with her baby. She gave birth to a little girl, with a mass of black, curly hair, who weighed just over five pounds.

"I'm going to call you Dawn," Eliza whispered in her baby's ear, kissing her soft pink cheeks. They would be in hospital for two weeks.

The matron was horrible. "Only one visitor allowed at each bed," she said. Ray was on shift work and was currently home during the day time.

"Come on, Mother, I will take you to visit Eliza in hospital," he said to Tilly after hearing Eliza had her baby. Ray popped in first. "Just a quick hello to see that you are all right. I won't stop long. Mother's waiting outside."

Eliza was really pleased to see her brother. "How's Marge?" she asked him.

"Fine! I'm off now. See you when you come home."

Eliza lay there, waiting for her mother to come in. "Hi there," she said, with a smile on her face. Eliza was overwhelmed as her mother sat by the bed. All of a sudden the Matron was standing behind Tilly. "Out now!" she said, with her hands on hips.

"Why?

"There is only one visitor to a bed!"

"Ray was only in here for five minutes, if that," replied Tilly.

"I'm not having anybody swapping," and, with that, she almost frog marched Tilly out of the ward.

Eliza was heartbroken. She pulled the curtains 'round the bed and sobbed her heart out. *How mean could the Matron be?*

In the meantime, Tilly went to the head of the hospital to

complain, but the administrator said that she must listen to the matron because she ran the ward, "and what she says must be obeyed."

Ray took Tilly back again the next day, but this time he stayed outside.

"I cried all the way home yesterday," said Tilly.

"I did, too," replied Eliza.

"Doesn't she have a lot of hair!" said Tilly, looking at the baby. "And isn't she tiny? She has more hair than Mo had when she was born. She's lovely."

"I know," replied a proud Eliza, "and she looks just like you, Mom."

The lady in the next bed crocheted a tiny bonnet for Eliza's baby.

"My mother used to do a lot of crocheting a few years ago when she had time," said Eliza, thanking the woman.

At last the day arrived for Eliza to be discharged from hospital. She had been there for fourteen long days. It was her brother Ray who came to collect her, taking her straight to The Tin House, where all her brothers and sister crowded 'round to look at the new baby.

"Isn't she beautiful!" they said as each one held her in turn.

"Can you take me home please, Ray? Joseph will be home from work soon and he won't like it if I'm not there."

Tilly gave Sam's pram to Eliza for Dawn It was high and very fashionable—a Silver Cross pram—that Eliza knew to be best. Even Tilly had felt lucky to have it. She saw it advertised in the local paper when she was pregnant with Sam, and she knew she had to have that pram.

Tilly hadn't seen Eliza for over two weeks and was worried about her. Meanwhile Eliza hadn't had much sleep since the baby seemed to want to be fed all the time. As soon as Eliza s put her down, she would start crying again. Eliza sighed and wished her mother was there. She would know what to do.

The crying went on day and night and created a problem for Eliza's father-in-law. He had to rise at four in the morning to do the milking and then the milk round after that, and Eliza worried that the baby disturbed his sleep. He had never spoken to Eliza all the time she knew him, but she thought he was the most horrible man she ever met.

At two in the morning, there was a tap on the door. Eliza unlocked it and her mother-in-law stepped inside. "What's the baby crying for?"

"I don't know, I think she just likes crying," replied Eliza.

"I think you had better try her on national dried milk, then you can see how much milk she had. I will take you to get some in the morning, and we will buy a couple of bottles and teats as well."

The next morning, bright and early, her mother-in-law called to take her to town. "Are you ready to go, Eliza? We will go and get the dried milk and bottles now."

Eliza mixed the dried milk, knowing how to do it because Tilly used dried milk for Sam, the first one of her children to be bottle-fed. The milk was ready. *"Here goes!"* Eliza crossed her fingers and popped the teat into Dawn's mouth. The baby only drank one ounce the first time, refusing any more. An hour later she was crying for milk again.

"You have to persevere with her. Try to make her take more milk at a time," said her mother-in-law. Eliza tried, but Dawn refused to take more than the one ounce. "I will just have to feed her every hour until she starts taking more a little at a time," she said.

Eliza was changing her baby. "Come in," she called, hearing a knock at the door, thinking it would be her mother-in-law. But it was Joseph's father. Eliza was petrified before he even said a word. The look on his face spelled trouble. This was the first time he had been in their room since Eliza moved in. He had never spoken to her, but suddenly he was shouting.

"You owe me twelve months milk money and I want it now!" he said while glaring at her. Eliza knew he always started drinking before he came home from the milk rounds and today was no different. She took a deep breath and reminded herself to be careful.

"I thought Joseph paid you. He's the one who brings the milk up," replied Eliza, trembling.

"You are the wife, you should pay," he shouted, pointing at her. Eliza could smell the drink on him.

"I will tell Joseph when he gets home," she said. "Please leave me alone. I haven't got any money."

Eliza locked the door as soon as he was gone. Leaning back on it, she stood there shaking as he plodded downstairs. *Pig!!*

When Joseph came in form work, Eliza told him she wanted to get out of there.

"What's up?" he asked.

She told him what his father had said to her. "I know he doesn't like me, nor does your mother. They think I'm not good enough because I came from The Tin House. "

"I will go and see my grandmother," said Joseph. "She's the only one that dares say anything to him."

After Joseph finished his tea, he headed to his grandmother's house. She was delighted to see her grandson in the middle of the week. "It's not really a social visit," he said. "I need your help. Could you please talk with father?" He then told his grandmother about his father's visit to Eliza and that she was terrified of him. "She's too scared to go down to the toilet. She's peeing in a bucket then putting it down the sink."

At home, Eliza thought about Joseph's grandmother. *What a lovely woman she is! How could she have had such a horrible son!*

The next afternoon, Joseph' grandmother got on her bike and cycled down to the farm to see her son. "What's this I hear about you upsetting Eliza," she demanded. "You should be ashamed of yourself. Don't forget how you got started, son!" She then went upstairs to see Joseph and Eliza. "He won't be bothering you again."

Joseph started a new job. It was not far from the farm so he cycled there on his bike. The same day, Eliza needed a few things from the shop, but she didn't have any money. Joseph had money in his tin, but Eliza didn't dare to touch it. He counted it every other day. She decided to walk to The Tin House to see her mother she might have a couple of bob to spare.

It was still bitter cold outside, but she believed the baby would be fine if she wrapped her up warmly. Filling a hot water bottle, Eliza wrapped in a couple of nappies and put it at the bottom of the pram well away from the baby. She then walked to her mother's house to borrow some money. She checked the baby several times on the way, and pushed the pram right inside The Tin House. The baby was toasty warm and comfortable. Snow melted off the wheels of the pram and left small puddles on the red quarry floor.

"I will clean that up," said Tilly, fetching the mop from the kitchen. Eliza had a cup of tea and a great chat with her mother before she refilled the hot water bottle. "I don't know when I will see you again," she said, setting off for home.

"Hang on a minute you wanted some money, didn't you? Here's four bob, get something for your tea on the way back home."

Eliza put the brake on the pram before going into the shop at the bottom of the road. She didn't know that this was the place Tilly used to wait for Jim when they dated years ago.

She bought what she needed and ten cigarettes before she continued on to the farm. When she got home, she twisted and turned the large ring that opened the dairy door, but it was locked from the inside. *Blast! It's not usually locked.* This meant that Eliza had to go 'round to the large kitchen, where her in-laws would be sitting by the blazing fire.

Eliza was greeted by icy stares when she walked in. Knowing she was in big trouble, she walked past them as quickly as she could, giving them a nice smile. She unlocked the dairy door, brought the pram inside and took her baby upstairs. The fire still had a spark of life left in it, and she prodded it with the poker. Putting some wood on it, she drew fire up by holding a sheet of newspaper to it. The draught soon had sparks flying as the wood caught fire. She finished by placing a couple more logs on the fire before she went back downstairs to mop the floor, where the wheels of the pram wet it. Then, she carried her shopping upstairs and started getting tea ready. Eliza prayed that her in-laws said nothing to Joseph.

Eliza looked out of the window, watching for Joseph to come down the long drive. She always put his tea on the table when she heard his footsteps on the stairs even though he always spoke to his parents before he came up. She glanced at the clock, noting that he seemed to be talking for ages. As he walked in she knew, by the look on his face, that his mother told him. Joseph didn't say a word. He looked at the baby, washed his hands, and then sat down to eat his tea.

Eliza was on edge. She kept trying to converse with him, but he didn't answer. They finished their meal in total silence—it was so quiet that she could hear the clock ticking.

Joseph finished eating. Then, without a word, he rose, walked around the table and hit her so hard that he knocked her off her chair onto the floor. Eliza just stayed on the floor. She knew he would hit her again if she got straight up. She learned that from the last time he hit her. After a while, Joseph left the room.

Eliza got up off the floor and cleared the table. She was going to steer clean away from him if she could. That night, Eliza lay awake a long time. She had heard that her father-in-law beat his wife. It now seemed that Joseph would do the same. The next morning Eliza waited until she thought no one was there. Then, she retrieved the hot water bottle from the pram and refilled it. She took the powdered milk tin and baby bottles, and a couple of changes for herself and the baby before she set off for The Tin House. She had decided to leave Joseph.

Eliza was walking as fast as she could. She felt that she had to get back to her mother and father and the safety of The Tin House, where she would be safe and welcome. Her mother and father would look after her and the baby. The last time Joseph hit her, Tilly told her "if he did it once, he will do it again."

Eliza's walked swiftly and thought of happier times. At first she didn't notice the car near her, but it pulled up beside her.

"Where do you think you're going?" a voice called out.

Christ! It's my mother-in- law, Eliza cringed.

"Joseph told me to keep an eye on you today, but you sneaked out when I was in the shop," she said.

"I'm leaving him. I'm not being a punching bag like you have been all your married life," Eliza couldn't believe she had actually answered her mother-in-law back.

CHAPTER 9

Eliza couldn't walk any faster! She was going uphill and had another two miles to cover before she reached The Tin House. Her hands were freezing, but she was sweating everywhere else as she hurried on. She reached the top of the hill, and, then, the pram was sliding all over the road as she sprinted towards the crossroads. Finally, she reached a downhill portion of the road, and she was able to run faster.

The car came up beside her so quickly that Eliza didn't realise it was there until it skidded to a halt. She looked 'round and tried to run faster, but she was not fast enough. Her mother-in-law snatched the pram and started walking back home. Joseph grabbed Eliza and virtually threw her into the car, his face twisted in rage.

Joseph's mother, Martha, had fetched him out of work and he was furious that Eliza had caused this interruption to his work day. He took her back to the farm and dropped her off outside the dairy door. Joseph knew Eliza would go into the house because his mother had the baby. He was sure his wife wouldn't go anywhere without her baby. He returned to work, but not before his mother promised to keep a close eye on Eliza and prevent her from leaving.

At last his Martha arrived and carried the baby up to Eliza. "You live here now, you belong to Joseph so don't try anything like that again." Eliza was terrified just thinking about what could happen when Joseph returned from work that night. She was sure she would get another backhander from him. Even though she was anxious and hurt, Eliza got Joseph's tea ready on time so that he would not have another reason to hit her.

When he arrived home, he sat right down to his tea without speaking. He finished eating, stood up, and walked toward Eliza. When he came close to her, she ducked—a reflex—something she didn't plan, but it was clear that his beatings took a toll on Eliza.

"What's the matter?" he asked. "I'm not going to hit you. I think you know the score now."

Their days continued in much the same way. Joseph went to work while Eliza cared for the baby and made sure the house was clean, the wash done and his tea and meals on time. She never knew which Joseph would greet her each morning and each time he came home from work. Would it be the pleasant man she fell in love with or the mean person who was impossible to please? She was always uneasy and on guard, wondering when Joseph would hit her next. She seldom saw her relatives because it was easier to stay away than to upset Joseph.

One day, Joseph informed Eliza that his mother made arrangements for Dawn's christening with the vicar at the Church of England in Fekenham, about four miles away, where her mother and sister were buried. Eliza had no time to invite her family because the ceremony was scheduled in two days. Martha made all the arrangements, and she never asked Eliza if she would like her family to come.

"You'd better go to town and buy a new dress," Joseph said, "I will give you the money for it." *He'll have to give me the money. I don't have any of my own!*

On the day of Dawn's christening, three weeks later, Joseph's family completely took over, making all the decisions—the type of church service, who was invited and the refreshments they would serve later at home. Joseph, his mother, his sister and his gran seemed to have a wonderful time. Eliza didn't complain—she had other things on her mind. She was pregnant again, and she knew that she would have to put any thoughts she had about leaving Joseph on hold.

Ken and Jean came to the farm to tell them their good news—they were getting married a week from Saturday in Jean's hometown. They invited Eliza and Joseph to come, saying they really wanted the whole family to be there. Ken told them their transportation was all arranged—they would ride in Ray's Bedford van that had seats on both sides. "The only thing you need to do is get a babysitter," Ken told them.

After they left, Eliza told Joseph she was excited about the wedding. "It's forty miles away," Joseph said, grumpily.

"Yes. Isn't it great that Ray has the van?" Eliza asked. Assuming that Joseph was glad to be going to the wedding, too, she continued, "Could you ask your mother to take care of Dawn? She knows her better than anyone else."

"I'm not coming with you," Joseph said. "I'm going to the local for a few pints." Eliza was stunned. Joseph never said anything about staying home when Ken and Jean were there. And now he was saying he would definitely not ask his mother to take care of Dawn. "If you want to go, you'll have to get your own babysitter."

Who can I ask? I hardly see anyone anymore. Eliza still didn't have a babysitter a few days before the wedding.

"I can't come to the wedding," she told Ray and Marge sadly. However, they didn't hear her because they were focused on their own news. They came to tell Eliza that Marge was pregnant.

"So am I," Eliza said, hugging Marge and congratulating them. "Anyway, about the wedding on Saturday," Eliza said with tears in her eyes, "I can't come. I don't have a babysitter."

"You have to come!" pleaded Ray. "Ken and Jean will be the first in our family to have a white wedding. It's going to be a lovely day." Noticing Eliza's distress and aware the rest of the family will be upset if she stayed home, Ray said he would see what he could do about arranging a babysitter for her.

"It will have to be someone who is used to babies and someone I can trust as well," Eliza said. "I won't let just anyone have her."

Ray came back the next night with a smile from ear to ear. "It's all sorted. May will look after Dawn."

Eliza was grateful to May and to Ray.

"Marge and I will pick you up first on Saturday, so we can take the baby to May's house," he said. "Then we will get mother, father and the other children on the way."

Eliza was so excited! No one knew how much she looked forward to this wedding. *I might even have a dance!* Eliza loved dancing, but she knew better than to share that fantasy with Joseph. *He would go ballistic!* She couldn't wait to spend an uninterrupted day celebrating with her family.

On Saturday, the day of the wedding, Eliza was already outside and ready when Ray pulled into the farmyard. She knew he would be on time, he always was. Eliza settled into her seat and Ray passed Dawn to her. As her brother closed the van door, Eliza looked up to the window of her apartment and spotted Joseph watching them. As they drove away Eliza let out a slow breath. *At last I can relax and be myself for a while.*

"Are you sure she will be fine, May?" Eliza asked when they got to her cousin's house. As much as Eliza wanted to get away, she was still a bit anxious about leaving Dawn—she had never left her before.

"She will be fine," May reassured her. "I still have our pram even though Kev has outgrown it, so I will even take her for a walk." She hugged Eliza. "Off you go and have a good time."

They got back into the van and headed to The Tin House for the rest of the clan. Tilly pinned on her buttonholes, small corsages for the women and single flowers for the men, which she brought for them on this festive occasion. Finally, they were off, singing all the way to the wedding.

What a wonderful day they had! Jean was lovely in her white, flowing wedding dress. Ken looked handsome standing tall at the church altar waiting for his bride to come down the aisle to him. Jim and Tilly were obviously proud.

After an amazing day filled with love, friendship, the glorious church wedding, good food and spirits, music, dancing and getting to know Jean's family it was time to go home. Tilly glanced over to Eliza as Jim struck a match to light his cigarette. *She looks like a scared little girl! She's only nineteen and already pregnant with her second child.*

"What's up, love?" she asked her.

"I'm wondering what sort of mood Joseph will be in when I get back home."

"You can come back with us to The Tin House," Tilly said. "We'll pick the baby up and you can spend the night with us."

Eliza gently tapped on May's door before going in. She knew Joe, May's husband, would be in bed since it was now after midnight—about one.

"How has she been," asked Eliza in a whisper.

"She was all right this afternoon, but she cried for two hours tonight," May said. "I took her for a walk 'round the block until she went to sleep."

"I'm sorry," replied Eliza, feeling guilty for leaving her baby for so long.

"As long as you had a good time, that's all that matters."

Ray helped Eliza back into the van with the baby and the inevitable bags of baby things. Then, Ray headed back to The Tin House to drop them all off.

As they rounded the bend in the drive leading to The Tin House, the van's headlights swept across another car parked by the house. It was Joseph's car!

"I hope he's not going to start," said Jim.

Joseph, who was reading a newspaper, smiled as they got out. "I decided to wait here for you," he said.

"It's a good job I never took her home first, or we would have missed you," Ray replied.

"How about a cup of tea first?" asked Jim. "We've had a long journey home."

Jim was playing for time he didn't want to upset Joseph but he was weighing him up. He wanted to see what kind of mood he was in.

Twenty minutes later Joseph, Eliza and the baby set off home. Joseph never mentioned the wedding at all, and Eliza knew better than to say anything about it.

Eliza woke when she heard Dawn crying, but she was tired. It seemed like she had just gone to bed. Rubbing her eyes to get used to the darkness, she got out of bed, fed her baby, settled her down, and then fell into a deep sleep. Joseph had already gone for his Sunday morning walk when she awoke again. He loved walking over the fields, seeing wildlife and listening to birds singing. *Why does he have to be so possessive? He can be lovely at times. It's like living with Jekyll and Hyde.*

Eliza wanted to ask Joseph about finding a house for them. She knew he had quite a sum of money because it took him a long time to count it now. She couldn't wait to get away from the farm and her in-laws. *Maybe Joseph would change if he was away from them.* Eliza hoped that would happen. She also wondered how she could manage two babies upstairs in their small apartment. Dawn would only be thirteen months old when the baby came. *Maybe I will be able to talk with Joseph tonight.*

Eliza was getting used to her new neighbourhood. She found a couple of shops that were fairly close to the farm if she walked away from instead of towards The Tin House. She walked up the lane admiring the view on her way to the little shop. She had some money left from the weekly amount Joseph gave her for food.

"Hello, fancy seeing you here," someone said to her.

Turing around, Eliza noticed and greeted Vera Bott, a woman she worked with at the laundry.

"I'm retired now," said Vera.

"I live at the farm down the lane," said Eliza.

"Do you fancy a cup of tea?" asked Vera. "I only live just there," she said, pointing to a house just up the road.

"Thanks, I would love that. It's lovely to find a friendly face 'round here. It's the first time I have been this way, but now I'm glad I came."

"Here, sit here," said Vera, moving a pile of washing off a chair to make room at the table.

Eliza drank her tea as they chatted. *What a nice person Vera is!* "I will have to be on my way now," Eliza said, as little Dawn waved goodbye. "I have enjoyed catching up with you."

"Just call in whenever you're up this way again. I'm usually in, I don't move far away from home."

Eliza thanked Vera before setting off home. As soon as Joseph came home from work that night, Eliza told him about meeting Vera while she was out walking just in case someone saw her going in or coming out of Vera's house, especially since the house was fairly close to Joseph's workplace. He didn't seem to mind her friendship with Vera. It was Tilly and her family that upset him. Eliza had tried to figure out why Joseph couldn't accept her family and just love them like her brother's wives did. She believed that the family's closeness—the way they loved each other and helped one another was a sore spot for Joseph. He seemed jealous of anyone who loved

Eliza, and he came from a family that seldom expressed love or worked together.

Eliza noticed that her in-laws went out twice a week. They left before noon when the milk round was finished and did not return until after evening tea. Eventually Eliza found out that they took their eggs to a market in another town and then had a meal and a few beers. Joseph never told Eliza where they went, but his brother did.

Eliza took full advantage of their time away. She used those days to go to The Tin House. She was chuffed to be able to spend time with her mother again, and delighted that she could do it on a regular basis. Eliza walked to her parent's house before lunch and one of her brothers accompanied her on the way home in time to make Joseph's tea.

Eliza's life was a lot better now. She had learned to keep her mouth shut about anything she heard or saw. Ken's wife Jean was pregnant as well as Marge and Eliza. Tilly and Jim would have four grandchildren while they still had toddlers of their own. Marge, Eliza's and Jean's babies were due about the same time so there would be three more family members to love.

Tilly's house was still filled with children all the time but now the friends came to play with Joseph, Michael and Mo. Tilly always said The Tin House was made for children, and most of the children in the village had played and eaten there at one time or another.

They got through winter once again, and finally, it was spring. Jean's baby, a son, was the first of the three babies to be born. Marge had a daughter soon afterward and Eliza's baby, a boy, was last to arrive.

Bloody hell! He looks just like my father-in-law! Eliza hoped he would look better when he had more hair. Joseph came bouncing in the hospital with a big grin on his face. *Maybe having a son will change him.*

"Guess what," he said. "I heard about a cottage coming up for sale." He explained that he had talked to the owner and got first option to buy it. Eliza was pleased. She had been dreaming of a larger house since she got pregnant again. She wanted to get away from the farm and her in-laws almost from the start, but she hadn't dared to hope they would own a cottage of their own. Joseph told her the cottage he was looking at cost one thousand, one hundred pounds.

Eliza's thoughts were miles away as Joseph drove her home from hospital. She couldn't wait to see baby Dawn, who was with her mother-in-law Martha. She was only thirteen-months old, and Eliza hadn't seen her for two whole weeks. It was breaking her heart.

As soon as the car pulled into the farmyard, Eliza's ran into the farmhouse. "Where's my baby, is she OK?" she asked her mother-in-law.

"She's in her pram in the back garden."

Eliza was gone in a shot, holding her arms out to her daughter. Dawn, naturally upset at having been left, just stared back at her, a blank look on her face. Eliza picked her up, cuddling her to herself, and carried her inside. She swore she would never leave Dawn again.

At last, Joseph legally owned the cottage. He bought it when Eliza was in hospital and only put his name on the deed. It lay down a long dirt track drive, surrounded by fields and a couple of orchards. The only running water was the tiny stream running along a ditch behind the hedge at the bottom of the plum orchard. The toilet was hidden in the far corner of the lot among trees and hedgerow.

"I won't be going out there on my own at night," said Eliza. Worst of all, the deepest well Eliza had ever seen was six feet from the front door. As much as she wanted to get away from the farm, she had no intention of taking her children near that well. "You will have to fill that well in, before I move here," she said to Joseph.

Eliza was walking up to The Tin House. She set out just after her in-laws went to market, as usual. The weather was great the sunshine glorious. Although it was only April, it felt just like a summer day. Eliza decided to ask her dad to help with the cottage. She couldn't wait to move because it was her back ached from running back and forth upstairs and down again to take care of the needs of her two babies, especially since she had to fetch water from the brew house. Two babies used a lot of water!

Just as she passed the Palmer Farm, she thought she saw a man walking towards her in the distance. She looked all around, though, and didn't see anyone, so she kept walking. She walked a bit slower, looking from side to side. She decided her eyes must have been playing tricks on her, and she reminded herself that she had been using this route for two years without problems. In fact, her mother, too, had used the same route years before without problems.

Eliza hurried past the drive that led to the farmhouse, and came to the only other house in the lane. There, Mrs Heath was hanging out her washing.

"Have you seen anybody about?" asked Eliza. "I could have sworn I saw a man, but he seems to have disappeared."

"No, I haven't seen anyone, love," she replied. "I will stand here by the gate and watch you out of sight."

Eliza thanked her and carried on 'round the next bend. She was out of Mrs Heath sight now, still looking from side to side, her heart thumping. She was frightened because she had to go up Botters Hill and that stretch of the road had no houses on either side. Once she got over the hill, there were houses again.

Eliza looked up and stopped. She was right, there had been a man watching her. Now he was standing in the shadows of a tree, his trousers down round his ankles, giving himself a *J. Arthur Rank*!

Eliza turned the pram 'round and ran back to Mrs Heath, who was still in the garden hanging the washing out. Eliza was shaking so much she couldn't speak for a minute or two.

"I was sure I wasn't seeing things!" she blurted out, shaking as she explained what happened.

"The dirty bastard!" said Mrs Heath. "Leave the children with me and run to the farm. Ask them if they will phone the police."

Eliza headed to the farm, looking over her shoulder as she ran. When the farmer rang the police one of them spoke to Eliza. "Go back to where your children are and stay there. We have a good idea who he is but we will come and pick you up."

Eliza was just finishing the cup of tea Mrs Heath made for her when the police arrived. "Come on," they said, "Jump in the car."

"First, we must take my children to The Tin House so my mother can look after them."

Eliza's sat looking at the photos in the police station. "I know him. He lives just five minutes away from the spot where she saw the man expose himself, but it wasn't him." She didn't recognize the man who exposed himself in any of the police photos.

The policemen, however, still believed they knew who the man was. "If you had continued walking towards him he would probably have run away," one of them said.

"I couldn't risk that, I have my children to consider!" replied Eliza.

A police officer took her back to The Tin House. "I am going to see the man we think it is. He matches the description you gave us," he said, driving off.

Ray was on the six to two shift so he and Marge were together at The Tin House visiting Tilly. They told Eliza they were surprised to see her two babies without her.

Eliza and Marge got on well. They usually swapped baby stories and hints and both of them enjoyed talking together. Marge and everyone else were eager to hear Eliza's story about the man she saw and the experience she had with the police.

"I will take you back to get the pram from Mrs Heath's house," said Ray, who took his role as eldest sibling seriously and always tried to help his sisters and brother. Even though the pram wouldn't fit in the car opened up, he volunteered to follow Eliza home while she walked.

Eliza said goodbye to her mother and then got into Ray's car.

"In the future, I will meet you by Palmer's farm," he told Eliza. "You won't have to come by the farm much longer. The route from the cottage should be safer."

"Will you ask Dad if he will help us?" asked Eliza, suddenly remembering one of the reasons she went to The Tin House. that day. "Why don't you ask Joseph if he will bring you up tonight, and then you can ask him yourself? I wouldn't mention today's episode, if I were you. Joseph might accuse you of leading the chap on."

"That's for certain. Don't worry. He won't even know I have been out." She answered."If I get him to come up tonight, warn the boys not to say anything."

Joseph was in a good mood when he came home from work.

"Fancy going up and seeing dad after tea to ask him if he will help do the cottage up, or we will never move in?" asked Eliza.

"Okay."

Eliza picked up Dawn, Joseph carried baby Mark in his carrycot and off they went in the old A40 car. Eliza, who wished she could drive, always watched what Joseph did when he was driving.

Tilly had already told Jim that Eliza and Joseph might be up. However, Jim never let on. He didn't like the way Joseph treated his daughter, but he would be civil to him. *Maybe the cottage is what Joseph needs—maybe he'll treat Eliza better when they move to the cottage.*

"Will you help us?" Eliza asked her father.

"I will get Ray to come and pick me up on Saturday so I can see what needs doing," Jim assured her.

Jim was drinking a cuppa tea when Ray came for him on Saturday.

"Come on, then, Dad," said Ray. "Let's see what this cottage is like then."

Joseph and Eliza were already there.

"Bloody hell!" said Jim. "It wants a bomb on it! It's worse than I expected, but there is one good thing—it already has electricity." Jim agreed to help on nights and weekends provided that Joseph worked, too, and that Joseph bought all the materials. "This is a good time of year for a rennovation since the nights are getting lighter," Jim said.

Joseph and Jim worked side by side. First they dug the trench for the water pipe.

"Christ! Jim, this is hard work," said Joseph. The only digging tools they had were spades and Jim's pick axe.

"You wonna try digging six feet deep holes for graves, if you think this is hard work!"

Even young Joseph and Michael came to the cottage with their father to help. The boys, Jim and Eliza's Joseph worked hard digging the trench they needed to lay pipe from the road to the cottage. It seemed like a long way while they were digging, but after a couple of days, the trench was ready. They could now lay the pipe, connect it to the system on the road and bring running water to the cottage. They put an old tap in the house, so at last they had running water.

"Anything leaking anywhere?" called Jim.

"No," replied Joseph, checking down the length of the pipe.

Finally, they filled in the trench. The next job was to fill in the well, but it was so deep that they could hardly hear the splash of the rock they dropped into it. Jim said they would fill it with the things they would throw away while renovating the house.

'There are two black leaded fire grates to replace, for a start," he said. So out they went straight into the well. Then, they ripped out the downstairs floors, and the debris followed the grate.

Because the cottage had been built into a slope, the back walls were riddled with water stains. Jim was certain that was the source of the dampness and the musty smell.

"We'll have to dig a trench all 'round the back and the one side of the cottage," he said.

"We will put loads of chippings around it to keep out the dampness."

With all the junk and the soil from levelling off the ground, the well filled up quickly. Jim put two new grates in—one in the small living room and the other in the front room. He then partitioned part of the kitchen off. They installed a sink in one half and made the other side into a bathroom with a flush toilet. "Now we will have to work hard again," he said. They had to dig a cesspit since there were no sewers in this area at all.

"Christ! Jim, how far down do we have to dig? My bloody back's aching," Joseph complained, mopping his brow.

"Until it's deep enough," said Jim, sympathetically. "It's harder because the earth's so dry and we've got down to clay. This must be one of the hottest summers we've had for a long time."

"That just about fills the well in," said Joseph, as he tipped in the last barrow of clay. "It will gradually sink, though, so we will have to top it up, that's for sure."

The floors were the last item on their long list of chores. They put buff-coloured tiles in the bathroom and the new, smaller red quarry tiles in the kitchen and living room. Everything looked new and shiny. The inside of the cottage was finished. All Eliza had to do was decorate, and she said she would do that after they moved in.

CHAPTER 10

Eliza stepped back to admire the pretty flowery curtains she had just finished hanging—her first step in decorating the cottage. A soft summer breeze blew through the open windows and rippled the lightweight curtains that added lively colour, reminding Eliza of a garden in bloom. She loved the numerous windows in the cottage. They provided plenty of light and cross ventilation, making the rooms bright and airy. Eliza was grateful to Joseph's gran, who gave her the old treadle sewing machine that enabled her to make the curtains. Most of all, though, she was thankful for the cottage—she loved living there.

Ripening Bramley apples weighed down the branches of the trees in the back orchards while plums and other types of apples ripened in front of the cottage. Several sheds held tools and stood ready to store the fruit and vegetables that Joseph and Jim grew in a huge garden. Eliza was delighted that Joseph seemed to mellow a bit more each week as he worked with her father. Her friends and family members also noticed the change in him.

"I'm going to get some pullets for laying and a pig," Joseph said. "I will make plenty of money selling eggs and apples when they're ripe."

Two months later he placed a sign up at the top of the drive. EGGS AND APPLES FOR SALE. Joseph soon had regular customers. He had worked hard on the garden. Jim helped him when he could, but he also tended his own garden at The Tin House. Both men had the same amount of land, but Joseph was more fortunate because he owned his land.

While Joseph took care of the outside chores, Eliza set about decorating the cottage, something she had never done before. Her father bought her some paint and wallpaper. The painting went fine, but her wallpaper paste just wasn't right. It was too thick and she couldn't get it completely smooth. When she applied the first strips of paper to the wall, the lumps in the paste showed under the paper

One evening Marge and Ray were on their way to see Eliza."Let's call in and see if mother wants to come," Ray said. Tilly consulted Jim and they agreed that everyone would go.

"Come on, kids in the back," said Ray as they piled in. They all wanted to see how Joseph and Eliza were getting on.

"What happened with the wallpaper, Eliza, it has lumps under it?" asked her father.

"I couldn't get the lumps out of the flour when I mixed it with the water. I think I should have used plain flour instead of self - rising," replied Eliza.

"You will learn," Jim said. He and Tilly laughingly told her about some of the problems they had the first few times they wallpapered rooms. Always concerned about Eliza's well being, Jim asked her, "How's he treating you now?"

"Fine" she said immediately. "He's been great since we moved here. Mind you, I've hardly been anywhere yet, and I have a few weeks family allowance to get and a tin of milk for Mark."

"The garden's coming on well, Joseph," said Jim, after walking up the garden to his son-in-law.

"Yes, I'm quite pleased with myself," Joseph replied. "It's only been a few weeks and you can see some shoots coming up already. I'm really pleased I got this cottage, I love it here."

"Eliza seems to like it here as well," said Jim.

"Yes, she loves it. We're getting on a lot better now. I was wondering if you could get one of the boys to baby-sit so we could take you and Tilly out one night. It's a long time since we went out anywhere."

Eliza was excited! She couldn't remember the last time they went out. When the day of the outing arrived, she had curlers in her hair all day. She was getting ready when Joseph left to fetch young Joseph, who would baby sit, and Tilly and Jim at the same time. Eliza gave her brother a list in case the children woke up, but she wasn't worried. Young Joseph was used to children. *He should be, there are enough of them at his house.*

Tilly put her glass down on the table at the pub and leaned

toward Eliza. "I'm going to the loo," she said. "Coming?"

When they were alone, she put her arm round Eliza before speaking. "I have been waiting to get you on your own," she said. "The police came to The Tin House today. They asked me to tell you that the chap, whom they think is the one who exposed himself to you, was found burned to death in his shed, or what was left of his shed. They think he committed suicide."

Eliza was pensive when they returned to the bar to Jim and Joseph. Soon after that, they finished their drinks and decided to return home, where they arrived by half ten. Joseph dropped Eliza first so he could pick up young Joseph, whom he was taking home, along with Jim and Tilly.

Eliza went into the house, and sent young Joseph to the car. "Take this key and lock the door on your way out," she instructed her brother. "Then, give it to Joseph and tell him I will be in bed when he gets back."

She lay in bed, thinking that she had a lovely night with Joseph and her parents, unaware of what would come next. Finally, she heard Joseph coming upstairs.

"Did you have any men in while I was gone?" he asked her, putting his hand up her nightie to feel if she was wet. Eliza didn't reply she just gently started to snore, while Joseph got into bed and was soon fast asleep.

It was family allowance day, so Eliza set out for the post office to collect it. The first mile was downhill, but then there was a huge hill to climb. The pram seemed heavier than ever and she struggled to push it. *Why are there so many hills? It's no wonder I have lost so much weight!*

Eliza got the family allowance and national dried milk for Mark. Then, she went to the butcher's shop, which was just over the road from the post office. She wanted some meat for dinner and brains as a treat for Joseph, who liked to eat them on toast.

"Two lamb chops and half a pound of brains please," she told the butcher.

"I haven't seen you around before," the butcher remarked as

Eliza smiled at him, her mind on something else. *Surely that's Daisy walking toward me!* Daisy was the girl she worked with on the milk rounds, but they lost touch after Eliza married.

"Eliza, what are you doing in these parts?" asked Daisy. "I haven't seen you about for a long time! I hardly recognised you, you're so thin. Are you all right?"

"I thought it was you," Eliza replied. "It's great seeing you." She explained that she felt fine and was not sick. "I think it's all the walking I do," she said, quickly changing the subject by focusing on Daisy's children "Are all three of those children yours?"

"Yes."

"Bloody hell! You have been busy, haven't you!" replied Eliza.

"I only live just down the road. Come on and have a coffee with me."

"Okay," replied Eliza, turning the pram 'round and walking alongside Daisy.

Eliza lit another cigarette up, in between sipping her coffee. She was smoking a lot more lately!

Daisy watched her. "Eliza, why are you shaking like that, you never used to be nervous!" Just then another woman walked in with two small children. "This is a friend of mine," said Daisy, introducing her as Janice. "She lives just round the corner. We met at the swings in the park just up the road."

Eliza thought Janice was stunning. She noted that she had a soft voice with a lilt to it, and her eyes twinkled when she smiled.

"Pleased to meet you," she said. The three of them were chatting away, while the children played nicely. The three younger children, still babies, were in their prams in the other room, with the door open so they could be heard if they woke up.

Daisy's house had no garden, just a tatty yard.

"I don't let them play out there very often," she said.

Eliza thought they would enjoy playing at the cottage in its beautiful garden. Before she could mention it, though, she told her friends it was time to leave because it was almost time for Dawn's dinner.

"That's no problem. You can have dinner here," Daisy said. "You can make a bottle for Mark, too. I have a spare bottle and teat you can borrow."

"Blimey!" said Eliza, noticing the clock later. "It's three o'clock! The time has flown by!" She explained that she really did have to leave this time because Joseph liked his tea on the table as soon as he came in. "Tell you what," she said. "Why don't you two come to the cottage tomorrow? There's lots of room to play," she said, explaining where she lived.

Later, Eliza told her husband that she bumped into an old friend, but she didn't tell him she went inside Daisy's house. The next day, Daisy and Janice and their children arrived about half eleven.

"Aren't you lonely and scared living down here," they asked. "It's a bit isolated."

"Sometimes, at night when Joseph goes to the pub, I'm a bit scared." Eliza replied. She didn't tell them that Joseph had started to go out more and more lately. "I lock the door and make sure the curtains are drawn," Eliza added.

Eliza cooked her friends a dinner of eggs and chips, using potatoes out of the garden and fresh laid eggs. She knew, though, that she would have to replace the eggs by getting more from the chicken coop before Joseph came home from work. He would go mad if he knew she fed anyone with them. Anyway, it would be best if he didn't know anyone was there.

Joseph had his tea, sat for a bit and then went to feed the pigs and chickens. "I think the chickens have gone off the lay a bit," he said, walking back into the house with the bucket of eggs. "There doesn't seem to be as many eggs as usual." Eliza was glad that Dawn was playing in the other room because she might have mentioned the eggs they used at lunchtime if she heard him say that. As they cleaned the eggs for market,

Eliza asked Joseph to teach her to drive the car.

"What do you want to drive for, you haven't got a car, and you won't be driving mine."

Eliza winced everything was his—never theirs.

She recently noticed the bus going past a couple of times when she was in the top orchard picking apples. She would have to find out the time and day it came by because she'd been having a toothache and needed to see the dentist. Although she often walked for miles, she didn't think she would want to push a pram with two children in it, all that way and back, after having a tooth out. Maybe Ray could take her. No, she wouldn't ask him he did enough for her as it was. *I need to try to stand on my own two feet.*

Eliza eventually learned that the buses ran three times a day, twice a week at nine a.m., noon and five p.m. She got the big pushchair her mother gave her and stood, waiting for the bus at the top of the drive. Apparently, there were no designated stops, but the driver stopped when he saw a person put an arm out. Holding Mark in her arms, Eliza stood there with Dawn at her side. *Bless her she's only nineteen months old and quite tiny! Mark, though at five months is big for his age.*

When the bus stopped Eliza put Dawn on first. Then, she had to struggle to get the pushchair on. By the time every one was settled, Eliza was exhausted. *Bloody hell! I won't be doing this again in a hurry.*

"I will have to take these two back ones out," the dentist told her. After that was done, Eliza decided it would be easier to walk home rather than repeat the hassle she experienced earlier on the bus.

When she got home, Eliza told Joseph about the struggle she had with the bus. "Please teach me to drive."

He was in a good mood. "I will give you a go at the weekend," he replied.

On Saturday afternoon, Derek came to visit them with his girlfriend.

"Dek, will you do us a favour and look after the children for five minutes, please?" Joseph asked. "I want to give your sister a driving lesson."

"OK," they both replied.

Joseph drove the car up the drive onto the road. "Come on then, let's have you," he said, swapping seats. Eliza wasn't doing too badly, but Joseph told her to drive down the very narrow lane that led to Fekenham. Joseph's car was a big sedan. Eliza neared a bend in the narrow lane. She was just on the little humpback bridge when a motor-bike came roaring past her in the opposite direction. It had to swerve to miss them. Eliza was quite shaken by the near collision.

161

"Get out, you stupid bastard!" Joseph shouted at her. "That's the last time you drive the bleeding car, you could have killed us!"

"It was your fault," replied Eliza. "Fancy taking me down that narrow lane!" When they arrived home Joseph went straight up the garden.

"That was quick," said Derek as Eliza walked into the house.

"Yes, it was a complete disaster!"

"Where did he take you?"

"Down the back lanes," she replied.

"I will come and give you basic lessons up and down the drive in my spare time," said Derek.

"That's great."

Derek passed his test the year before, and now the only thing was, the nights were starting to draw in so it might have to be next spring before he would be able to teach her.

On Monday, Eliza fed Dawn and Mark their dinners and settled them down for their afternoon naps. She sat down and reached for the book she was reading. She felt the car keys, which Joseph must have left near her book. He heart started racing—beating a mile a minute—as if she were in danger. She was determined to learn to drive even if she had to do it behind Joseph's back.

Taking a pillow with her, she unlocked the car door, put the pillow under her bottom as she sat down and then, started the car. She slowly reversed up the drive and then drove back down again. Eliza was careful to lock the car again before she returned to the house. She was so chuffed with herself that she decided to tell Marge about her adventure when she called in on her way to see Tilly at The Tin House. From that day on, Eliza drove the car back and forth in the drive whenever she got a chance. She became quite an expert at reversing.

Eliza was upset when winter finally brought snow. She wasn't able to drive the car any more because she didn't dare leave any tracks up and down the drive for Joseph to see. *I will have to leave it for this year. That snow buggered it for me!*

What a Christmas it was! The snow made every place seem calm and tranquil, while the frost left pretty patterns on the windows.

"Look at all the lovely shapes that Jack Frost has done for you," Eliza said to her two children. "I will ask daddy to make a sledge for you."

Joseph made a small sledge then sat on it. Eliza passed Dawn to him and he slid down the slope with Dawn on his lap, using his feet to slow them down. Then he did the same with Mark. The children were laughing and giggling. Eliza would have liked to have a picture of her children enjoying themselves in the snow, but no one in the family had a camera. *It would have been a lovely picture,*

They hadn't been out for such a long time that Eliza grew bored, but the snow would be gone soon because spring was just 'round the corner. She made up her mind to walk to Daisy's house tomorrow with the children in the pram if the weather was not too bad.

The next morning Eliza set out. It was hard going but she made it, with Mark and Dawn tucked up in the pram, all nice and warm. They wore teddy bear all-in-one suits which Joseph' grandmother bought them for Christmas, among many other things. Dawn's was red and Mark's was blue. Daisy was excited that Eliza came to visit.

"I'm so pleased to see you. I haven't been out much either, but I'm luckier than you," she said. "I have the shop next door to my house, and I'm on a regular bus route if I want to pop downtown." She explained that she and Janice exchanged babysitting when one of them wanted to go to town. "She goes one time and I go the next— our kids know each of us well, so they are never scared."

It had been so long since she drove the car that Eliza almost forgot her quest to earn her license. The weather would be better soon, and she enjoyed walking. It was mostly on wet, rainy days that she wished she could drive. After all, none of the women she knew drove.

Eliza continued to walk to her mother's house, and sometimes she and her sister-in-law Marge walked to town as well. Marge always carried an extra bottle of freshly made-up baby milk—not for her own baby, but for Mark—who had an enormous appetite.

Tilly still worked at the same place. Biron was in school, and Sam had only another year until he started school. Jim suggested they resume their Saturday nights out again, now that the weather was better, and Marge and Ray decided to go as well.

The six of them sat 'round the table, in 'The Nag's Head Pub. They had drinks and chatted, the three men sitting opposite the three women. Eliza smiled as Marge talked to her, but the smile froze on her face as Joseph suddenly jumped up and spit at her straight her in the eye.

Ray jumped up and grabbed hold of him. "What the fuck did you do that for?"

"She smiled at that fucking chap over there."

"I swear! I never!" said Eliza. "I was smiling at what Marge said to me."

"For Christ's sake! Get a grip on yourself, man, you're paranoid! If' you're going to be like this, we shan't come out with you again!" said Ray.

Jim and Tilly were disgusted with Joseph, and they drove home in silence.

"You're nothing more than a fukin' slut," Joseph ranted, poking her in bed. "Whore!"

The onslaught carried on well into the night. Joseph called Eliza every dirty thing he could think of while she pretended to be asleep. Although she tried to appear calm so Joseph would believe she was asleep, Eliza cringed waiting for the blows she feared would come to her head and back. She hated the verbal abuse more than the physical.

How much longer can I take it? I don't want to leave him. When he's in a good mood, he's a lovely chap, but he changes in a flash! Eliza loved their cottage, too, and she didn't want to leave that either. However, she knew the cottage would never be hers. Joseph bought it when she was in the hospital and put the deed in his name only.

Eliza left Joseph a couple of times before. Since they have been living at the cottage, she and her two children had slept at Marge and Ray's house a few times. If Ray was on nights, Eliza and the children slept in the bed with Marge, and if he was on one of the

164

other shifts, Eliza and her two babies sleep on a mattress on the floor in the landing.

"Why do you keep going back for more?" Marge asked her.

"Because I love him and I am still hoping he will change."

The day after a fight, Joseph would come for her, promise to change, or swear blindly that he never did or said those things to her. Once he got angry over chickens of her own, then a pig. Joseph always came to persuade her to go back, and she always fell for it.

Marge would look at her as if to say, "Fool!"

Saturday night arrived again.

"If you act up this week I won't come again—neither will the others," said Eliza

"I can't remember much about last week," replied Joseph. "I think you must have dreamt it all."

Young Joseph was planning to sleep at the cottage this week, and Eliza believed that would help Joseph to behave. She thought Joseph would be on guard since someone else would be there. Indeed, they had a brilliant night out.

"I'm going up to bed, are you coming?" asked Eliza.

"In a minute. I'm having a glass of wine first."

Eliza was fast asleep, but she woke when Joseph dug her in the ribs and started again—calling her a dirty slut and other awful names.

"I'm off now!" said young Joseph coming downstairs the next morning. "I'm off before that bloody maniac starts again, he's crackers."

"You mean you heard him last night?" asked Eliza.

"He has a screw loose! What are you doing living with a maniac like that? I'm off before he comes back in the house. I lay in bed this morning, until I heard him whistling on his way up to feed the chickens. I will walk home."

"Don't tell mom or dad, they will worry about me."

"They already do worry about you!"

Eliza continued visiting with her two friends twice a week and on other occasions, they came to her house, too. She also continued her visits to her mother twice a week. If Joseph found out, he abused her verbally, but sometimes it escalated to physical abuse as well. Now, it was worse than ever.

"Why didn't you tell me you were going?" he would say. Even when she did tell him where she was going, he abused her anyway. She couldn't win either way.

Eliza was making an apple sponge pudding, which Joseph and the children loved. She mixed the sponge and then walked up to the shed where the apples were stored. Putting the apples in a bowl, she bent over.

"Who're yer meeting in here then?"

Eliza jumped. "You scared me to death, you bloody idiot. You are absolutely barmy. When are you going to stop this?" she asked him.

"Just checking," replied Joseph.

Eliza started driving the car up and down the drive again, like she did before. She knew she would be safe on the road now since she was a good driver now. But she needed to practise on the roads— to get road sense.

On the day after Dawn's second birthday, Eliza had her first professional driving lesson. The man from the driving school was really nice. He picked Eliza and the two children up at the cottage and then brought the children to The Tin House so Tilly could look after them. Eliza had half-an-hour's driving, and then it was back to The Tin House to pick up the children. Tilly came out with the money and paid the man.

"I'm quite impressed with your driving," the instructor told her. Eliza had already told him how she had learned. She had to be discreet because if Joseph knew she took driving lessons, he would go ballistic. He wouldn't allow her to get in a car with another man.

After the next lesson, a week later, the instructor told Eliza to register for her test.

"You will be ready by the time it comes through," he said/He also suggested that she get someone to babysit in her own house next week so thtat they could go on a longer run.

Eliza walked up to her mother's the following day, calling for Marge on the way.

"How's the driving going, have you told Joseph yet?" Tilly greeted her.

"You must be joking! He would swear blind that I was knocking the instructor off."

As they turned down the drive to The Tin House, Eliza said, "How about a cuppa, Mom, I'm thirsty. It's a long walk up here."

The three of them were sitting in the living room with the door open, drinking their tea, nattering away, while their children played outside. All of a sudden, one of the children screamed. It was Dawn, and she was lying on the ground.

She said she was walking along the little brick wall and fell off, even though the wall was only two bricks high.

"I think one leg's broken," said Tilly.

"Surely it can't be that bad, it was only a tiny wall," Eliza said, but Dawn was still screaming.

"I will run up and get Ray out of bed," said Marge. "It's a good job he's on nights."

Both Eliza and Tilly were trying to console Dawn but she wouldn't stop crying. Ray was there in ten minutes with Marge, in their brand new mini car. Tilly offered to look after Mark while Eliza took Dawn to the hospital.

"The poor child's broken her leg," said the doctor, looking at the X-ray.

Dawn's crying turned to little sobs as Ray carried her gently to the car after the doctor put her leg in a cast. Then, they went back to The Tin House to get Mark before Ray took them home. Carrying Dawn into the cottage, Ray put her gently on the settee.

Eliza dreaded telling Joseph what happened. He might be horrible to her at times, but he loved the children. He never raised a finger to them. When Eliza heard him come in, she started shaking. She still sat with Dawn on the settee, while Mark played on the floor.

Immediately, Joseph noticed that the pram was missing.

"We're in here," Eliza called out, and he walked in the front room.

"Where's the pram?" then he spotted Dawn's leg. "What the bloody hell's happened to her?"

Eliza cringed and her head nodded uncontrollably, as she explained about Dawn falling off the wall.

"Why weren't you watching her, you bloody idiot, and what the hell were you doing up there anyway? I've told you before your place is here!"

The next day Tilly asked Ray to take her to see Dawn. She wanted to check on Eliza as well as her granddaughter.

Eliza told her that she slept on the floor all night. "I didn't want to move Dawn too much," she said. "I didn't want to hurt her." She asked her mother to get in touch with the B.S. School of Motoring to cancel her lessons. "I won't be having my lessons for a bit, but I will let them know when I can resume them."

Tilly hoped the accident wouldn't put her daughter off driving. She wanted Eliza to be more independent.

A week later Derek was playing football when he got kicked so badly that his leg was broken—the same leg he broke when he was a little boy.

Eliza's test date came through. *Thank goodness I got to the post box first!* It was for scheduled in three weeks time.

Tilly popped in to see the driving instructor on her way home from work. She cancelled the next lesson, but she told him about Eliza's test date. Between them, Tilly and the driving instructor arranged to pick Eliza and the children up, the same as on the previous occasions, for a future lesson.

"She can have an hour before her test," he said. "I don't think she will pass, though, she's only had one lesson."

Derek, though, decided to help his sister even though his leg was in a cast.

"Are you ready?" he asked. "I will sit by you and you can drive my car, but you'd better not go over any bumps."

"Gee, thanks, you're a brick," replied Eliza.

"Don't change the gears so fast, you're jerking my leg," said Derek.

"Sorry," Eliza replied, thinking about getting out of the car, and leaving him to it. But she couldn't. Derek couldn't drive with his broken leg.

"Why do you shout at me? I get enough of that at home," she asked.

"Because I want you to pass your test," he replied.

When the day of the test arrived, Ray came for the children. "I'm taking them to The Tin House for you. Mother's thought you could have a longer lesson then."

"I've got to pass. Mom said there's a fiver in it if I do," Eliza said to Trevor, her driving instructor. But, Trevor just smiled.

Eliza wasn't a bit nervous because she knew she could pass if only she kept calm. During her lesson before the test, though, she kept making stupid mistakes.

"Stop the car!" said Trevor. "Now, calm down a bit. The trouble is, that husband of yours has knocked the confidence out of you."

"I'm useless," replied Eliza.

"Stop putting yourself down all the time. Have you got any lipstick in your bag?"

"Yes."

"Well, put some on and put a smile on your face, then, we will try again."

"Well, here we are then," said Trevor, as she pulled up at the test centre. "Now, don't forget keep calm. The examiner is just a man doing his job."

The examiner climbed in beside her and directed her to the route that he wanted her to drive. Eliza was quite calm as she turned up Plymouth Road. All of a sudden, a dog ran out in the front of them! Eliza slammed the brakes on, just missing the dog. This made her nervous as she drove on. Then, turning left a bit higher up, she had a massive hill to climb.

Now it's the hill. Start. Take your time. Blast! I've stalled the car Eliza restarted the car. *Blast! I've stalled again. That's it! I've ruined my chance now.* She set off again, handled the car perfectly on the hill and drove back to the test station.

The examiner asked her several different questions. Finally, he turned to her. "OK, you passed," he said. Eliza couldn't believe it, and she started shaking. She was so hot on this glorious day in May.

When Trevor came back to the car, she squealed, "I passed! Can I drive home?"

"Not on your life! Look at the state you're in," Trevor said. "I have finished my job now, but, Eliza, remember. Don't let that husband of yours treat you like dirt all the time."

"I thought I failed on the hill start," she said, ignoring the remark he made about Joseph.

"You kept control and never rolled back. The examiner was highly impressed with your reaction when the dog ran out."

Tilly came running out to the car. "How did you get on?"

"I passed!" replied Eliza, dancing past her into the house.

"I knew you could do it," said her mother, following her in. She passed her a five-pound note. "Well done, I told you I would give you a fiver if you passed."

Five pounds! That was two weeks housekeeping for Eliza.

Now Eliza knew she must tell Joseph that she passed her test, even though he didn't even know she had driving lessons. She knew she had to tell him. She was so excited and scared at the same time, but the sooner she told him the sooner it would be over with! *I will tell him after tea, after he has finished feeding the hens and pigs, if he's in a good mood,* she decided.

In he came, carrying a bucket of eggs. "That's it for tonight. Let's have a drink," he said, reaching for a bottle of home-made parsnip wine out of the cabinet. He poured one for himself and then filled a glass up for Eliza. She knew she had to tell him before he had his drink. "I have something to tell you. I passed my driving test today," she said quickly, the look on his face turned to one of disbelief.

"Liar!" he replied.

"All right," said Joseph before leaving for work the next morning, "if you think you can drive, you can fetch some pig and chicken meal today, from Richmond Stores up the Cross, and don't think you can go gallivanting anywhere else. I've checked the mileage," he added as he tossed the car keys on the table. Then, he went out, jumped on his bike and pedalled off to work.

Eliza didn't care that he checked the mileage because she was taking the children to see Daisy and Janice and their children, and that was on the way to the corn stores.

"I am surprised to see he let you have the car," said Daisy.

Yes. I am too, but the only reason he's let me have it is to save him a journey. I have to get meal for the animals."

As Eliza tried to pick up the bag of feed, she was surprised it was so heavy. *Christ! This is heavy!* Eliza tried to pick the bag up a second time, but each bag weighed half a hundredweight.

"Can you put them in the boot for me, please?" she asked the store clerk.

"I will help you this time but in the future you will have to do it yourself, we're very busy."

"I hope there's not a next time."

"That's one thing you're useful for. You can fetch it every week," Joseph told her, humping the bags up to the shed.

The next day Eliza walked up the lane to The Tin House, with her two children in the lovely pram her mother gave her after Dawn was born.

"I want to get a job, Mom. I can't manage on money I get."

Marge and Ray came in and got in on the conversation. "What on earth do you want to go to work for?" asked Ray.

"Because I can't manage on the money Joseph gives me, and he won't let me have the car," replied Eliza.

"Tell you what! You can borrow my car while I'm doing the night shift," Ray offered. "I will pick you up at eight a.m. and you can bring it back at four thirty. That will give me a chance to drink a cuppa since I get up at four p.m. Then, we will pick mother and the kids up. I will have to take mother to work, before I take you home." Ray was only doing nights until Marge had the baby.

Ray had always been a brilliant brother, but even Eliza was amazed at his generosity. For him to be doing all that for her! He has only had his brand new mini car about six weeks and it was the first new car he had ever owned. True to his word, her brother was at her house smack on eight on Monday morning. He drove to his house and then got out. Eliza took the driver's seat, and then took Dawn and Mark to her mother's and then she was off to work at the laundry where she worked from the time she left school until she got married.

Joseph, however, hated her going to work. He moaned about it every night, accusing her of having affairs. "Who's been shagging you today?" he asked every evening.

Eliza stood it for three months. Then, after a particularly vicious outburst of verbal abuse from Joseph, she gave her notice. She had enough. She couldn't cope with the rows every night, and she was "a complete and utter nervous wreck!' She also just discovered that she was pregnant again. Joseph was chuffed at least he was in a better mood.

A few weeks later, Marge had a little boy, and Ray, Marge and their two babies came down to the cottage to see Eliza and Joseph.

"I'm swapping my car in for a Bedford van next week," said Ray.

"We've got exciting news! We are planning a holiday in Cornwall and we want you to come with us. Could you?"

"Who's going?" asked Joseph.

"Mother and Father, with the youngest four and ours," replied Ray.

"Wow!" said Eliza, who had never been to the seaside. "Can we go?" she asked her husband excitedly. "The children would love it. We have never been to the seaside."

"OK," Joseph answered, shocking Eliza who expected him to say no.

Dawn and Mark were so excited, even though they didn't know what the sea looked like. On the night before the holiday, Eliza started packing a few clothes in a clean sack.

"What are you doing?" asked Joseph.

"Putting the clothes ready for the holiday tomorrow, she said. "They're coming quite early as it's a long way to Cornwall."

"You can take them back out, we're not going. I've changed my mind."

"Well, we are!" Eliza replied firmly. "The children and I are looking forward to it. I'm sorry, Joseph, but I'm standing my ground on this one!"

"I promise you won't be saying this tomorrow night when you're still here."

Eliza quietly got up early the next morning. She put their few clothes in the sack bag in the pushchair, and then, quietly pushed the pushchair up to the shed, looking over her shoulder as she went. Then, she crept, back into the house.

Ray pulled up in the van that already held Tilly, Jim, Marge and their children—all in a festive mood. He came into the house and approached Joseph.

"Come on," he said. "You can sit in the front with dad and me."

"We're not coming now. I couldn't get anyone to look after the animals," he said.

"I'm going!" Eliza piped in. "So are the children." She knew Joseph wouldn't dare to hit her with her family there.

"Oh no, you're not!" yelled Joseph, trying to grab her arm.

Jim and Tilly heard the shouting.

"What's going on here?" asked Jim, walking in behind them.

"We're not going!" Joseph repeated.

"Do you know what, Joseph? You're bloody pathetic!" replied Jim.

Eliza saw her chance and, as Joseph let go of her arm, she grabbed hold of the children and ran to the van, climbing in the back of it. Marge was holding her hands out to help Eliza and the children, as Eliza shouted back to tell her father where her things were. He fetched them while Ray kept Joseph talking.

Jim threw the bags of clothes into the back of the van and closed the doors. "Get in, dad!" shouted Ray, jumping in the van. He started the van up and drove off.

Joseph stood shouting, waving his fist at them. Eliza breathed a sigh of relief—two weeks without Joseph watching her every move! It was quite dark in the back of the van, but quite comfortable. A double bed mattress lay on the floor for them to sit on.

This would be their bedroom for the next two weeks. It now held a pram, the pushchair, eight children, two dogs, Marge and Eliza! The children slept most of the way.

"This reminds me of my childhood days, going to the hops fields with my mother and brother," said Tilly. "I wonder how Billy is getting on." She had only seen him that once—the day he had come with her sister now years ago, and she hadn't heard from her sister at all, even though they had promised to keep in touch.

The family stopped several times along the way so that everyone could stretch their legs and pee, and so that Ray, especially, could rest a bit from driving. Finally, they reached their campsite at the shore.

CHAPTER 11

There were a few tents and small caravans in the field where Ray and Jim started erecting the two tents.

"Fancy seeing you here!" a voice called out to them.

They both turned 'round.

"Blimey, it's Pete and Jessie," Jim said as they continued pitching the tents right next to them. "Fancy coming all this way and pitching next to you."

After they all had a good look 'round, they made their way down the steep winding road to have a drink at a small pub. Ray had Michael and Biron sleeping in his tiny tent, and Sam was going into the same tent as Tilly and Jim. The rest of the family would sleep in the van. Marge and Ray's youngest baby at only six weeks had his own bed in the pram.

The next morning the children woke early, eager to get to the beach.

"Hang on, you have to have breakfast first," said Tilly. "You can't go on your own anyway."

The camp was quite high up, so they could see for miles. The sun was brilliant, and Eliza noticed that the ocean seemed to sparkle as sunlight danced on its rippling waves. She took deep breaths of the clean, salty air as she looked over the beach from the campsite. It was a lovely sight.

Mo and Michael went to a nearby farmhouse to buy some milk, while Ray and Jim fetched the water that Tilly put in a saucepan on the primus stove for their morning tea. When it boiled, she made a pot of tea, and they all sat around the camp fire drinking their tea and toasting bread for breakfast.

After breakfast they donned swim suits and made their way down a winding path to a small cove. They all piled onto the beach with Jessie, Pete and their two children. It was the first time they had ever been on a beach. The smaller children just sat and played, letting the golden sand filter between their fingers and toes.

The older children ran in and out of the waves, splashing and laughing. They loved it and were having a wonderful time. By dinner time, the beach was packed with people swimming, digging in the sand and laying out in the sun.

After Marge and Tilly fetched chips from the mobile chippie, they sat on the beach eating them, along with a few grains of sand with every bite. All of a sudden, they realised that half the people had disappeared.

"Where's everybody gone," asked Tilly.

"Maybe the noise we're all making drove them away," suggested Marge, laughing. "We soon cleared the beach." The children were used to making noise. They lived in open spaces and were always playing and laughing. They could make as much noise as they wanted in and around The Tin House. Now, they were so excited in the water and on the beach that they were making more noise than ever.

Eliza was swimming in the sea and she said later that it was "sheer bliss." She hadn't been swimming since before she left school.

"Give you a race," said Ray, splashing her.

"I've got no chance of beating you. You're twice my size."

They used the same little beach every day. Nighttimes they sat by the glow of the fire, chatting away while the older children explored the fields and woods near the campsite. After four days, they were all quite relaxed. Everyone agreed it was four days of joy. They were, as Eliza said, having a "brilliant time."

"You're looking good, Eliza, with a bit of tan, and it's nice to see you more relaxed than you usually are," said Tilly.

Eliza did feel relaxed, and she was delighted to be with her family in such a perfect spot. She did miss Joseph—at least the Joseph who was a good chap—and she hadn't yet started worrying about returning home again. For now, she and her children loved being part of Tilly and Jim's large, spirited family.

"It has gone dark very early tonight," said Jim, going into his tent. "I think we may be in for a storm—it looks mighty black over there."

"Good night all," they call to one another as they settled down for the night.

Later, Marge nudged Eliza awake.

"Listen, something's happening. It's a wonder the shouting never woke you."

Eliza realised the van was rocking like a boat. It was so strong that she and Marge prayed it wouldn't overturn.

Suddenly, the door opened and a soaking wet Ray clambered in.

"Just look at Dad," he said, laughing as the wind and rain lashed his face. He pointed at a lone figure. They could just make him out in the headlights of different cars.

There lay Jim, in the middle of the field, a Mac raincoat over his head, trying to smoke a cigarette.

All the tents had blown away and most of the caravans were overturned. The wind was tremendous, howling and blowing so much so that it was difficult to walk without getting blown off course. The rain pelted down in torrents, thoroughly soaking Ray and the others who were outside near the tents in a less than a minute. It lashed the van severely.

Ray passed Mo and the three boys to Marge and Eliza.

"Rub them down with a towel, will you please." They were absolutely soaking wet, looking like little orphan children! Ray Tilly and Jim quickly got in the front of the van, and the dogs jumped in behind them.

Jim cussed when the dogs shook their wet coats, dousing the cigarette he took pains to light up. His children had never heard their father use bad language—the nearest he got to swearing was "bucket" or "bucking." On this occasion he said, "If this is what you call a bucking holiday you can keep it."

As daybreak arrived, the torrent stopped and the sun shone brilliantly, but all of them were aching all over from being cramped up. The baby was the only one who had plenty of room as he slept in the pram. Their outer clothes and tents were scattered all over the field, sopping wet, and everything was swimming in the water. It was a hilarious scene.

They realised they had no alternative but to pack up and return home. "At least we had a few great days here," Tilly told them as they gathered all the wet clothing. The van skidded and slid all over the place, while they all helped each other. Ray laughingly compared the scene to a "Carry On" film.

On their way out of the camp ground, the farmer, who owned the place, told them that the storm was actually a hurricane. He said many whales had washed up on the beach. The older children were stunned by that news and hoped the whales survived. They didn't need to know that beached whales seldom survived.

Ray dropped Eliza and her two children off first after the long journey home. Eliza was glad Joseph was still at work because she longed for a soak in the tub—the children needed a bath, too. She immediately filled the boiler with water and stripped her sweat-soaked clothes off and the children's clothing, too. The heat in the van had been unbearable and they were all grateful that Ray stopped several times on the way home.

Eliza lifted Dawn and put her in the bath and then Mark before she slid in herself at the other end. It was wonderful just to lay there. After fifteen minutes the water was getting cold, and Eliza decided they had better get out "or we will be shrivelled up like prune."

She stepped out of the bath, wrapped a towel 'round her, and then, wrapped the children in two towels, sitting them on the settee. She dried and dressed herself, then, she dressed the children. The kitchen was cool, so she opened the window, feeling the warm breeze blowing on her cheeks. She peeled potatoes, and then cut them up for chips. They would have chips and eggs for tea. She then put the boiler back on. The washing would have to be done tonight.

"Hi," said Joseph, walking in from work. "It's great to see you back. I'm sorry about the trouble I caused," he added. "I don't know what comes over me. I don't even know I'm doing it. I didn't think you would be back this time."

"You've got to stop being like that, Joseph, or one of these days I won't come back."

"How come you're back early anyway?" he asked.

Eliza told him all about the holiday, and the two children were all over him, telling him about paddling in the big water. Dawn was now three and a half years old, Mark was thirteen months younger and Eliza was four months pregnant!

Ray and Ken still took their families down to The Tin House every Sunday and the toddlers just played outside, while Ray and Ken usually messed about with Derek's car. There was always something going wrong with it. They all cleaned their cars there, but Tilly and Jim didn't mind at all. In fact their motto could have been "The more the merrier."

Edna and Bill were moving out of the bungalow up the drive from Tilly and Jim. Tilly hadn't seen much of them the last two years, because Edna worked all day and Tilly worked mornings and nights. They were moving to a flat in a new council estate, something they later regretted doing. Edna liked the flat since it had a nice little bathroom and an inside toilet—something they never had before. They would discover, though, that it was noisy living in an apartment building close to other families.

Tilly and Jim were going to Blackpool for the weekend with Doll, Bert and some of Tilly's other friends from work. It would be the first time Tilly was away from her family. She was excited, but she also worried about leaving her children.

"Go on, enjoy yourself," said Ray. He and Marge were going to stop at The Tin House with the kids. "Just enjoy the freedom while you can."

Tilly and Jim had a fabulous time. They danced in the pubs and relaxed while sitting on deck chairs on the beach singing. As they sat there watching boats at a distance as the tide came in, they vowed to take a holiday together every year.

Jim entertained everyone in the coach on the way home by whistling popular and old favourite tunes. Tilly gazed at him lovingly—she hadn't heard him whistle like that for ages. Everyone clapped when the bus neared home, and Jim graciously stood up and bowed. As they came up the drive from the bus stop, their children ran out to meet them. Tilly was prepared with rock candy for each of them and she handed it out as they walked home. "

"Wow, that's pretty, mom, what is it?"

"Its rock candy," she said, as Mo admired the big stick Tilly had given her. "You can eat it off the stick or break it into small pieces." Each child had a separate stick to himself.

In the middle of the night, Tilly woke Jim. "I'm in agony. I had this niggling pain all yesterday, but it's worse now," she said. "I can't stand it any more." She rushed to the bathroom and threw up.

Jim jumped out of bed, threw on his clothes and ran to Ray's house, praying that his son was at home. Jim couldn't think what shift Ray was on this week, so he breathed a sigh of relief when he saw Ray's car parked in its usual place. He banged on the door, and Ray looked out the bedroom window.

"Who's there?" he called.

"It's me, your dad. Your mother's ill. I want you to take her to the hospital."

Ray dressed in a flash, then they jumped in the car and raced down to The Tin House. They ran inside and Ray asked, "What is it, Mother? What's the matter?"

"My tummy hurts all 'round. I'm in agony. I feel so sick." Jim grabbed the jug off the dressing table, just in time. Jim wiped Tilly's face while Ray draped a blanket 'round her.

"Come on, Mom, let's get you in the car and get you to the hospital," he said.

At the hospital, the doctor saw her right away. "I think it's her appendix," the doctor said. "We will have to operate straight away, she's very poorly."

Ray and Jim waited until they brought Tilly out of the operating room. It was her appendix and the doctor said they operated just in time.

They arrived back at The Tin House just before it was time to get the children up for school. They didn't know that anything happened during the night, when Jim got them up and ready for school, leaving Sam in bed since he hadn't yet started school. Jim didn't say anything to them since they were used to their mother not being there that time of the morning. He decided to tell them when they came home from school in the afternoon.

Ray needed to call the office where Tilly worked to tell them she was in hospital. He knew his mother loved her job and had many friends there. However, before he did that he decided to go tell Eliza before Joseph went to work. He wanted to ask Joseph to allow Eliza to have the car that day so she and Marge could sort out who would look after the children.

Marge took Joseph and Eliza took Biron while Jim insisted that the others would be okay because he could come home early to look after them.

Later in the day, Eliza called at the hospital to visit her mother, who was still a bit sleepy from the anaesthetic.

"How do you feel, Mom?"

"Tired and sore."

"Go back to sleep, the children are all right so don't worry. Dad will be in to see you later."

Marge waited eagerly for Eliza's report. "How is she?" she demanded as soon as Eliza got in the door of The Tin House to collect Biron and her two children. Marge had looked after them while Eliza visited her mother at the hospital.

"All right, she's still half doped and she will probably feel it more tomorrow," Eliza reported. She herded the children into the car and drove back home, thinking how much easier it was when she had the car. She turned the tiny television on for the children before she started preparing tea. She was grateful that Joseph was in a good mood tonight.

He, too, sought a report on Tilly. "How's your mother?" Eliza told him she seemed okay, but was still a bit sleepy. Then, she remembered Biron. "I hope you don't mind Biron being here," Eliza said. "He's no trouble."

"It's a wonder your father let you bring him here."

Biron liked being with Eliza and the two children. He loved playing with them but he was pining for his mother and father. Eliza tried to comfort him and gave him extra attention. Somehow, they all managed, and Tilly was soon out of the hospital.

"That's it," said Joseph. "You can't have the car any more." He had let her have it all the time Tilly has been in hospital and never moaned once, but Eliza had grown used to it and liked having the car at her disposal. She was disappointed. *Tight bastard!*

Tilly made a good recovery and she was telling Eliza about the pains she had before the operation. "When the pains first started I thought I was in labour, having a baby—so, I was quite relieved that it was my appendix. I don't want any more children."

"I should think not. You're forty-six and you already have nine."

Uncle Jack was retired now, so he went down to The Tin House more, helping Jim with the garden. Ray pushed his baby son in the pram, and his little girl toddled beside him. The house was still so full of different children it should have been called 'The Happy Open House.'

It was November, the month Derek and Val chose for their wedding. Val looked stunning. She was a beautiful girl and a lovely bride in her gorgeous white, flowing gown. The entire family would be at the wedding with one exception—Eliza's husband Joseph, who, of course, wouldn't go.

The wedding reception took place at The Star and gave both Jean and Eliza, who were pregnant, a chance to dance. They had a whale of a time and seemed to forget they were pregnant for the day.

Derek and Val were going to live with Tilly and Jim for a while until their names came up on the council list for a place of their own.

By the second week of January, it was freezing cold. Tilly had just finished her morning shift and was glad it was Friday. She decided to pick up a few groceries in town before she headed home on the 9 a.m. bus. Ever since she arrived at work in the early morning hours, though, she had a gut feeling that all was not well with Eliza.

That morning Eliza woke up at six o clock with labour pains. A single bed was already in the front room, ready for the home birth.

Joseph heard her and came downstairs. Lighting the fire, he said, "It won't take long to warm the room up. It's bitter cold out there today."

As he came back inside with a bucket of coal, Eliza made a pot of tea, and sat shivering in the cold kitchen.

"Will you put some newspaper against the fire, to draw it," she asked, huddling in the chair. The fire was soon blazing away, so it wouldn't take long to warm the small front room. Eliza drank her tea, stopping as another spasm of pain gripped her. It was now seven o clock.

"I think you'd better go and ask the nurse to come," said Eliza.

By the time he came back with the nurse Eliza lay on the bed in full labour.

The nurse washed her hands. "Let's sees how you're doing. It looks like I got here just in time."

Ten minutes later Eliza and Joseph had another little girl, whom they named Ann. Eliza felt fabulous—what an easy birth she'd had. It was a lot different from when she had the other children in the hospital. Eliza gave the credit to the midwife and her experience, which was superb.

The nurse was gone only about ten minutes when Joseph announced that he was going to return to work. Eliza was shocked! She thought that he would at least have taken the day off so he could help with the children. When she gave birth in the hospital, she had two weeks rest and the nurses looked after her. Now, Joseph expected her to do it all alone.

She lay there, looking at the bloodied sheets that were in a heap on the floor. There was only one thing she could do. Getting out of bed she collected the sheets, and put them in the bathtub, ran cold water on them and swished them 'round in the freezing water.

She rinsed off most of the blood and, then, left them to soak. Her hands were frozen, because the bathroom was extremely cold.

Eliza called her other two children downstairs, "Come and see what we have got in the front room. Isn't she lovely?" She told the little ones they could kiss the baby on the cheek if they were careful. When Ann awoke, Eliza promised, they could hold her.

Eliza washed them both, got their breakfast and then put the television on before she got back into bed, shivering. She was cold and tired. It was freezing cold in the kitchen, but in here the fire was blazing lovely. Eliza made sure the fireguard was secure before she got back into bed and dozed off.

She awoke when she heard *tap, tap* on the window, and heard Dawn saying, "Nana, Nana."

Eliza got out of bed and unlocked the door for her mother. She was with Tony Steers, a chap who worked with Derek. Tilly had asked him to drive her to Eliza's house because her gut feeling told her Eliza needed help.

"I knew you had the baby I had these pains at work this morning, and had this gut feeling about you." She made tea and toast for them all. "I can't stop long, but, do you want me to take Dawn and Mark with me?"

"No," replied Eliza. "They might think I don't want them."

"OK," said Tilly. "I know what you mean."

"Tony, will you get some more coal in before you go?" asked Eliza.

Tilly washed the crocks, dried them and put them away, while Tony brought the coal in.

"We will have to go now, Jim will be wondering where I am. And Tony has to get on with his deliveries, but I will see that Marge and the others know." Tilly kissed the children, and then she was off.

It looked so icy and cold outside, Eliza thought, as she lay cuddled up in bed. By this time, Mark and Dawn had gotten in with her, and both have fallen asleep. Eliza looked out at the large snowflakes gently coming down, some of them sticking to the window and melting as they slid off the warm windowpane. She counted her blessings beginning with her three beautiful children, and moving on through loving parents and brothers and sisters. She also had a lovely cottage and a husband who loved her. *If only he wasn't so jealous and possessive, everything would be perfect!*

When Joseph came home from work he was in a brilliant mood. He got their tea, saw to the pigs and hens, washed the children, and finally, put them into bed. Eliza couldn't believe the change in him! The next day he was still in a good mood. *Maybe the time I went to Cornwall without him made him realise that I could leave him if he mistreats me!*.

The next morning she sat on the toilet, looking at the sheets still soaking in the tub. Eliza knew she had to wash them because the other washing was piling up as well. As soon as the nurse came and went, Eliza started scrubbing. The water in the bath was turning bright red her hands were freezing as she wrung the sheets out as best she could. However, Eliza was dreading the next part—she had to hang them outside.

Slithering and sliding on the ice, she made her way up the slippery slope in the field that led to the clothesline. The sun was shining brilliantly by this time, despite the bursts of snow flakes. It was freezing, but the sun and wind would partially dry the sheets.

Eliza returned to bed absolutely frozen, thinking she would never get warm again. She dozed for a bit then woke with a start. The fire had gone low and the children needed feeding. She got back out of bed and placed more coal on the fire. Then, she got some dinner for the children and herself. Her back was killing her, and she was glad to get back into bed.

Joseph's brother's wife called in to see them. "Yoo Hoo!" she called out. "I see Joseph did the washing for you. It looks lovely and clean blowing out there." she said. "It must be nearly dry so I will get it in for you before I go."

"Joseph doing washing? You must be joking," Eliza said. "He never did it—I did it myself."

Her sister-in-law proceeded to give her a lecture about doing everything herself.

"That's a laugh," replied Eliza. "Who's going to do it if I don't?"

"I don't know."

Two days later Eliza was crying. She said she was in agony and that the pain in her breast was unbearable. One breast was swollen and bright red—even under her arm. She couldn't sleep lying down, so she sat up by the fire all night.

When the nurse arrived to check on her and the baby she asked what was wrong. Eliza quickly wiped her eyes, because she didn't want the nurse to think she was a baby.

"It's my boob," Eliza said. "It's killing me. I sat here all night!"

"Let's have a look. My goodness, that looks very painful! I'm going to have to phone the doctor up when I get home. I think you have got the cold in it. Have you been outside at all?"

"Yes," she replied. Then, Eliza reluctantly told the nurse about the washing she had to do.

"You poor girl!" said Nurse Stanley. "I will wash the children for you." She washed and gave them their breakfast, and then dressed them.

Eliza got back into bed. *What a super nurse she is!*

When the doctor looked at her breast, he said, "It looks nasty." He diagnosed her condition as "milk fever," and he blamed it on her going out in the cold. "Warm a napkin, fold it in half and put it in your bra, and take these tablets. You must express the milk off this side, and throw it away," he said. "I know it will be painful but it has to come away from you, or it will get worse." Before he left, the doctor told Eliza to feed the baby from her other breast until the sore one was better. "And don't forget the warm napkin wrapped 'round it."

Eliza winced at the thought of expressing milk from her sore breast.

Ray and Marge had been to the council to see if they could get a council house because the little house they live in was too tiny. It wasn't even as wide as Uncle Jack and Aunt Eve's house, but it was a bit longer. "It's a shame it's so small, because it's in a lovely spot," Eliza said. "You can see The Tin House over the fields from the bottom of the garden."

The workers in the council office took their name and address, and put them on the housing list. Ray wanted to stay in the village, if he could.

"Don't rely on it," the workers replied, when Marge made that request. "There are already people waiting for one of those." They explained that there were only about thirty council houses in the village, and they don't come empty very often. They told Ray and Marge that the council started building a new estate that should be finished next year. They said Ray and Marge had a good chance of getting one of those new houses.

"Well, at least we have our name down," said Ray. "That must be where Edna and Bill moved—they said the first phase was completed last fall and that's when they moved."

Tilly didn't want Ray to move, because he did so much for her. He was doing three different shifts now, ten till six, two till ten and six to two, and on two of these shifts he took Tilly and her mate to work before seven in the morning. She couldn't ask for a better son than Ray, and Marge was quite happy to let him help out. She loved Tilly and Jim as well, getting on better with them than her own parents.

Ken was doing all right, though he didn't come to The Tin House as often, now that he moved away. He bought up sacks of potatoes from a farm, washed and dries them, then, put them in five pound bags. He also bought trays of eggs to sell. He had worked up quite a large route. He also started up a repair shop in an old garage with a mate. They were doing quite well. Years ago, Ken said he was going to be wealthy. He just made his mind up, and now he seemed to be on the right rack and his wife was with him all the way. They even bought a small house, fixed it up, and were ready to sell if for a good profit. They were in the process of buying a lovely old bungalow.

Tilly's children were growing up now—the youngest was nearly six, only two years older than Dawn. Young Joseph was seventeen now. Blimey, how time flies! He said if Ray moved he would get up early and take Tilly to work. He already took her on the weeks Ray couldn't.

Derek and Val were expecting their first baby. *Look what you started, Mother.*

Summer had finally arrived. It was Sunday morning—an absolutely beautiful morning! Eliza's baby was asleep in her cot. Dawn and Mark were playing on the lawn the dinner was slowly simmering on the cooker, and the roast was in the oven sizzling.

Eliza ran out of ciggies. *It won't take me five minutes in the car,* she thought to herself. Picking the car keys off the rack, she shouted up the garden to Joseph, "I'm just popping down to the paper shop for some ciggies, the children are playing nicely on the lawn. I won't be more than ten minutes. Do you want any?"

"Then you will have to want or walk!" he shouted back to her. "You ain't having the bleeding car!"

"OK, I will walk then. But you know it's over two miles there and back to the shop, and the dinner's cooking. Keep an eye on the children."

Eliza got to the top of the drive and started running, knowing if she took a long time she would be in for it when she got back. She stopped at the little bridge to catch her breath. The bridge always reminded her of her mother. It was just like the little bridge by the church where Eliza's grandmother used to live.

She was just about to walk on, when a horn tooted and, looking 'round, she saw it was Joseph. Getting out of the car, he opened the back door, and passed the baby to her, off the back seat of the car. Then he shouted to Dawn and Mark to get out. "If you're going to see your bloody fancy man you can take the bloody kids with you!"

"But they haven't got any shoes on," said Eliza.

"Tough!"

She was half way between the cottage and Janice's house. If she walked back home the footpath stopped half the way up, and the road would hurt the children's feet. Eliza knew she was probably in for belting when she got back. *Bugger him! Why should I bow down to him?*

"Come on," she said. "We will walk to Janice's house, you can play with Gay and Nick for half an hour" She asked the older kids to look where they stepped because she didn't want them hurt by stones. Eliza was disgusted with Joseph for using the children as weapons. He hadn't done that before. *For Christ's sake, I was only going to the paper shop! Well, I left the dinner cooking—I hope it burns!*

She knocked on Janice's door.

Janice opened it, wondering who it could be on a Sunday morning.

"Eliza!" she said. "What a surprise!" Then she noticed the children's feet and gasped. "No need to ask you what you are doing here," she said. "What did he do this time?"

"I only popped in to see if you will do me a favour." Eliza didn't know Janice's husband but she did know he didn't like her to have her friends there when he was home. He told her she had all week for friends.

They were trying to keep their voices to a whisper in the back kitchen. Janice had a lovely large kitchen, and her children were playing on a large mat on the floor. Eliza sat down, with Dawn and Mark hanging on her skirt.

"This was the nearest place to come. The children's feet are sore. I wanted to know if you would just watch them while I run to Daisy's. Her husband will probably give us a lift up to The Tin House."

The door to the lounge opened, and Eliza held her breath as Janice's husband walked in. He hadn't seen Eliza before but he had heard about her.

"You must be Eliza," he said, looking at her.

"Yes," she replied nervously. She only looked like a kid herself and she looked as if she weighed about seven stone, he thought. He then noticed the children's bare feet.

"I'm only here for a minute," explained Eliza, "then, I will be on my way!"

"What happened?" Janice's husband asked her. He was furious. How could any man treat a woman like that?"

Eliza was still shaking.

"You don't have to go anywhere," he said. "You can stay here." He was a big chap with very broad shoulders, and his name was Gareth.

Janice gave Eliza and the children dinner. About six o' clock, someone knocked on the front door. Janice and Eliza were still in the kitchen, listening to Gareth talking to someone.

Janice walked into the hall. "What's going on?" she said, knowing it was Joseph.

"She isn't' going back—she's an absolute bag of nerves. What do you think you are doing to her?" Janice, then, walked back into the kitchen to Eliza.

"I had better go back with him. I didn't mean to drag you into it," she said, walking into the hall and biting her nails. "OK, I will come back, if you promise you won't hit me."

"I promise," replied Joseph.

"If you lay a hand on Eliza at all, I will personally come up and give you a bloody good hiding. As far as I'm concerned, you're nothing but a bully and a control freak."

Joseph could see he meant it, and he didn't want to cross him. He was a big man, with a gentle, soft voice.

Eliza was quiet on the way home, praying that Joseph wouldn't go back on his word. It would be a long time before she forgave him for making Dawn and Mark walk along the road with no shoes on.

As promised, Janice came to see her the next day and she had Daisy with her.

"Did he hit you last night?"

"No," replied Eliza. "I think Gareth scared him."

"He meant every word of it," said Janice. "He's not a violent man but he hates women being ill treated."

The next day Eliza was going to see her mother at The Tin House, but she decided not to mention what happened to her on Sunday because her mother already worried about her.

Marge was already down at The Tin House, having a cup of tea with Tilly.

"Have you heard anything from the council yet?" asked Tilly.

"No," replied Marge. "I think you have to be on the waiting list two years first."

Michael started his first job. He was in the building trade. There was plenty of building going on in the area. Michael's big ambition was to be able to build his own house one day. He was not going to work for peanuts, like his dad did. If he couldn't make it there, he said he would go abroad somewhere. Michael certainly worked hard.

He had started going out with his brother Joseph, and they were both good looking men, so they had plenty of girls after them.

Uncle Jack and Aunt Eve moved to a three-bedroom house, just a few yards along the road from where they lived in the tiny cottage. All their children had gone—married with children of their own. The reason they got the house was that the row of tiny cottages was about to be knocked down. They were condemned and should have been knocked down years ago. However, Uncle Jack and Aunt Eve were happy enough there for all those years.

Eliza and Marge called in to see them on their way home.

"How do you like it?" asked Marge.

"It's like a palace compared to the old house. We love it," replied Eve. "The best thing is the indoor toilet and the bit of garden for Jack. We've even got a back door and gate leading to the garden."

Both Eliza and Marge were pleased for them. They continued walking home. Marge's house was only a few yards past Jack and Eve's new home.

Eliza was pregnant again, but her mother was not pleased about it. She thought Eliza would be better off without Joseph, but she wouldn't interfere. Tilly believed any move away from Joseph had to come from Eliza. Tilly did worry constantly about Eliza, though. Tilly thought the situation would improve if she could drive. Then, she could go to the cottage more often to check on Eliza and her children. Alternatively, they could have lived closer so she could have kept a better eye on them.

CHAPTER 12

At midnight, Eliza lay awake in bed. Joseph had not come home from the pub yet even though it closed at ten thirty. *Where could he be? And what could he be doing?* It was about three o' clock when he finally came in, but Eliza pretended to be asleep.

"What happened last night?" she asked him. "It was three a.m. when you got home."

"Well, I was driving down Botters Hill when I missed the bend in the road and ended up in the ditch. I couldn't drive out of it so I walked down to the farm," Joseph said.

This was the same farm Eliza went to when the man exposed himself to her.

"I knocked on the door and got the farmer up and asked him if he would get the tractor to tow me. I can show you the dent in the car."

Taking her hand, Joseph led Eliza outside and showed her the bump on the front passenger side. Eliza never said any more she wasn't going to get into an argument with him because she knew she would never win. But, she did wonder why he took that route home since it was twice as far away as the direct route.

Eliza walked up the drive to check the mail in the letter tin and to get the milk. She noticed that the gatepost looked as if it had been hit by something. *Perhaps the milkman did it?* she thought.

"Joseph, did you notice the gate post? It looked as if someone hit it with something."

"Yes, I noticed it a few weeks ago."

"Did you? It looked like a new mark to me."

A few weeks later, Eliza was up at The Tin House visiting her mother, when Jessie came in.

"Will you join us in a cuppa?" asked Tilly. They sat chatting in between sips of tea.

"Did Joseph cop out when he came home late the other week?" asked Jessie.

"How do you know Joseph came home late?" Eliza replied. "I didn't tell anyone."

"Because he was with me. I told him I would tell you."

"The bastard!" replied Eliza. "He told me a lot of bullshit, and I believed him. Wait till I get home."

Joseph had deliberately run into the gatepost just to put a dent in the car so he could make up the tale about going into the ditch, when all the time he had been with Jessie.

"You call me a dirty slut and every name under the sun and you're knocking married women off!" Eliza said as Joseph came in from work. He didn't answer. Instead, he turned his back on her and walked outside to feed the pigs and the hens.

"Guess what!" said Marge a few days later. "Ray and I had a letter from the council," She was excited as she finished her news. "We've been offered a brand new house and we can move in next week."

Eliza was pleased for her, but she had mixed feelings. "I'll miss you, especially all the time we spend together at The Tin House," she said "I am sure mother will miss you, too. I doubt that you will want to walk all that way."

"I will miss you as well," replied Marge, "but I will still come up with Ray."

A few days later Daisy got her letter from he council. She, too, was offered a house on the same estate. Her current house had to come down because it was in the way of the new roundabout road planned for Crabs Cross.

"It's a good job you won't be moving," Eliza said to Janice. "If you did I wouldn't have one friend close by." Janice's house was over a mile from the cottage, but it was closer than The Tin House.

"You will always be welcome here, Eliza," said Janice. "Gareth asks me every day how you are. He says you are stupid to stand for it."

"I know. I keep thinking he will change, but anyway, where could I go? Mom and dad can't afford to keep me and my three children. And I reckon I'm pregnant again."

"Christ! Eliza, you will finish up like your mom if you don't watch it!" replied Janice.

"Come on," Joseph called up the stairs. "You have to get up early today."

Eliza jumped out of bed. Dawn would start school today, and she had to get all three children ready. Dawn was so excited that she danced 'round the room. Eliza dressed Mark and Ann, and at last they were ready, but it' was quite a walk. The school was up by the playing fields, and there was that massive hill to walk up.

Janice's eldest daughter also went to school, so at least Dawn knew someone there. It was about a mile if they took the short cut, but it was still hard going as there was a big hill to walk up that way, too.

Dawn soon made friends with a couple of girls who lived just down the road. They walked to school on their own.

"Do you think Dawn could walk with you, please?" asked Eliza as they reached the girls the next morning.

One girl took Dawn by the hand. After that, the neighbourhood girls waited for her each morning a short way from the house. Eliza could watch her from the gate as Dawn walked down the road to meet them. Then, Eliza would fetch her from school in the afternoons.

"That was far better," she told Joseph. She no longer had to get Mark and Ann up early.

One night Daisy and her husband came to see Joseph and Eliza. Joseph saw them coming down the drive. Before they even came in, he addressed Eliza,. "What the hell are they coming here for?"

Before Eliza could answer, the couple walked into the house. "We are having a little bit of a house-warming party, only a handful of people. Do you want to come?"

"That's my night out," replied Joseph.

"What if she can get a baby sitter?" asked Daisy.

"Yes, she can come if she can get there."

Blimey! What's come over him?

"I will fetch you and bring you home," said Daisy's husband.

Eliza was so looking forward to the house warming that she asked her sister Mo to baby-sit for her, but Joseph wasn't pleased when the night came. He changed his mind.

"You're not going!" he said.

Eliza guessed that this would happen so she washed and changed earlier on. She didn't need to put make up on as there are only going to be a few friends, and she knew Joseph might try to stop her when Daisy's husband came for her.

Eliza was right. When the car horn tooted for her to go, Joseph stood in front of her.

"You're not fukin' going!"

She evaded him and walked into the front room the only way out of there was the small window. Eliza quietly opened it and started squeezing herself through the small opening, wearing her best red tartan coat.

All of a sudden Joseph was in the room, grabbing the bottom of the coat, trying to pull her back in. Eliza heard a tearing noise as her feet touched the ground. Her best coat had ripped! A piece of the coat's flapping stuck on the window catch, but she ran and got in her mate's husband's car.

"Quick, drive!" she said, shaking.

"Fancy living a life like this!" he said, pulling off.

At ten o'clock Eliza was getting uneasy. She asked Daisy's husband to take her home, explaining that she wanted to be back before Joseph came home. *He must surely have gone out!*

Daisy asked one of her friends to listen for her children, knowing what Joseph was like. If he saw Eliza alone in a car with a man, he would go mad, even if it was Daisy's husband, and she didn't want him to cop out.

They turned into the drive where Eliza lived.

"I will be all right from here," she said, getting out of the car at the top of the drive. The car lights were shining down the drive, casting eerie shadows. Eliza ran inside as the car lights disappeared in the distance.

All of a sudden, wallop! She was on the floor, and someone was on top of her, strangling her. She was gasping for breath. This is it, she thought to herself. I've had it! The hands released their grip on her throat, but they grabbed her head and smashed it into the ground. Eliza lay there, gasping for breath, and sobbing at the same time.

The next minute Joseph was bending over her.

"Who did this to you?" he asked as he guided her into the house.

Her sister Mo was terrified, and so was Dawn. Still in a daze, Eliza made her way to the kitchen, and washed the dirt and blood off her face while Mo and Dawn screamed.

Then Joseph was hitting her again swinging her 'round, he put his hands 'round her throat, then started squeezing. Eliza could feel herself blacking out. She put her arms out in desperation, and then her hand felt a hard object. Grasping hold of it, she swung it up and over. She hit him on the head as hard as she could.

Joseph loosened his hold on her. Then, to Eliza's amazement, he started to cry. "You cut my head open! It's bleeding, you bastard!" He then sat down, his head in his hands.

Eliza still had the object in her hand. Without looking at it, she knew it was the glass sugar basin. There was sugar everywhere, but the basin remained intact. However, she would not put it down—not until Joseph was in bed, sleeping off his drink.

Mercifully, the two younger children were still in bed fast asleep. Eliza knew she had to calm down and stop crying for the sake of Mo and Dawn. They watched it all and were terrible frightened. Eventually, Joseph went up to bed. Eliza, her sister and her daughter went into the third bedroom and pushed the dressing table against the bedroom door.

Eliza knew the other two children would be all right Joseph might be horrid and abusive to her but he never touched the children.

The next morning Joseph was a different person, asking Eliza, "How did you hurt your face?"

She shuddered as she looked in the mirror. What a sight she was!' Her eyes were swollen and bloodshot her nose was twice as big as it should be, and she was hurting all over. She reckoned her nose was broken! *Joseph has certainly done a good job this time!* Eliza knew she couldn't show her face to her parents or they would go ballistic.

She would have to stay in the house until the bruises went down a bit.

"Come on, Mo, I will take you home," said Joseph.

"Please, Mo, don't tell mom or dad!" begged Eliza.

"Okay."

The next day Eliza was hurting so much that she couldn't get out of bed, so the children more or less looked after themselves, while little Dawn tried to mother them.

Two days later there was a knock on the door. Eliza had remained in bed since the beating. Every time she tried to move she was in agony, not knowing where she hurt the most. Dawn had been just like a little mother to the other two children and knew enough to lock the door when her father went to work.

"Who is it?" she called out as someone knocked on the door.

"It's Nanny Tilly," came the reply. Eliza could hear the noise of the chair scraping on the red tiles as Dawn dragged it over to the door, and unlocked it.

"Where's mommy?" she asked when Dawn opened the door.

"I'm up here, Mom," called Eliza.

Tilly walked upstairs. "Oh, my God, Eliza!" she said. "What on earth's happened to you?"

"I fell down the stairs," replied Eliza, not daring to tell her the truth Joseph said he would kill her, and she knew he was capable of doing it. Tilly tenderly bathed Eliza's face after she helped her down the stairs.

"How did you get here?" asked Eliza.

"Derek bought me in the laundry van, he will pick me up later." Tilly explained that she thought it odd that Eliza didn't make her regular visit the day before. She also noted that she did not believe Eliza story of falling down the stairs. "He did it, didn't he?"

Eliza never answered.

"I will see to the children, but when Derek gets back, I am going to get him to take us to the doctor to get you checked over."

"How did you get like this?" asked the doctor. "You're in a right state, aren't you?"

"I fell down the stairs," was her reply.

He gave her a knowing look. "I can only prescribe strong painkillers. You have broken blood vessels in your eyes, and your nose could be broken. Come back in a few days so I can take a better look after the swelling goes down."

Eliza knew she should leave, but she genuinely thought Joseph would find her and kill her if she did. So she would just have to put up with it. Joseph always swore blindly that he hadn't done it. He hadn't always been like that.

A few days later, Joseph came home with an old piano, which he had bought second hand, for her. Eliza was chuffed to buggery, maybe Joseph wasn't too bad after all. But, wait. He always bought her something after he knocked her about. Perhaps when the children were older, she could have piano lessons. She still remembered the piano and the tunes she learned to play as a child all years ago.

By the last week in June, it was quite hot, and Eliza had grown quite big carrying this baby. On this Sunday afternoon, Dawn and Mark squabbled all day, and Joseph was getting annoyed. "For Christ's sake, take the bleeding car keys and take the bloody kids up to your mother for a bit! I might get a bit of peace then!"

Eliza didn't really want to move since she had been having niggling pains in the bottom half of her back all morning, and she had terrible piles as big as grapes. She reckoned she was in the early stages of labour.

"The only time I can have the car is when it's beneficial to you," she told him.

"Are you all right, you don't look too good?" asked Tilly.

"I think I might be in labour."

"Do you want a nice cuppa?"

"Just cold water, thanks. It's getting on a bit I'd best get back and get the children ready for bed early. These pains are getting quite strong now."

"You can leave the eldest two here for the night, if you like," said Tilly.

"Are you sure?" replied Eliza. "I have to go, I'm in agony."

"Why is it so hot? I'm sweating buckets," she said to Joseph. "I think you'd better go and tell the nurse I have got really strong labour pains." She wearily lay on the bed glad that baby Ann had fallen asleep in the pram.

"Blimey! I think you're ready to have it, except the waters haven't broken yet," said the nurse. "And look at your piles. You poor thing, you must be in agony."

"Joseph, will you go down to the phone box and call the doctor? I need a hand here."

"What's the problem?" asked the doctor

"I can't break her waters the baby's that low, and the poor girl's got terrible piles."

The baby was soon born after the doctor broke Eliza's waters. It was boy, and they named him 'Thomas.' The nurse was brilliant, as usual.

Every day after washing Eliza and Thomas, the nurse put little Ann in the bowl in the sink and combed her lovely curls. Ann was eighteen months old.

When Tilly brought Mark and Dawn back, the nurse saw that Mark was dressed. He was four and a half now and Dawn was a year older. Joseph was in a good mood, putting the children to bed at night while Eliza was laid up. Her friend Daisy came to see her.

"I have missed you so much," said Eliza. "I have missed popping in for coffee and a natter when I go to the butcher's."

"Guess what!" said Daisy. "I'm expecting twins!"

"Bloody hell, you will have your hands full!"

"I will manage." Her husband was kind and wonderful to her, and he had a very good job. She didn't smoke but she very often bought packets for Eliza and Janice when they ran out.

True to his word, Ray still often visited at The Tin House with the children, the same as he had always done. He knew they loved it up there as much as the rest of the family did. He thought of the place as a magnet that drew people to it. Tilly's friends still went there even though their children were grown up or married and many had moved on.

Tilly and Jim still went out with Doll, but Bert had died a few years earlier. Jessie and Pete still visited The Tin House on occasion, but Eliza and Joseph no longer went out with Jim and Tilly on Saturday nights. Eliza couldn't cope with the abuse she had received. She found it easier to stay at home.

Joseph now had a new job working nights. He started going out with his brother to the local on Saturday and Sunday night. He still only allowed Eliza to have the car on odd occasions, mostly to suit him. Eliza decided that in future she would do the housework and washing at night, after Joseph had gone to work. That night, after he had gone, she set about doing the washing, which wouldn't take her long to hang out on the line in the morning.

"Come on, children, it's time for bed," she said, taking them upstairs. After settling them down, Eliza folded a sheet up and placed it on the red Formica-top table. She then stood there, doing the ironing. Finally, making sure everything was switched off, she went to bed exhausted. She had a plan she knew it might mean a good hiding, but she was getting used to that now.

The next morning Joseph came home, fed the animals, had his breakfast, and then went up to bed. Eliza knew Joseph would be in a deep sleep for about the first four hours. Waiting until she heard him snoring, she then warmed her hands. She wanted the car keys, and Joseph slept with them in his hand.

Eliza crept upstairs, missing the step that creaked, then crawled on her hands and knees into the bedroom, her knees scraped on the rough wooden floorboards. Her heart beat faster and louder every second. She hoped Joseph couldn't hear it. Then, slowly she slid her hand under the bedclothes, and very slowly pulled the keys out. She made sure she had hold of both keys, so they didn't rattle against each other, and then crept back down the stairs, glancing behind her as she went.

Dawn and Mark were at school. Eliza put Ann and Thomas in the car before she climbed in herself, hoping Joseph wouldn't hear the car start up. She kept glancing up at the bedroom window as she reversed up the drive. She checked once more to make sure Joseph wasn't watching out the window. Eliza was to repeat this caper many times.

She went either to The Tin House to see her mother or picked Janice up so they could go to see Daisy and Marge in their new houses. Sometimes, she picked Janice up and took her up to The Tin House. Janice loved Tilly and Jim. Her own parents were very religious and were always very strict with her as a child and still were. Even though she was married, she didn't dare let them know she smoked.

After a couple of hours Eliza knew she had better make her move back home since she had to get back before Joseph woke up. After dropping Janice off, Eliza would drive very slowly down the drive, knocking the car out of gear and turning the ignition off. She silently steered into the exact spot where Joseph had parked as the hairs on her neck stood on end in fear that Joseph might come out, she finally turned the mileage back on the clock. Eliza was not going to let him break her spirit no matter how hard he hit her, she wouldn't bow down to him.

She would quietly go into the house, knowing that Joseph was still in bed otherwise he would have flown out to her by now. Next, came the hardest part. She had to try to put the car keys back in the bed. She made a cup of tea for him, carried it quietly upstairs, popped the keys just under the sheet, and then gently shook him awake. "Here you are, Joseph, a nice cup of tea."

It was Saturday, and Joseph has just come back from visiting his mother, having taken the three biggest children to see their granny. "Guess what, Eliza?" he said. "My aunt's coming home from Norway where she lived for twenty years. She decided to sell up and come to live with Gran."

Joseph's aunt had married a Norwegian whaler, but apparently he had died at sea and had been in the freezer for months until the whaling season was over.

"Nobody likes her, do they?" asked Eliza.

"No. She's worse than my dad, and that's saying something. Gran was dreading it, and she hoped her daughter would get bored and go back. After all, she lived in Norway for twenty years."

"You must be Joseph' wife," she said to Eliza, giving her the once over. "You haven't got much meat on you, have you?" she added, making Eliza feel much smaller than she was. Joseph' aunt reminded Eliza of the horrible matron who sent her mother out when Dawn was born.

"I wouldn't like to cross her path," she told Joseph.

"No, neither would I."

A few days later Eliza was standing at the sink, washing the crocks in the bowl, when she saw Joseph' aunt walk past the kitchen window! *Oh, blimey! What does she want?* She tried to remain calm, but she cringed inside. Just the sight of her was enough to scare her.

"I will put the kettle on and make you a cup of tea," said Eliza with a smile on her face, but she was shaking underneath.

"No, you carry on. I will make the tea!" she replied briskly, grabbing the tea towel she started to dry the crocks, while waiting for the kettle to boil.

Eliza tipped the water out, swilled out the bowl, and then, put the potatoes in. She was going to scrape them.

"What do you think you are doing?" Joseph's aunt bellowed.

"I'm going to scrape the potatoes," replied Eliza, wishing she would piss off.

"What! In the same bowl you just washed up in?"

"What's wrong with that?" asked Eliza.

"Sheer filth!" she said. "I've never seen anything so disgusting in all my life. If you haven't got another bowl use a saucepan. I will have to have a word with Joseph about this!"

"Everybody I know only has one bowl!"

"What sort of people do you mix with?" she asked. "Were you dragged up, or what?"

"Take no notice of her," said Joseph when he arrived home. "My mother only has one bowl. Perhaps they are different in Norway."

"It's the bossy way she speaks to you. It's quite frightening."

The next day she was back carrying a new bowl in her hands.

"Here, there's no excuse now," she said.

Two years after that Joseph's gran found her dead in bed.

Eliza managed to get the car keys and called for Janice. "Come on, we will go to Daisy for a couple of hours."

Daisy and Janice were talking about the win they had at bingo the Friday before.

"Why you don't come with us, Eliza?" said Daisy.

"You're joking! Joseph hates me going anywhere in the day, let alone at night."

"He needn't know," said Janice. "If you get one of your brothers to bring your sister Mo to baby-sit for you and then pick her up after you get home Joseph won't even know."

"He'd kill me if I did that." A few days later Eliza was telling her mother about bingo.

"Well, it's about time you had a night out. If you do decide to go, call in the Plough and Arrow. Dad will buy you a drink."

And so, for the next few months, Eliza went to bingo, her brother brought Mo down to baby-sit, picked Eliza and Janice up, and then dropped them outside bingo to meet Daisy.

After bingo they made their way to the pub to have a drink with Tilly and Jim. Then, Eliza's brother Joseph took them all home in his new mini van. After he dropped Eliza home, her sister Mo jumped in the van, and off they went.

Eliza had been going to bingo about seven months, but she would have to stop when the winter came, or there would be wheel tracks down the drive in the snow.

"The Friday night shift is ending this week," said Joseph as he came in from work one morning. "The hours are four to eight."

That's goodbye to bingo! "Perhaps we could go out and have a drink with Mom and Dad then?" she asked.

"Okay."

Two days later, he changed his mind, saying he was going to the local pub with his brother.

So, after a couple of weeks, Eliza asked Joseph, "Seeing as you go out Friday, Saturday, and Sunday night, can I go to bingo?"

He ignored her, turned his back on her and walked outside.

"I think I will pop down the farm to see mother before I go to bed," he said, when he came home from work the next morning.

Eliza knew he was going to arrange Friday night out, with his brother, who worked on his father's farm, He had been telling his brother that Eliza wanted to go to bingo.

"You can go to bingo Friday, but my brother's wife will go with you," he said, coming back in the house. "And Mo can look after their two children as well. I will drop you off at bingo."

When Friday arrived, Eliza knew better than to put make-up on. Joseph dropped them at the bingo hall, but her sister-in-law had to join as she hadn't been before so they were a bit early. Eliza led the way to where she usually sat, and they were there when Janice and Daisy arrived with Daisy's other friend, Jan.

"How long have you been here?" asked Janice.

"About ten minutes."

"Well, Joseph is still outside in his car," said Janice.

"I'm not a bit surprised," was Eliza's reply.

Eliza had never won, not once, in all the months she went, but Janice, Daisy, and her friend won nearly every week.

Bingo over, they made their way to The Plough and Arrow Pub to join Tilly and Jim, who are having a drink and a laugh with them. Young Joseph, Eliza's brother, then took them home, unaware of what was to come. Eliza and her sister-in-law went into the house and sent Mo outside. She was going home with young Joseph. Eliza made coffee for her sister–in-law and herself. She noted that the four younger children are asleep, three on the settee and the youngest one in the pram.

Eliza and her sister-in-law sat drinking their coffee, idly chatting, when their husbands walked, in, both men laughing. *Thank God they're in a good mood!* Eliza went back into the kitchen to make coffee and sandwiches for the two men, humming a tune to herself.

What's going on? She wondered when she heard raised voices. "Oh no!" she said as she carried the coffee in. It was her brother-in-law shouting at his wife.

"Stop shouting!" cried Eliza, "You will wake the children up!"

Grabbing the cup of coffee out of Eliza's hand, he threw it all over his wife, as some of it shot up the walls and over the fireplace.

The fire hissed as coffee fell on the flames. Joseph was trying to calm his brother down, which he finally did, after a few minutes.

Eliza got some warm water, cotton wool and a towel to bathe her sister-in-law's face, which was a right mess. Joseph was watching her and she could see he was getting agitated.

All of a sudden, he jumped up, grabbed her and started belting her! Eliza fell as he smashed his fist straight in her face, then his hands were 'round her throat, squeezing.

This is it! Eliza thought, as she started to blackout. The children were screaming, the noise had woken them up.

His brother then started hitting his wife again, and then, all of a sudden, he seemed to sober up, stopped hitting his wife and pulled Joseph off Eliza.

"Leave her now, she's had enough," he said.

Eliza was trying to get up off the floor, and all the children were crying. Her brother-in-law pulled her to her feet.

"I can't stay here any more!" Eliza cried out. "He will kill me. He has that look in his eye."

"Give the keys to the car to her, Joseph, and let her go. You can talk tomorrow," said Joseph's brother. Even he knew she wouldn't be safe alone with him. Joseph, however, didn't want to do that, he wanted her to stay. After more arguing, he threw the car keys at Eliza.

"Here, now fuck off, you slut!" he yelled at her. "And don't come back."

His brother was standing between them, shielding her from her husband. He wouldn't go before he saw Eliza and her children safely to the car. She grabbed the children.

"Quick!" she said. "Get in the car before he changes his mind."

As soon as they were safely in the car, she locked all the doors quickly as she was fumbling for the ignition slot. Finding it, she put the keys in, turned it on, and pressed the starter. The engine burst into life, but before she could move, her brother-in law needed to move his car, which was parked behind her, blocking her in. She was sobbing and shaking!

Pull yourself together, be calm! She had to reverse up the drive. As soon as the other car was moving, Eliza reversed as fast as she could, almost touching the other car's bumper.

Joseph had now changed his mind, so he was running by the side of he car, shouting to her, "Get out of that car, you fucking old bag." He tried to open the locked door.

Eliza kept reversing up the drive, but he was still hanging on, shouting. She could feel the blood trickling down her face, but she didn't dare to stop now. At last, she reached the top of the drive and swung the steering wheel 'round. While the car was spinning, Joseph lost his grip on the door handle.

Eliza wiped the blood off her face with her sleeve as she drove up to The Tin House. At that moment, she realised Joseph would never change. As much as she loved him and the cottage, at the moment she hated him and she knew she would never go back.

It was 2 a.m. and she was banging on her parent's door, waking them. They guessed who it was—the children were crying, and Eliza was crying.

Jim looked at her. "This has to be the last time," he said. "He will kill you one day. This is the last chance you have. Your mother and I worry about you every minute of the day and night, waiting to hear he has killed you."

"I swear I won't ever go back again!" Eliza sobbed. "I don't even know how it started. I was in the kitchen making coffee."

They all climbed in bed with Mo, in the front room. Eliza and her children were safe in The Tin House. The next day one of her brothers took the car back to the cottage.

Eliza would have to get a job to keep them here, as her mother and father couldn't afford to keep an extra five mouths. Eliza started to relax a bit. It was a week since she came back to The Tin House. It was all quiet in darkness, with everyone in bed asleep.

Suddenly, Eliza woke with a start! She could feel a hand on her leg. She was scared stiff! Then someone was kissing her. She froze. *Only one person should be doing that, but how did he get in?* She slid her left arm out until she was touching her sister, then she pinched her. Mo screamed out, which startled Joseph, who gave Eliza a quick punch and ran out of the house.

By the time Jim came downstairs Joseph was gone, without a trace of him. Jim fixed a bolt on the front room door where Eliza and Mo slept with Dawn and Ann, all in a double bed. Thomas has a cot by the bed and Mark slept upstairs with Eliza's brothers. Jim also secured the outside doors better.

Eliza was looking for a job, but it had to be nine to four. She worried about the children and how she would get to work. Thomas was sitting in the bowl in front of the fire in the front room, while Eliza bathed him.

Someone knocked on the door, and Eliza heard her name mentioned. She watched as Tilly walked in followed by a man in a business suit. "This man says he's from Social Services," her mother said. "I have been sent to see you because we had a complaint saying you were not looking after your children properly."

Eliza knew it was Joseph up to his tricks. After talking to her for half an hour, he said, "I can see this little chappie's healthy enough and scrubbed spotless. I've also just seen Ann playing with some toys in the other room with your mother, so you don't have anything to worry about. We have already had a report about Dawn and Mark from school, and we are quite satisfied they are being looked after. In fact, the teacher said they seemed happier, more settled than before."

Eliza was fuming. Joseph had no intention of having the children himself. He wanted them to go in a home rather than allow her to have them.

Eliza got a job in a spring factory, after asking if she could work nine to three thirty. Each job had a price on it so much a thousand. She soon picked it up and was earning good money, but she had to get up at half past six every morning, the same time as her mother. Tilly had to be at work for seven, and young Joseph usually took her.

Eliza had to get the children, washed and dressed, and then take her brother Joseph to work. He was lending her his van. "See you at five," she called out as she dropped him at the building yard. Then, she drove back to The Tin House to do a bit of washing before she took Dawn and Mark to school. After all that, she carried on to work.

Eliza let them stay at the same school as before, so that they weren't any more disrupted than necessary. She loved her job, and the boss was very pleased with her work.

"Do you know anyone else who would like a job?" he said to her one day. "I will ask my friend Janice. But she will have to do the same hours as me because I will have to pick her up."

So, Janice started working there as well.

The boss allowed them to leave a few minutes before three thirty so they wouldn't be late picking the children up from school. He was a great boss.

After she dropped Janice off at home, the three of them headed back home to The Tin House to her mother, Ann and Thomas. They shared a quick cup of tea and a wash, and then Eliza and Tilly started preparing the tea, making sure they all had a home cooked meal at night.

All the greens and potatoes came from Jim's garden the meat was mainly lamb chops or belly draft. After she popped it all on to cook, Eliza sat the children on a blanket in the back of the van, because she had to take her mother to work for her second shift of the day. Then, she picked her brother Joseph up from work. Tilly would have her cooked tea when she came home later at night.

Eliza blushed as Joseph's workmates started wolf whistling at her. Joseph told her one of the men had asked him, "Who's the gorgeous redhead driving about in your van?"

"How old is he?" she asked.

"Same as me," replied Joseph. "He asked me to fix him up with you."

"Thanks, all the same," she replied, "but he's too young for me, and I don't want anyone at the moment."

Eliza stayed in most nights because at first her husband still prowled around The Tin House at times, and she didn't want to risk him catching her out at night. On the nights Tilly and Jim went out, Eliza went with them. She didn't dare to go out without her father in case her husband came around.

One night when young Joseph came to pick them up from the pub, he had a friend with him. A few days later the chap asked Eliza to go out and have a drink with him and her brother. They went in a foursome with her brother and his girlfriend, Donna. Eliza learned the chap's name was Dean. She couldn't understand why he wanted to go out with her—a married woman with four children.

Another chap who worked with her brother fancied her as well. He began to come up to The Tin House regularly. He was the same chap who told her brother she was gorgeous those few weeks ago. His name was Larry.

Eliza had been going out with Dean about four months when someone told his mother, who was not at all pleased. And who could blame her? Her only son was going out with a married woman, who had four children. As a result, he and Eliza split up.

The other man, Larry, still came to The Tin House all the time. One Saturday Eliza was busy in the kitchen. She had just washed her hair and put her rollers in, when Larry came in. He was a little bit like the furniture these days since he was at The Tin House so often.

"Is it true that you're not going out with Dean any more?" he asked her.

"Yes, it's true, but I still fancy him."

"Will you come out with me tonight?"

"Okay, but no strings attached."

"No, I promise."

Larry had a car—nothing posh. It was a big green Consul with the gear stick by the steering wheel. He picked her up at 7.30 and took her to a pub in the country. The two of them got on like a house on fire she was so relaxed with him. He told Eliza he fancied her from the first time he saw her, but he didn't have the courage to ask her out. Then, when he got the courage, she was going out with Dean.

Larry was smashing, and Eliza couldn't understand why he wasn't already spoken for. He would do anything for her. He let her use his car and got a lift to work himself with a mate who lived near him. He treated her like a princess.

He took her to meet his parents, who were great to her. Eliza had already taken Larry to meet her friend Janice, and then she took him to meet Daisy.

"Crikey, Eliza! Where did you find him? He's gorgeous!"

"I know, and he's so good—he lets me have his car, and I can't believe my luck."

However, she knew her heart was still with Dean. A few weeks later Eliza was at home at The Tin House, when Dean knocked on the door.

"Can I have a word with you outside?" he asked her.

"What is it you want?" she replied, going outside with him.

"I think about you all the time. I told my mother how I feel and she said, 'DO whatever makes you happy.' I want to go out with you again, if you will have me."

Eliza wanted to see him again, but she was in turmoil. She liked Larry a lot, and he had been so good to her and her children.

At one point, Larry was sitting in the front room and Dean was in the kitchen. Each man was keenly aware that the other was there. In the end, Eliza chose Dean, although she wished she could have them both.

Eliza had been legally separated from Joseph for over a year now. He was even back on speaking terms with Tilly, Jim, and the family, and he often came up to The Tin House to see the children. He had finally accepted the fact that fact that the marriage was over. He, too, was getting on with his life—seeing other women. Eliza was glad that he was enjoying life. She was especially happy that he now left her alone.

"It's your birthday next week, Eliza. How about coming out with me for a drink, for old time's sake?" Joseph asked her. "No hankie panky."

"No thanks."

"Come on," he said. "Just to show there's no hard feeling, and then we can both move on."

"Okay, but no pissing about."

Eliza met Joseph at the top of the drive. Her mother and father would go mad if they knew she was going out with him. They still didn't trust him one hundred percent .He was taking her to the country pub where they used to go with her mother and father years ago. Once they were out, he started telling her about all the women he had been with in the last twelve months.

"Have another drink?" he asked her.

"No thanks." Eliza's was on edge. He had that glint in his eye! She should have known better than to go out with him. He was okay so far, but she wanted to get back to the safety of The Tin House.

"Are you ready to go now?" she asked.

"What's the rush?"

Eliza was worried. "I have to get up early in the morning and I have got to get the children's clothes ready for school when I get back." She said, almost pleading.

"Okay, let's go."

Eliza began to relax. They were nearing home, just driving up Botters Hill, almost at the same place where that man had exposed himself to her a few years before. She cringed as Joseph brought the car to a halt, and tried to put his arms round her.

"Stop it! Don't spoil a good night," she said, trying to pull away from him, but he grabbed hold of her wrists and tightened his grip like a vice. Eliza knew she had to get away fast. She frantically tried to open the car door. Just as she got it open, he drove off, flinging her to the side of the road.

She didn't stay there. She was up in a flash, running over the road to the gate opposite and into the field. She lay there in the dip for about half an hour, not daring to move.

Joseph had turned around. She could hear his car driving up and down the hill for ages! Then she made a move as she heard the car door slam shut. He was out of the car, calling her.

"I'm sorry, Eliza. Come back."

But Eliza wasn't ever going to fall for that again. She was half-way across the fields that she knew them like the back of her hand. She carefully made her way back to The Tin House. Thankfully, her parents didn't see her come in. She winced as she bathed her knees and hands. The disinfectant stung as she tried to get the bits of gravel out of her scrapes.

Tilly's son, young Joseph, was still courting Donna. One night Dean, Eliza, young Joseph, and Donna went for 'chicken in the basket' at the pub where John Bonham (who later became the drummer in the Led Zeppelin band) played. They went to listen to him a lot, and they had become big fans

Afterward, they drove Donna home first. Dean and Eliza were sitting in the back of the mini van outside Donna's house, waiting for Joseph to come out. Suddenly they heard a noise at the back of the van, so Dean jumped out and saw a man. He grabbed hold of him.

"A peeping Tom, are you!" he said, pulling him towards the light. "I should have known. Piss off!" said Dean.

It was Joseph.

"And if you follow Eliza again I will give you a hiding," said Dean, throwing him to the ground.

Dean bought a mini van for Eliza to make things easier for her.

"That chap deserves a medal as big as a bucket," said Jim, "taking you on with four kids. I hope he knows what he's doing."

About the same time, the family had bad news. Uncle Jack was ill in hospital, and Jim was beside himself. Uncle Jack had always been like a father to him and his family was always at hand when Jim or any of the family members needed him. The doctor said he was seriously ill. A few days later, Aunt Eve told them Uncle Jack's kidneys were failing.

Jim hurried to the hospital, but he was too late. H is beloved Uncle Jack had passed away. Jim, Tilly and their six eldest children went to the funeral, but Aunt Eve was too distressed to attend her husband's funeral. Everybody at The Tin House would miss Uncle Jack. He was such a big part of their family, a pleasure to know and a brilliant man. After the funeral Jim, Tilly and their children went straight home instead of returning to Uncle Jack's house.

CHAPTER 13

Come on, Eliza, hurry up," said young Joseph. "You know the Boat at Wixford always gets choc-a-block, especially when Johnny Bonham plays!" He also reminded her that they had to pick up the others. They were a little late, but they managed to get a small table they could all squeeze around.

Eliza had been thinking of getting her own house for several months. She decided she must see about getting a house to rent, but she was a bit wary. She had never been on her own before, and the prospect made her nervous. Eliza was also worried because she didn't have any furniture or other things she needed for the house. She had walked away from Joseph with nothing, but she now had peace of mind and for that, she would give up any possession. She decided to take the day when the rent man came off work.

On the day the rent man came, she was waiting for him so she could ask if he had any empty houses. "Not at the moment," he said, "but I will put your name on the list." He explained that most of the houses he let were town houses, and he suggested that she put name down on the Council's list, too.

A couple of months later Eliza arrived home from work. Her mother heard the van coming and greeted her at the door.

"Look what the rent man left you, the keys to a house on Archer Road down town. You must take the keys back tomorrow if you don't want it! If you do want it, the rent is two pounds, ten shillings for the first two weeks."

Tilly and Jim went with her to see the house. The kitchen was six feet by four feet and had a big old sink and an old cooker. The floor was all uneven there wasn't any hot water—only cold water—and the toilet was down the yard.

"The living room isn't too bad at all," said Jim, "but it is a bit dark."

"Come in here," said Tilly, who was ahead of them, exploring the front room that had lovely bay windows. "It's beautiful in here," she called out.

Jim and Eliza checked the upstairs. "The two bedrooms aren't too bad," said Eliza. There was also an attic bedroom, which was very dark. Eliza knew she had to take it. It wasn't fair to her mother and father to keep crowding The Tin House, especially now that she had been working for a while. Scared as she was to be on her own, the time has come to stand on her own feet. What would she put in the house? She had no money, so how could she buy furniture?

She need not have worried! Her family and friends soon rallied around her, and she had plenty of furniture, even if most of it was odds and ends. Daisy was first.

"We are getting a new three-piece suite for the living room," she told her. "You can have my old one."

"Old one!" replied Eliza. "You've only had it about twelve months." Eliza swore her friend only got a new one to help her out, as Daisy had a heart of gold.

Then different friends and relatives found things they weren't using or could do without. In no time at all, the house was furnished. Eliza had furniture and pots, pans, knives, forks and spoons as well. All of it was given to her by her family members and friends.

Two weeks later Dean moved in with her. His mother had gone to Blackpool for two weeks, and she wasn't pleased when she got back. Dean left a full pisspot under his bed when he moved, and it smelled the house up by the time she got back. "You might have emptied the jerry," she said to him in her matter-of-fact voice.

The children didn't like the house at first because there was only a tiny garden that led to an alleyway. It was perfect to park the van in, but there wasn't too much room to play. They were used to all the garden space at The Tin House and this garden was decidedly smaller.

"Never mind," said Eliza. "I will take you up to Nan's on weekends."

Dean and Eliza managed to get some new things together for the house. They were the first on the road to have a colour television and fitted carpets in their two downstairs rooms. Eliza now lived only about a half mile from Ray and Marge, Daisy and her husband,

and Jan, the friend Daisy introduced to her.

"Do you want to go on holiday to Blackpool with us? Of course, we will be taking Mom and Dad and the little ones?" said Ray. *What a lovely couple Ray and Marge are. They always look after Tilly, Jim and the younger ones.*

Dean thought a moment before he replied. "We will come next year," he said. "Young Ann will start school next January and she'll need a uniform. We also want to give the children a good Christmas this year after all the upheaval they've had."

"Fair enough," replied Ray.

The next morning when Eliza took Ann and Thomas to The Tin House, she could see that her mother had been crying. "What's the matter?"

"It's Michael. He said he's immigrating to Australia. That means we will never see him again." She explained that he was going with a mate and that she worried because they were so young and had only ten pounds each to take with them.

Ray would take them to the airport, and Tilly and Jim would also go to see them off. However, a few days later, Michael's friend changed his mind. Tilly begged Michael not to go on his own.

"No one's going to say I'm chicken," he answered.

Ray was still trying to talk Michael out of going, as he drove to the Airport.

"You can still change your mind, you know!"

But, Michael wouldn't have any of it. "Don't worry, I will be back when I've made some money," he promised.

None of them had ever been so close to a plane before.

"It's not too late to change your mind, son," said Jim, making a last stab at convincing Michael to stay home.

"I will be all right."

They stayed until Michael was ready to board his plane. He turned 'round and waved as he went in the departure lounge.

It was three months before they heard from him—three months in which Tilly and Jim worried about him every day. They were almost frantic wondering why he hadn't written and imagining all sorts of mishaps he might have had, by the time the first letter arrived. The letter described his flight, mentioning that the stewardess gave him champagne because it was his birthday, and that he had been in hospital with pneumonia.

He said he was fine now and had a job on a building site. "I'm doing very well so I might be a millionaire after all!"

Michael wasn't the best correspondent. The next time he wrote, almost a year later, he was about to get married. He had a nice house and planned to bring his bride home to meet his family in a year's time.

On a Saturday afternoon, Derek, his children and his Alsatian dog, Sheba, were at 'The Tin House along with Eliza and her children, who were usually there on the weekend. Derek always brought Sheba with him. She was very gentle with the children, but she was Derek's dog—his pride and joy.

Jim asked Eliza to run to the store for milk. They were always running out. Jim, still addicted to his tea, said he would make a pot for them when she got back. Eliza was soon back with the milk. As Eliza took the milk into the house, Derek said, "Sheba's dead!"

"Fancy saying a thing like that!" Eliza answered. "Sheba was running around outside when I just went to the shop."

"It's true, take a look over the fence in the field," he repeated, but Eliza still thought he was joking with her. Her jaw dropped when she looked over the fence. There lay Derek's beautiful dog, the one he loved so much. She had been running about with Tilly's dog, Butch, a few minutes ago. Now she lay dead at his feet. Tilly and Jim had always had dogs, and they had always been all right.

"I'm taking her to the vet," Derek said with tears in his eyes. "I have never seen anything like it before. One minute she was playing the next minute she was dead."

The three of them struggled to pick her up, gently laying her in the back of Derek's van. Then, he drove off to the vet. "I want you to find out what she died from," he said.

A few days later Derek had the results. "Hi, mother," he said, as he walks into The Tin House. "We have a problem. Sheba was poisoned with strychnine—it only takes a few seconds to kill once it's ingested." Tilly and Jim were worried sick.

The children's dogs and chickens had played in the field for thirty years, and nothing like this had ever happened before. Also, Sheba had only been a couple of yards into the field, so she wasn't far from their garden. They searched the field in that area, but they couldn't find anything suspicious at all.

"I'm going to see the farmer," said Jim. "He has cattle in the field so he needs to know what's going on."

"It wasn't me, Jim. I have my cows in those fields," the farmer said when he heard the news. Jim assured him he never suspected him of foul play. He just wanted to alert him to the danger his cows could be in. The farmer and Jim reported the incident to the police, but no one ever found out where the strychnine came from. The children were forbidden to go in that field, so they played in the one adjacent to the drive.

A few weeks later Eliza was visiting at The Tin House when Thomas shouted, "Mom, Nana, come quick!'

Tilly and Eliza ran outside to find Butch convulsing and peeing at the same time, then he, too, died just outside the back door.

The police come down, thinking this must be the work of a maniac. No one in their right mind would put strychnine down so close to where people lived, especially knowing that children played there. Whoever did it would have to have done it in the dark or someone in the family would have seen them.

The area was closed off. When it was examined and analysed, they found a piece of liver coated with strychnine. They managed to find the food that killed Butch, but they never found out who poisoned her or Sheba. After a couple of months Tilly got another two dogs, which she loved. She named them Chip and Tyke.

During the hustle and bustle of Christmas and buying the children new school clothes, Eliza forgot to get her birth control pills refilled. Six weeks later she knew she was pregnant again. She had been so careful up until then or thought she had. *I must be like my mother—I only have to look at it to get pregnant.* She continued to work until she was seven months pregnant.

A month before her baby was due her friend Janice and her family left. They decided to live in Canada. Janice gave Eliza lots of bedroom furniture and wished her all the best for the future. They both cried. Tilly and Jim were also sad that Janice was going—they considered her one of the family.

Young Joseph's girlfriend, Donna, walked in with chips "You've done the bread and butter, I see," she remarked, glancing at the table.

"Haven't I always? And the coffee's ready."

They had a good natter as they made and then ate their chip butties. Donna worked in town and came to Eliza's house every day, sharing her chips with Eliza and her children.

"We ought to be as big as barrels eating chips every day," said Donna. "We're both as thin as rakes."

Eliza was sick—she hadn't felt well for a while.

"You could be in slow labour," said the doctor, examining her. He wrote on the chart, "Wait and see."

About four o'clock, the door opened and Nurse Wooldridge arrived. "You got your nightdress on?"

"I don't feel very well today," replied Eliza.

"Does this say 'Wait and See for the heartbeat?'"

"I think so."

"Let's get you upstairs to see what's going on," said the nurse. "I know what the doctor means. You are in slow labour your water has been leaking, and that's why you thought you kept wetting your pants" She went on to tell Eliza that the baby's heartbeat was "very weak." The nurse decided to stretch the cervix to get her labour going. "I will do my other calls and then I will be back."

"You don't remember me, do you?" asked Eliza, "You were my mother's midwife for years."

"What's her name? I might remember, but I have delivered hundreds of babies in my time and I'm coming up to retiring age now."

"Tilly," said Eliza.

"Oh yes, The Tin House," replied the nurse. "One of the nicest couples I ever went to."

It wasn't long before Eliza's pains started, and they were very strong. She was trying to take her mind off the pain, when Dean came home. She was lying on the bed. "You had better make sure we have water boiling on the stove," she said to him.

When the nurse came back, her first words were, "Let's see what happening."

"Bloody hell!" she yelled. "I didn't think it would be this quick—a bit different from your mother when she gave birth. I can see what the doctor went on about. The cord is knotted, and the baby has looped the cord. As the water's been leaking, it's been tightening the knot." She explained that very little oxygen was getting through to the baby. "You're lucky he's alive."

Eliza sent Dean to, "Phone the bloody doctor and tell him I want him here now!" She muttered to herself a bit and then said, "I'll give him 'Wait and See'!"

Eliza and the baby were there, all snugly wrapped up with the window open to let plenty of air in the bedroom. The nurse then started giving the doctor a piece of her mind.

"That isn't the doctor who came to see me this morning," Eliza butted in. "The doctor who came this morning was a new one."

If Nurse Wooldridge hadn't come the baby would have died. Dean was delighted to have a son, and so was his mother, who by this time had warmed to Eliza, They called the new baby 'Jay.'

Eliza wrote, telling her brother Michael and his wife about the baby. She also wrote to her friend Janice, whom she misses very much. Daisy and Jan called in regularly, and so did Marge they only lived a half mile away since Eliza's house was in the town. In fact, she had lots of visitors, calling in for coffee every time they went to town shopping. Eliza called it 'The Dropping-In Place.'

It was January again, the month young Joseph and Donna got married. Dawn, Ray's daughter Mo, and Donna's sister were bridesmaids. They all looked lovely in their red velvet dresses trimmed with white fur. Matching muffs completed their outfits. Donna was a stunning bride, graceful and radiant in her fitted white gown with train. They had a wonderful time laughing, singing and dancing at the reception that was held at 'The Star,' the same place where Derek's reception was held.

Dean and his mate were doing plenty of work, but they were not getting much money. Like Jim years ago, they found it difficult getting their money in. People wanted the work done, but they didn't want to or couldn't pay. Now, the weather was getting bad, and that meant they couldn't do construction projects again until spring. Dean had borrowed so much money from his mother that they didn't know how they were going to pay it back.

"I will go back to work until we get out of this mess," said Eliza, asking her mother to care for Jay.

Always ready to help, Tilly agreed immediately.

So Eliza started working in a spring factory, and at the same time Dean left the building work and went to factory work as well. He loathed working in the factory, but the money was good and could be counted on every week. They finally paid off their debts and were soon saving to go on holiday. Joseph and Donna had a baby boy now so they would come on holiday, and, of course, Ray and Marge would be there.

Eliza was having a lot of trouble with her back. It was so bad that she could sometimes cry with the pain. Jay cried every time she left him at her mother's house, and Eliza couldn't bear to see him like that.

"It's no good, his crying is tearing me apart." She told Dean. "I will have to give my job up, but we should be all right now."

Dean had a good job and agreed that Eliza should stay home with Jay. All the time she had been working she'd been having money stopped out of her wages, going straight to the bank on pay day. It was the only way she could save for the holiday, and she was confident that there was enough for their holiday now.

Tilly and Jim now had only three children at home. Every Sunday Ray and his family, Eliza and her family, Derek and Joseph all went up to The Tin House Their hearts were still—and always would be—there. Ken, too, came with his family but not so often. It was a long way for them to come. The children played in the fields, just like they did when they lived there. Out came the buckets and any old rags that Tilly had. Then, they cleaned their cars while the children played. Jim was proud of his children—all of them were hard workers who would get on well in life. Tilly and Jim would miss the holiday with the family this year. They decided to go back to Blackpool with their friends, and Tilly's workmates. They had a wonderful time the last time.

In June, Ray, Marge, Eliza, Dean, Joseph, Donna and all their children set off for Paignton, a beach town, in a three-vehicle convoy, with Ray in the lead. They were headed for the shore and would stay in three small chalets. The children wanted to go straight to the beach since it was the first time for some of them. Their squeals of delight were worth every penny they paid for the holiday. They made sand castles and drew pictures in the sand, ran in and out of the ocean with the water for the moats 'round the castles they built. It was no trouble putting the children to bed. They fall fast asleep, absolutely exhausted.

The next day, they were all on the beach when Ray felt a tap on his shoulder. He turned his head and looked 'round. It was Mo and her boyfriend! And just behind them were Biron and his girlfriend.

"We've come to stay with you."

Ray chuckled as they shared hugs all around. "I knew you would find us somehow," he said, remembering that the same thing happened when they went to Dawlish Warren, the year before.

It was so hot, and poor Joseph had lain in the sun so long that he has got sunstroke on the second day. He also had a raging toothache. They managed to find a dentist, but he wouldn't touch the tooth until the abscess cleared. So, unfortunately, Joseph suffered with the toothache for a whole week before he could have it taken out.

Every afternoon, as they were coming off the beach, they stopped at a little hut that sold sweets, candyfloss, chips, and fried banana fritters on sticks. Yummy! They were all addicted to them, and they had one every day as they left the beach. They ate them on the way back to the chalets because they couldn't wait to dig into them.

"If you give me some money I will pop down to the shops to get something for tea," said Dean, holding his hand out as they walked back. Eliza fumbled in her bag. "Where's my purse?" she said, becoming alarmed as she rummaged even further in her bag. "It's not here! Blimey, I must have forgotten to pick it up off the counter when we bought the fritters and candy."

"I bet that will be gone," replied Dean.

Eliza ran back to the stall, passing lots of people walking towards her, eating their goodies from the hut. *I've got no chance of finding it, and all our money is in that purse!*

She reached the hut breathless, but she gasped out a sigh of relief. She couldn't believe it. There was her purse—exactly where she put it down. *Thank goodness for honest people!*

Mo was getting married soon. She wanted Ray's daughter, Lynn, and Eliza's two daughters, Dawn and Ann, to be bridesmaids. Derek's youngest boy and Joseph's little boy as well as Eliza's youngest boys, Thomas and Jay, would be pageboys. That posed a problem. There was no way Eliza and Dean could afford to have the clothes made.

"I will have to get a job again," said Eliza, wondering if her mother would look after Jay again.

Marge was working, doing packing at a car components factory. Both of her children were at school now.

"Come and get a job at our place," she said. "The money's brilliant, but the work is very hard. It's piecework, so you get what you earn." She arranged an interview for Eliza with the personnel manager, who was about sixty years of age with red rosy cheeks and a twinkle in his eye. He eyed her up and down, almost flirting with her. The interview was going quite well, until Eliza said she could only work from nine until four.

"Our hours are eight thirty to four thirty," he said.

"That's a shame. I have to get my four children to school first, and then take youngest one up to my mother's house. I couldn't possibly send the children out before eight forty." Eliza stood up to go.

"You don't look old enough to have five children," he said. "But I like your face, so I'll give you a job. You will be on a month's trial," he said and added, "If anyone mentions the time you get here, tell them to come and see me."

Marge was right. The work was hard and some components were very heavy, but the money was great. The big clutch plates were one of the best jobs, but, also one of the heaviest. The women had to bend over the crates, pick them up and place them on the table. Then they packed them in sleeves and made up the box to pack them in. They finally lifted them onto the conveyor belt. For each sleeve, they were paid a penny, and they used to pack one hundred in an hour. Eliza thought earning a £1 an hour was absolutely brilliant at that time.

The brake shoes and break pads were brilliant jobs as well. With asbestos dust flying all over the place, the women leaned over the crates, picked the boxes up and threw the pads on the table as if they were feathers. In fact, they were really heavy. Each box had forty-eight pads in it. A couple of the women always wore tiny mini skirts, and all you could see were legs and knickers. They looked hilarious when they leaned over the crates.

After working the month, Eliza expected the personnel manager to let her know if she was staying or not. She guessed it was okay, judging from the money she was earning—she knew she kept up with the others since they compared paychecks. Whenever the manager who hired her passed by, he winked!

Eliza's back was killing her, but she had to keep working to pay for the wedding clothes. She also wanted a good life for her children. When she had working there about six years, the company started putting leaflets that warned the buyer about the dangers of asbestos in with the brake shoes and pads.

The gaffers then decided to supply the women who packed them with masks. Often there weren't enough for everyone or there were none available, so they continued packing them the way they had for years.

Michael and his wife Catharine were coming over from Australia for a few months so he could catch up with everyone and his wife could get to know his family. They would stay at The Tin House with Tilly and Jim. The family wondered what Catharine would think of The Tin House and the family that started out there.

His wife Catharine was a bit overwhelmed when the whole family arrived to see them.

Michael opened his suitcase. "Look what I have here. I brought presents for the children." He then offered the suitcase to the children, calling them over "Here you are, the girls have fluffy koala bears, and the boys have boomerangs." He promptly took the boys out to the field to show them how to throw the boomerangs. The boys loved them and played for hours.

The next Saturday Michael called in Eliza's house.

"I told you I would do well, didn't I?" he asked, pulling a massive wad of money out of his pocket and throwing it on the floor.

Eliza had never seen so much money.

"Do you want to count it?" he asked Thomas and Jay.

"We can't count that much," Thomas replied.

"Have a go," he said, watching their eyes light up. But, they gave up when they lost count. "Come on, Eliza," Michael said, getting to his feet. "Let's go 'round town. I want to buy you a present, something for your house."

"I like that beautiful lamp stand in that window," said Eliza, "or is it too dear?"

"You can have it. You can have those four stools for the kitchen as well, if you want them."

"Only get two, there's not enough room for the four. Gee, thanks, Michael," she said, stretching up to kiss him on the cheek. "I won't forget this." They made their way back to Eliza's house. She carried the lamp stand and Michael carried the stools.

"How do you manage in this house?" he asked, observing, "You've gone back to living like we did years ago."

Eliza admitted going outside to the toilet wasn't nice. "The worst, though, was emptying the tin bath with a saucepan, after we've had baths on Sunday night." She explained that she had to boil the water in the twin-tub washing machine and then pump it into the bathtub, and then, refill it to do the washing. She did the washing every night, but she was used to that. That was how they got hot water at The Tin House and the cottage she had lived in when she was married to Joseph. If only she had a pound for each time she had done this.

Eliza decided to book a day's holiday at work so she could go to the council office, although she had been several times before and gotten nowhere. She dressed in the bright green dress she wore for Mo's wedding because she knew the colour suited her. However, as she stepped outside, the heat hit her. She hadn't realised it was so hot, as it was quite cool in the house.

Eliza, therefore, decided to change the dress, which was quite heavy, because she didn't want to walk into the council house department stinking of sweat. She opened the door that led to the stairs. She could smell smoke, but she thought someone must have a bonfire. As she climbed the stairs, the smell of smoke got stronger.

She ran up the rest of the stairs, flung opens the girls' bedroom door, and found the middle of the girls' bed engulfed in flames. *How the fuck had this happened?* Eliza smothered the flames with a couple of blankets, then ran downstairs for a bowl of water, and then ran back and threw it over the middle of the bed on top of the fire. Thank goodness she decided to change her dress, or the whole house could have gone up in smoke. She knew who the culprit was—he was hiding behind the settee! Eliza hoped she wasn't late for her appointment. That wouldn't have been a good start. She has planned to walk up with Thomas and Jay, but now she would have to drive.

Near to tears by the time the man called them in, she was thinking about the mess the bed was in. She would have to clean up when she got home. She decided she would ask her mother if she would have the two girls up there for a few days while she sorted a new mattress and blankets out for their bed.

Her thoughts were interrupted when her name was called. She sat down, with the two children at her side, and explained her position.

"How long have you been living there?" asked the housing inspector.

"Over five years."

"I feel sorry for you with five children and no bathroom, nor hot water," the man said. "As soon as I find you something suitable I will let you know."

Dean was getting ready to go out to the darts match he was playing on the team tonight. "Are you coming to watch me?" he asked Eliza.

"Not this time. You go ahead," She said. "I'm too knackered." She told him she wanted to soak her feet and manicure her nails for an hour. Eliza looked at her nails, all chipped and broken and remembered when they were lovely and long. *That's the price I pay to earn all that money packing car components!* She decided it didn't matter because the main thing was that she was happy enough and her children were happy.

Eliza looked 'round the room .It was quite cosy with a lovely thick carpet, the colour of autumn leaves, and a colour television. All she really needed was hot water and a bathroom. She put her feet in a bowl of hot water and experienced what she later told Dean was "sure bliss." Her children were sitting 'round her watching the 'Miss World Competition.'

She glanced down at Jay as he said, "You would win if you were there, wouldn't you, Mom?"

Bless him! All her hard work seemed well worthwhile when she heard him say that. She settled down, cuddling Jay to her.

Another wedding was being planned and this time the groom would be Biron. It was hard for Eliza to think of Biron as a grown-up, never mind as a groom. She still pictured him as a shy little boy hanging onto Tilly or Jim. When he left school, he helped his father do odd jobs, but no grafting was too hard for him. People started to notice his good work and called him often. His coming wedding was quite a surprise to the family. Biron and his fiancée planned to follow the family tradition of having the reception at The Star.

It was nearing the end of October. Eliza had just come home from work after she had already fetched Jay and taken her mother to work. She was very tired and flopped down on the couch.

"Here you are, Mom," said Dawn, handing her a cup of tea. "Here's the post," she added, passing her mother a couple of letters. Eliza was proud of Dawn. She was so good, and she helped out a great deal.

"Bills I suppose," Eliza said.

"Well, one gas bill, but the other is a letter from the Council," Dawn replied.

Eliza held her breath as she tore the envelope open. Her dreams had come true. A three-bedroom house had come empty, and it would be hers if she wanted it. Eliza' was excited as she handed Dean the letter.

"You can forget that!" he said after reading the letter. "I'm not moving down there."

"At least we can look at the house."

"I suppose," he said, pulling a face.

It was dark, but there was a street lamp shining right outside the front garden. There was a nice neat lawn at the front of the house, with a border of flowers 'round it and a privet hedge about seven-foot high all round, making it very private. They tried peeping in the window.

"We can't see much in this light," said Dean.

"I will collect the keys tomorrow," replied Eliza.

"Please yourself, but I'm not moving there."

Eliza fetched the keys and then went to pick up her mother, who went with Eliza to look at the house. On entering the front door, the first thing they noticed was the dark green paint in the hall. Then Eliza spotted the phone and picked it up. It still had a dial tone, so it worked. That was a bonus to start with. Eliza thought only the posh people and Daisy had phones, although her brother Ray was about to have one put in his house now that he had moved to Crabbs Cross.

Tilly followed Eliza down the hall into the kitchen. "Blimey, it's no bigger than the one I have!" she remarked to her mother. Next to that was the bathroom with hot and cold running water and a radiator. "I love this, it's sure bliss!" said Eliza. "Can you imagine sitting in that bath, just topping it up with hot water by turning the tap on? You can come down here for a bath, Mother," Eliza told her. The whole house had central heating, and the front room had a gas fire as well.

"Look at that beautiful big back garden, and there's a driveway at the side of the house," yelled Tilly.

"Well, Dean can please himself if he is living here or not." Eliza definitely was moving in. She would have been a complete idiot to turn it down. Tearing herself away, she drove back to the Council.

"I will take the house. When can we move in?" Eliza said.

"As soon as you like, you can keep the keys now if you want."

When Dean came home from work that night Eliza was already packing, putting some things in boxes she collected from a shop on the way back home.

"What are you doing?" he asked.

"Packing our things together. We're moving!"

"I haven't seen it in the light yet and, besides, I don't want to move down there."

"Please your bloody self! This time I'm doing what I know is best," replied Eliza.

"Okay, let's go and see it then."

"Two of the bedrooms aren't very big," he said, but the children loved the house. They didn't know anyone who had a phone. Dean had to admit it was a hundred times better than the house they lived in, and the garden was lovely.

They moved in on the 5th of November when .Jay had just turned five, Eliza went to the local school to see if Thomas and Jay could go there, and she also changed Ann's school—the local school was just round the corner from Eliza's workplace.

Jim was worried. he had just received his income tax bill, and they reckoned he earned eight hundred pounds this year. "I ain't earned that much!" he said. "They say I owe six pounds twenty and they want it in two instalments of three pounds ten pence. I don't know where that's coming from."

It was the children's first day at their new school. "Come on, kids, I've two schools to go to," Eliza said as the children got in the car. She took Ann and Thomas first. Then, she headed to Jay's school. Eliza knew she was going to have trouble with Jay who was adamant about school—he insisted that he wasn't going. He wanted to stay with Nanny Tilly at The Tin House.

"I'm not staying here!" he said. As Eliza took him by his hand, almost dragging him in, he cried and hung on to her for dear life. Once they were in the classroom, the teacher took him by the hand.

"He'll be all right," she said. Eliza didn't drive Dawn and Mark. They took the bus.

As soon as Eliza got into work, she ran to the toilet and shed a few tears she hated seeing her baby like that. She was glad that she had eventually managed to get him to school. Some time later, an office worker put out a call for her to "Come to the office please." Going into the office, the worker saw her and pointed towards the window. She looked outside and there was Jay, leaning against her car.

"I don't know what I'm going to do with you," she said, putting him back in the car and taking him back to school. This went on for weeks and weeks.

Years later Eliza discovered that Thomas often played truant as well, but he played with Kevin, a boy he had befriended.

"You will both be as thick as two short planks when you get older," Dean said to them. Eliza could see herself getting the sack— she would get Jay back in the car and take him back to school, but at noontime, he would be there again. *What on earth am I going to do with him?* she thought.

Ann, who was devoted to animals and had a gentle way with them, always wanted a pony. It didn't help that her father, Joseph, promised to buy one for her, but kept putting it off. She had no pets at home, but she loved to play with the dogs at 'The Tin House.' Most nights she sobbed herself to sleep thinking about the pony she wanted so much. Eliza felt really sorry for her, especially on the days Ann visited her friend's pony, and sobbed again.

"We will have to buy her one," said Eliza. "The poor child's heart is breaking."

The problem, as Eliza saw it, was that Joseph shouldn't have said he was going to buy her one when he didn't have any intention of doing so. Ann came home excited after she saw a sign on the gate to a field 'round the corner. It read. "The Horse Sale will take place in this field." It gave the date and time of the sale and not much more information. Even though the family lived on a council estate, the open country was nearby, so there were a lot of farms and horse people in the area.

"Will you take me please, Mom?" she asked.

"Come on, Dean, let's go' round to see how much they are."

"Oh, look at that one!" said Ann. "He's so cute."

He was a greyish brown colour with a white blaze on his forehead. "Can we buy her that one?" Eliza asked.

"Where the bloody hell will we keep it?"

"At 'The Tin House, 'of course. "

They bought the pony and called him Blaze. He was just a yearling and as wild as they come. When they borrowed a horsebox to take him up to The Tin House it took six men to get the pony into the shed at the top of the garden. The poor thing was scared to death. It was a long time before Ann was able to ride him, but she didn't mind. She had a pony at last, and she loved him.

Within weeks Ann had the pony eating out of her hand. When she put the bridle on Blaze, he trotted behind her as sweet as a nut. She left the pony standing by the back door of The Tin House while she spoke to her Granddad, Jim, in the kitchen, but the pony poked his head in the doorway.

"That's it, you might as well come in, everybody else does," said Jim to Blaze, and with that, the pony walked in—*clippety clop* on the red quarry tiles! After that Blaze had the run of the drive and one field.

Ray, Marge, Dean, Eliza and their children were all going on holiday, but Donna and Joseph were really disappointed because they couldn't afford to go this time. Jim and Tilly were broke as well. They had received the final bill for electricity and owed five pounds, ten pence, a higher sum than they had ever paid before.

"How did we use that much in half a year?" asked Jim. "That really buggered the holidays up for this year."

Most of the family—Jim, Tilly, Ray, Marge, Eliza, Dean, Joseph, Donna, Derek and his wife—all went up to The Star on Saturday nights. They loved listening to the chap who played the piano, and they enjoyed a good sing song. One of the women who usually sat with them always brought loads of sandwiches with her. They munched away in between drinking and singing and always had a good time there.

"This is how all pubs should be—just like The Star," said Jim.

It was 1972 when Michael announced that he and his wife Catharine were expecting a baby. Since they decided to stay in England until after the baby was born, he decided to put his money into a house, buying a little terraced one just down the road from Ray and his family. They bought their house the year before after they moved from their council house. Michael and his wife decided to remain at The Tin House, though, until after the baby came since he wanted to make improvements in the house they purchased.

Michael soon started repairing the house, knocking walls out and adding windows. The results were amazing! It looked like a show home by the time he was finished. Eliza worked with the couple who sold the house to Michael. When they heard what Michael has done to it, they asked if they could see it. When they did, they couldn't believe the change in it.

"It's an investment for us," Michael explained. "We shall sell it when we go back to Australia, and we should turn a profit."

With Christmas nearly there, Eliza had been working lots of overtime shifts. The last few months, her children's Christmas lists seemed to get longer, and she also liked to get gifts for the other children in the family and her parents. Since there were so many cousins, she and Dean needed her extra shifts to afford all the gifts. But, Eliza seemed to more on edge lately, and she agreed that her nerves were frayed with tension. Tilly noticed that Eliza was losing weight and looked tired. "I think you should cut down on the overtime a bit."

"I keep having this anxiety and choking panic attacks, they're very frightening," Eliza said. She always confided in Tilly and listened to her advice.

"Don't leave it! Promise me you will go to the doctor."

"Okay, Mom, just to put your mind at rest, I will go in the morning."

The doctor was also concerned. "You're doing too much by the sound of it, and you should slow down a bit," he said, writing a prescription for Ativan, a tablet usually used for anxiety, when he heard all of her symptoms. "This medicine is supposed to be marvellous!"

Eliza took the small blue tablets, and in no time at all she felt on top of the world. So she kept working overtime shifts and even added a few more hours. She told Tilly and Dean that she "feels fabulous and full of life—as if she could conquer anything."

The next day she was working away, feeling full of beans.

"Hey, slow down a bit," said the woman working next to her. "Leave some for us to do. How many have you done today, anyway?"

"Three thousand."

"Three thousand? I'm usually faster than you and I haven't done that many." She was furious and thought maybe Eliza was exaggerating. So, she called for the end-of-line packer to check Eliza's count against the others.

"She's right!" the packer called back. "She did a few more than three thousand." The woman bit her lip and tried to catch up to Eliza all day—without success.

A few weeks later Eliza was taking Jay up to The Tin House via the town.

"Watch out! What are you doing Mom?" he asked, a bit agitated.

"What are you talking about?"

"You just drove through those traffic lights on red."

"Oh God! I never did, did I?" she asked.

"You honestly did, Mom."

Eliza carefully made her way home, making sure she drove slowly after leaving her mother's house. She prepared the tea and then cleaned up after every one was finished eating. Opening the fridge, she took out a can of lager, got a bowl of hot water and soaked her feet.

As she put her feet into the water, she sighed. Opening the can of lager, she took a long hard swig from the can and then sat there until the water was nearly cold. She was just drying her feet when the phone rang. She hopped over to answer it, drops of water dripping on the carpet from her other foot.

"Hi. Mo, how are you?" she asked her sister on the other end of the line.

"I'm all right," she replied.

As they chatted, Eliza told her sister about the traffic light incident.

"That's unusual for you, Eliza, you are usually a very observant driver. You'd better be more careful in future," Mo said. She then said she called to ask if Eliza and Dean would be going to Marge's at all that week."

"I don't know if I'll have time. I haven't been there for over three weeks because I've been doing a lot of overtime."

"You were there last week," said Mo. "I was there, and we said how well you looked."

"I never!" insisted Eliza.

"Have it your own way," replied Mo. "I think you're losing the plot."

Eliza replaced the phone in its cradle, a frown on her face. *Am I going mad?* She picked up the phone again and dialled Marge's number.

"Hi Marge. It's me, Eliza. How long is it since I came to your house?"

"You were here last week," replied Marge. "Surely you haven't forgotten!"

"You're joking, aren't you?"

"No, I'm not."

"You must remember. You were telling Ray and me your latest jokes."

Eliza was devastated she still couldn't remember going there. "Did I seem all right?" she asked. "I'm extremely worried now."

Later when she told Dean, he had a ready answer. "It's those bloody tablets! There are a lot of things you can't remember over the period of time you've been taking them. "And, he continued, "You're hyped up all the time."

Eliza realised she would have to wean herself off the pills. It took a few weeks, but eventually, she was off them.

Eliza stopped at The Tin House with some extra milk she picked up for her father's tea. Jim greeted her with his usual enthusiasm, but his voice was hoarse.

"What's the matter, dad, have you got a bad throat?" Eliza asked.

"It's a bit sore."

Two weeks later, Jim's voice was still rough, "I'm taking you to the doctor," Eliza said. "Don't be silly. I haven't been to the doctor for over thirty years."

After a few more weeks went by, Eliza noticed that her father hardly spoke at all nowadays. He always seemed to be lying on the settee in the kitchen by the fire.

It was the Easter holiday and school was out, so Eliza took her three youngest children up to The Tin House so her mother could look after them, as usual. She drove straight up to fetch the children after finishing work, and was surprised to see her father in his best suit.

"Going anywhere nice?" It had been a long time since Jim donned his best suit. And he hadn't been out with them on a Saturday night for weeks either.

"I want you to take me to the doctor," he said.

Eliza looked closely at him, and suddenly, she noticed how old he looked. His blue eyes look dull, and had lost their sparkle. She knew at that moment that her father was definitely ill, and she was very worried.

Tilly didn't seem worried at all she seemed to be oblivious to the way he looked. Living with Jim and seeing him everyday, she failed to notice the changes in him.

The doctor's surgery was on the same route as Eliza's house, so she dropped the three children home first.

"Dawn, will you watch them until I get back?" she asked her daughter, who was just fifteen then.

Eliza dropped her mother at work, then, she took her father to the doctor. Jim didn't say anything until they were inside.

"I will go in on my own," he said.

"No way! I'm coming in with you."

"What can I do for you?" asked the doctor. "I haven't seen you before."

"No," replied Jim gruffly. "I haven't been here for over thirty years."

After a lot of questions the doctor examined him, after which, picking his phone up, he called the hospital. He asked someone if they would see Jim the next day. Neither Eliza nor her father spoke as she drove him back home, but she wondered what her father was thinking. *It must be serious, because the doctor wants him to go to hospital so quickly.*

Back at The Tin House Jim got out of the car.

"I will book a day off work tomorrow, Dad," Eliza said to him. "I will phone work first thing in the morning before I pick you up to take you to the hospital." Eliza didn't get out of the car. She watched him as he slowly walked into the house. Then, she drove back home.

Eliza put on the twin-tub washing machine, loaded it, and started cooking the tea. Tears started to trickle down her cheeks and all at once, she was sobbing uncontrollably. She couldn't bear the thought of anything happening to her father!

"Come back about five o'clock," said the nurse next day, as she left Jim to a bed at the hospital. "The tests will take all day."

Tilly walked up the road to her friend's house. "Will you tell them at work I won't be in tonight?" she asked. "I'm going with Eliza to fetch Jim out of hospital." She also asked the woman she had worked with for many years to pick up her wages.

"I hope it's nothing serious," replied her friend.

"So do I," said Tilly.

As Tilly and Eliza approached the ward where Eliza left Jim earlier that day, a nurse beckoned them into her office.

"I'm sorry, but Jim must stay another day," she said. "The doctor wants to talk with you tomorrow morning in his surgery." She sent them in to see Jim after warning them that he might doze off as they talked because he was sedated earlier for his examination. "His throat is very sore," she added.

235

The next morning, Tilly and Eliza sat in the waiting area at the doctor's surgery. They waited less than ten minutes before the receptionist told them to go in. Eliza could tell by the doctor's face that it was something serious.

"I'm very sorry, but Jim has cancer of the gullet," said the doctor, lowering his eyes. "The surgeon tried to put a tube down his gullet yesterday for two hours without any success," he continued. "It's a wonder he's been eating anything at all."

Eliza recalled that her father had been mashing his dinner, but she hadn't taken much notice.

"You can go and get him from the hospital now," he said. "There's nothing else we can do for him." Rising from his desk, he handed Tilly a prescription.

"Does my father know?" Eliza asked.

"No one said anything to him, but your father's not a stupid man—he probably knows."

When they went to get Jim, he was very quiet, but he hadn't really said much for weeks. Eliza lowered her eyes as she asked him how he felt. She couldn't look him in the eye. She blamed herself for not noticing how ill he was, beforehand.

All of the family members were gutted. They simply could not face the fact that their father was going to die—in a very short time. It had been a few weeks since Jim came out with them on a Saturday night, and now they knew why.

Several days later, someone knocked at the door of The Tin House.

"Who's that?" Tilly wondered, since everyone they know just tapped and walked straight in. It was the receptionist from the doctor's surgery, who lived just over the road from them.

"I have a letter from the doctor," she said to Tilly.

Tilly opened the letter and then went to the phone box to phone Eliza.

236

"I have a letter here. It says to take Jim up to the Q.E. Hospital tomorrow. There's a chap there who reckons he can do something to help him."

The next morning, Eliza noticed that Ray was there when she got to The Tin House.

"I'm coming as well," he said. "I will drive. I've been studying the road on the map and it's not far from where I work."

"Jim, I'm going to admit you for a few days. I have a surgeon who thinks he can help you," the doctor said after taking a few notes.

Ray and Eliza saw their father settled in the ward. They walked out together, but neither of them dared to look back because they had tears in their eyes.

The next night Tilly and all the nine of them visited their father. They had to take turns going in to the ward, but they all waited and left together. They found Jim heavily sedated again. The whole ward was full of cancer patients, so, if Jim didn't know his diagnosis before, he must have figured it out by now. Ray and Eliza went into the office to ask how their father was doing.

"They managed to get the tube down," said the doctor. "We are going to give him twenty doses of radium over a course of the next four weeks. Jim will be able to come home on the weekends, but all his food will have to be liquefied. The doctor explained that he would also need to be careful not to throw up because that could dislodge the tube.

On Friday, Eliza went to fetch her father, who looked a shade better. "How are you?" she asked him.

"A bit better than I went in, I'm going to have a salmon sandwich when I get home. I just fancy that."

"You can't, Dad. Your food has to be liquefied."

"I will chew the bread very fine and keep sipping a drink to swill it down with," replied Jim.

Eliza was watching him cautiously, praying her father didn't choke while he indulged in his salmon sandwiches. She sliced the bread as thin as she could and cut the crusts off.

"That was bloody lovely!" he reported, devouring the last crumbs off the plate.

"Good," replied Eliza, a lilt in her voice. She felt happier now that her father looked a lot better. On Saturday night, Jim got ready to go out with them. "Are you sure you feel well enough?" Tilly asked.

"I will be fine." Michael and his wife, who was nearly six months pregnant then were going as well.

Jim seemed fine. He felt much better than he had for ages, and he wanted a brandy to celebrate.

"Please don't have any more, Dad," Eliza pleaded. "Why must you have it? You don't usually drink brandy!" pleaded Eliza. "If you're sick you might move the tube."

"Don't be so bloody stupid! The tube's not there now."

"Have it your own way," she replied, but, she knew the tube was still down his gullet.

The next day was Sunday, so Eliza got her family's dinner early. Then, without eating her own, she was off to The Tin House. It was a ritual—Sunday dinner was nearly always roast beef and Yorkshire pudding. But now, Eliza had to make sure her father's dinner went into the liquidiser.

"It looks like shit!" Jim said as she handed him the mug of light brown thick liquid.

"It doesn't taste like it, I've tried it," Eliza replied.

The summer holidays had been booked from the previous year, at a holiday camp at Minehead. Tilly and Jim were supposed to come this time, but it didn't look like anyone would be going at the moment, as Jim kept having his treatments, but he was getting thinner and weaker every day. They could all see that. His children went to see him, either at home or in hospital, every day.

"I don't want any more of that treatment," he said one day. "It's not doing me any good."

A few days later, after work, Eliza was on her way up to see her father. Rounding the corner of the drive, she stopped. There was Jim, in the garden, trying to put stakes in for the runner beans he planted earlier in the year. He looked so thin and gaunt. He had always been thin, but now he looked like a skeleton. As she sat watching him, Eliza knew he wouldn't be with them much longer. *That's Dad all over. So ill he can barely stand, yet there he is— still worried about stringing the beans up! How has he mustered up the energy?*

Eliza got out of the car and ran to him. "I will help you," she said desperately trying to hold the sticks in place for him.

"I can manage, myself," was his reply.

A couple of days later Jim took to his bed. He would get up occasionally to sit in a chair next to Tilly, but he seemed to be cold all the time, and he would return to bed after a short time. He ate very little, and went on that way for a few weeks.

Thomas wasn't well. Eliza took him to The Tin House even though she had misgivings about leaving him there while Jim was so ill.

"I have lost so much time from work, we're having a job to pay the bills," she said to her mother. "Don't let him go in dad's room, will you?"

"Okay." Tilly was so laid back that she still didn't seem to realise how ill Jim was.

Later that morning, Eliza was working hard. She hoped that throwing herself into the physical labour of her job would help erase the picture of Jim trying to string the beans from her mind.

Suddenly, her thoughts were broken by her name being called out on the loud speaker. "Could you report to the office? To the office please."

Not Jay playing truant again! Eliza thought he was over that. An office worker pointed to the phone, and. Eliza picked it up.

"Can you come straight up to The Tin House?" the voice on the other end of the phone said. "Come as soon as possible. Your father's being sick."

Eliza ran, grabbed her bag, and fumbled for the car keys and ran to the car. It took less than ten minutes for her to get there. She ran to the door and was greeted by her Aunt Lou.

"Tilly went to town, and I said I would look after Jim. Thomas is reading a book in the kitchen. I haven't let him near your father at all."

Eliza flew into the front room, where her father was lying in bed, wide-awake with blood trickling down his chin and neck. It was coming from mouth and nose. She dashed back to Thomas in the kitchen.

"Quick, Thomas, run to Mavis, the woman at the top of the drive. Ask her to phone the doctor and ask him to come quick. It's urgent!"

The bleeding had slowed down a bit by the time the doctor arrived. Biron had also arrived. Jim was still conscious and knew exactly what was going on. Mavis had phoned Ray as well.

"I'm sorry, I'm afraid this is going to be the end!" said the doctor.

Did he have to say that so loud with father still having all his faculties? Eliza thought.

With that, the doctor walked out and said, "Call me back when he's gone."

"I want to go to the toilet," said their father.

Biron and Eliza looked at each other as Jim started bleeding, from the mouth and nose again.

"Please take me to the toilet!" he begged.

Eliza was panicking by this time, looked at Biron, then pulled the bed covers back and gasped. Her father was just skin and bone, and the bed was full of blood their beloved father was bleeding everywhere. He was bleeding to death and they couldn't do a thing about it. He looked at them, unblinking. Then, his head rolled to the side, and he was dead.

Eliza and Biron just sat looking at him.

Oh, why did this have to happen? Eliza thought. *He was due to retire at Christmas, and he so looked forward to it.*

A few seconds later Ray came rushing into the room.

"You're too late!" said Biron.

"I had to come on the bike Marge went out earlier in the car. I came as soon as I received the phone call."

Someone went to phone the doctor again. He hadn't come home yet from the visit to see their father, so he came straight back.

When Tilly arrived back from town, she asked, "What are you lot doing here so early, and why the glum faces?"

"Sit down, Mom," said Ray gently, as Lou poured Tilly a cup of tea that had been brewing on the stove. "Dad has passed away," he told her as Tilly sipped the hot tea.

Tilly got up off the chair and slowly walked into the front room to Jim, shutting the door behind her.

Thomas, hearing all the commotion, ran screaming down the field. He adored his granddad, who always called him "little pudding. "Come here, pudding, let me give you a rub of brush," he would say, and then he would rub his whiskers on Thomas' belly before having a shave. Thomas used to squeal and laugh.

Eliza and Biron were desperately trying to straighten their father's face, but it keeps lolloping.

"I can't do it," cried Eliza.

"Leave him," said Lou, "the funeral people will do it later."

Eliza had to get Thomas home before the funeral directors came to fetch her father's body. She took her mother with her as well. Ray waited to sort things out, he was the head of the family now.

"We've got to clean the bedding and take the bed out of the front room," Ray said to Eliza the next day. The Tin House was so quiet when they went inside. "Let's get the windows open, it's stifling hot in here."

"It's stifling hot everywhere," said Eliza. Opening the front door to the front room, she caught her breath as she walked in—she could still smell her father in the room.

"The mattress and bedding will have to be burnt," said Ray. "It's all covered with Dad's blood."

Tilly stayed with Dean and Eliza, as she didn't want to go home for a few weeks. Meanwhile, they all took turns going to The Tin House to look after the dogs, chickens and Blaze, the pony. They had stopped raising pigs ages ago. Eliza had already arranged for Blaze to go and stay for two weeks at the farm where Tilly did her service all those years ago. They were supposed to be going on holiday, so she arranged for Blaze to be at the farm the same weeks as their holiday. The farm had different owners now as the Palmers sold up and left years ago.

"What are we going to do about the holiday? It's paid for, we are due to go next week, but Dad's funeral is tomorrow," Ray said.

Now that Jim was gone, none of hem felt like going on holiday.

"We have to go," said Tilly. "Your father would hate it if we never went."

It turned out to be he best thing they could have done. The group included Ray, Marge, their two children, Tilly, Sam, Eliza, Dean and their five children, Joseph, Donna and their two children. Ray was in the lead, as usual, and the others followed behind.

When they arrived they were shown their chalets, and the first thing Donna did was go to the shop to get some cleaning equipment and disinfectant to clean her family's rooms. She spent the whole day cleaning while the others explored the place.

"There's a boating lake with an island in the middle, which will be fun!" said Mark, so they all made their way over the road to the beach. "I'm not going in the sea," he complained, "the tide has washed up loads of filth." The rest of the day was taken up with exploring.

Sam and the three elder children fancied a go in the rowing boats as soon as they finished their breakfast, and Tilly, Marge and Eliza decided to have a go as well to keep their eyes on the little ones.
"

"Shall we get a boat out as well," asked Marge.

"Sounds good to me," replied Eliza.

Tilly stood, clutching her handbag, watching them, still dressed in her black mourning clothes.

Eliza sat in one end of the boat with Marge at the other end. They were just about to row off when Tilly called out, "Can I come with you?"

"Sure," replied Marge. "I will move up, and you can get in this end."

Marge budged up a bit as Tilly, who had put on quite a bit of weight over the years, stepped in and plonked herself down the one end. As she did, the boat tipped up.

"Christ!" she shouted, as the boat started to sink at her end. Before anyone could do anything to help her, she was up to her chest in water, still clutching her handbag. Everybody sitting by the lake started laughing. It was a hilarious sight so even Tilly, Eliza, and

Marge joined in.

After Tilly got herself dry, Ray put the iron on and ironed her money. This was the best tonic they could have had. It was the first time they laughed since the death of their father two weeks ago!

Three days later, when they are sitting on the beach, they turned 'round as a voice said, "Hi there, it's us again."

It was Mo and her husband with their two little ones, and standing behind them was Biron, his wife, and their baby.

Where are they all going to sleep? Eliza thought.

Mo brought her pram with her, so her youngest could sleep in that.

"You sniffed us out again," said Ray. "It's all right for you, we have to save all year, and the lot of you come for nothing."

Ann suffered from asthma, and the air down at camp didn't suit her at all so she had a terrible time with her breathing.

"Come on, I'm taking you to see the camp doctor," said Eliza.

"We're in the Channel, that's why she is having a reaction," he explained. "Here's a different sort of inhaler. Try this—it should make things easier for you."

But the inhaler did not help poor Ann, who continued to cough and wheeze. It was a fairly certain fact they wouldn't bring her there again.

"Come on," Sam told the other kids, "it's our last morning at the camp. Let's go to the lake and get one of the boats out before we go home." He jumped into a nearby boat. "Come on, Mark," he called out. "Get in this one with me."

"Okay," Mark replied, while Dawn got in another boat with the others.

"Let's have a race!" one of them shouted.

So they started to race. "Hey!" shouted Dawn. "You're getting too close to us."

Crash!

"That's torn it!" said Dawn as they collided. They started splashing the water over each other's boats. It was hilarious. The shores on both sides were getting more and more crowded. People sitting there were cheering, and egging them on. The more they cheered, the more the children splashed.

Suddenly the boats started sinking. The manager heard all the cheering and came to investigate. Soon he was standing at the water's edge, waving his fist, shouting for them to come out. They tried dragging the boats out, but the children couldn't hear the manager shouting because of all the cheering. Fortunately, however, the water was not very deep, and at last, they dragged the boats back to the side.

"Bravo!" the holiday makers shouted from the banks

"Get out of this camp immediately!" the manager shouted. "And don't ever come back."

It was a good thing that they had already packed their clothes in their carrier bags that morning, ready to head home, but the children were soaking.

"Come on, let's get these wet clothes off," said Eliza and Marge, rummaging in the bags for dry clothes.

"Oh, no, you don't!" shouted the manager. "Just get off this property and clear off!"

"Okay we will change on the beach."

What a holiday!

On their return, the family got back to life without Jim. Tilly didn't want to stay up The Tin House on her own, so her grandchildren took turns sleeping there with her. Sam still lived there, but he was seventeen now and into girls, so he didn't always go home at night.

The family still went up to The Tin House, but the place wasn't the same without Jim.

"Can you bring Blaze back?" asked Tilly. "I know I have the dogs but I could do with a bit more company."

So Eliza and Ann went to get Blaze from the farm, but he looked like he lost quite a bit of weight, so Eliza phoned the vet.

"He wants worming badly," said the vet. "They're all suffering from worms down there, so try to keep him here. He needs gelding as well, I will do it in a month's time when he's put a bit of weight on."

It was ten months since Jim died. Michael and his wife had a little girl eleven months old, born prematurely a month before Jim died. He had never seen the baby because she was in the hospital for the majority of Jim's last month on earth.

Michael decided to put Australia on hold again, since he couldn't bear to leave his mother now that she was alone.

Blaze looked more like his old self as he ran in the field that the elder boys fenced off for him. The vet would come to geld him later in the day.

"Can I offer you a cuppa tea?" Tilly asked.

"Thanks. I won't take long," said the vet, stroking Blaze's neck.

Tilly made the tea and carried it out to him.

"All but finished," he said, sipping his tea. "Blaze should be all right," he added, collecting his gear. "If you have any worries phone the practice."

By the end of the week, Eliza was quite concerned about Blaze. he was terribly swollen where the vet gelded him, and the swelling seemed to be getting larger.

"That's never right," she said. "I will ask Dawn's friend to ask her father. He knows a lot about horses." He lived just down the road from The Tin House, and Eliza has been a friend of his wife, Brenda, from when they were children.

"Could you come and have a look at Blaze, please," asked Eliza.

"Sure. They do swell like that sometimes," he said, looking at Blaze, "but if it hasn't gone down in a couple of days I would get the vet back out to him."

Two days later Eliza phoned the vet, "I'm extremely worried about my daughter's pony," she said, explaining about the swelling.

"The vet you want is on holiday, but I will ask the other vet who cares for domestic animals to come and see him for you," someone at the vet's office replied.

"He looks all right to me," the new vet said. "Sure, he's swollen, but it will go down."

Eliza was still worried as she led Blaze back into the field.

"The vet should know what he's on about," said Tilly.

"I know, but Blaze seems so weak. He was fine until he was gelded."

The phone rang suddenly and woke Eliza. Who can that be on a Sunday morning? She was having a lie in—Sunday was her only chance to get extra rest. "Let it ring!" said Dean.

"It isn't going to stop," replied Eliza, getting out of bed. She ran downstairs and picked the phone up.

"It's Blaze!" said her mother on the telephone. "I went to give him some titbits and found him rolling about banging his head on the floor."

Eliza phoned Donna. She had always had horses. When she was a child her family was quite wealthy, before her father left home. Donna and Eliza arrived at The Tin House at about the same time. They walked into the field together, where Blaze was lying on his side.

"Is he dead?" asked Eliza.

"Just stunned! I think he knocked himself about all 'round his head. He might have a twisted gut," said Donna. "We must get him standing up. Come on, Blaze," she said, trying to coax him to stand up.

Two men, who were walking by with their dogs, saw the two women struggling, and came over and to help them. At last Blaze was standing.

Eliza thanked the two men as they continued walking their dogs. Donna and Eliza gently coaxed Blaze slowly down the drive to The Tin House, but he was so weak he was actually leaning on Donna. She was having a job to keep him standing even though. Eliza was holding him up from the other side.

After settling him down a bit, Donna ran down to the phone box to phone up the vet, who was not going to like coming out on a Sunday

"Sorry about calling you out so early on a Sunday morning," said Donna. "I think he might have a twisted gut."

"Okay. I will be straight up." It was the same vet who gelded Blaze a couple of weeks ago. "Let's have a look at you," he said to the pony as he examined him. "Well, he hasn't got a twisted gut. I think he must have an infection from the gelding."

"I called the other vet out last week," said Eliza, "and he said it was normal."

"Well it's not normal," he replied. "Blaze is so weak that he looked like he could have leukaemia," he added, giving Blaze an injection. "You must keep him on his feet, and I will come back later on to see how he's doing."

Ray arrived for his usual visit with his mother. "You two are early this morning," he said, looking at them holding Blaze and trying to keep him standing. "What's up with Blaze?"

Donna explained the situation to him.

"I know. I will get one of the boys to help me out with the settee from the kitchen for you to sit on. You can't just stand there all day." The rest of the family rallied 'round, taking turns to keep Blaze standing.

It had just turned seven o'clock, when the vet came back.

"Will one of you pop up to the pub to get some Guinness. They should just about be open. If we can get that down him he might perk up a bit."

Eliza ran up the pub for the Guinness, opening the bottle as soon as she returned.

"Can you two hold his head up while I pour this down his throat?" asked the vet. He was pouring the beer down Blaze's throat, when Blaze started peeing. His fluids are coming straight out off him. "I think his kidneys have packed up. See if you can get him back in his shed for the night. I will come back in the morning."

Donna and Eliza were exhausted. Eliza looked at her watch. It was coming up to two a.m. It was Monday morning, and they both had to get their children's clothes and things ready to wear for school.

"We'd better go home now. I don't know about you, but I can't keep my eyes open and we have to think of the children," said Donna. "I will come up to see Blaze after I have taken my son to school."

Eliza was up, and she had the children all ready for school. She was just going out the door when the phone rang.

It was her mother, and she was crying.

"What's the matter, Mom?"

"It's Blaze. I went to check on him. Oh, Eliza he's dead!"

It was exactly eleven months to the day since Jim died. He died the 9th of July, 1973, and this was the 9th of June, 1974.

Eliza phoned Donna. "Don't bother coming to The Tin House."

Both Donna and Eliza blamed themselves for leaving Blaze alone. Eliza slowly walked into the shed. Blaze was lying on his side, stone cold and rigid. *The poor thing must have died soon after we left him.*

Kneeling down, she lovingly stroked his head, then slowly walked to the phone box and spoke to the vet.

"I will arrange for him to be picked up. I'm going to do a post mortem to see what he died from."

Poor Ann was hysterical when she heard her beloved pony was dead. Three weeks passed by without Eliza hearing anything from the vet. "I will give him a few more days, but if I haven't heard by then I will phone him up."

Then, the local paper arrived with this headline. **LOCAL VET AND WIFE FOUND DEAD—SUICIDE.**

CHAPTER 14

The Tin House was about to be demolished to make way for a new road.

Tilly and Jim were dreading it when the Council told them before Jim died. But, now, she was grateful that Jim never saw the end of the home where they had been so happy. It would have broken his heart to leave The Tin House, but it no longer mattered to Tilly. She simply wasn't happy there without Jim.

She finally received the letter that offered her a council flat, where she moved with Sam. Both mother and son hated the flat, and Sam complained to the council members so much that the Council moved them to a house just up the road from Eliza. Tilly quite liked it there and Tilly still had her two dogs, Chip, and Tyke. She went up town on the bus and did shopping for herself and Eliza. Tilly did her garden beautifully, still planting gladioli, her favourite flowers.

Sam was seldom there, sleeping more and more at his girlfriend's house, and Tilly was getting a bit scared when she was on her own. She had trouble with the woman living nearby. That particular neighbour kept asking her for fags, and she borrowed money but never returned it. Tilly was too soft to say anything to her.

One day Eliza called in her mother's house, to find her crying about the situation.

"I've tried not answering the door, but they know I am in."

"I will go and see them."

"No, don't do that!" begged Tilly.

"Okay, I will come up and sit with you for a few nights."

That night, Eliza sat and watched television with her mother, drinking the can of lager she brought with her. After a while, there was a knock on the door. Eliza opened it.

"Yes?" she pleasantly asked the woman standing there.

"I want to speak to Tilly."

"Can I give her a message?"

"Well, I was wondering if she could lend me ten bob."

"She can't!" replied Eliza evenly. "Her son has taken the finances over so my mother doesn't handle the money any more. Sorry!" She walked back into the front room to her mother. "I don't think she will bother you again, Mom."

The woman who lived next door to Eliza told her she and her family were moving. Ironically, they were moving up to the village where Tilly lived all those years in The Tin House, though that was long gone now.

"The house next door to us is coming empty," she said to Dean.

"Which one?"

"The one that shares our drive," replied Eliza.

"Why don't you see if your mother can move there?"

Eliza has already asked the Council for a move for her mother because of the grief she was getting from the neighbour, so she got on the phone to them again.

"Hello, can I help you?" asked a man's voice. Eliza started to explain about the house, when the man on the other end of the phone stopped her.

"Do you know who you're talking to?" he asked.

"I seem to recognise your voice, but I can't put a face to it. Did you used to come to The Tin House to play?"

"I sure did—I almost lived there. What a fabulous time we had!"

"Is that you, John?" John used to live with his mother and two sisters, Sheila and Jill, just up the road from The Tin House. "I thought it sounded like your voice. How did you get a job at the Council?" asked Eliza.

"It's not what you know as much as whom you know," he replied. "I worked my way up the ladder."

A few days later Tilly got a letter telling her she could have the house. It was an exact replica of the house she was moving out of, so she didn't do anyone out of a home.

"I felt so lonely living up there, I didn't get visitors like I did at The Tin House" said Tilly.

"Never mind, Mom. You won't be lonely any more."

Tilly loved living next to Eliza. She was always popping 'round Eliza's or one of Eliza's children went 'round there. It was great, except for the thing—she no longer had Chip and Tyke. They had both died, but they lived until they were eighteen years old.

Tilly seemed to have new zest for life, and she was far happier than she has been for ages. She walked up to the shops, got the shopping, and stopped to sit on the bench by the lake, feeding the ducks. When she got home, she peeled the potatoes, cleaned the veg and put the meat in the oven to start cooking, timing everything so it would be ready when Eliza and Dean got home. Tilly ate with Eliza and her family every day.

That made life much easier for Eliza, who worked many hours.

Michael bought a piece of land and he intended to build his own house on the top road in the village overlooking the spot where he was born, where The Tin House once stood.

If only his father was alive to see how well he was doing, Michael knew Jim would have been proud of him. It took him about six months to build the house. It turned out to be the most posh and fabulous house on the street. It was better by far than the other houses on the road—and they were beautiful homes, too.

The house had a giant hall with a gallery stairway leading from it. It included four large bedrooms, two of them with suites. There was a massive lounge with a large open log fireplace and lovely, large French windows. A large dining room, equally large kitchen, and a utility room completed the house. His family had never seen anything like it before. They were all proud of Michael. No one ever thought their son or brother would build and live in such a stately house.

Tilly wondered what the people who talked about them before when the children were young thought about them now.

Dawn was babysitting for Eliza even though the children weren't actually babies any more.

After having a couple of lagers, though, Eliza decided to go home—she had a bit of a headache.

"What's going on?" she asked, walking in the lounge. Dawn wasn't there, but her friend Lucy, from over the road, was there instead, and she had a young man with her. "It's okay, Mom "she said to Eliza, walking out with the young man.

Before Eliza could say anything, they were gone.

"Shan't be long, Mom," she called out, shutting the door

Half-an-hour later, Dawn walked in. Eliza asked her to explain why Lucy started calling her Mom.

"Lucy told her boyfriend she lives here, because our house has carpets and a phone, and she wanted to impress him," replied Dawn.

A few months later, the same boy came home with Dawn.

"What did your boyfriend think of the house?" asked Eliza, but Dawn just laughed.

It was Mothering Sunday, and Tilly and Eliza got the usual flowers, but there was a big box in the kitchen with 'Love from Thomas' written on it. Eliza opened the box, and inside was a wooden clock with a pendulum hanging from it. "It's lovely," she said, giving him a big kiss.

He and Jay were always hanging on her skirt. Thomas was always bringing Eliza little presents home but the clock must have cost quite a lot of money.

"Where did you get the money from to buy it?" she asked.

"I paid for it weekly at the little shop up the road! The shopkeeper kept it for me, until I had paid for it."

Eliza gave him another hug he was so loving and thoughtful, as were her other children.

On Eliza's birthday in April, she had a hard day at work, and her back was aching worse than ever. As she pulled her car into the drive, Eliza couldn't miss the new net curtains hanging up in the windows of her house.

"Happy birthday, Mom," Ann called out as Eliza walked in the door. "Do you like the new net curtains? I bought them for your birthday." Ann had saved her babysitting money to buy them. Every room had new net curtains, and she put them up herself. She was handier than a handyman!

"Play your cards right," said Eliza, "and you will be able to get a good job when you leave school."

Dawn and Mark bought her a lovely pair of shoes. Thomas got some brasses, and Jay gave his mom a giant box of chocolates.

What lovely children I have, Eliza thought.

Tilly often told her they were a credit to her.

Dawn walked into the kitchen with a smile on her face. "Guess what, Mom! I'm getting married!"

"I don't want you to get married yet, Dawn! You're only eighteen, and look what happened to me! Why don't you stay engaged for a couple of years first and give yourselves a chance to save some more money."

"Why don't you want me to get married, Mom?" she asked. "I know he's the one for me."

"Because I don't want you making the same mistake I did."

"I'm not making a mistake, Mom. I'm eighteen now so I can get married if I want."

"I won't stop you. You have to make you own mind up. I like your boyfriend, he seems a very nice young man," replied Eliza.

Dawn had recently passed her driving test, and Eliza was hoping she would enjoy herself and go on holidays with her friends. She worried about her being tied down at such a young age like she had been. However, she also believed Dawn knew what was best for her.

Dawn booked the church and the reception, but she didn't want it to be at The Star as had other her family celebrations. She wanted to try a new place.

Dawn was married in the church in the middle of the town. Her bridesmaids all dressed in light and dark lilac, and the combination looked lovely.

Eliza was quite proud of both Dawn and her new husband because they paid for their wedding all on their own. *How beautiful Dawn looks in her bridal dress!* Eliza thought. *She looks so much like her grandmother, Tilly.* Only Dawn wasn't as tall as Tilly had been in her younger days.

After the reception, they were off Blackpool for the honeymoon. Dawn bought Eliza a beautiful framed picture of a lovely young woman.

"That's you when you were younger, isn't it, Mom?" asked Jay, looking admiringly at the picture

I don't think I was that pretty, but certainly Jay thinks so. Eliza was flattered by the attention.

Tilly's youngest son, Sam, and his girlfriend, bought an old, derelict cottage down a lane in a very small posh village and had started to do it up. He reckoned if Michael could build a house, then he could renovate the old cottage. Thomas was always helping Sam, and, though he wasn't very old, he didn't mind working for pocket money. He got on well with Sam and his girlfriend. Dean, Mark and Jay were helping as well, but it took them ages to do it up in their spare time. They started stripping it first.

Eventually after they moved in, Sam asked his mother if she wanted to visit for a few weeks. Tilly jumped at the chance, because, even though she loved living next door to Eliza, she really missed the countryside. She stayed there for weeks on end, and then went home for a few weeks. After that, she was off to Sam's again.

Tilly loved Sam's place. A local chap called in to have a chat and cup of tea with her when she was at Sam's. He told her about his childhood and Tilly told him about hers. They chatted for hours as if they had known each other all their lives.

However, she also liked to get back home, to the hustle and bustle that went on at Eliza's house, and she missed the children, too.

Dawn chatted with Biron, "Why don't you buy your council house?' she asked. "You might struggle a bit, but after that you won't look back."

A few weeks later Biron told Dawn that he and his wife were in the process of buying their house.

"I hope you're right," he said to her.

Dawn and her hubby bought a house too.

Eliza was glad for them, as they seem to be managing their lives very well. Mark had a job now. *Oh how time flies!* It seemed like yesterday that she had been pushing him and Dawn up to The Tin House in their pram.

Mark went to work every morning. When he came home at teatime, he had a bath, ate his tea and then went off to the youth club. He was very bright and quite brainy—he always had good reports at school, and Ann did, too. Mark had stayed at school an extra twelve months and was the school's champion at chess and draughts. He was proud of that as was his mother. Mark was easy going, and he had never been any trouble. He was quite happy to potter about. As long as he had an old bike to mess with, he was completely happy.

Ann tidied the house for Eliza when she came home from school like Dawn had in the past. Ann didn't mind. She loved doing housework, knowing that if she did it well she would be rewarded at the end of the week.

Eliza dreaded the days that Ann rang her while she was at work in the factory. One of the office girls would come out of the office, or call her over the intercom "Eliza, it's Ann on the phone," she'd say, as Eliza walked into the office.

What's gone wrong now? Eliza would wonder as she picked up the phone. She hated to take a call in the office because the five people who work there could hear her whole conversation. She could feel their eyes on her.

"What's the matter?" she asked, trying to speak in a calm voice.

"It's those two, they're playing me up," said Ann.

"Put Thomas on the phone," replied Eliza in a quiet voice.

Ann passed the phone to Thomas. "Mother wants to speak to you."

"Now be a good boy and go in the garden with Jay. I will be home in half an hour," said Eliza calmly. She was actually dying to shout at them because she could hear them in the background, shouting at each other. Eliza was sure the women in the office could hear them as well. "I will kill the little buggers when I get home!" she said to the woman she worked with, as she returned to the packing line.

By the time Eliza arrived home, the two boys were playing in the garden and Ann had already started to get the tea ready. Eliza called the two boys in.

"Sit down! Right, do you like going on holiday every year and having a nice home? If you do, you will have to be good when you come home from school. It's only for thirty minutes, and then I'm home." Eliza continued without even taking a breath, "Do you know what I feel like in that office at work every time they call me in there? When Ann phoned me today, I felt two feet tall. If you don't like the nice things you get I will pack my job in. Okay?"

"Okay," they both replied, "We want our holidays."

"We were all going to Bournemouth this year, but Ray had a lot of trouble with his stomach lately. He was waiting to go in hospital for an operation. I don't think we should go on holiday with Ray being ill like this," said Tilly, worried about her son who had lost so much weight lately. "Shall we forget the holiday until next year?"

"No way!" Ray said. "The children are looking forward to going, and I'm not going to disappoint them."

They all threw their clothes in the carrier bags as usual, and were off.

"It's about time we bought some suitcases," said Eliza.

"Don't be silly, we would never get them in the boot with all the things we have to take," replied Dean.

Ray was in the lead as usual, followed by Joseph, and then Dean.

What a beautiful place Bournemouth was—so pretty! After getting settled in their holiday accommodations, it was off to the beach. It wasn't long before they get a good-sized stretch of beach.

"What's the matter with some people, don't they like to see children enjoy themselves?" said Marge.

Ray just lay there. He had two lightweight tee shirts, one navy and one an oatmeal colour. Their patterns were identical, and he wore them on alternate days. The shirts were patterned with holes, and he never took them off to sunbathe, he just wore them all day. However, Ray was not himself at all he was hardly eating or drinking anything, he was feeling so poorly.

With the holiday over, they arrived home on Saturday about six p.m.

"This letter looks as though it might be from the hospital," said Ray, picking the brown envelope up off the porch floor. He opened it up and called Marge, who had gone straight through into the kitchen to make a pot of tea after their long journey home.

"Guess what! I have to go in hospital Monday morning," he said.

"Blimey!" said Marge. "I will have to nip to the little shop round the corner in the morning to get you a few toiletries." It's about the only shop that opens on Sundays."

When Monday arrived, Marge drove Ray to hospital, which was quite a long way—about fifteen miles.

"Get undressed and put your pyjamas on," said the nurse.

Ray had just taken his shirt off when the doctor opened the curtain. Ray looked a hilarious sight with his back and chest dotted with spots of suntan.

"You're one of the healthiest-looking sick men I've ever seen," the doctor said, and they all laughed together.

Within a month Ray was fit and back at work.

"Thank goodness it wasn't cancer," he said. "I was dreading that."

Eliza took Tilly to the pub with her every Tuesday and Friday night, and they met Dawn, and another friend, Rainy, at 'The Rose and Crown'. Sometimes they played cards, sometimes darts. Eliza and a couple of other women were on the pub's darts team, which went all over the area to play in competitions. The best part was after the match, when they were served cheese and ham on crusty bread with the pickled onions and black pigs' pudding, a large-sized sausage made with fat, meat and blood.

"Mmm! It was delicious!"

Dean went to a different pub, where he played darts and dominoes.

One afternoon, Dawn came to see her mother at work. "Guess what, Mom! I'm pregnant. I've gone three months, but I never said anything because I thought you might get upset."

"Well, you have been married three years," replied Eliza.

Eliza went straight to Tilly when she got home.

"Congratulations, Mom," she said. "You are going to be a great gran. What do you think of that?"

"That's bloody marvellous!"

Thomas bought himself a little 'put-put', as Eliza called his tiny motor-bike. He worked on a farm just up the lane, not far from where they lived.

"I'm going in the army," he announced one day, after opening the letter he received that morning. "I have an appointment to go to the recruitment office at Bromsgrove. Will you take me there, Mom?" he asked Eliza.

"If you're sure this is what you want to do." Eliza was quite surprised at his sudden interest in the military since he never mentioned going into the army before. She booked a day's holiday from work to take Thomas for his interview.

"I don't want you coming in with me," he said as she pulled up in the car park.

Eliza brought a book to read, thinking he might want some privacy. *He's become quite independent lately.*

"Okay, off you go. Good luck!" she said, watching him as he walked over the road and 'round the corner. Then, she settled down to read her book. Eliza glanced at her watch, thinking that Thomas had been gone for ages. Just as she looked up, though, she spotted him almost swaggering across the road. At that moment, she realised how fast her children were growing up.

"I think I will be accepted," he said, getting back into the car.

A few weeks later, Thomas was packing his gear.

"Mom, will you take me to the train station?" he asked.

"You know I will."

Eliza shed a tear as she waved him off. *He's still a baby!*

Thomas stood waving back as the train moved off. Eliza watched, her eyes full of tears, as his train disappeared in the distance. He went to do his training in a place called "Deepcut."

When his training was over, Thomas phoned up. "Mom, are you coming to my passing-out parade?"

"Try and stop me," Eliza replied, so proud of him.

"Hi Marge, it's me," said Eliza, ringing her sister-in-law up. "It's Thomas' passing-out parade next week. Are you coming?"

"We sure will!" replied Marge. "Ray will come as well."

Eliza then phoned Mo.

"Yes we will come."

So they all went off to Deepcut.

The ceremony was touching, and Dean and Eliza were quite proud of Thomas.

"Jim would have been so proud of his 'pudding'," said Tilly.

The parade over, they were ushered to another room where there was a buffet laid out, after which they were on their way home with Thomas, for a well-earned leave. He seemed to have grown two inches and he hadn't been gone that long.

And so, Thomas settled down to army life.

Jay joined the Territorial Army.

"I wonder if he's going to follow in Thomas' footsteps," said Dean, but Jay's girlfriend had different ideas about that. He had his passing-out parade, but then he seemed to lose interest in it and jacked it in.

Ann went to work in the Isle of Wight, with a friend, as a chambermaid. "It was just for the summer season," she said. She phoned her mother every week right up to the end of the season.

CHAPTER 15

E liza answered the phone.
"It's me. Ann. It's the end of the season. Can you please come and pick me up tonight, Mom?"

"Bloody hell, Ann! That's a long way for me to come!" replied Eliza. "I just got home from work!"

"But Mom, I am scared to travel alone!"

"What about your friend, Lucy?"

"She's not coming home; she's staying here with a friend."

Eliza reluctantly agreed to pick up Ann, but she asked Dean to go with her. "It will be dark, and I will have that big forest to drive through."

"You must be bloody joking!" he replied. "It will take you all night. Tell her to find her own way back. It's not as if it's a few miles away—it's hundreds of miles."

Eliza then phoned Dawn and asked her to come, too. "I know you're pregnant."

"The things you do for us kids!" replied Dawn.

"I'll pick you up in ten minutes," promised Eliza.

"You must be out of your bloody mind to drive that far. You will be lucky to get a ferry," said Dawn's husband, Dave. "It will take you three hours or more to get to Yarmouth!"

Eliza and Dawn set off with a map, but it was a tatty thing. It was absolutely pissing down with rain and darkness came early. They finally reached New Forrest; however, it was raining so much that they had to stop for a minute.

"Which way now?" asked Eliza.

"I don't know," replied Dawn, trying to read the map. "It looks like we are lost."

"Oh, no, that's all we need! What a place to get lost—the middle of a bloody forest!"

As they were trying to figure out what to do, a man on a bike appeared.

"I can't believe my eyes," Eliza said. "What on earth is anyone doing on a bike in this kind of weather in the middle of a forest?"

"Maybe he's a blessing," Dawn replied. "We can ask him for directions."

"Lock the doors of the car," said Eliza, pulling up beside him.

Both their hearts were going ten to the dozen as Dawn wound her window down a fraction and asked the man the way. He pointed his finger in a direction, and Eliza drove off, hoping he told them the right way. They reached the port just as the last ferry had gone, and they stood, watching it move out of sight.

"The story of my bloody life!" said Eliza. "That's all we need—now what?"

To make matters worse, both women needed to pee. Seeing no alternative, they peed by the side of the car. Then, they tried to make the best of the situation and attempted to get comfortable enough to sleep in the car. *What a night!*

Neither of them got much sleep, but they were first in line for the ferry the next morning. By this time, Eliza and Dawn felt like partners in a caper and laughed at themselves.

"You know we are fucking crackers doing this, don't you agree?" said Dawn.

"Yes. I thought about getting a job at Jacobs. Dean says I'm fucking crackers, running after you children like I do."

Eventually they got to the hotel where a well-rested Ann wondered why they were late.

"What kept you?" she asked. "I was ready last night."

"Just get your things and get in the car. We want to get the next ferry back. Dawn and I are knackered," replied Eliza. "And, Ann, don't ask us to do this again!"

They arrived home at teatime. It took them twenty-one hours to fetch Ann!

"I am serious, Ann. Don't ask me to do that again!" said Eliza. "Dawn and I were shit-scared driving through that forest."

The factory where Eliza worked was moving. They had already moved once before, and then moved back again. This time, they were moving to a building that was just round the corner from Dawn's house.

Dawn had a little boy, who was lovely with loads of dark hair. It looked just like Dawn's hair when she was born.

Perhaps Dawn will walk round at dinnertime to see me then during her half-hour lunch break at work, Eliza thought.

Thomas phoned. "Don't worry, Mom, I have got to go to the Ascension Isles because of the war in Argentina."

Of course, Eliza was worried stiff since she knew she wouldn't hear from him for a long time. To her, he was still a baby. He was only eighteen years old, and she had no idea how far the Ascension Isles were from the combat in Argentina.

Dean decided to add an extension to the house. The plans were approved, and he soon got started, working in his spare time. At last that pokey kitchen would no longer exist. The new one would be a lot larger, and Eliza wouldn't have to keep the washing machine in the pantry anymore. Dean decided to get rid of the pantry entirely. Derek, who had been working for himself quite a few years doing plastering, gave Dean a hand with it. Derek was doing all right, but he had a hard time saving any money. Like Eliza, he spent all his money on his family of four boys.

It didn't take long for Dean to complete the extension with Derek's help. They bought a new carpet for the lounge area, and Eliza thought it looked lovely.

"Can we afford to have the same carpet running through the hall and up the stairs and landing like the posh people do?" asked Eliza.

"I suppose we can just about afford it," Dean replied.

When Tilly returned from one of her visits to Sam's house, she was amazed. "The house looks fantastic," she said, "but it makes the furniture look small."

"I know," replied Eliza. "It looks drab as well, but we will have to wait a few months to get new furniture."

About the time that Dean finished the kitchen, Ray decided to go into the building business. He had been putting money away for ages, and he asked for his redundancy from the factory where he worked for years and years to help finance his new business. They were thinning the workforce down a bit.

"Are you sure?" asked his boss.

"Yes, I am. I have something in mind."

Ray could see that his brothers, who built homes and restored flats, were doing well. He bought a new van, and the work started to come in.

"Any chance of a job for me?" asked Jay.

"Sure, I will give you a job, but you will be on a three months trial and, if you're no good, you will be off. Nephew or not, you will have to pull your weight," Ray said. He liked Jay. "He's a good lad," he said. "Mind you, they're all nice kids."

Ray tooted the horn in the mornings when he came to pickup Jay for work. Tilly heard him and opened her window to speak to him.

"Hi, Mom," he called back too her. "How are you?"

"I'm okay," Tilly called back.

Business fell off in the factory where Eliza worked. "It was so bad that there were rumours going round that the whole factory was going to close. A few days later they were all told they were being made redundant. All of the employees were gutted and shocked. They all thought the place would run forever. Eliza, who had been there for twelve years, would miss the people she worked with. She felt sorry for those who had been there since they left school and were about to retire.

Eliza had been suffering with a chest ailment for some time. Her cough was so bad that she actually cracked a couple of ribs coughing, and she had been drinking far too much. She had been going up the road to the outdoor at the Brockhill and getting a bottle filled with sherry every night. She hated the taste of it, but it was a cheap way to get drunk. More importantly, it was the only thing that stopped her cough so she could get some sleep. Eliza answered the phone one afternoon and heard a sound she had been longing for—Thomas' voice.

"I'm back in England," he said. "I landed yesterday and shall be home at the weekend. By the way, Mom, is it okay to bring a friend with me?"

"What's new?" replied Eliza.

Thomas arrived home with his friend on Friday, as scheduled. The boys went out on the town.

On Saturday, Eliza said, "Why don't you come out to *The Sugar Brook* with us tonight? We'll have a good sing song?"

Dean told him that other family members—Nanny Tilly, Mo, Marge and Ray—would also be there. "We'll have a brilliant night," he concluded.

"Okay," Thomas replied.

"Come on, drink up. The towel's on," said the publican.

"It's time we left and went home," said Tilly.

"Not us," replied Thomas. "We're going on the town tonight."

The next day, Eliza cooked the traditional Sunday roast while potatoes and greens simmered on the stove. She always made plenty. Her Sunday dinner had become a bit like that meal used to be at the Tin House. They never knew who would turn up.

"That's my favourite. You're the best cook in the world," remarked Thomas, making Eliza smile even though he always said that.

"Flattery will get you nowhere," she replied.

The next morning, someone was shaking Eliza.

"What's going on?" she said, opening her eyes. She noticed that the clock read five a.m.

"Shush," said a voice, whispering in her ear. "It's Thomas."

Eliza got out of bed and followed him downstairs. "What's the matter?"

"You're not going to like it," he replied, "Mom, we need a lift to Bicester."

"You've got to be bloody joking!" replied Eliza.

"I'm not. We have to be on parade at eight."

"I get some bloody good jobs, don't I?" she replied, lighting up a fag. She drank the rest of her tea, and Thomas asked her to leave the others a note explaining where she was because he didn't want to worry them. Eliza was not looking forward to the return journey since she had no sense of direction and often got lost when she drove in unfamiliar places. She was hopeless when she didn't know the way. To remedy that, she asked Thomas to write down every village and town they passed through so she could reverse the route on the way home.

Young Jay had a car now, so he sometimes ran Thomas back, but Eliza always went with him.

"You do everything for these kids," her friend said to her. "It's about time they learnt to stand on their own two feet."

"I know, but like my husband says, I'm a soft touch where the children are concerned. He always says I'm as soft as butter with the children."

Dawn had started a part time job, and Eliza looked after Dawn's little boy, Brett. He was no trouble at all. Tilly loved taking him for a walk up the road and always took some bread with them so they could sit and feed the ducks. However, the child was usually asleep by the time Tilly brought him back.

"I wish I could go back a few years to when you were little," said Tilly.

Eliza, who was quite sensitive to Tilly, told her she wished they could all re-experience the years at the Tin House again.

While they were talking, Dawn came home with a new idea. "Do you fancy running a shop?" Dawn asked her mother.

"What sort of shop?"

"A grocery shop," she said, noting that she knew of one that was for sale.

"I haven't got any money to buy a shop."

"You get a mortgage for it," Dawn told her.

That night they discussed it with their husbands. Dean was adamant about checking the store's books before they considered buying it and Dave agreed. After seeing the books and the bank manager, who would have to approve a mortgage, they put down a large deposit. Then, they went off to see a solicitor.

"I've had a good look at the books, and I wouldn't advise you to carry on with the purchase. I wouldn't touch it with a barge pole," said the solicitor.

"We can't back out," replied Dean "We paid a large deposit." He thought the solicitor was wrong. "It can't be that bad. The chap has been running it for forty years."

"It's up to you, but don't say I didn't warn you," said the solicitor, sticking to his first assessment.

In the end, they carried on with the purchase, regardless of what the solicitor said.

The weekend before they were due to take over, Dawn went to help in the shop. Then, on the Saturday, her husband went to help deliver the orders. That night they were both exhausted—Dawn from putting the deliveries up and working in the shop and her husband from learning the delivery route and carrying boxes of groceries.

"It was ever so busy," Dawn said, "and the worst part was getting the bread order right. I never knew there were that many kinds of bread. I shall be dreaming about bloomers all night."

She managed to get her little boy into the nursery school near the shop, and she and Eliza agreed to take turns fetching him after school. They would have alternate afternoons off, and Tilly would care for the child on Fridays and Saturdays.

Monday morning arrived—their first day in the shop. Eliza was tired because she had a terrible dream about bread the night before and awoke several times. She took the estate car they bought especially for the shop. It was second-hand but they thought they had a nick. Eliza had to pick up Dawn and take her grandson to school. She started the car up and slowly reversed into the road. She was being very careful because there was a nasty bend just up the road, and other drivers seemed to speed by it.

Is that a wobble I can feel? Eliza wondered, getting out of the car? "Oh, no!"

The front wheel on the passenger side was as flat as a pancake.

"No, it can't be!" Eliza said out loud.

She got a foot pump out of the car and tried to use it, but the tyre didn't budge—it was completely knackered. Eliza kicked the wheel then trotted back in the house, puffing and panting. She phoned

Dawn to tell her what had happened.

"I'll get a taxi so I can greet the bread man, and you get there as soon as possible, okay?" Dawn asked.

Eliza got the spare wheel out. "Oh! That bloody thing's flat as well! What a start." She would have to ring one of her brothers up and hope at least one of them had not yet left for work. Derek only lived a half mile up the road, and Eliza knew he often stayed a bit later than the others to see his youngest child off to school.

"Give me ten minutes," he said when she reached him. "This is a fine start. Why didn't you check the spare when you bought the car?"

"Don't give me a lecture!" replied Eliza. "I'm already a bag of nerves, and the little one can't go to the nursery school until I get there."

"That's a fine start to a new venture, isn't it!" said Dawn as Eliza walked into the shop. "But you haven't missed anything."

"How much money did you take in?" asked Eliza.

"I've only had one person in and that was for his bread. He walked in and asked for his bloomer, then walked out saying, 'Put it on tick.'"

"Tick!" replied Eliza. "I didn't think anyone had grocery on tick anymore."

"Well, we do—right here—it seems."

The first day was over.

"It didn't take much counting, did it?" said Dawn, holding the day's taking in her hand—the grand total of three pounds twenty-five pence! "This does not even cover the cost of the petrol, let alone anything else."

Oh God! What have we done? Eliza and Dawn hoped it was just a bad day because the people who did come in had the goods mainly on tick.

Tuesday came and went, Wednesday came and went, still no better. By Thursday, things were not much better, but Friday was a little better.

Saturday was busy because of the orders, but most of these were for elderly people who had been customers for years. Quarter pound of cheese, two eggs, and two slices of bacon was a typical order. It cost more for the wrappings than they made on the goods they were selling. At the end of the week, they had taken in about eight hundred pounds. That only just covered the cost of the goods they bought and the petrol and electricity they used, never mind paying anything on the mortgage.

They were working every day, and they were not able to take any wages from the store, not being paid any wages themselves. Ann was helping as well on Saturday, even though she was pregnant, and Sam's wife helped as well. The main items sold were bread, sliced ham, cheese, sugar and lovely fresh greens. The only thing was that the greens soon went bad if they weren't sold in a couple of days. Then they were left with a lot of waste, and that was costly.

Ann answered the phone one afternoon and asked who was calling. Holding the phone out to her mother and Dawn, she said. "The bank manager wants to talk with one of you."

They both knew what he wanted. They hadn't paid anything on the mortgage since they took out the loan.

"Eliza speaking," she answered.

He told her he wanted both of them to come to the bank on Tuesday at ten o'clock. "On that day, Ann went to look after the shop, but it was a certain fact that she wouldn't be rushed off her feet. Dawn and Eliza were nervous, as it was a different loan officer they would see that day.

"Come in," he said opening the door to his office. He sat looking through some papers. "I've been racking my brain," he began. "I don't know what you're going to do." He explained that he had examined the paperwork on their loan that included their income levels and ability to repay the loan. "Whoever gave you a mortgage of this amount, on the figures I have before me, has a lot to answer for." His face wore a pitying look as he softly explained that their houses were in jeopardy if the mortgage wasn't paid.

"We don't know what we're going to do," said Dawn. "We have tried selling loads of different things like pens, pads, and combs."

"I think you'd better sell the shop if you can—that is, if anyone will buy it," the banker said. "The interest is piling up by the day." He promised to give them a month's time and asked them to pay as much as they could in the meantime.

"I have a friend," said the bank manager one day on their monthly visit to see him, "who's an independent financial adviser. He's a good friend of mine and is prepared to see both of you, to advise you on the best way out."

Should they go bankrupt or what? The man they would see was doing so free of charge, as a favour to the bank manager. He advised them to sell one of their houses until they could get rid of the shop.

After talking to their partners, they decided to put both of their houses up for sale, and whoever sold first would move in with Tilly. They closed the shop and put it up for sale. It was useless to carry on with it because they were getting deeper and deeper in debt.

Three months passed, and no one even inquired about either house or the shop.

If only we had listened to the solicitor last year! If they had pulled out then, they would only have lost a couple of thousand pounds. Now they were going to lose their homes.

The bank manager felt that sorry for them, and he phoned Dawn. "Dawn, I know this won't help much, but do you want a part time job?"

"What doing?" asked Dawn.

"I have been talking to my wife, and we could do with a cleaner a couple of times a week."

"Thank you."

"Call in tomorrow night, and we will give you a key to the house."

Dawn couldn't believe they were going to trust her with a key to their house. He only knew her through the bank.

"I don't want to do this, Mom," she said. "I feel so embarrassed, but if I don't do it, he will think I'm not bothered." Dawn went to collect the key and to meet his wife with mixed emotions.

The next Monday, she took her son to playschool. He would soon be starting the infant school. Feeling like an intruder as she unlocked the bank manager's door, Dawn walked into the kitchen and saw the note of instructions with an envelope that had *Dawn* written on it. When she finished the work, she made sure the door was locked, fetched her little boy from playschool, and then drove down to her mother's house.

"How did it go?" asked Eliza.

"Okay, but I felt like an intruder."

Following her mother and carrying the coffee, Dawn walked outside, and both sat on the swinging hammock together. But they were interrupted when Eliza got up to answer the phone. It was her sister-in-law, Janet.

"You've done spring work, haven't you?" she asked.

"I sure have."

"Well, my gaffer wants to know if you want some outwork, but it means having a press in your kitchen," she said.

"That's fine."

Dean wouldn't be happy or impressed about having a press in the kitchen, especially now that it looked so nice because he liked things neat and tidy. He knew, though, that Eliza wasn't strong enough to go to full time work. Her back was that bad. She couldn't stand for long. Eliza didn't think Dean would make much of a fuss, however, because they certainly needed the money.

When the man arrived with the outwork, Eliza was surprised. "Blimey, the press is quite big, isn't it?" she said.

"Where do you want it?

"It will have to go on the table," replied Eliza, pointing to the white-topped round table that her sister-in-law, Viv, had given to them.

"Now I will show you what to do," he said, taking a handful of springs in his hand. "Just loop the ends like this." Eliza did a handful. "That's right, keep those few separate, and you can check them occasionally."

"How much for a thousand?" She asked.

"Two pounds fifty for the small ones and three pounds for the larger ones. These are the large ones."

Eliza soon got the hang of doing the springs. She expected to be work for peanuts but this was a great price. She wondered whether the chap has made a mistake, but she would soon find out when she got her wages. Eliza loved the job, and when Dawn came and tried doing springs. "This is a good job, isn't it?" she said.

Ann went into labour and soon gave birth to a little girl—Eliza's second grandchild and Tilly's second great grandchild. Tilly asked if she could come with Eliza to see the new baby.

"Of course you can" Eliza answered.

They were surprised to see Ann standing by the crib, discussing the electric bill with her partner.

"I thought you would be lying in bed," said Tilly. "You only had the baby an hour ago."

"I'm fine. It wasn't any big deal."

"I wish I could have had mine like that all those years ago," replied Tilly, "but then, all nine of my babies were bigger than that little one lying in the crib." She noted that she now had two great grandchildren—one boy and one girl. She grinned at Dawn and added, "I'm pleased as punch."

A couple of weeks later Dawn announced that she thought she was pregnant.

Eliza worried that Dawn and her family still had the worry of the shop hanging over their heads, as she did. *What are we going to do?*

The situation wasn't good. The only way Eliza could make sure the mortgage would be paid was to so swallow her pride and ask Ray to help. Getting in her car, she drove down to her brother's house. It seemed a bit cheeky since he had helped her so many times in the past, but she couldn't see any other way out of the nightmare caused by buying the shop.

Eliza sat at Ray's table, drinking the cup of tea Marge made for her and trying to pluck up the nerve to ask him to help them.

"What's happening with the shop?" he asked.

"That's why I came—to see if you would help us!" she blurted out.

271

"What have you got in your mind?" he asked.

"The bank manager suggested turning the upstairs into a self-contained flat and titivating the shop up a bit. Then, it might sell as a shop with living accommodation above. "

"It's going to take a long time. I can only do it nights and weekends," he said, agreeing to help her. They discussed the project. Ray told her she and Dawn would have to save as much as they could for materials and their husbands would have to help too. He would allow them to pay for any materials that he could provide when the shop sold.

"Thanks, Ray. You saved my life—and Dawn's."

And so, they started knocking the shop all about, gutting nearly to the ground. They worked every evening and at least one full day, but sometimes two on the weekends. Slowly, the flat started to look inviting. Eliza and Dawn still saw the bank manager every month to update him on their progress. But now they owed twice as much as they borrowed. Eliza feared that selling the shop and flat might not be enough to cover their debt.

Chapter 16

Mark started courting!

He described his fiancé as a "lovely girl" as he came into the kitchen to talk with Eliza. She looked up to answer him when she noticed the girl behind him.

"I can see that," said Eliza. After that, Wendy spent all her spare time at Eliza's house. They were saving their money to get married, as well as organizing and planning for it. The wedding, they decided, would take place at the big church uptown where Dawn got married. Whenever Eliza saw them together, she had the same thought: *They really are a handsome couple.*

Just as Eliza was getting ready to go to bed around ten o'clock, Dawn telephoned. "Mom, can you come down? I'm in labour, and I'd like you to baby-sit."

"You can sleep in our bed," said Dawn when Eliza arrived.

"No, I will lie on the settee. I don't think I will be sleeping much anyway."

Dawn and her husband left for the hospital as soon as Eliza arrived. But they had only been out of the house an hour when the phone rang.

It can't be them. It takes at least half an hour to get to the hospital. Eliza reached for the phone, wondering who would call this late.

"It's a girl!" yelled Dave.

"That was quick!" replied Eliza excitedly. "A little girl!"

Dawn and Dave now had one of each, Eliza thought, smiling. She was glad her daughter had a happier marriage than she had when she gave birth to her.

Meanwhile, Dave was still on the phone. "Yes, it was quick," he said, adding, "They took her straight to the delivery room. She had the baby straight away."

"That's the way to have a baby!" replied Eliza.

"She's lovely, and just look at all that hair! It must be an inch long," said Eliza, cradling the baby in her arms the next day. Tilly, too, was delighted with the new arrival.

When Mark's wedding day arrived, he looked handsome in his silvery blue suit. He was very tense and so nervous he kept pacing up and down the room. Suddenly, he stopped and looked alarmed. "What's this on the front of my jacket?" he cried out. There were a few speckles of orange there.

Eliza gently wiped it off. "I wonder where that came from?" she asked. A few minutes later the stains were back again.

"It's from that lily on that coffee table. Every time you pass by, it brushes your jacket," she said as she moved the flowers out of the way.

Both Eliza and Tilly agreed that the bride was stunningly beautiful, the groom was ruggedly handsome and the bridesmaids, who wore delicate blue gowns, completed an elegant wedding party. After the wedding, Mark and his wife planned to live with Eliza and Dean for a while.

Eliza had a bit of a break from her money worries during the wedding festivities, but she had to return to the worry of trying to sell one of the houses. There were a few people looking at their homes, mostly though, they did just that—look. Those people wasted Eliza's time. She said they just wanted a nose. The housing market was slow, and that added to their burden.

Dawn took Tilly to see Biron, whom she hadn't seen for ages. They noticed a *For Sale* sign outside the house.

"Where are you moving to?" asked Dawn.

"The old post office and cafe. We are going to do it up a bit, run it as a going concern for a couple of years, and then we hope to get permission to build on the car park."

"I hope you do better than we did," said Dawn.

"We're in a different position than you were," Biron said, thoughtfully. "We will be living there, and I will still be working."

"You're a jammy bugger! Everything seems to fall in your lap."

His house sold easily, and they soon moved into the café. Biron did it up, and his wife opened the cafe and small shop. They gave Dawn a part-time job. She was no longer working because she stopped cleaning for the banker and his wife before she had her baby girl.

The café was quiet, and so was the shop. However, one day a builder walked into the shop and ordered a number of breakfasts to take out. He was part of a large crew that was building an estate down the lane opposite the café. It was the lane that led to the church where Jim and Tilly were married many years ago.

It didn't take long until the café business was booming—nothing seemed to go wrong for Biron. He and his Viv decided to run the cafe until the builders finished the estate, but they had to hire more staff for the morning shift.

Tilly and Eliza looked after Dawn's baby between them while she worked in her uncle's café. Tilly often took the baby for a walk up to the shops. They sat and watched the ducks by the lake while Eliza continued her outwork for the spring company on the press.

Friends asked Dean and Eliza to Tenerife for a week. They were pleased to be invited, but Eliza thought taking a trip was next to impossible.

"No," replied Eliza. "I will give you two good reasons. First, I'm shit-scared to fly, and second, what would Ray and the other ones who are helping us think if we were to clear off on holiday?"

Dean came home from the pub the next night, with a surprise for her. "Send for our passports, Eliza, we're going on holiday."

"I don't want to go! I told you, I am scared of flying."

"Well, I already told them to book it now."

So reluctantly, Eliza set off with Dean to get photos for their passports. They filled the forms in and posted them. In no time, the passports arrived. Eliza started drinking more heavily and she was smoking more and more, too. She kept calling Dean every nasty name she could think of because she blamed him for "making" her fly. The nearer the holiday came, the worse she got.

Because Thomas came home on leave that weekend, Eliza and Dean postponed their holiday a few days and left on Monday instead of Friday night or Saturday. They were going on holiday on Monday at dinnertime. On Monday morning, though. Thomas woke her up, again,. "Come on, Mom, I want you to take me back to the camp!"

"For Christ's sake, Thomas! I can't! I'm going on holiday at dinnertime."

"You will be back by then," he begged.

He was at a different camp now, and Eliza had no idea how to get there—he knew she hated driving when she didn't know the way.

"Why do you do this to me?" she asked Thomas. As she was driving, she asked Thomas how far it was to camp.

"It's about a hundred miles or just over."

"Bloody hell! I will never get back in time. Dean will think I did this on purpose. Just make sure you write down the way correctly."

As Eliza at last pulled up at the camp, Thomas jumped out. "Bye," he said, kissing her on the cheek. "I have ten minutes to get on parade." With that, he was gone.

. She turned the car round and drove back the way she came, humming to herself as she drove along. She remembered the first thirty miles or so. Then, she stopped and looked at what Thomas had written down for her.

She must have taken a wrong turn somewhere, because she couldn't remember coming down the large open road she found herself on. At the first opportunity, she stopped. Then, restarting the car, she carried on. "Excuse me," she called out to a man after stopping again. "I think I'm lost. Can you put me on the right road?"

"You're miles out of your way," he said after he heard where she was going. "You're going in the opposite direction!" So she turned around again and retraced the last twenty or so miles. She finally found he right route home. At last, a weary Eliza drove into her driveway in time to see Dean and their friends just leaving the house

"Where the bloody hell have you been?" they chorused together. "We were just about to leave without you.

Eliza was so nervous she was biting her nails, as well as starving and dying for a drink. They arrived at the airport late, booked in, and then they had to go straight to the departure lounge. Dean had to push Eliza up the steps to the plane because she was shaking all over and her breathing was bad.

When the plane taxied out to the runway before it took off, Dean looked at Eliza and worried. *She's going to faint! She's gripping my arm so tightly that she is almost drawing blood.*

However, after they were in the air, Eliza began to relax. They were amazed by the clouds.

"They look like balls of cotton wool, don't they?" said Eliza, who was a bit calmer now. She was just beginning to enjoy the flight, but when they landed, she didn't like the landing and was glad to get off.

A few days later Eliza phoned Dawn. "How's everyone at home?" she asked.

"Okay," Dawn replied, but Eliza knew by the tone in her voice that something wasn't right.

"What's the matter?"

"It's the baby. She isn't well. I took her to the doctor, but he said she's all right."

"Just see that she drinks plenty of fluids, and if she's still poorly tomorrow, take her back," said Eliza.

"Okay, Mom."

A few days later Eliza and Dean returned from their holiday.

"I've got to admit, I really enjoyed the holiday," said Eliza, who donned her black leather skirt and got ready to go to Dawn's house.

She didn't unpack or do anything else. She first wanted to check on the baby.

"She's very pale," she said, picking her up and cuddling her. "This baby is very ill, she's just limp," she added, trying to get her Holli to stand on her lap.

At eight months, the baby was usually full of life, but now she lay limp in Eliza's arms. "We have to get her back to the doctor."

A few minutes later, Eliza felt something wet on her hands. When she looked down, there was a puddle in the lap of her skirt that began to drip onto the floor.

"Look at this," she said to Dawn.

"I know. But it's not from her bladder, it's from her bottom. She has terrible diarrhoea."

Eliza was appalled. "It's just water!" she said.

"I have taken her twice and I have had the doctor out as well," Dawn explained, "and they just said to give her plenty of fluids."

"Come on, get in the car."

Eliza got into the driving seat, and off they went to the surgery. Eliza's sister, Mo, was with them.

"We brought the baby to see a doctor," said Mo.

"I'm sorry. We are fully booked up," replied the receptionist.

"We will take her to hospital if she can't see a doctor," Mo continued. "She saw three different doctors this week, and the baby's getting worse."

"Wait there. I will see if a doctor will see her."

Mo waited in the waiting room while Dawn and Eliza took the baby in. Dawn was too scared to go in herself. She thought she was a nuisance.

"How dare you speak to my receptionist like that!" said the doctor as they went into his surgery.

"Like what? Let me tell *you* two things—one, we didn't speak to the receptionist, and two, we have to get the baby better."

Finally, the doctor turned his attention to the baby. "Why haven't you brought her before?" he asked.

"This is the fourth time she has seen a doctor in ten days," Dawn replied.

The doctor's voice softened. "Give her this," he said, handing Dawn a prescription. "Make sure she takes it, and I guarantee she will be lots better by tomorrow. If she isn't, bring her straight back."

Eliza was up early the next morning, had a quick cup of coffee, and dragged hard on her cigarette as she jumped in her car. She went straight to Dawn's house. "How is she this morning?" she asked, picking up Holli out of her pram.

"She doesn't seem any better," Dawn replied.

"Get your clothes on, then. We're taking her to hospital," Eliza said, decisively as she wrapped the baby in a blanket.

Although it was summer, there was still a nip in the early morning air. As Dawn carried the baby to her mother's car, her coat brushed against the pampas grass as she walked past it, catching the early morning cobwebs on her sleeve. She brushed them off as she got in the car. Once at the hospital, Dawn told the doctor the baby's symptoms and about all the doctor and hospital visits.

"This baby is slowly starving to death," the doctor on duty said after examining her. "We will have to keep her in. She's very poorly." While she was in hospital, they slowly started feeding her as they treated her diarrhoea. Eventually tests revealed that she had salmonella food poisoning.

Where can she have got that from? Eliza thought.

After eight days, Holli was discharged from hospital and was almost back to normal. Later that day, Eliza read the daily paper, which Dean fetched for her every morning before he went to work. She turned the page to an article that described salmonella poisoning in babies. Some babies died from the infection, but others, with stronger immune systems, survived. Eliza was shocked to learn that the source of the salmonella was dried milk.

Eliza phoned Dawn immediately, "Throw the baby's milk away. It's the milk that made her ill."

Needless to say, Dawn never used that product again. Her baby was lucky to survive.

279

Finally, after more than six months, someone made an offer on Dawn's house. She was a bit dismayed that they wanted her to be out in a month. Although Dawn and Eliza will be glad when they had paid back the bank, the victory was both bitter and sweet." It was heartbreaking for all of them, especially Dawn and Dave.

Eliza felt guilty about still being in her house while her daughter was losing hers. She and Tilly helped Dawn pack her belongings together. All their furniture was going to be stored in different places wherever friends and relatives had room.

After the mortgage on the house was taken out of the sale, the bank took the rest of the money. The two families still owed more than they borrowed. Instead of paying the mortgage on the house, now, the four of them were paying off the shop.

What a nightmare! And, it seemed to be getting worse! Still nothing was happening at the shop or at the flat. Both were still unsold, although people had inquired about the flat on its own. They had been trying to sell the two together.

Eliza approached her other brother, Michael, about turning the shop part of the building into another flat. "We will have to get a permit for change of use as well as a planning permit," Eliza told him. She knew permits cost money too—costs that seemed never ending. When Eliza phoned the town's planning department, the woman in charge told her they could draw their own plans as long as the measurements were accurate. Eliza thanked her since that information would save them a fortune.

Within two weeks the plan passed. Michael didn't mess about. He soon had it done. The top flat sold first. The bank took the money, and the two couples still owed more than they had initially borrowed.

"We have to sell the bottom flat quickly, or we will owe the bank all that we get for that. We can't let that happen because we still owe Ray and Michael."

The next few weeks were filled with highs and lows. Each time someone said they wanted it, they were elated. But when the financing didn't work out, they were depressed. It happened three separate times.

Meanwhile, Dawn's father lent her the deposit for a house that was to be built in a small housing estate. At last the bottom flat sold. But, after paying the bank what they owed, there was still not enough money to pay Ray, Michael and Joseph, Dawn's father, back.

Dean and Eliza, therefore, took a second mortgage on their house, borrowing sixteen thousand pounds. They needed fifteen thousand, but Dean decided they all needed a holiday after the nightmare they went through.

First, they paid their debts, and then they tried to get into a holiday mood. They booked the holiday for Dean and Eliza, Dawn and Dave, and Brett and Holli, their two children and Ann and her little girl Sadie. Ann's partner was long gone.

With the nightmare over, Eliza took stock. They bought the shop four years ago, and closed it within a few months of purchasing it. It cost about ninety thousand pounds when all was tallied, even though they only borrowed twenty-five thousand pounds to begin with. It was a four-year nightmare that was finally over. They were ready to celebrate.

The eight of them boarded the plane, and they were off. At last, they were free of that bloody shop! The nightmare was over. They couldn't have been happier.

They arrived at the hotel, called Holidays in Evia. The hotel was nice, and the food excelled, but any decent place would have made them happy. This was a holiday in heaven because they were finally free of their worries. They didn't have much money, but the burden of the last four years was over thanks to Ray and Michael.

After washing and changing, they went for their evening meal, both of the little girls in their pushchairs. Eliza pushed one, as it helped her to walk. She could lean on it, and ease the pressure on her back—her breathing, too, was a problem.

Ann walked ahead of them, idly kicking the stones. They were going to see the show offered by the hotel. As Ann walked she kicked something, so she bent down to investigate. "Look at what I have found," she said, waving a wallet in the air. The wallet bulged with Greek and English money. Ann looked to see if there was a name inside. "Ah here it is," she said.

"Are you going to give it in?" asked Eliza.

"Of course I am! The poor chap's probably looking everywhere for it."

The show over, they return to the hotel, and Ann went up to the receptionist.

"Can you tell me the number of this gentleman's room, please?"

"Why do you want to know?" the clerk countered.

"I've found his wallet."

"Just give it to me. I will return it," said the receptionist.

"If you don't mind, I will give it to him myself," replied Ann.

Ann tapped on the door, and a tall man opened it.

"I believe this is yours," she said to him.

"Thank you very much," he replied, with an element of surprise in his voice. "I hadn't a clue I'd lost it. Thank you very much," he repeated.

The next morning, they sat eating their breakfast, when a man walked over and put a large bottle of brandy in front of Ann.

"Thanks again," he said to her.

The rest of the holiday was smashing. They all had a brilliant time. The sea was lovely and warm, and the three children swam in the pool. What a fabulous holiday it was! It seemed no time until it was over. They returned home renewed. They would continue to plan for the future, but Eliza and Dawn sincerely hoped there were no shops in it.

Eliza and Dawn had little spare time, but they made time to take the children, all of whom could swim, to the swimming baths. Michael's wife Catharine and their little girl came along. She was their second child, but she was ten years younger than her sibling. Eliza was glad they took Ann on holiday because she had helped out in the shop and was never paid a penny. Sam's girlfriend was a good help to them too.

Tilly would be seventy-five soon, and the family pulled together to do a surprise party. It was scheduled later in the week at Biron and Viv's cafe, which would be closed to the public while the family celebrated together.

The day of the party, Eliza and her siblings were excited about the surprise that was in store for Tilly. They found her brother and sister. Tilly had seen her brother, Billy, on a few occasions, but had lost touch years ago, and she had only seen her sister Mary twice. However, Sam's wife had found her and fetched her from Oxen in Oxford. She took Mary straight to Biron and Viv's café, and left her in the living room, catching up with Billy. After the party, Mary and Tilly would sleep at Eliza's house so they could get to know one another better. Billy would stay with Sam at his house.

Mark's wife was expecting a baby that was due on Tilly's actual birthday. "Let's hope you don't have it tonight!" said Mark.

Tilly was delighted with the party and seemed elated to see her brother and sister. They all had a wonderful night celebrating Tilly and telling stories about her—especially the things, large and small, about their relationships with her that meant the most to each of them.

A couple of days later Mark's wife had a little girl, born on Tilly's actual birthday. Naturally she was beautiful, like all their babies, but Tilly considered her "birthday present" to be especially lovely with her ivory complexion, rosebud lips and delicate fingers. She was overjoyed. Eliza, too, was thrilled to have another grandchild.

The next morning, Tilly and her sister, Mary, walked up to the shops together. Eliza had bacon sandwiches ready for them when they came back. "I will take mine with me, if you don't mind," said Mary, disappearing upstairs. She had a very small briefcase with her, which she carried wherever she went, even to the toilet.

"Perhaps she has all her money in it and thinks we will steal it," said Tilly.

That night the four of them—Tilly, Mary, Dean and Eliza—were watching television, when every now and then, there was a rustle of sweet papers. Tilly could see what Mary was doing.

Eliza walked past them on her way to the kitchen. "Anyone for a cup of tea?" she asked.

Tilly followed Eliza into the kitchen. "She's not like us, is she?" said Tilly.

"What's happening with the sweets?"

"Mary's trying to eat them without anyone noticing. She bought them at the shop this morning."

"Fancy a trip to Oxford, Dawn, to take Mary home?" Eliza asked her daughter the next morning. "Mother doesn't like her very much, and, you know, Mother usually likes everyone."

"I can't say I'm very keen either, I saw her hit Ann's little girl this morning," replied Dawn.

Dawn decided to drive, and she and Eliza figured it would take about three hours to bring Mary home and come back again. As they were riding along, Mary told them she had a daughter who died in her late twenties. She added that her daughter's sons—her two grandsons—were in a home because their father remarried and didn't want them anymore.

"How could you let them go into a home?" asked Eliza. "I would never let that happen to any of my grandchildren!"

"We are all different," replied Mary. "Stop. This is it," she said. "This is where I live."

Dawn carried Mary's bag in, and they all said goodbye, perhaps forever. It rained all the way back and took a lot longer than they thought it would. So it was a good job Dawn had asked her friend to get her little boy from school. Her daughter was cuddling with Eliza in the back seat.

"I have been looking out of the window for you," said Tilly. "I've got the kettle on. It's such a horrible day."

"No tea for me, thanks," said Dawn, "I'm off."

"Thanks for taking Mary home," Tilly called out to Dawn, but Dawn was already driving away to fetch her little boy.

"Did you enjoy seeing your brother and sister?" asked Eliza, sipping her coffee. But she knew what the answer would be.

"The party was wonderful. I enjoyed seeing Billy, but I don't particularly want to see my sister again, though it has put my mind at rest. I've never missed anything not knowing her all my life. She's nothing like my parents or my brother."

"Never mind, you don't have to see her again."

Tilly was a wonderful mother. She never would have seen any of her grandchildren in a home.

Tilly and Eliza called in to see Mark's new baby. They lived just round the corner so they saw a lot of Mark and his family.

Dawn's house was finished, and at last, she and Dave could move all their belongings to their new home—they were moving the next day, so tonight was he last night Dawn and her family would live next door to Eliza and Dean. Eliza dreaded it, as she and Tilly were now closer to the children—in fact, Brett called Eliza *Mom*.

"She's not your Mom," Dean would tell him.

"She is," he replied. "I have got two Moms."

This would be the last night that Eliza could put the children to bed, while Dawn was at work. *Sod it! I'm keeping them up tonight. It's a lovely evening, and it's their last night staying next door.*

Eliza was gutted because they were moving. She loved having them next door and knew she would miss them. At eight forty-five, Dawn pulled onto the drive, spotting her mother sitting in the garden with the two children on her knees, singing a lullaby to them.

"Why aren't they in bed?" asked Dawn.

"I wanted to savour my last moments with them living here."

The next day Dawn took the rest of their things, and Eliza and Tilly said goodbye to them. Eliza thought the children would cry at leaving her and Tilly, but they just waved. Eliza walked in the house and broke her heart, crying.

"For Christ's sake, woman!" said Dean. "They've only moved four miles away."

Eliza was pleased they had a house of their own at last, but she would really miss them, and she would also miss having a late night drink with Dawn.

Tilly was staying at Sam's again and had been there for a few days when Sam's girlfriend phoned Eliza. "Something terrible happened. I found Tilly on the bathroom floor in a pool of blood. I called for an ambulance straight away, and they've taken her to hospital in Bromsgrove."

By the time Eliza got there, Tilly was in the operating theatre. Hours later, they were allowed to see her. She had suffered a burst ulcer.

"Your mother's very lucky to be alive," said the doctor. "She lost a massive amount of blood."

Tilly was heavily sedated for several days and it took a long time for her to recover.

"We are going to keep a better eye on you in future," the family members told her. "We don't want that to happen again."

On a Tuesday night, Tilly, Dawn, and Eliza were in the pub having a drink with their friend Rainy, when Ray walked in. They waved to him, but he ignored them.

"He couldn't have seen us," said Dawn. "He would probably come over in a minute." He always bought his mother a brandy and pep, and there was no way Ray would snub them. The next time they looked up, he was gone.

"Thar ent like Ray, is it?" remarked Rainy, who had a real old Webheath accent.

"I will phone him up tomorrow," said Eliza. After she got home, she told Dean about the incident with Ray. "I'm sure he saw us."

Jay walked in just as she was telling Dean. "It's because of the letter," Jay butted in.

"What letter?" asked Eliza.

"He had an anonymous letter off someone, saying you and Dawn were overheard saying he was a tight-fisted greedy bastard."

Who could have written the note saying those things? Who hated them that much? Hadn't they suffered enough over the last four years? Ray was as good as gold to Eliza and the family all his life, and no way would she or Dawn have said a thing like that. The next morning Eliza was listening for Ray to pip the horn for Jay. When she heard him, she ran out to him. "What's this about a letter?"

"Just fuck off," replied Ray.

Eliza' racked her brains. *Who would write a letter that upset my brother so much?*

Later that day, Eliza and Dawn talked about it, and between them, they could only think of one person with enough malice to do that. It was someone who liked to see them down all the time. The person they thought of had caused lots of trouble before on many occasions, and unfortunately, they were stuck with them.

Eliza phoned Marge. "What does that letter say?"

Marge told her.

"That's terrible! Do you honestly believe either of us would say a thing like that, after all the help you two have given me over the years?"

"I honestly don't know what to believe," replied Marge.

"Can we come and see if we can recognise the writing on the letter?"

"Ray has it in his pocket, but I can tell you the writing's scrawled, and the spelling isn't too good either. Ray's adamant he's finished with you and Dawn."

"I will see him up the pub on Friday night," said Eliza.

"You will be wasting your time. He's absolutely gutted."

"He's not on his own. Dawn and I are gutted as well."

They sat in the pub, having a drink when Ray walked in with the elderly person he brought out with him every week. Eliza waved, but Ray ignored her.

How long will this go on?

Dean could see that Eliza and Dawn were extremely upset. "I will go and speak to him and explain it's just spiteful malice." Dean approached Ray, then he came straight back. "He told me to fuck off as well. He was adamant about it."

Tilly was oblivious to the problem. Every time they saw Ray they waved, but he was not having any of it.

One night Eliza walked up to Ray. "You can ignore me as much as you like but I will always speak to you," she said.

It was almost time for Jay's birthday. *Is it really, twenty-one years since he was born?*

Tilly, Dawn and Eliza were going to do the food at Eliza's house, and Mo was doing some at hers, but they hadn't told Jay—it would be a surprise for him. The room was booked, so was the disco. All the invitations had gone out. Now, just how could they get rid of Jay while they prepared the food? The party was a week away, and Jay took Dawn's son up to the woods.

Arriving home, he walked into the lounge. "How many are coming to my party, Mom?" he asked.

Eliza looked at him blankly.

"Don't try to think of an excuse, I saw Biron's two boys up the woods and they told me. I hope you've invited my new girlfriend."

"Of course we have, we've invited her parents as well."

The party had swing and flair as a man, also called Ray, did the disco, and Allen did a video. There were old friends and new friends, all having a whale of a time. They had a great time together.

Eliza's oldest friend, Jill, her husband, Graham, and her daughter, Julie, were there. They had a fine time catching up with one another. They would all sleep at Eliza's house so they could have a drink together after the party since Jill and her family now lived about fifteen miles away. In fact, the only people missing were Ray and Marge!

What a fabulous night! Jay loved it. One of the highlights was Dawn's little boy's rendition of Michael Jackson's "Moonwalk." He was brilliant, yet nobody knew he could dance. He had been secretly practising. The results were terrific. The boy seemed to have music in his soul and rhythm in his feet. Dean asked Ray, the disco chap, if he wanted to come back for a drink.

Eliza and Tilly went to bed about four a.m.—absolutely knackered. "We're leaving you to it," they said to those who were still partying.

Jay moved in with Tilly, and it was not long before his girlfriend moved in with her as well.

"Have you ever thought of buying Tilly's house with her, Jay?" Eliza asked him.

"That's a good idea," he said, and soon the wheels were in motion. Once Jay had the mortgage, he started knocking the place about. It would be a cracking house by the time he was finished!

Eliza had a phone call from her friend, Janice, in Canada. They called each other up from time to time and always sent Christmas cards.

"Guess what, Eliza! Gareth and I are coming over to see you."

"I can't wait," replied Eliza.

"We have already booked the hotel just up the road from you," said Janice. "We are bringing two friends with us. You will love them, they are just like you."

Tilly and Eliza sat in the swinging hammock in the garden when Gareth and Janice arrived. They all started crying. They counted twenty-two years since they had last seen each other. Janice cried with Tilly over Jim's death.

"I loved him like my own father," Janice told Tilly.

"It's sixteen years since we lost Jim," replied Tilly.

"I know, but I'm sure he's in a nice place."

"I hope so."

Gareth and Janice made a fine couple.

"Let me introduce you to our friends," said Janice, as the couple had been standing on the side, watching the reunion. "Oh Eliza!" I think about you so many times. I tell all my friends about you and how you will always be my best friend. Gareth still can't understand why you stayed with Joseph for eight years."

"I can tell you, I was looking over my shoulder for two years after I left, and I genuinely thought he would kill me. Mind you, that's all in the past now. We have to get on because of the children."

Two days later Gareth and Janice were off to see relatives down on the coast they had promised to visit. That was the last time Eliza ever saw Janice!

Biron got his planning permission to build on his car park, and he planned to build two luxury houses. After the first one was finished, he and his wife moved in. He then planned to turn the café and the shop into one large luxury house and sell it. With this project, Biron would move into the big time, building more and more.

Who would have thought little Biron, the second youngest in the family, would be the first to make his fortune?

Everyone thought Michael would be first because he was already on his next house, but everything seemed to fall just right for Biron. Everybody wanted a page from his book.

On a Friday night, Thomas was home on leave. He finally bought an old car so he could make his own way there and back now that he was stationed in Scotland.

Imagine! He had been half way round the world in the army.

Mark brought his daughter to visit on Saturday. The little girl loved to come to Eliza's house—especially to play with her cousin, Ann's little girl, who came to spend the night. They all loved to sleep at Nanny's. Mark put both girls in the pushchair and started running up and down the lawn with them. They squealed with delight.

Both of their mothers were up town, where they spent hours every Saturday. Mark was still running up and down the lawn and the two girls giggled their heads off. Suddenly, Mark stopped quickly. His little girl was screaming although she had been laughing a few seconds before. As Eliza ran to her, she could see that her hand was bleeding. *"Oh, God! Her finger's hanging off!"*

Eliza unfastened her, and Mark picked her up and ran in the house. She grabbed a clean towel then placed the finger where it should be and wrapped the towel round her hand.

Thomas was already in the car with the engine running, waiting for Mark, who jumped in with her in his arms. Then, they were off to the hospital.

After a couple of hours, they returned.

"They managed to sew her finger back on," said Mark. "They said it will heal quickly."

A few days later, the doctor checked the finger, which was healing up nicely. A week later there was hardly a mark there.

CHAPTER 17

The sun was shining brilliantly in a cloudless blue sky—it was the first perfect day in a long time. It was also Bank Holiday—a Monday at dinnertime—and everyone was pleased that this glorious day started the summer season.

"Who wants to come to The Queen's Head for a drink?" asked Thomas.

"Shall we all go?" replied Dawn. "We could sit outside with the children. They will love it playing on the swings."

"I'm not coming," said Dean. "I'm going to mow the lawn."

Ray's son joined them as they sat outside in the garden at the pub, watching he children at play. Soon they noticed hundreds of gnats.

"The gnats are biting well today!" said Thomas.

Ray's son suggested that Eliza light another fag to keep the bugs at bay.

"I'm going to pack up this smoking," she replied. "I've been coughing my guts up lately, and with everybody cutting their lawns today, my chest hurts even more."

"Sure you'll quit. That'll be the day!" the others replied together.

Eliza had tried to quit dozens of times, because she knew it did her no good. She reckoned her bad chest started from the asbestos dust she inhaled when she worked packing brake shoes at the factory. However, she loved her fags, even though she knew they were killing her. Ray once smoked more than she did, but managed to give it up a few years ago.

He smoked like a chimney so if he did it, I could too.

Dean had just finished mowing the lawn, and the smell of the new cut grass sent Eliza into a coughing fit when she got home. "Here, Dawn, take these cigarettes away with you when you go home. I shan't need them. I'm never going to smoke again," Eliza said to her daughter, in between coughing and gasping for breath.

"What's the use, Mom? You will want them back tomorrow!"

"No, I won't. I'm adamant. I will never smoke again."

But, after a few days, Eliza was dying for a smoke, and to makes matters worse, Tilly smoked. Tilly only started to smoke when she was forty.

"How come you started smoking when you were that old, Mom?" asked Eliza.

"I can't remember," she replied. "But it's the stupidest thing I ever did."

Eliza knew she had to find an incentive to keep herself off the cigs. "Thomas, when you go up the club tonight, will you ask if they have one of those giant whisky bottles empty?"

"Here you are, Mother," he said, returning home later. "It cost me fifty pence so make sure you use it."

The next morning Eliza headed straight to the green grocers. She was going to buy some celery, carrots, and apples to chew on. She knew she had a battle on her hands and that her very life was in jeopardy. From then on, whenever she felt that she wanted a ciggie, she reached for the celery, and each day, she put the amount of money that she would have spent on cigarettes into the whisky jar.

After two months, Eliza opened her first savings in many years. Her ambition was to go to the Caribbean. She had looked at travel brochures many times, and it seemed inviting and quite beautiful. Her aim was Barbados. Thomas was stationed in Canada and he would be off to America next. At least she had one child who understood her desire to see far away places.

Eliza and Dean scheduled a week's vacation in Tenerife with Tilly and his mother. Eliza still wasn't overly keen on flying, but she had done it before and was not as scared as she used to be. She had been to Tenerife several times.

The trip didn't start well. Tilly was sick on the coach on the way to the hotel. Then, Dean's mom bought her a neat gin on the plane, but Tilly's tummy couldn't take it. She still suffered the effects of the ulcer she had a few years ago.

Once there, wherever Eliza and Dean went, they came too.

"I want to go to bingo," said Dean's mother.

"That's not our scene," replied Dean. "But you and Tilly go. We will see you in."

"No." she said. "I'm sticking with you."

And so, the four of them lay on the terrace sunbathing.

"I'm starving, Dean!" shouted his mother.

"Well go and eat!"

"Come on, Tilly, before we starve to death," she said, catching Tilly's arm before she trotted off and to the restaurant. Tilly, who was kind and pleasant to everyone, went along without complaint.

Dean and Eliza chuckled to themselves.

"We can have a bit of peace now," he said.

An hour later both mothers were back. "Here we are," said his mother, as the two of them lay on their lounges in the shade of their parasols.

In no time at all they were both asleep—and snoring—in the shade.

"Come on," said Dean, "Let's nip to the bar down the road for a bite to eat," and they tiptoed off like two naughty children.

They sat eating and enjoying their food, when a voice called out. "Thought you got rid of us, didn't you?" It was Dean's mother, with Tilly in tow. Dean's mother was a good woman, but a pain in the neck sometimes.

Tilly wisely didn't say a word.

~

When they were home again, Thomas phoned Eliza up. "Mother, I met a girl in America."

"Oh yes!" replied Eliza. "What's new?"

"I'm serious about this girl. I want you to book our wedding. I want the same church that Joseph and Donna were married in."

Tilly, Eliza, Mo, Donna, and Dawn all got involved, and so did her children's stepmother, Eliza's ex husband's wife. There would be five bridesmaids.

Cher, Thomas' girlfriend, had a little girl from a previous marriage.

When Thomas came home on leave, he told them, "Cher's little girl is the same age as Ann's, but she may be a touch bigger."

"We will have to have her measurements for the bridesmaid's dress," noted Eliza.

"Cher will arrive a couple of weeks before the wedding and will bring her dress with her," said Thomas.

Tilly, Eliza, Dawn, and some of the others rallied round to arrange the wedding, while Joseph and Donna sorted out the church. They were all waiting for the bride-to-be and her little girl. Thomas planned to leave the army as soon as he could because all he wanted now was to be with his new family. He approached the appropriate officers who stationed him back in England for the last couple of months of his enlistment.

Everyone was excited because Cher would arrive today.

Before Thomas headed to the airport to pick her up, he asked a favour of Eliza. "Please don't have everyone here when we get back. Ask them to come round after we've had a chance to get settled." Thomas was afraid his large family might overwhelm Cher and her daughter if they appeared all at once.

Hours later there was a *pip pip* outside, and Tilly and Eliza went out. The first thing they noticed was Cher's mass of beautiful curly, red hair and then, her delicate frame. She pulled the seat forward to help her little girl out of the back seat. The child coyly held on to her mother and practically hid behind her. She seemed quite shy.

"Come on," Thomas said to her. "This is Nanny Tilly and Nanny Eliza."

"Come on in," said Eliza, taking the little girl's hand. "I have a present for you."

"Watch her," said Thomas, disappearing with Cher next door. "Cher needs a shower," he explained.

"Yes," replied Eliza. "I bet you need one as well, don't you?"

Thomas laughed. The three of them were going to stay with Jay and his girlfriend, and Tilly would sleep at Eliza and Dean's house.

Eliza and Dean had gone to Majorca with Biron and Viv a couple of weeks earlier, and Eliza bought Spanish dresses there for her three granddaughters. She got one for Cher's little girl as well because she wanted her to know she was one of the family.

Eliza had the dress all ready for her in a bag in the front room.

"Come and see what I have for you," she said, passing the bag over to her.

When she opened the bag and pulled the dress out, her little face lit up.

Ann brought her little girl to play. The two girls, who would both be five years old the next week, played well together. Thomas and Cher gave Ann some money to provide a double birthday party for them.

Finally, the day of the wedding arrived. Thomas looked smart in his evening suit, complete with tails and a top hat, and the five bridesmaids were lovely. But Cher, with her flaming red curls and tiny waist, looked like she stepped out of a bridal magazine.

Dean stood in for Cher's father at church to give the bride away. She was stunning, as were the bridesmaids—all six of them. Cher's mother and sister managed to come over to see them get married. The wedding took place in the beautiful church at Coughton, and Jay was best man. It was a wonderful day filled with beauty, love and happiness.

Jay managed to be best man even though he had a bad back from an injury he got at work. He was waiting for an operation to fuse his discs and had been unable to work for a few months. He would be the fourth one in the family to have a fusion done. That's what the building trade did for them. It was hard work.

In October, the Blackpool Illuminations started. Dawn, her husband, Eliza, her husband, Biron, his wife, Derek and his partner, as well as a lot of their friends were going. There were about twelve of them who had been going there together for a weekend in the last few years. They always had a brilliant time, and all of them got along well.

They started at the pub where they ordered fish and chips as soon as they arrived on Friday night. On Saturday morning, after having a huge fried breakfast, they shopped and played games in the arcades. They only returned to the hotel to change their clothes and have their tea.

Then, they were off to the fair, where they just ambled along. There was no hurry, and Eliza couldn't move fast, anyway. They had all night to wander round the fair. Their favourite thing was a competitive game where they tried to get balls into a slot to make camels race to the finishing line. Whoever got the most balls into the slot moved his camel the farthest and eventually won. They also enjoyed the rides.

Dawn and Biron got on a ride.

"Coming on, Eliza?" one of them called out.

"I don't think so."

"Chicken!" The reply—or maybe the challenge—came back.

"Okay," said Eliza, getting on the ride. As they reached the top, it stopped unexpectedly, giving all the riders a huge jolt.

"Christ! My back!" Eliza gasped. She felt as though her back was broken. She couldn't move or speak. The pain was excruciating. She prayed for the ride to stop, but it seemed to go on forever. When it finally stopped, she couldn't move.

"Come on," said the man running it. "Get out! I have to keep the ride moving."

"Can't you see she's unable to move?" replied Dawn, looking with horror at her mother's face twisted in agony.

"I have to keep the ride moving along!" the man repeated. "For Christ's sake, pull her out!"

It took several of them to get Eliza out, but they managed. The ride was back in motion before they left the platform. They half-carried and half-pulled Eliza along. She wished she could pass out so it wouldn't hurt so much. The pain was that intense.

"Where's the first aid surgery?" Dean asked one of the fair men.

"I think it's over there," he replied.

But it was a struggle to get her there. Every move they made caused more pain for Eliza. When they finally reached the first aid hut, they gently lifted her onto a bed.

"What happened to you?" asked the nurse.

Eliza was so miserable that she couldn't talk so Dean explained what happened.

"The man on the ride should have sent for us," she said. "We would have sent a stretcher."

When the ambulance arrived, the emergency team took Eliza and Dean to the Queen Victoria Hospital. Eliza's pain radiated round the middle of her back, but she couldn't describe which part hurt the most. The hospital was packed with casualties of one sort or another. Eliza felt like she was in a queue like the one at the supermarket when it was especially busy.

At last, it was her turn to see the doctor.

After taking x-rays of her lower back, the doctor came to her. "Nothing shows up on the x-ray."

"I'm sure I felt a crack when it happened," Eliza said.

"Well, nothing shows up on the x-ray," he repeated. "Take these for the pain," he added, dismissing her as he handed her two tablets of Parasetamol.

Eliza was still lying on the bed. It was quite late, and rain was tipping down in torrents outside.

"Off you go. Hop off the bed," said the doctor. "We need it."

Eliza attempted to get up, but she hurt so much that she still couldn't move.

Dean left the cubicle to find the doctor again. "She can't move," he explained.

"Well, get a wheelchair then," he said. "We x-rayed her and checked her over, but we didn't find anything broken," he said. "I'm sure she will feel a lot better tomorrow."

Dean somehow got Eliza off the bed into a wheelchair and pushed her toward the door. They couldn't walk anywhere with Eliza in so much pain, so he rang for a taxi. It seemed an eternity that they waited for the taxi in the hospital's busy entrance way.

"At last," Dean said, pushing the wheelchair to the cab.

Eliza screamed as Dean pushed her over the ramp, off the kerb, and into the road.

"Can you give me a hand, mate?" Dean asked the taxi driver. "My wife's in great pain and she can't stand up."

The taxi driver obliged and asked how Eliza was injured. Dean explained and the two men managed to get her into the cab. They agreed that the filthy night only made matters worse. The taxi driver also helped Dean to get Eliza inside the hotel.

"Thank goodness the stairs are just inside the door," Eliza said.

"How the bloody hell am I getting you up there?" asked Dean, scratching his head. Eliza was kneeling on the stairs. "You try to crawl, and I will push your bottom up."

At last they reached the top, where Eliza crawled on all fours to their room. Then they struggled together until Eliza was on the bed. She was settled only a few minutes when she needed to use the toilet.

"Why didn't you say before?" asked Dean. "Hold on, I will go down and see if the others are back yet. They might be in the bar." He came back with Dawn and her friend Lorraine, and the three of them managed to get Eliza to the toilet and back.

Lorraine drove to the fair with her husband in their estate car. She arranged to take Eliza home the next day so she could be "more comfortable lying in the back seat of their car." Once home, Dean fetched a blanket for Eliza, who would sleep on the settee.

Thank goodness the toilet is downstairs! At least I can crawl there.

The next day Dean and Tilly took Eliza to the hospital after struggling to get her into the car. The doctor asked to see the x-rays taken in the other hospital. "Did they give them to you?"

"No," Eliza replied, lying on the bed.

"Can you pick your leg up?" he asked.

Eliza picked one leg up and then the other.

"I don't think there's anything broken, but I will give you a cortisone injection and tablets to help with the pain." Turning to Dean, he said to "get a mattress downstairs for her and let her lie on that for a couple of weeks."

The next few weeks were hell for Eliza, especially when she wanted to go to the toilet. She crawled on her hands and knees to the bottom stair, and then eased her way round the toilet door. *Thank goodness Tilly's here to help.*

Gradually, the pain eased a bit, and Eliza realised it was a lot higher than where she had been x-rayed. "I don't think I will ever get better," she said to her mother. "It's one thing after another. I have two bad backs now, one at the top and one at the bottom."

"You seem to be as bad as I am," said Jay, who was still out of work waiting for his operation.

"Poor Jay needs that operation," Eliza told Dean.

Christmas came, and Jay still waited for his operation. He could hardly stand, even after he spent two weeks in hospital in traction. It didn't help at all. When New Year's Day arrived, Jay was determined to go out with them." He thought he could manage if he stayed seated.

The pub was jam-packed, with no sign of an empty seat anywhere. One of the men rose and gave Tilly his seat—their friends and neighbours had a great of respect for Tilly. Jay stood, but he was stooped over and obviously uncomfortable. Eliza managed to squeeze in by her friend, and eventually someone brought a chair over for Jay.

"Poor Jay!" said Tilly, looking at her grandson. "He's in a terrible amount of pain, isn't he?"

"Dean and I are going to pay for him to get it sorted as soon as possible," replied Eliza. The next day, she phoned the surgeon's secretary. "Is there any chance that Jay can see the surgeon any earlier?"

"You mean private?"

"Yes, please."

A few days later Jay had his operation.

Dean walked into the ward ahead of Eliza and Jay's girlfriend. "How are you, son?" he asked.

"I'll be glad when the next few days are over," replied Jay, wincing as he turned his head to speak to his father. "I'm due some more painkillers now." Jay was rough for a few days and then he recovered very well. In a short time, he was back at work.

"He's a tough nut, is young Jay," said Tilly.

Eliza, however, worried about him—she thought he went back to building too soon after the operation. "Be careful!" she told him.

"Stop worrying, Mother. I'm as good as new."

"I wish they could put mine right like that," she replied. Her back bothered her all the time, and she would give anything to make it better.

Mark's family grew again as his wife gave birth to another baby girl. Of course, she was lovely. Tilly and Eliza rejoiced over the newest member of the family. They were never too busy to make a fuss over the babies or to baby-sit and help out whenever they could.

The money in Eliza's savings account grew month by month. She had enough money saved for that trip to the Caribbean, but she wasn't sure her bad back would behave while she took the trip. That was on her on her mind when Rainy asked her and Dean if they fancied a trip to the Dominican Islands.

"I have enough saved but I'm a bit worried about my back and breathing." It had been three months since she hurt her back, and it still hurt like hell.

"You have to make your mind up. It's a bargain, but the holiday is next month, so I have to book it tomorrow if we are going," said their friend, "I am afraid if we wait, it will be snapped up."

Dean wondered what to do. "Shall we go for it? It's your dream trip, and your back might be better by then," said Dean.

"Okay, we would love to come."

In the meantime Thomas and his wife got a council house on an estate the other side of town. Apparently, they got it so quickly because he served in the army for nearly ten years. Dawn did the decorating, at which she had a dab hand for them. Family members and friends rallied round to help them, just as they always did. Thomas and Cher took the time to visit each person who helped to thank him or her for the hard work.

Eliza and Dean were off to the Dominican Republic with Rainy and her husband, and they were all excited since none of them had been there before. Tilly, who would look after Eliza's house while she was gone, was happy to have the house and she invited Ann and her daughter to stay with her.

In the Dominican Republic, Dean, Eliza, and friends were a bit unnerved at the airport as townspeople came from all sides, rushing up to everyone and grabbing their travel cases.

What the hell's happening?

Eliza and Rainy clung to their husbands as they were bundled into a little truck. They could have been going anywhere. *Bump. Bump. Bump.* Eliza could feel every dip in the road, and it didn't help that the driver was going fast and seemed to hit every pothole in the poorly paved roadway.

"Oh, my back!" cried Eliza.

At last they reached the hotel, where they were happily surprised that their room had two giant beds. "We don't have to share, do we?"

"No," replied the porter, beckoning their friends to a room a few doors down.

Eliza and Dean had never seen beds as large as these before. They would have one each.

"We will see you after we have washed up and changed," Dean called out to their friends.

"You will have to go on your own," said Eliza. "I'm just going to lie on the bed to rest my back. I'm absolutely knackered."

They had, after all, travelled for twenty hours or more. Eliza soon fell asleep, but she was awakened by the sound of the rain—*pitter patter*—on the large leaves outside. Groaning, she got up, went to the window, and peered behind the curtain through the patio doors. The rain sounded lovely as it plopped on the shrubs with giant leaves near the window and the palm fronds in the distance.

"Food's not bad," announced Dean as he handed her the cob he brought. The next morning they awoke to more rain, tipping down again.

Dean pulled the curtains back. "Look at the size of those raindrops!" he said to Eliza.

An hour later the sun was shining. It was glorious, and drying everywhere.

Eliza hung on to Dean for support as they went downstairs to breakfast. The restaurant was smack on the beach, just like Dean had told her. He guided Eliza to a table on the edge of the restaurant. She took her sandals off and dug her feet into the golden sand, letting it trickle through her toes. Dean went to get their breakfast, leaving Eliza gazing at the blue ocean as glorious sunlight danced on the waves and dolphins leaped in and out of the water. What a beautiful sight! Dean rejoined her, carrying their breakfast on a tray.

"Looks scrumptious," she said, eyeing scrambled eggs on toast and freshly cut fruit.

A girl followed Dean, carrying their juice and coffee.

"That looks nice," said their friends, sitting down beside them.

"Quick, look at those whales going past. What an experience!" said Dean.

After eating, they lay on the beach in sun and then in shade to cool off a bit. The locals came round, flogging their goods.

Dean teased them. "Happy hour—two for the price of one," he called out.

The locals loved it.

Later that evening they decided to walk to the village, which they had heard was about a mile away. Eliza dreaded it because she knew she couldn't walk that far. Dean was caught up in the fun and didn't seem to realize that she was still in pain. They started walking while Eliza hung onto Dean's arm for dear life.

"Hang on a minute," she said. "I have to stop for a rest. She was having a job to breathe, and her back was giving her some stick.

"For fuck's sake!" said Dean. "This is a waste of time. We've only just started out." He beckoned to a local youth who had a small motor-bike. "Can you give my wife a lift to the village please?"

"Fine," replied the local boy. "Five pesos please. I will take her to PJ's Bar. That's the most popular place."

"So they tell me."

The boy stopped outside PJ's and took Eliza inside.

"Wow!" said Eliza. "It looks like something out of a movie. How wonderful!"

The bar was decorated like an old saloon in an early western film, and the local people were quite friendly.

"Drink?" asked the barman.

"Half of lager please," she said.

"Try this bottle of Presidenty," said the barman.

Eliza thought it was lovely the way the cold liquid hit her parched throat.

Finally, Dean and the others arrived. "I see you didn't waste any time," he said, looking at the bottle in her hand. "What's it like?"

"Brilliant, it's got a good kick to it."

That night they all got blotto, not realising that the lager was so strong. They had to take a taxi back to the hotel.

"When we get back home, I'm paying you to see someone about your back and breathing," said Dean.

The holiday was fabulous. Each day, they finished up at PJ's Bar. Even though they tried some others, they ended up there. It had a great atmosphere that seemed to take them back in time.

On their final day on the island, Dean packed the suitcases, while Eliza lay on the bed. He looked at her and sighed. "I'm taking you to see a specialist when we get home."

~

After a couple of days back home, Dean made an appointment for Eliza to see an orthopaedic consultant. The hospital was a lovely place, with plush pink seats, a coffee percolator, and china cups. It was more like a hotel than a hospital.

Dean and Eliza had just finished their coffee when they were called into another posh room.

The doctor examined Eliza. "I think you have a crush fracture to one of your discs, but I will get you x-rayed to make sure."

"Have you injured your back at any other time?" asked the woman doing the x-rays.

"Not really. My first husband used to use me as a punching bag, but I can't say if he damaged my back. I used to hurt everywhere when he hit me." She explained that she suffered from the lower part of her back for years, but it was much worse now. "I'm sure I heard a crack at the time of the accident at the fair."

"You can go now. You will be hearing from us."

"Is that it?" replied Eliza.

"Yes, we don't have you booked for treatment—only diagnosis."

On Saturday morning two weeks later, Dean was just leaving for work, when the postman popped the letters through the door. *This one looks like it's from the hospital*, thought Dean, opening the letter and reading it as he walked upstairs to Eliza. "Wake up," he said, waving the letter in his hand. "Good grief, Eliza, no wonder you have been in agony all these months. You have loads of things wrong with you." Dean listed a crush fracture of the eleventh and twelfth thoracic vertebrae, kyphosis of the lower thoracic spine, and some scoliosis. "Well, at least we know what the matter with you is."

"I told you I heard something crack at the time. At least I know why I have been suffering with my back all these years."

A few mornings later while Dean was getting ready for work, Tilly fell. He heard someone coming down the stairs and called out, "Who's up this early?"

"It's only me," Tilly had replied. "I'm just getting up for a pee."

The next minute, Dean heard a loud noise like a couple of *bumps*, and he found Tilly on her back at the bottom of the stairs. "Are you all right?" he asked, helping her up.

"I'm not sure yet, but I have got to have a wee."

Dean got her to the toilet, waited for her and then helped her to an armchair in the front room.

"I've hurt my back," said Tilly.

Eliza, too, heard the *bump* and went down to investigate. "You carry on to work or you will be late. I will make Mom and me a cup of tea," she said. After drinking their tea, Eliza tried to help Tilly to her feet. "Do you think you can stand up now?" she asked, as she pulled Tilly's arm. Tilly managed to stand, and they both laughed.

"Who's helping who?" said Tilly.

"I think we better get you checked over at the hospital just to be on the safe side." Eliza phoned her sister, explained the situation, and asked her to take them to the hospital.

"Sure I'll be there in fifteen minutes," replied Mo.

They helped Tilly into the car, and were at the hospital in ten minutes. They were laughing, as they couldn't get her out of the car. Eliza was no help, anyway, with her back. Also, Tilly was heavy. She had put a lot of weight on over the last twenty years and weighed about twelve stone now.

Mo went inside to ask for help, and two porters came with a wheelchair to get Tilly out of the car.

"Come on love," they coaxed as they helped Tilly into he wheelchair.

Inside, the nurse who assessed Tilly gave Mo an x-ray slip and they got x-rays taken before they saw the doctor.

"You haven't broken any bones, Tilly, but because of your age we, think you had better stop in for a few days bed rest," he said.

"Okay," she replied.

Mo and Eliza saw their mother settled in the ward.

"It's just for a couple of days, Mom," said Mo. "We had better tell the doctor about mum's diet before we go," she said to Eliza before they left.

Since she had the ulcer, Tilly wasn't allowed to eat fried or acidic foods or aspirin.

The next day, when Mo and Eliza visited, a nurse approached them as they talked with Tilly. "Can you excuse me for one minute please," she said, "while I give Tilly her injection?"

Mo and Eliza left the ward for a few moments.

"I wonder what the injection's for," said Mo.

"It would be for the pain, I expect."

When they returned to the room, Mo approached the nurse "Nurse, can you tell us what the injection was for?"

"It's for thinning Tilly's blood while she's on bed rest," replied the nurse.

"She can't have that. We have nearly lost her once from an ulcer, and no way should they be thinning her blood."

They waited to see the doctor, but it was a different doctor than who they saw the day before. They explained their concerns

"I will cross them off Tilly's chart," he said. "We will have to get her moving about a bit."

The woman in the bed opposite Tilly heard the conversation and called them over. "I will keep my eye on your mother," she said. "I used to be a nurse."

"Thanks," they both replied. Mo and Eliza couldn't believe the doctor authorized those injections. Between the two of them, they kept their brothers and other family members informed.

Later that day, a nurse from the hospital phoned.

Dean told them a nurse from the hospital wanted them to come back straight away. "Apparently Tilly isn't very well."

Mo, Eliza, and Dawn rushed to the hospital wondering what was wrong. They were shocked when they saw Tilly. She was asleep, but she looked dreadful—extremely pale.

"Tilly has a burst ulcer," a nurse said.

Just then, a doctor arrived to look at Tilly. "We are going to move her into a side ward," he said. "We have the blood team coming up to transfuse her."

"If you had listened to us in the first place, none of this would have happened!" fumed Eliza. "She's only here on bed rest and now here she is, dangerously ill."

"We will go down for coffee in the coffee shop, but we will be back in a tick," said Mo.

The three of them phoned the rest of the family to share the bad news. After they had their coffee, they went back to Tilly's side. She was in a side ward where there was extra space having a blood transfusion.

"How bad is it?" asked Mo.

"Well, she's still losing a lot of blood from her back passage but it has slowed down a bit. We are hoping it might heal itself."

Later that night Mo and Eliza were back to see Tilly. The nurse met them, saying the doctor wanted to see them. She said she would page him and tell him they were there.

The two women continued to Tilly's room. "Call us when the doctor gets here," they said.

What a shock they had as they entered the room! Tilly lay unconscious with transfusion drips in both arms and a nurse by her bedside. The door opened.

"The doctor's here," said a nurse, poking her head round the door. "He will see you now."

By this time, Biron and Sam had arrived, and they all went into the doctor's office.

"Hang on," said the doctor. "Just two of you please."

"We all stay!" said Biron.

The doctor could see they weren't going to move. "Okay," he replied. "You know your mother's gravely ill, don't you?"

"Yes, we do. We've been down this road before—this would be a laugh if it wasn't so serious."

"We have two options," said the doctor, ignoring the remark. "One is to take her down to the operating theatre to try and cauterise the ulcer, sealing it via her throat. " He explained that it would be traumatic since the patient had to swallow a camera to guide the surgeon.

"She probably won't make it, she's losing so much blood," he continued, hardly pausing for a breath. "The other alternative is to take her off the blood transfusions and just let her slip away." His last words angered them intensely. "We don't give her any hope either way since she's getting on for eighty—her age is against her."

"You don't know our mother!" Biron replied. "She's as tough as old boots, and we're certainly not going to let her die without a fight." Biron reminded him that the hospital was to blame, anyway. "She only came in for bed rest because she slipped downstairs and now she's dying." With his eyes blazing and his jaw set, Biron finished. "Tell the surgeon to get his gown on. No way are we going to sit and watch her just die if there's the slightest chance of saving her."

Eliza and Mo nipped home for something to eat and then they went back to the hospital. Tilly was still in surgery, so Mo and the others waited in the side ward where their mother received the transfusions and settled down, ready to spend the night if necessary.

Mo and Eliza both dozed off in armchairs, as it was hours since their mother was taken to the operating theatre. They woke as the door opened and stood as Tilly was pushed back into the side ward in her bed. She still had the two drips on her arms.

"We sealed it. All we can do is wait and hope it doesn't start off again." Mo and Eliza stayed with their mother while the rest went home. They sat up all night holding Tilly's hands, willing life back into her.

Gradually Tilly got better and stronger, but at least one family member was with her at all times, making sure she ate the right food. Two weeks later, Tilly was home again, living with Eliza. She couldn't remember any of the trauma and drama she went through.

～

Dawn's husband got Thomas a job as stores manager at the place where he worked. He was pleased with the job, but he was also keen to start his own business one day. Eliza wondered what happened to her shy little boy. *He's not shy anymore.*

Thomas built a bench in his garage and started making mirrors and photo frames, and then he started framing pictures, too. Thomas spent every bit of spare time in his garage working, but he still worked his other job as well. Thomas and Cher had a little boy as well now.

Thomas approached Dawn's husband. "Dave, will you give me a hand to do a boot sale to see if I can sell any of my pictures?"

On Sunday morning at five thirty sharp, they were off to the boot sale. They left early because they wanted to get a good pitch. They didn't do too badly, but they were absolutely frozen to the core by the end of the day.

This became a weekly thing until, one day Thomas decided to open a small store next to the other small businesses in a courtyard at a farm. He went there straight from work, spending every bit of his time working at one job or the other. Then he got a better paying job as manager of another factory—that included a company car.

"Well done, son," said Eliza.

"I'm not stopping there," he said. "This is just a stepping-stone."

Eliza smiled to herself. She still couldn't believe the change in him.

~

Tilly would be eighty soon. The question was, "Shall we do mother a big party for her birthday again—eighty is a milestone birthday!"

All nine of Tilly's children decided to pool a certain sum of money from each of them to put on a good bash for her. It wouldn't be at Biron's café this time, as that was long gone. He built two houses on his car park and turned the café into a large house. They would hire a room at the Alloys Club and invite many of the people who had played down at The Tin House as children. Of course, they were all grown up now with children and grandchildren of their own.

Tilly hadn't seen her brother Billy since her seventy-fifth birthday and wanted to see him again. He was now eighty-three. Eliza knew he was in a nursing home, because his daughter phoned Tilly earlier in the year. He's been in a home a couple of years.

Eliza rang Irene, Billy's daughter, to ask, "Is it all right for Uncle Bill to come to Tilly's eightieth birthday party?"

"Sure," she replied.

"You're quite welcome to come as well," says Eliza, but Eliza knew as she asked that they wouldn't come. They has been invited before but has never turned up, and Bill's wife died years ago.

So, it was all arranged, Thomas would go to pick up Tilly's brother on Friday night, and Mo's husband John would take him back on Sunday night.

On Friday, the eve of the party, Uncle Billy arrived with Thomas about seven thirty. He would stay at Eliza's house this time in the front bedroom. It was a pretty room painted in a light, delicate green with a matching duvet and curtain set. Eliza's grandchildren used the room when they spent the night there.

When they arrived, Eliza was in the kitchen doing her outwork while Tilly sat by her, laying the springs out for her. Thomas came in carrying a small suitcase, a grin all over his face, and Uncle Billy followed behind him. "What are you grinning about?" asked Tilly.

"You will soon see," replied Thomas. "The best of luck, Mother. I don't think you know what you let yourself in for," he said, winking his eye. He started to leave, but retraced his steps. "By the way, here are Bill's tablets. The home said he mustn't keep them himself," another wink, then he was gone.

By this time, Billy was sitting next to Tilly. He started fiddling with the springs, then turning to Tilly, he asked, "How long have you worked here?"

Tilly and Eliza looked at each other. So that's what Thomas meant, poor Uncle Billy had lost his marbles.

"What's your name?" he asked Tilly Eliza and Tilly looked at each other, again. They couldn't help laughing. Bill passed his packet of cigarettes to Eliza, saying, "I want them back tomorrow."

"There's no smoking in this house," stated Eliza. Tilly had given it up when she had been in hospital.

All of a sudden, Billy jumped up, asking who pinched his money. "Oh, there it is, rolling under the table," he said.

"There's nothing there," replied Tilly.

Dean, who was watching TV in the front room, hadn't seen Bill yet, so Eliza went in to him. "Just come and see Bill, he's completely barmy."

Dean walked into the kitchen, holding out his hand. "How're you going on, mate?" he asked.

Bill stood up, shaking Dean by the hand. "Pleased to meet you, now if you'll call a taxi I will be off," he said.

"You're staying here the night," added Tilly.

"Am I?" he replied.

Eliza made a milk drink for Uncle Bill and her mother and then opened a can of lager for herself. *I'm in for a long night tonight.* She started to laugh as she took a swig of lager from the can.

"I want a ciggie now!" demanded Bill, standing up. So, Eliza let Bill have a cigarette in the kitchen because she didn't dare let him to have one outside. He might bugger off. They would just have to put up with the smoke.

Tilly and Eliza both wondered when Billy started smoking. he hadn't smoked the last time he had been here. Eliza watched as he sucked the smoke down his lungs—the smoke twirling 'round the light that's hanging over the press she was working and making her cough and sputter. She hoped he wouldn't want another one before he went to bed.

"Come on, Uncle," I will show you to your bedroom," said Eliza, handing him his tablets. She sat on the bottom of the stairs by the toilet, waiting for Bill to come out.

"Whoops! Missed again!" she heard him say.

Christ! I bet he's peed all over the seat and floor. She managed to get Bill upstairs into the bedroom, watching as he put his pyjamas on. She pulled the duvet and sheet back for him to get in.

"I a' sleeping in that bed?" he said in his Black Country accent. "There be no bloody blankets on it. You do know I stopped with gentry the last time I was over here."

Dean heard the commotion and came up to investigate. "He's not that barmy if he can remember sleeping at Sam's house the last time he came, that was five years ago. Come on, Billy, be a good chap and get in bed," said Dean.

Bill reluctantly got into bed. "But what about the blankets?"

"I will go fetch you one," replied Dean, and he was soon back with the blanket.

"It's a good job you kept some," Bill said.

Eliza sat in the window seat, not moving until Bill was asleep. Eventually, when Bill dozed off, Eliza quietly closed the door and crept downstairs.

"He's bonkers, isn't he?" said Tilly.

"I didn't know he was like this," replied Eliza. "God knows what will happen tomorrow night. Someone will have to watch him all the time."

They all went to bed, and Dean peeped in to check on Bill, who was still fast asleep.

"Thank God for that!" replied Eliza. "I'm knackered."

What's that!" asked Eliza, waking with a start.

It was two in the middle of the morning, and Bill was shouting, "Be anybody there? Is anybody there?"

"Shut him up, Eliza! I have to go to work in the morning!" said Dean.

"What on earth's the matter, Uncle?" she asked, going into him."

"I want a cigarette!"

"It's the middle of the night!" replied Eliza. "Be good and go back to sleep."

"No, I don't care. I'm not getting back in bed until I have had a ciggie!" he said. Eliza tried to reason with him but he kept shouting.

"For Christ's sake, take him downstairs and give him a bloody fag, then maybe we can all get some sleep!" said Dean, coming in the bedroom. "I have work in a few hours time."

"Come on, Uncle," said Eliza, taking Bill downstairs and leading him into the front room. "Only one," she said as he sat down. Getting a cigarette out, she held the match to light it. He started puffing away, but he was not inhaling the smoke, just puffing in and out.

Eliza coughed, and in no time at all the room was full of thick smoke. "Come on, Bill, let's go back to bed," she said, yawning.

"Not until I've had another ciggie!" he stated.

"You just had two, let's go to bed and have another in the morning," replied Eliza.

"I want another one now!" he insisted, grabbing hold of the phone. "And if you don't give me on, I will phone the police. I mean it. It comes to something when I can't have one of my own cigarettes."

"I give in," said Eliza, passing him another cigarette. At that, moment she knew she was up for the night.

Morning came at last, and Eliza heard Dean coming down the stairs. "Bill's fast asleep in the chair, snoring his head off. What a bloody night I've had!" says Eliza.

"I would phone Mo, if I were you. See if her husband will take him back to the home," said Dean. "You've got no chance of watching him all day."

"I'm going to phone Uncle's daughter first to give her a piece of my mind," replied Eliza. "Fancy letting him come, knowing he's like this."

Dean went off to work. "See you just turned twelve," he said, going out the door. "Oh, and good luck."

Dean left work at twelve on Saturdays, and he always said he'd see Eliza after it "just turned twelve" because he insisted he could walk home from work in five minutes or less.

Eliza picked up the phone and rang Bill's daughter. "Why didn't you tell us Uncle's mind has gone? He should never have been allowed to come, he's had me up all night, and I'm not in very good health myself."

"O a, e a naughty boy", she replied, in her Black Country accent.

"Is that all you have to say?" replied Eliza. "You'd better get on to the home and tell them he will be coming back today." She replaced the phone, but soon picked it up again to ring her sister, Mo. "There's a change of plans, Mo. Billy will be going home today." She then proceeded to tell her about the night she had with him.

Eliza gave Tilly and Billy their breakfast, then Tilly and Eliza tidied up before Eliza sat down to do some more presswork. She could do with going to bed really, but there was no way she dared to leave Bill. Tilly sat beside her, and Bill sat beside Tilly.

Despite being tired, Eliza couldn't help laughing at the things her Uncle was doing and saying. She cast her mind back five years ago, when they had last seen him and he had been perfectly all right then.

Tilly suddenly burst out laughing. Bill was looking for his money again.

Eliza crept out of the front door, quietly closing it behind her, and then she went next door. "Come with me," she said to Jay's girlfriend Zoë. "I know it's a shame but Uncle Bill has had us in stitches."

Zoë followed Eliza through the back door, where Tilly and Bill were sitting. As Eliza walked back in, Bill looked up, and said "Ai sin yow sum were afor?"

They all burst out laughing, with Bill joining in.

At last Mo and her husband arrived. "What's going on?" asked Mo.

"I'm just waiting for a lift home," replied Bill. "I only came for the party."

Mo laughed as she opened the car door for Bill to climb in. He turned to Tilly and Eliza. "Thanks for 'avin me! I will come and stop again some time."

They all laughed.

"Not if I see you coming first," replied Eliza under her breath.

"I hope I don't go like that when I'm older," said Tilly.

"I'm sure you won't," replied Eliza.

The hairdresser came to do their hair for this special night with Tilly. She knew she would have a good night, although she had no idea about the number of people who would be there. Tilly looked radiant as she walked into the room.

"Surprise, surprise!" Everyone shouted at that moment. She was surrounded by family and friends, as well as a lot of the kids who used to play down The Tin House. They all said what a fabulous place The Tin House had been, and Tilly was elated! It was a wonderful night, and Tilly slept like a log that night.

Only a few weeks later, Bill's daughter phoned with the news that Uncle Billy died. Biron's son took Tilly and Eliza over for his funeral—the first time any of them ever went to Bill's house.

Thomas was interested in a pair of four hundred year old cottages for sale in Sambourne, but they were in a terrible state—worse than the one his Granddad Jim did up for Joseph and Eliza years ago. The cottages had holes all over the place so rainwater poured in just about everywhere. It was hard to imagine people still lived like this in the nineteen nineties. Thomas was determined to buy them, even though he had only owned his council house for a couple of years after leaving the army.

"I hope you know what you're doing," Eliza said to him. "Don't run before you can walk, son."

"You worry too much," he replied. "You have to speculate before you accumulate."

"I know that, but look what happened to us when we bought that shop!"

"That's not going to happen to me."

"It's only a couple of weeks ago that I had to give you your little girl's dinner money," said Eliza.

Thomas approached Michael about the caravan he had, although it's more like a mobile home.

"Sure you can have it," he replied, so Thomas and Cher bought the two cottages and moved into the caravan on the land with their two children. It took him months and months to get the cottages finished. Finally, though, he had two absolutely beautiful homes in his name.

"There's credit due to him," said Dean.

Thomas' houses were in small posh village where Sam lived. Jay was doing his house up, the ex council house he bought with Tilly. He still worked for Ray, who still refused to speak to Dawn and Eliza after all these years.

"Ray hurt himself at work today," said Jay, walking into his mother's house after work, explaining that Ray fell down a ladder. "He broke his back! You should have heard the thud. You know how big he is."

"Don't tell Tilly, until I speak to Marge," said Eliza, who then, picked up the phone and dialled. "Is that you, Marge? What's this about Ray breaking his back?"

"Yes, he has a fracture in his back," replied Marge. "I will give you a call tomorrow to tell you how he is."

"Do you think I can come and see him?" asked Eliza hopefully.

"No, don't do that. He's still refusing to see you."

Eliza took Tilly to Ray's house to see him, but she remained outside in the car, thinking about the letter. *Who,* she wondered, *sent it, and do they realise the heartache they caused us over the years?*

315

Eliza waited for about half-an-hour, knowing her mother would have asked Ray if she could have gone in. He must have said no again. Eliza would never give up her brother. She still remembered that he helped her often in the past, lending her pounds, letting her drive his new car, and housing her children.

At last, Tilly came out of the house. "He wouldn't see you, Eliza," she told her.

"Never mind. At least he knows I'm asking about him. Surely he's not going to let this feud last for ever."

Three weeks later Ray was driving the van again.

"Blimey! He recovered quickly," remarked Tilly. "I remember when you did yours, Eliza. You were in agony for months."

"I still am, Mom."

Jay came home from work. He had a work van now. "Mom," he said, popping in to see her. "I think something's wrong with Ray he hit the kerb twice on the way home, one of the chaps says. He actually hit the bumper of the van in front of them. The chap made Ray stop and change places with him. Ray didn't realise he had done it."

Marge made an appointment for Ray with the doctor for the next day. "I will make an appointment at the hospital for some tests," said the doctor. "You shouldn't wait very long you will probably hear in a few days. I'm going to phone them myself after surgery."

"Let's get the fish and chips on the way home. It's chip night tonight," said Ray.

"You remembered that then," replied Marge.

Ray loved his fish and chips. Marge did the bread and butter and put it on the table in the kitchen. Ray was already tucking into his dinner. Marge sat opposite him. Then she noticed that when he tried to stick the fork in a chip he kept missing it. At that moment she knew something was seriously wrong with him.

"Eat it with your fingers," she told him.

A few days later Marge took Ray to see the specialist at the hospital, holding onto his arm as he was very unsteady and kept walking over the flower bed. At last, she got Ray inside.

"He will have to do a scan and some other tests on you," the specialist told Ray. "You will have to stay in hospital for a few days."

Marge went home, made herself a cup of tea and then got on the phone. She told her son and daughter first, and then, she phoned Eliza. "Be careful what you say to Tilly. Don't worry her yet. We won't know what's wrong with him until he has those tests."

On Saturday, Eliza lay on the settee because her breathing was bad, while Tilly napped upstairs. Dean and Jay were building a wall and putting new gates up for both houses. Kelvin, one of Jay's mates, who also worked for Ray, was outside helping with he gates. Eliza was on pins and needles because this was the day Marge had an appointment with Ray's doctor to learn the results of his scans and tests. Eliza was just dozing off when Marge phoned.

"I have bad news. Ray has two tumours on his brain, and they have given him three months to live," she said quietly. "They think that's why he fell off the ladder and broke his back and also why he never felt much pain."

Eliza didn't know what to say, but she managed to tell Marge how sorry she was and to offer to help in any way Marge needed her. Marge immediately accepted.

"Do me a favour. Will you tell everyone else for me? I just can't cope talking to anyone at the moment."

Tears were already streaming down Eliza's cheeks before she got outside. She tried to tell Dean, Jay, and Kelvin, but she couldn't speak. She was sobbing uncontrollably by this time.

"What's wrong?" asked Dean, guiding her back into the house as Jay and Kelvin followed behind. He put the kettle on. "I will make some coffee, and then you can tell us what the matter is."

"It's Ray!" Eliza blurted out. "He has two tumours on his brain. Oh, God, he's going to die!"

They all went silent, but then Jay disappeared next door, absolutely gutted. Soon he was back with his girlfriend Zoë, and she was crying as well.

"Marge wants me to tell the others for her," said Eliza. "I can't face telling anyone at the moment."

"Would you like me to do it?" asked Zoë.

"Thanks," she replied, between sobs. How on earth could she tell her mother, when she came down from her afternoon nap? How could this be happening? Ray was such a big strong, strapping chap, and this was a bolt out of the blue. *Please, don't let it be true.*

Eliza was in the front room lying back on the settee when she heard Tilly coming downstairs. She could hear the *bumpity bump* as she came down on her bottom. She had done that ever since her fall. Eliza then heard the click as her mother switched the kettle on and the clatter of the cup on the saucer as she made herself a drink. *I will wait until she's finished her tea before I tell her.*

Tilly came into the front room and got settled in her favourite chair.

Eliza asked, "Did you have a good sleep, Mom?"

"Fine," she replied. Looking at Eliza's flushed face, Tilly asked," Have you been crying?"

"Oh, Mom," burst out Eliza. "It's Ray, they reckon he has a tumour on his brain," not telling her he had two and that they were secondary tumours, meaning that they came from cancer elsewhere in his body .

"He's not going to die, is he?" cried Tilly.

Eliza never answered, she walked back into the kitchen to get some tea on, and then she made a few sandwiches.

"Ray's such a strapping chap," said Tilly, sitting at the kitchen table. "I can't believe this is happening."

Eliza put her arms round her mother, and they both cried together.

The family usually went out Saturday nights, but tonight no one felt like going out. Marge called Tilly to arrange to take her to see Ray the next day.

"How is he?" asked Eliza, as Marge brought Tilly back.

"He's ever so cheerful. it's as if he doesn't know what was wrong with him. Oh, and Eliza, he finally asked to see you and Dawn. You can go tomorrow if you want."

The next night Eliza and Dawn cautiously walked to the entrance of the Ray's ward. He was looking at the door, and his face lit up when he spotted them and beckoned them in. Dawn and Eliza sat by the bed. Ray was talking away as if nothing had ever happened between them. But whether he had put it to the back of his mind or had just forgotten the letter, they would never know.

"I'm glad I'm not a diabetic," Ray said out of the blue.

They knew his mind was playing tricks on him although sometimes he said things that were quite normal. Earlier, the specialist told Ray he would give him radium treatments to reduce his brain's swelling, but then he changed his mind.

Ray's son was furious and went to see the doctor. "How dare you raise my dad's hopes up like that and then refuse to treat him?"

As a result, the doctor reconsidered and arranged the radium treatments.

At this time, Biron's sister-in-law was also battling a cancerous brain tumour. She was only in her thirties and was very ill. Every day the phones were going non-stop as family members and friends checked on both of them.

Ray was home again, but he went every day for a radium treatment. Marge was combing Ray's once thick hair, which was just starting to go grey. She gently retrieved the thick clumps of hair that came out in the comb and placed it on the patio table. Then she sat and watched blue tits fly down and pick the hair up in their tiny beaks. They took the hair, to line the tit boxes that hung from both the apple trees in the middle of the lawn. Loss of hair was one of the side-effects of radium treatments.

"The birds love your hair, Ray," she called in to him.

Ray now spent most of his time in bed now, hardly moving out of the bedroom at all. Tilly and Eliza were sitting by Ray's bedside when Ray asked if they'd like to hear him play the organ. The electric organ was in his bedroom.

He struggled to get out of bed, but he was determined to play his beloved organ. Finally, he managed to sit on the stool, putting his hands on the keys as he tried to play, but his fingers wouldn't go where he wanted them to go. He couldn't understand why, and quietly flopped back on the bed, looking puzzled. Ray bought the organ about fifteen years ago when had packed up smoking. He used to smoke about eighty cigs a day so he did well to pack it in. He had gone cold turkey and was still Eliza's inspiration.

Two weeks later, Ray's bed was moved downstairs since he and Biron's sister-in-law were deteriorating rapidly. By Friday of the same week, the sister-in-law passed away, and Marge cautioned them not to tell Ray.

That same night, Tilly, Eliza, and Ann went to see Ray, who seemed to be fast asleep.

As Ann said goodbye to him, he opened his eyes and said, "I never realised you were here, Ann. Wake me up the next time you come." He liked Ann, as most people did.

On Sunday, Michael, who was always popping in and out, called in to see Ray. He found his brother shouting, saying his legs were killing him. He was already on morphine tablets, but he could no longer swallow, so he couldn't take any. Marge phoned the doctor, who decided to put a line straight into his veins. When Eliza and Tilly came by later and asked about him, Marge said, "He's fast asleep at the moment but he was in terrible pain this morning. He hasn't murmured since the line has been in his chest."

When they stood up to go, Eliza asked Marge, "Do you want me to come back, and sit with you?" Marge said she would be all right.

Eliza went in to say bye to Ray. It had been a scorching hot day, so the window by Ray's bed was open, and there was a gentle breeze drifting through it. "Blimey, Marge! It's quite cold over here," said Eliza, touching Ray's arm. "Ray's freezing cold."

Marge came over, felt Ray's leg, and shut the window. "I didn't realise it was that cold over here. It's been such a hot day." She pulled the blanket up over Ray.

"We're off now don't forget to phone if you want me to come back."

Jay heard his mother's car pull up and came into her kitchen, just as she was putting the kettle on. "How is he, Mom?" he asked.

"I don't think he's going to be here very long," replied Eliza, stifling a sob. She switched the kettle off before answering the phone.

"It's me, Marge Ray's dead!" she cried. "I poured myself a stiff drink after you went, sat on the settee to relax a bit, and then it dawned on me—I couldn't hear Ray breathing." She said the doctor was on his way and refused Eliza's offer to come back, saying, "I don't want to see anyone."

Eliza had to tell Tilly that her first born son was dead. She looked at Tilly, but her mother spoke first.

"It s Ray, isn't it?"

Eliza just nodded her head. They hugged each other and sobbed their hearts out.

"I can't believe it," said Dean. "What must it be like for Biron and his wife? She has lost her sister and he has lost his brother two days apart!"

They were both in the same mortuary. What a horrific week! The funeral for Biron's sister-in-law was Thursday, and of course, they all went. Ray's funeral followed on Friday. The majority of the mourners were the same people at both funerals.

As they followed the hearse on the way to the cemetery, Eliza thought of all the times they went on holiday. Ray was always in the lead then. This would definitely be the last time he would lead them. As she dabbed at the tears that ran down her cheeks, she realised this was the saddest week in twenty years—that's how long it was since their father, Jim, died.

Tilly became a bit absent-minded after Ray's death, so when Dean and Eliza went out on a Saturday night, they got two of the grandchildren down to look after her. Eliza has put notes on all the plugs. PLEASE DO NOT SWITCH OFF OR ON. Tilly had switched the freezer off the week before, and they hadn't noticed it for a few days, so Eliza had to throw the contents away. She has also put a note on the bottom of the stairs. DO NOT GO TO BED. The family thought it was the shock of losing Ray he had been her rock, as well as her beloved eldest son.

Most of in the family went to a medieval night at a castle, and they hired a coach. They sang all the way there, and Jay was full of beans. He had just told Eliza his girlfriend was pregnant.

They were all eating and drinking. The main course was over, and they were just starting their desserts, when the gang of women who sat at the next table started throwing bits of bread at them.

All of a sudden, a big blob of cream came flying across to the table. The women were laughing, and that was all it took to set everyone off. Tilly's gang could never resist a laugh. So they all started throwing it back and then at each other. The cream and jelly was flying everywhere.

It was hilarious, but the people running the place didn't think it funny. "Come out, you lot," they were told. "Out!

"We started it!" yelled the girls on the other table.

"This is how a medieval banquet should be. But don't worry, we're leaving," said one of the women sitting on the other table.

At that moment, a clot of cream hit one of Tilly's daughters-in-law smack in the face. From the way she looked, she was fuming. She stood up, wiping the cream off her face. Then she walked round the table to Mark. *Whack!* Straight across his face!

Mark didn't see it coming and was furious. Only a couple of them were aware of what was going on. he jumped up as if to hit back, but then saw who had hit him. "I should have known it was you. You're fucking crackers," he said to her.

At that moment, Jay flicked some cream at Mark, oblivious to what had happened. It hit Mark smack in the centre of his face. Mark was furious, and there was another big row.

"You ought to be ashamed of yourselves," said Eliza. "We are all grieving for Ray—he just died."

After she had a shower the next morning, Eliza thought she had better go to see if Ann was all right because she was blotto the night before, absolutely out of her brain. As Eliza neared her house, she saw that the door was wide open. She called Ann's name, but there was no answer.

Eliza went upstairs, and there was Ann fast asleep. She still had the pale blue medieval maiden's dress on, and her hair was matted with jelly and cream. The room reeked—the smell was just terrible—a mixture of vomit and the cream in her hair.

Eliza shook her awake. "Are you all right? Come on, I will run you a bath." She went downstairs to make Ann a cup off tea while the water was running in the bath.

"Drink this up," she said, going over to the bedroom window. "Let's get rid of this stench."

They spent the rest of the day trying to wash their clothes. Later that day, Ann phoned Eliza. "Mom, how can I get the grease marks out of this dress? It's all stained where the cream had been."

"I don't know. Let's hope they don't notice when we take them back. I think everyone's going to be in the same state."

Eliza developed terrible chest pains and had a job to breathe.

"Come on," said Dean. "I'm taking you to the hospital."

They examined Eliza and gave her a nebulizer, a machine that converted a liquid medicine to a fine, moist spray. She had to take in the mist by inhaling it through a tube attached to the nebulizer to ease her breathing.

"You have pleurisy," said the doctor. "You will be in for about two weeks."

"What exactly is the matter with her?" asked Dean.

"Well, the good news is she hasn't got cancer. The bad news is her lungs are knackered," replied the doctor.

"Will they get any better?" Eliza butted in.

"I'm sorry, but no they won't."

Derek and his girlfriend came to see her. He and his wife had parted years earlier, and Derek had problems with his throat for ages. He'd been back to the doctor's several times, and each time he was told there was nothing wrong. Everybody else knew there was something wrong—he talked as if he has gravel in his throat. The last time he went, his girlfriend, Gill, went with him and insisted he see a specialist about it.

Derek had just had his second visit with the specialist.

"How did you get on?" asked Eliza.

"Not very good," he replied gruffly. "The doctor says it is cancer of the pharynx. I've got to have radium treatment at the Q.E."

Derek was scheduled for twenty radium treatments, and after a few treatments, they said it was shrinking. "I'll tell you what," said Derek. "It still feels like the lump is still in my throat. Mother doesn't know, does she?"

"No, we don't want to upset her."

A few weeks later Eliza was back in hospital with pneumonia and the chest infection, again. Back on to the drip. *I'm not going to beat this. It's two weeks and I'm no better at all.* After a couple more days, the pneumonia was gone, but the infection persisted.

Her sister-in-law, Karen, her brother Sam's wife, came to visit her.

"You know what you need?" she asked.

"What?" asked Eliza.

"A bloody good holiday!"

"I think you may be right. Book one up somewhere nice and hot."

The next afternoon Eliza's sister-in-law was back. "I found a brilliant bargain so I booked it up. We fly to Antigua a week Monday."

"Wow! That's super," replied Eliza, "but I have to get out of here first."

When Dr. Vathenum came on his ward duties, she spoke. "I'm going on holiday a week Monday, I need to get out of here," she told him.

"I agree. You need to go home, but I wouldn't recommend that you go all that way on holiday," he replied. "You just seem to be picking up everybody else's germs in here. You can go home today." It was Friday, and the doctor gave her antibiotics to take for a week, but he insisted that she come back on Tuesday for a bronchoscope so he could see what was happening in those lungs.

Eliza improved slightly over the weekend, and when Tuesday arrived, she had bronchoscopes. The doctor came to see her in the recovery room.

"I'm sorry," he said, "Your lungs have had it. Are you still going on that holiday?"

"I certainly am!"

"I can only give you one week's supply of antibiotics, so go to your own doctor and ask for enough to see you all right for two more weeks, and I will see you when you get back."

On Thursday, Eliza asked Dawn to take her to see a one of the doctors in the local practice, a woman's doctor, because she had not been able to get in with her own general physician.

"What can I do for you?" she asked, but Eliza couldn't answer for a few seconds. She was still trying to catch her breath. "You're in a bit of trouble, aren't you?"

Eliza was gasping every few seconds as she slowly explained everything to her. The doctor looked at Eliza in amazement. "You're never going on holiday in that state, are you?"

"Yes, my sister-in-law organised a wheelchair to take for me. I look at it this way. if I'm going to die, I will die happier in the sunshine, enjoying myself."

"Well, I have got to admire you, but I still don't think you should go," she replied.

Tilly was going to Thomas and Cher's to stay. While Eliza was away in hospital, though, she stayed with Dawn. However, Dawn was ready for her own holiday. She was going to Blackpool to see the lights. It was Sunday night, and Eliza lay in bed, wheezing with every breath she took.

Dean turned to her. "Eliza, we can't go to Antigua with you in that state, You can hardly breathe."

"Don't worry, I will be all right."

They were taking one of their granddaughters with them— Sadie more or less lived with them anyway, as her mother, Ann, and father split up when she was a baby.

Dean pushed Eliza up the steps to the plane and her brother pulled her. *What a sorry state I must look as I board the plane!* Eliza looked out of the window, wondering whether she would see England again. *Antigua, here we come!*

The hotel was wonderful—right on the beach, and their rooms were near the pool. The place was quite deserted. There were very few people near by. After all, it was November, a quiet time in the islands. The holiday was booked "room only" and they got a shock when they went for breakfast. A slice of toast cost a pound. Christ! They weren't going to get very fat at these prices. It was a good thing that they had packed crisps and biscuits to bring with them.

"Will you push me to the side of the pool by the steps, I'm going in for a swim?" asked Eliza.

"Be careful what you're doing," replied Dean, as she eased herself down the steps and slid into the warm water.

"It's wonderful!" she called out, as she started to do a bit of breaststroke. "The pool isn't big. It's fabulous."

"The water's really warm," she called out to the others. Eliza managed to reach the other side, where she had a rest. Then she swam back.

"Come on out now," Dean called her. "I will help you out."

Eliza lay in the sun. Its hot rays were invigorating, warming her whole body. She felt a lot better already. *What a beautiful place this is!*

That evening they ate in the hotel. The food was expensive, but it was also first class.

The next day Eliza swam even farther.

"At this rate, you will be swimming the channel," remarked her brother, Sam.

Dean came back from a walk up the beach, saying, "There's a restaurant and bar up the beach. The menu looks quite good and it's a lot cheaper than here. Shall we try it tonight?"

"How will we get Eliza there?"

"We will push her in the wheelchair" And, so that night they pushed Eliza up the beach. What a laugh!

"Christ! This is hard work!" said Dean.

"Try to push her along the harder sand, by the edge of the water," replied Sam.

All of a sudden, the tide came in, and Dean left Eliza in the wheelchair, the water running all over his feet. He moved up the beach a bit until the tide waned.

Sam's little boy started to cry, "Don't leave her!"

"I'm not," said Dean. As the tide waned, he pushed Eliza out of range of the water.

"Can I push the cripple-chair?" a little voice called out. It was a local boy.

"It's too hard for you to push," replied Dean, and they later found out the boy was the son of the man who looked after all the boats for the hotel. He lived with his father, and they lived and slept in the boat shed. The boy's name was One-Love and he was ten years old, the same age as Eliza's granddaughter. He played in the sand with Sadie and Sam's son.

When his father called him away, One-Love kept looking at them, so Dean called him over. "Do you want a drink?" he asked him.

"I can have a drink, but I mustn't play with the children," he replied.

"Why not?" asked Sam.

"My father thinks you will not like me playing with them."

Sam went over to his father. "One-Love is welcome to play with the children if he wants to. By the way, do you know anyone that does taxis?"

"I will find out for you," and he was soon back with an older man. The man said he had a limousine, so they negotiated a price for him to take them out for the day, hoping there would be room for the wheelchair.

The next morning after breakfast, they went out to the front of the hotel, looking around for the limo. The only car there was an old banger, with a man polishing the bonnet. The man had his back towards them. Then all of a sudden they laughed .

The man turned round. "This is my limo," he said with a proud look on his face, still polishing as he spoke. It was amazing that the car held together so well there were bits of string holding one of the doors on.

"Come on then," he said. "Get in." They all climbed in. There were holes in the seats, with all the stuffing coming out, and one could see the road through the floor.

"We will be lucky if we get anywhere in this," remarked Sam quietly. "Are there any cheap stores about where we can get beer and food?" he asked.

The man started the car up and off they went. The first stop was a giant warehouse. "You wait in the car," Dean said to the women and children as he and Sam make their way inside. While they were in there, the driver again polished his car, which really was his pride and joy. Dean and Sam were soon out with the food and bottles of pop and beer.

The driver took them to lots of different places and wonderful beaches their favourite was Blackwood Beach, where there wasn't a soul in sight—just the sea and them! The water was crystal clear. On the way back, they stopped at the warehouse again and stocked up with drink and biscuits before they made their way to the hotel. They took their own drinks to the poolside in buckets of ice.

What a fabulous holiday it had been. Eliza's chest infection was entirely gone, and now it was time for her appointment at the hospital.

The doctor was amazed at how much better she seemed. "The climate there certainly suited you," he said.

"It certainly did." I think the swimming in the warm water helped."

On Christmas Eve, the family usually went out—except for those who had small children and usually met at one of the pubs. They had a good sing song, but Eliza was coughing her head off.

"I'm sorry," she said. "I'm going home. I can't sit in all this smoke. You stay," she said to her mother. Eliza knew someone would bring Tilly home.

"No, I will come with you."

By March, there were lovely flowers in the garden. Eliza said the spring flowers had the loveliest colours. Tilly sat in the armchair, while Eliza lay on the settee next to her, watching the birds fluttering on the patio and lawn in the early spring sunshine.

CHAPTER 18

E liza relied on the telephone.
There was always a phone by her side whether she lay on the settee, was in bed, or anywhere else in the house. She was grateful that she could talk with her sisters, daughters, or friends when she was lonely and, more importantly, keep tabs on her family at large. She never mentioned her worries. Since she had been sick, though, she knew her life—or even someone else's life—might depend on immediate access to emergency care. So there were several telephones throughout the house.

Eliza and Dean were fast asleep when the phone rang. She glanced at the clock, then picked up the phone. It was twenty to six.

"Hi ya, Mom. It's me, Jay. We have a baby boy. He was just born."

"I never heard the car," said Eliza.

"No, I rolled it back onto the road so as not to wake you."

"Come on, Eliza, let's go and see the new baby," Dean said later that night.

"You will have to push me to the ward in a wheelchair," replied Eliza. "I can't walk all that way."

The baby was adorable. He lay on his back asleep, snuggled in a blue blanket with one arm thrown up next to his head. His mouth moved in a sucking motion as if he was dreaming of food. Dean and Eliza were happy to welcome the newest member of the family. Later, they were at home watching television with Tilly when the phone rang.

Dean answered, but Eliza could tell by Dean's responses that somebody was upset. "I will pass you over to Eliza," he said, finally handing her the phone.

It was Jill's husband Graham, and Eliza immediately told him she had been thinking of them. "I was going to give you a ring tomorrow about our good news."

Dean was trying to get Eliza's attention, by putting his hand to his mouth and shaking his head as if to tell Eliza to shut up.

She sensed from Dean's motions that she was on the wrong track, and quickly and quietly added, "What's the matter, Graham?"

"It's our Steven," said Graham, referring to his son. "Jill found him dead on the kitchen floor this morning!"

Eliza was shocked. Steven was twenty-one years old.

Graham went on to say his wife was in a "terrible state."

"I can imagine. Tell her I will be over first thing in the morning," said Eliza.

"What is it you were going to tell me?"

"I don't think I can tell you now," Eliza replied.

"Come on, I can take it."

"Jay's girlfriend gave birth to a little boy this morning," replied Eliza.

"What time was he born?" asked Graham.

"About twenty to six."

"That's about the time they think Steven died!"

The next morning Eliza picked Dawn up to go over to Jill's house.

"What happened to Steven?" Dawn asked, but Eliza didn't know what caused his death.

She was so shocked that she hadn't asked Graham, and she knew that Graham and Jill might not have known that then, anyway. Jill and Eliza both had five children, and they even gave birth on the same day with their third babies, which for her was Ann. At last, they reached Jill's house about twelve miles away.

Jill looked up as Eliza and Dawn came into the kitchen. She was surrounded by family members, and the air was thick with smoke. Graham walked over to the window.

"Let's get some fresh air in the room," he said, opening it as he thanked Eliza for coming. "I'm really pleased to hear about Jay's baby. I needed some good news."

Eliza put her arm round Jill and patted her on the back. "What happened?" she gently asked. She hated seeing her friend like this. They had been friends since they were old enough to toddle as infants, and this was the first time she didn't know what to say to her.

Apparently, Steven came home in high spirits the night before he died after he had a few drinks with his mate. He joked with his parents and fell asleep on the carpet by the radiator in the kitchen. Jill went back into the kitchen about an hour later and covered him with a duvet and popped a pillow under his head as she had many on many occasions. Then she went to bed.

When Graham got up at five a.m. for work, he actually sat by his son and drank his tea before he left for work at six. It was light when Jill got up later, and she could see her son as she walked in the kitchen. She knew straight away that he was dead.

Jill couldn't forgive herself for Stephen's death. She thought she should have prevented it somehow. Steven was well-known, and well-liked, and there were hundreds at his funeral. Now, Graham didn't dare to leave Jill alone now so he asked for his redundancy from work, in order to stay at home with her.

"It's only me," Dawn called out as she walked into her mother's house. "Fancy going to The Crown for a drink and a bite to eat?" she asked Tilly and Eliza.

"I have a load of greens and potatoes left from yesterday," replied Eliza. "I'm just going to fry it up. We can have it with some corned beef and brown sauce on it"

"Yum, that sounds good. You sit there. I will do the dinner," Dawn offered. "Tilly can't have sauce on hers, can she?" she asked.

"No," replied Eliza. "We don't want her tummy upset again, do we?"

"Pass me a pickled onion will you please," said Eliza, when lunch had started.

Dawn passed the jar over.

"I will have a couple as well. I could just eat one of those," said Tilly, licking her lips.

"You know you can't have one, don't you, Nan?" Dawn piped in. She was just about to pop another forkful in her mouth.

"Stop!" said Tilly. "Don't put that in your mouth. Look, it's crawling with ants." Dawn dropped the fork back on the plate.

"There are no ants," replied Eliza, crunching on her pickled onion.

"There!" Tilly was pointing to a speck of sauce.

"It's nothing," said Eliza.

"I can't eat it now, I was really enjoying it, too," said Dawn, walking up to the top of the garden, scraping the food off her plate for the birds. "Poor Tilly! I hope she doesn't get any worse."

"I do too. I hate to think the time might come that I won't be able to cope with Mother."

Except for her brain, Tilly was incredibly fit. She tried to keep busy with little chores like peeling potatoes.

Another day that week, Eliza tapped on the bathroom door. "How much longer are you going to be in there, Mother?"

"I can't get out. I'm stuck in the bathtub," she said. "Could you come in and help me?"

Eliza gingerly opened the door. Her mother was sitting in the empty bath, naked, with a big grin on her face. She had pulled the plug out with her toe. Eliza tried and tried but she couldn't budge her.

"I'm not strong enough, Mom, I will have to phone Dawn," she said. "Let's hope she hasn't gone out."

Dawn laughed when she heard about the situation. "I will be with you as fast as I can," she said.

Eliza got two towels, draped them 'round her mother, and then made them both a cup of coffee. She sat on the edge of the bath, waiting for Dawn to arrive.

"Have you got a film in your camera?" Dawn, asked, laughing. "This is a hilarious sight!"

"I think I have," replied Eliza, going in the lounge to fetch her camera. Snap! "I got you on film, Mom."

"Bloody hell, Tilly!" said Dawn, puffing and struggling, trying to pull her out while Eliza sat on the bottom of the stairs watching, and crying with laughter. In fact, all three women were laughing Dawn finally managed to get her grandmother out.

"That's the last bath you'll have!" said Eliza. "In the future, I will get someone in to help you shower."

Biron was known in the building trade now, and at the moment, he was doing the best of all Tilly's children. He was a well-established builder, but the others weren't far behind. Jay and his mate took over his Uncle Ray's business just before he died, and his brother Mark worked with him, too.

Thomas decided to make a go at the packing business. He had started to get a lot of outwork from a factory and then sublet it out to outworkers. He still did other jobs as well. Thomas was doing well enough to employ three full-time people.

Tilly was napping, and Eliza was doing the crossword in the paper. All of a sudden Eliza was racked with pain. It was just like electric shocks running all the way down her chest and back, and she struggled to breathe. Eliza managed to grab the phone at her side to call Dean's workplace.

"I'm dying!" she gasped and ten minutes later Dean was taking her to hospital. Eliza was admitted straight away. They immediately started a drip and put her on oxygen. At night, they added a breathing treatment that included moist steam mixed with medicine that she breathed in and out on a special tube. Her pain continued.

One day she cried because the pain was unbearable. Michael and Catharine, who were visiting before they left for a six-week visit to her family in Australia, were so alarmed that they called for the nurse. She assured them that she had already called the doctor, who was on his way.

The doctor soon arrived. "You will have to have some morphine. I don't know what the pains are." He told her he would have to do another bronchoscope tomorrow.

He paused a moment and suggested that he could give her lungs a rest by sedating her and putting her on a ventilator for a few days, if she liked.

"Not on your life!" was Eliza's answer.

The next day, the bronchoscope revealed "loads of black muck" on and in her lungs and an infection with the pseudonymous Aeruginosa bug. Again, the doctor said that her lungs had had it.

That same day, Thomas and Dean asked to see him. The doctor arrived, shook their hands and asked why they sent for him.

"I want to know if my mother can have a lung transplant." said Thomas.

The doctor looked at him. "I can ask," he said, "but I already have two people on the list at the Queen Elizabeth Hospital."

Eliza recovered enough to go home with a prescription for one antibiotic tablet a week to try to prevent infections.

"Take one at the same time each week," the doctor said, giving her an appointment in two weeks time. During this period, Dean bought her a nebuliser. the machine that delivered a moist, medicated air to her lungs to help her breathe. Two weeks later, Eliza kept her appointment with her doctor.

"How do you feel?" he asked.

"No worse. I have my Ventalin and Atrovent in my nebuliser." She gasped with every breath she took. "It's horrible being like this. I was always full of get up and go—I loved dancing before I had this bad chest and back."

"I can imagine," he said sympathetically. "You know your son asked me about a lung transplant. Do you still want to see about it?"

"I'm not sure," she replied. "It sounds very frightening."

"I have been in touch with a very good consultant in Weymouth Road, London. He says he will see you, but he's private so you will have to pay. Do you want to see him? It's your only chance."

"Okay," replied Eliza nervously.

While Eliza was in hospital, Jay and Zoë, his girlfriend, moved into a newly built two-bedroom bungalow they bought from Michael. Michael, who had become a shrewd businessman, bought the parcel with an old bungalow and the land from an old man who owned it. When he sold the bungalow to Jay and Zoë, for the same price he paid for the bungalow and the land. Jay and Zoë had to sell the house Jay bought with Tilly in order to buy the bungalow, which was in the posh area of the village where The Tin House was and near the farm where Tilly did her service as a young girl. Michael was going to build a large house on the nearby land later on.

Jay wondered what the stuck up people who shunned his grandparents would think about that! There were still a few of them around.

Two weeks later, Eliza and her husband were on their way to London. Dawn's husband, Dave, was taking them. He did long distance driving and knew his way 'round most places. It was the middle of June—maybe the hottest day of they year—and they were in a traffic jam in the middle of the capitol city.

"I have to open the window," said Dean. "It's so hot in the car."

A few seconds later, Eliza was choking on the fumes that were coming in the window. "For Christ's sake, close the windows! The fumes are choking me!" she shouted. So they wound the windows back up.

After a few minutes, they had to open the windows again. "I shall be dead before we get there at this rate," said Eliza.

"It's a good job we made an early start this morning," said Dean. "There are traffic jams everywhere."

Finally, they arrived at Weymouth Road.

"Here we are at last!" said Dean. They easily found a parking spot, and Dave suggested that he and Dean go in to find out exactly where Eliza needed to go. She sat in the car while the two of them walked off down the road. A few minutes later they were back.

"What a piece of luck! This is the place. We parked right outside," said Dave, noting that they went to a big establishment down the road and asked a porter to point it out to them.

The porter came out side and pointed to the building where Dave parked. "There it is," he said. "Where that red car is parked."

Dean and Dave chuckled because that was their car. They thanked the porter and returned to Eliza. Dean helped an elated Eliza out of the car and up the steps of a magnificent Victorian house. She was chuffed because she didn't have far to walk, but she wouldn't be happy for long.

"You're a few minutes early," the receptionist said, directing them to a waiting room on the other side of the hall. It was old-fashioned and smelled musty.

About ten minutes later, a very tall, thin man came into the room.

"I'm Mr Geddus," he said, shaking hands all around. "Follow me."

Dean helped Eliza up off her chair to follow him back into the hall and to the bottom of some steep stairs.

"After you," Mr Geddus said, pointing to the stairs.

Eliza was horrified. *How the bloody hell does, he think, I can walk upstairs! "I can't possibly make it up there!"* She gasped, already out of breath just walking from the room into the hall, and she had hung onto Dean for support.

"Take your time, it's the only way to my examination room," he replied, noticing her anxiety.

Dean pulled her up with one hand and Eliza pulled herself up using the stair railing with her other hand. She had to stop for breath ever few seconds. Finally, they reached the top of the stairs, and straight opposite was a small room.

"In there," he said where another receptionist sat waiting for them.

Mr Geddus went into the room next to it while Eliza flopped on the chair gasping for breath. She fumbled in her handbag for her inhaler, her heart thumping in her chest.

"I just have to ask a few questions," said the receptionist.

Dean answered the questions while Eliza's chest eased a bit, then Mr Geddus called them into the next room.

"Sit down. I want to ask you about the treatment you have been having," and he started asking different questions.

Dean started to answer for her, but Mr Geddus waved him off. "I want Eliza to answer herself," he said.

"She hasn't got her breath back from climbing the stairs yet," Dean answered, protectively.

"That's all right, she can take as much time as she likes."

After talking to Eliza for about twenty minutes, Mr Geddus walked round the desk and took hold of her gently under her arm. "Come on just over here. I want you to go on the breathing machine to test how much oxygen is going into your lungs before I examine you."

A few minutes later he sat back at the desk. "I'm sorry I made you come up the stairs and answer the questions yourself, but I had to assess how bad you are." He said she was on "the best treatment you can get in the world," adding, "In fact, it might be a bit too good. See if you can get by using the nebuliser a bit less. "

Mr Geddus agreed with the hospital doctor that a lung transplant was her only chance. He told her the procedure for transplant patients included rigorous tests for which he would set her up at Royal Brompton Hospital. After that, he would be in touch. Before he sent them on their way,. he told them to call if they had not heard from the hospital within two weeks.

They stopped to eat on the way home, but Eliza didn't eat much. Her lungs were so swollen that they pushed on her stomach, making her very uncomfortable when she ate—there wasn't much room in her stomach and it was hard to breathe and eat at the same time.

"Penny for your thoughts?" asked Dean.

"I'm bloody petrified at the idea of having a lung transplant," she admitted.

"It's got to be better than dying."

Back home, her mother, Tilly, met Eliza at the door.

"How did you get on?" Eliza looks at her in amazement.

"It's all right, I told her," said Jay, coming in. "Nan asked where you were so I told her you had gone for a check-up."

It wasn't that they didn't want Tilly to know. they just didn't think she would understand what a transplant meant.

The phone never stopped ringing all night as family members called for the report. Within a week, the letter arrived from Royal Brompton Hospital. It gave her an admission date and told her to plan for a two-week stay.

On the way to the hospital, Eliza was a complete bag of nerves. She worried about being such a long way from her family for two whole weeks. They arrived on Sunday the twenty-fifth of June, 1995.

In they went, and then up in the lift. Eliza has never been so scared in her life and she had been through some scary things in her time!

"Come this way," said a nurse. "Just follow me," to Dean, who was pushing Eliza in the wheelchair. "Have you come far?"

"About a hundred and forty miles," replied Dean.

"I'm dying for a pee," said Eliza.

"And me, too," replied Dean.

The nurse pointed out the toilet, and Dawn, who insisted on accompanying them, pushed Eliza up the corridor. The windows in the toilets and passageway were so enormous that they could see their car across the road.

"Harrods is over there," said the nurse, pointing in the distance.

"I would love to go 'round Harrods, if ever I get better," replied Eliza.

"You never know," said the nurse. "There are a number of variables. There has to be a suitable donor, but first the surgeon has to make sure you are fit for a transplant. Sometimes people have to wait a while for a donor."

. The ward had six beds in it. Eliza shivered, even though it was hot outside.

"It's quite cold in there, but you needn't get into bed," said the nurse. "Put your things in your locker and I will show you the sitting room."

The sitting room was quite nice with sunlight shining through the window. There were armchairs, a table and chairs, coffee tables and a television.

"We will have to be off in a minute," said Dean, giving Eliza a hug.

"Okay, have a safe journey home. I will phone you later." She noticed a pay phone on the wall in the passage by the toilet.

Eliza stood looking through the large window, watching them walk across the road, to where the car was parked, and finally, she watched them drive off. Then, she went into the toilet and sobbed her heart out. For the first time in her life, she was totally on her own.

As she sobbed, she thought about how her mother must have felt when her father sent her to the convent all those years ago when Tilly had been a little girl. *I would have been petrified at just ten years old.*

Monday wasn't too bad. First, Eliza had a scan, then they took swabs from her ears, nose and throat as well as numerous blood tests for which they drew many tubes of blood. She was also fitted for a

24 hour tape to measure her heart's activity. The food was horrible. *I won't be eating much of that!*

She had more tests on Tuesday, Wednesday, and Thursday. On Thursday afternoon, the doctor came to see her.

"We have to do an angiogram on you tomorrow," he said.

"What's that?" asked Eliza.

"We put a camera in your groin and feed it through the veins into your heart and lungs to see how bad they are, but you have to lie down for six hours afterward," he added.

"I was hoping to go home tomorrow night. My niece is getting married on Saturday and I desperately want to be there."

"I will try and arrange for you to be done first," he replied. "We will see how it goes. By the way, the x-rays have shown a crush fracture in one of your vertebrates."

"I was hoping you wouldn't notice that. I thought it might jeopardize my chances of a transplant."

After the doctor was gone, a male nurse came to her. "I have to give you a shave down below," he said.

"Not on your life!" replied Eliza. "I will do it myself."

When Friday morning arrived, Eliza was scared. She had to be taken to another part of the hospital, which was down the next road. They put her in a small ward with three more people, all waiting for angiograms. .The lady in the next bed went first, and then it was Eliza's turn.

Eliza shivered as the operating theatre was quite cold. There was lots of equipment and a large screen.

"What film are we watching today?" Eliza joked, putting on a brave face.

"Sleeping Beauty," he replied, laughing.

"Are you going to put me to sleep?" she asked him.

"You will miss the show if I do that. Now lie on here for me," he said, helping her on the bed, although it wasn't a bed—it was very narrow and hard.

The man was chatting away to Eliza as he prepared the equipment, putting a cover that looked like a hair net over a part of it. There was another person on the other side of the room having the same procedure done.

"Right, we're going to put a small nick in your groin," the man said as he prodded about. "I can't get the blooming thing up through the vein," he called to the man doing the other person.

"Hang on!" the other chap replied. "I'll come and have a look." He asked Eliza what job she used to do, and she told him about packing the car components and about all the asbestos that used to fly off the brake shoes.

Just then, the other chap came over. "Let's have a look. You're hitting the walls, she's bleeding too much. You have to stop!"

The nurse dressed the wound and put Eliza back in the corridor, where she remained for about ten minutes, when the second man came out to see her.

"I'm sorry about what happened. we can leave it and try again Monday if you like or try again now, but in the opposite groin. It's entirely up to you?"

"I will have it done now and get it over with. I don't want to worry about this all weekend."

They wheeled her back inside and were about to start, when Eliza noticed that they hadn't put the net thing over the equipment as they did before. "Don't you have to put that cover on there first?" she asked.

"A good job you noticed that," he replied. "I can see what made you a good packer."

They put the cover on and proceed with the angiogram. Eliza lay there, watching everything on the screen. It was an amazing sight.

"You might feel a little bump as it enters your heart."

Eliza was intrigued, just watching.

"Now we are going through into your lung, and then back though your heart, into the other lung," he said, providing a running commentary. He explained that they would inject some dye that might taste something like iodine, "… and it might make you feel as if you had wet yourself."

"I've wet myself," she said after a few minutes.

"You certainly have!" he replied.

Later that night, Eliza was on her way home, but she had to return to hospital on Sunday night.

"Who's been looking after Mom?" asked Eliza on the way home. "I've been so worried about her even though I know you will all look after her."

"Tilly's fine. Cher and I have been taking turns looking after her," replied Dawn. She couldn't go to Sam's house, as she had before, because his wife worked quite long hours, and Tilly couldn't be left on her own that long.

The tops of Eliza's legs were black and blue, especially the right one.

"I don't think you should go to the church," said Dean. "We will go straight to the reception."

Eliza phoned Michael to explain about her legs since his daughter was the bride. Of course, that was fine with Michael—he was delighted that his sister could be there at all after all she had been through.

The bride was radiant on that glorious summer's day. Eliza was glad to see her family together again—that was one of the nice things about being in a big family—there were plenty of birthday parties, showers, weddings and anniversaries to celebrate. This day belonged to Michael's family and, especially, to his daughter, Eliza's niece. She was grateful that Michael and Catharine never returned to Australia to live so she knew his family well.

Before they sat down to eat, Michael said grace and offered a beautiful speech remembering Ray and Biron's sister-in-law. They celebrated for most of Saturday, but it was a rather early party for Eliza since she had to return to the hospital early on Sunday.

Eliza and Thomas set out at five a.m. because he had to drive all the way back again. As she said goodbye to Tilly, who was staying with Dawn that day, her mother asked, "Why do you have to go back to he hospital again?"

"They are doing some more tests to see if I can have a lung transplant," Eliza said, telling her the truth.

"Who of?" asked Tilly.

"I don't know yet," replied Eliza, shivering at the thought.

"You can have one of mine."

"Thanks, Mom, but it doesn't work like that. People donate them after one of their loved ones dies."

"Sounds morbid, doesn't it? The people that donate must be

very lovely and brave to do that. It doesn't bear thinking about. You've lost me now," admitted Tilly.

"Don't worry about it, Mom. I will be back in a few days and then you can come home again."

Eliza only needed a few more tests, and then she would come home. The next evening she was pleasantly surprised. She was sitting by her hospital bed reading, when her niece Debbie came in with her boyfriend, Richard. Eliza's face lit up.

"I've never been happier to see you in my life," she said to her niece. "Is it all right if we take Eliza for a walk round the corner to that little pub?" they asked the nurse.

"Sure, I will fetch a wheelchair for you, but don't buy her too many drinks, will you?"

They pushed Eliza 'round to the pub and bought her a meal, which tasted fabulous. "Thanks so much for coming," Eliza said, kissing her niece good-bye.

"You can probably go home on Wednesday," said the doctor, "but first you have to go before the panel."

"Why, is there a beauty competition on then?"

On the Tuesday, the porter came for her. "Come on, you have to see the big knobs now."

"What for?" she asked

"Your guess is as good as mine," he said, pushing her into a waiting room where, Eliza sat wondering what they would ask.

Two men dressed in smart suits sat behind a large desk.

"How long have you been ill?" one of them asked.

"I can't really recall," she answered. "It's a long time. it sort of came on gradually at first, then it hit me with a vengeance. I'm gasping like this all the time now."

They asked her to tell them what her days were like. So, Eliza told them how she lay on the settee all day.

"My granddaughter stays at my house. When I get up in the morning, she has already put one of the phones, a pad of paper for notes, and the newspapers on the coffee table by the settee ready for when I eventually get downstairs," Eliza said. *Bless her She's only eleven and she does it before she goes to school.*

"Do you ever feel dizzy?" asked one of them.

"Only when I'm pissed!" she replied.

Both men laughed..

"When do you want the operation?" the other chap asked.

"Have you got the right person?" replied Eliza shuddering as she spoke. "Someone has to die, don't they? That sounds horrible."

"You are right," he replied, "but, unfortunately, that's what happens."

On the day Eliza was due to go home, Liz, the co-ordinator, asked to see her, Thomas, and Dean. She explained that it might be weeks or even years before an organ became available.

"It might not happen at all, there have been hundreds of people who died while on the waiting list, and you're in the rare blood group. Have they decided whether they're giving you just lungs or heart and lungs?" asked Liz.

"They did mention it could be either, depending," replied Eliza, "but they say there's nothing wrong with my heart."

"I know, but sometimes it's better to fit the three together in one unit, then they give someone else your heart."

Eliza shuddered again. It seemed terrible to be talking about it. The person whose lung she would have, if she got one, was still alive at this very moment, probably enjoying life to the fullest.

Liz noticed the expression on her face and said softly, "I know it sounds morbid, but it's your only chance to live. Look at it this way. Someone's not going to die just to give you an organ. This person, whoever it might be, will probably have an accident or die tragically—not because you need a transplant."

Liz gave Eliza a letter. "Call in at Harefield Hospital and give them this letter on the way home. They will give you a bleeper. Test it every so often to make sure it's working. The best of luck," she said, shaking their hands as they goodbye.

When they arrived at Harefield an hour later, Thomas and Dean took the letter in, leaving Eliza sitting in the car outside. Dean came back out to her. "The co-ordinator wants to see you."

343

Can't everyone see how hard it is for me to move? Gasping, she got out of the car, and Dean helped her inside. She had an appointment with the surgeon at Royal Brompton.

On the night before her appointment, Eliza lay on the settee watching television as usual. there was not much else she could do.

"Are you ready for bed?" asked Dean. "We have an early start in the morning."

"I just want to finish watching this first. There's a programme on television. The surgeon's performing a heart transplant, and Ruby Wax is in the operating theatre with him," she replied. "It's at the Royal Brompton Hospital." Eliza watched it with great interest.

"How can you sit and watch that when you might be having it done to you?" asked Dean.

"That's makes it more interesting."

The next day Eliza and Dean waited to go in to see the surgeon, and at last the nurse called them in.

The surgeon introduced himself. "I'm Mr Pepper," he said, shaking their hands. "I have to measure you."

"What do you have to measure me for?" she asked.

"To see how big you are round the top half," he replied, getting a tape measure out of the drawer of his table.

Dean told him about Eliza watching the transplant on television.

"And do you know who the surgeon was?" he replied. "Me!"

"What a coincidence!" replied Dean.

CHAPTER 19

All the time that Eliza was sick, she prayed that her brother Derek, who was undergoing radium treatments for the cancer in his throat, was getting better. Never one to dwell on her own problems, Eliza worried about him and became sad and frustrated because she was unable to cook for, visit with, or otherwise help to care for Derek. When he came to see her and Tilly, Eliza was delighted.

"Have you finished your treatments?" she asked.

"Yes, I have to go for a check up in a few weeks' time," he said. Since Tilly was napping, he confided in Eliza. "To be quite honest, I don't feel any better, but I suppose they know what's happening better than me."

"We are a bright pair between us, aren't we?"

Tilly, who was just getting up from her afternoon nap, still didn't know Derek had cancer.

"Hi there, Derek. Want a cuppa?" she asked.

"Okay two sugars, please."

"Have you got a sore throat?" asked Tilly, noticing his rough voice.

"Just a bit."

Tilly was looking forward to Ken's birthday. A party was coming up and all of the family members were going over to a club at Stretton-On-Dunsmore, where he lived. His two boys were doing a surprise party for him.

"Shall we hire a coach out?" asked Mo. "We can all have a drink then." So most of them went in the coach, but a few of them took their own cars.

Eliza had her beeper with her, which she placed on the table in front of her. "I will never hear this if it goes off with this music so loud," she said. "So I will have to keep my eye on it."

The night went well, and everyone had a great night. Eliza usually thought it was smashing when the family got together.

A couple of weeks later Mo's daughter got married—another radiant bride—all of the family's brides were beautiful. "That's another one added to the family," said Tilly. "I will never remember all the names."

"What's new?" replied Eliza. "There are so many of us I have a job to remember my own name half the time."

Cher's mother came from America to visit for a few weeks. When Cher brought her to visit Tilly and Eliza, she offered to do Eliza's nails.

"Great, she can do them while I shower Tilly." Cher said.

Eliza's, daughters-in-law, Cher and Wendy, and Tilly's daughters-in-law, took turns helping Tilly with her shower since the incident in the bathtub.

"That's brilliant," replied Eliza. "I haven't had my nails done for ages, I will enjoy that." Eliza had lovely nails, but she had neglected them lately.

Cher's mother chatted with Eliza as if they were old friends. She sat down by Eliza.

"Put your hands in here," she said, placing in front of her the bowl of warm water that Cher has brought in from the kitchen. She painted Eliza's nails in two different golds, diagonally across each nail, with a thin line of gold leaf in between.

"They look fabulous, you should do that for a living," said Eliza.

Eliza showed her them to Dean as soon as he walked in the door at five o'clock, "Look at my nails, Dean."

"Very nice, you have perked up today."

"Yes, and guess what, I fancy going to eat at The Fox.

"You know I don't like that place."

"It has easy access to it," said Eliza. "We can park straight out by the door, and sit just inside."

"No! Ring Dawn up and see if she and her husband want to go. I will cook Tilly's tea for her."

Miserable git! Eliza picked up the phone to ring Dawn.

"It's a bit short notice," she replied, "but if you feel well enough to go we will meet you outside."

Eliza staggered to the car, sat in the driving seat and rested to get her breath back before starting the car up. She was all right driving the car, as it was automatic and very easy to drive. Eliza was already waiting in the car on the car park of The Fox when her son-in-law arrived with his two children. They loved to see their Nan, and Eliza adored them. She loved and enjoyed all of her grandchildren, but every time she saw them, she wondered if she would live to see them grow up.

"Dawn's not coming," her son-in-law said, giving her his arm.

Eliza hated anyone to notice that she couldn't walk far. So, every couple of steps, she stopped to look at the notice boards when really she was just getting her next breath. "I will have Caigon chicken, chips and peas and half a lager, please," she said, getting the money out of her bag. "I feel ravenous tonight."

"You won't eat all that!" said Dave. "You hardly eat anything these days."

"I will have a good try."

"I can't believe you ate all that!" he remarked, as Eliza was putting the last forkful in her mouth. "This must be one of the best days you've had for ages."

"I think I deserve another half," she said as they sat chatting.

"It's getting on for nine o'clock, we have to go home. It's way past the children's bedtime," Dave said.

After saying good night and kissing the two children, Eliza settled herself into the car, drove home, got just inside the kitchen, and flopped on a chair for a rest. Then, she moved to the bottom of the stairs in the hall. She sat on the second from bottom of the stairs, for another rest. *Only another two steps to the toilet. I hope I reach it before I pee myself!*

Eliza heard the phone ringing and Dean talking as he carried the phone into the hall, where she was sitting on the stairs making her way back to the living room. "It's someone from the hospital," he said, passing her the phone.

"Is that you, Eliza? I'm one of the coordinators from the hospital," a voice said. Eliza's heart started beating so fast she thought she would have a heart attack any minute. "Are you still there?"

"Yes I am," replied Eliza quietly, her hands sweating and shaking.

"I haven't had time to talk to you before."

Eliza's heartbeat slowed down a bit. The coordinator only wanted to talk to her.

"How you are feeling?" the voice went on.

"I'm feeling quite a lot better today—better than I have been for ages. I've just this minute walked in from going to the pub. I had Caigon chicken, chips and peas and two halves of lager."

"Well, let us worry about that," the voice said. "We have a donor lung for you. How long will it take you, to get here?"

Eliza started shaking uncontrollably. "But I've had a meal!"

"I told you, we will sort that out when you get here. How long will it take you?"

"About two and a half hours, I think."

"See if you can make it a bit sooner, I will be waiting for you."

"I must wash my feet before I go!" says Eliza, in a panic. "Can you get me a bowl of water and my nail varnish remover?" The beautiful nail polish had to come off! "I have to phone Mo up first, her husband's driving us to the hospital." She asked Dean to phone their children.

Eliza had her feet in the bowl and was cleaning the nail varnish off at the same time. Dean seemed to be running round in circles. Tilly was holding the nebuliser to Eliza's face, unaware of what was going on. They had never been in a flap like this before! Eliza's husband, Dean, was even worse than she.

"Have you got my case?" she asked as he helped her into coat on. "Mo's a long time, isn't she?"

The door opened as Thomas arrived, quickly followed by Dawn.

"I will take Tilly back with me," she said.

"I'm going with Mother, said Thomas. "But if Mo's not here in a minute, we will have to go without her. I don't want to drive but I will if I have to."

Just then, Mo and her husband John arrived—Mo with dripping wet hair.

"I was in the hair dresser with lather on my hair when we got the call," she said. "They had to rinse it off."

They all climbed in the car. "Can we stop up the shop up the road for some cans of lager?" someone asked. "I think we are in for a long night."

Christ! I will never get there in time! Eliza worried about being late as she sat in the car waiting for them. "What kept you?" she asked when they came back. "It must be over half an hour since the hospital called, and we're not even on our way yet."

Rain was absolutely peeing down, but it eased up a bit as they got on the motorway. Then, as they approach Oxford, the rain tipped down with a vengeance. The traffic was crawling by this time.

"I can't see us getting there!" said Eliza, as John passed other cars when he could. All of them were panicky by that time, but, at last, they reached the hospital, where a porter waited with a wheel chair. It was eleven thirty.

"Eliza?" he asked.

She nodded. "

In you get," he told her. "I will take you up. Turning to the others, he added." Park the car, then catch up."

The porter was almost running with her in the wheelchair, up in the lift, then into a room. It was like a bedroom—with a man sitting on the bed.

"Get on," he told Eliza.

"Is this your bed?" she asked.

"No. I'm a registrar. Drink this," he said, passing her some thick liquid.

"It's horrible!" she said, sipping it.

"Knock it back quickly, we haven't much time."

"Can I have a wee first?" Eliza asked.

"There's a toilet in there," he replied, pointing to a door.

So, Eliza got off the bed and panted as she entered the bathroom. She quickly did her wee and wet one of the paper towels to quickly wash down below. She didn't want to smell when they put the catheter in.

It was ten to twelve when they wheeled her into the operating theatre. Eliza glanced back at her family. *Is this goodbye? Will this be the last time I'll see them?* A tear slid down her cheek, but she quickly wiped it away.

Eliza lay in the outer theatre, while the anaesthetists talked and did the final preparations. "Did they tell you I had Caigon chicken, chips, peas and two lagers about seven o' clock? I hope my breath doesn't smell too much."

"Don't worry," one of them replied.

Dean, Thomas, Mo and John settled down in the waiting room, drinking their cans of lager. It was going to be a long wait. Hours went by, then at last, about seven in the morning a nurse came in and fetched Dean and Thomas.

"Only two at a time," she said. Dean and Thomas were relieved to see that Eliza came through the operation all right. However, they were shocked to see all the wires and tubes coming out of her body. Dean held her hand and spoke to her, while the surgeon stood at the bottom of the bed.

Eliza briefly opened her eyes and tried to speak, but she couldn't because she was on a ventilator. Eliza pointed to the tube in her mouth, then tried to say, "Take it out."

The surgeon told the nurse to turn the ventilator off a bit later on in the day, and if she could breathe on her in a half hour's time, the nurse could take the tube out and take her off it. The morphine knocked Eliza out again, and she was glad of that.

The next time she opened her eyes, Dawn and John were standing by her bed, as well as the surgeon, who had popped back in.

"You're doing well," he said to her.

Eliza was delirious. "You can't have sex tonight!" she said to her husband, and even the nurses laughed.

Later that day, Eliza was breathing so well they moved her to a room of her own. She couldn't remember much about the next few days, It was all delusions and blankness and pain. All she knew was that she didn't want to wake up until she was better. She hated it when they got her out of bed to have X-rays.

"It has to be done," said the nurse who was looking after her.

Mo, Dawn, and Dean were staying at the hospital's motel nearby. "Are the children and Tilly all right?" asked Eliza.

"Don't worry, Mother, they're all right. I go back to see them every two days." Later, a doctor came to see Eliza. "Has anyone told you what you have had done?"

"I can't remember."

"You have one new lung, and we took half the other lung away. I'm afraid that one's causing us some concern, so we will have to take you to the operating theatre again to investigate the problem."

It was costing Dean a bomb to rent a room out for Dawn, Mo, and himself at the hospital's motel, but they would never leave Eliza there on her own.

Eliza was half-unconscious as they took her back to her room after the second operation—the investigation.

Dean and Dawn were there waiting for her. "Have you sorted the problem out, Doctor?"

"I think so. Keep your fingers crossed. You heal quicker from a transplant than from having part of a lung removed."

A few days later Eliza had to go back to surgery to correct another bleeding problem with her remaining half lung—they used the bronchoscope to find and stop the bleeding. It was her third operation.

"Just give me a massive dose of something, and put me to sleep forever," said Eliza in despair. "I've had enough."

"Don't give up," said David, her doctor, who was a smashing chap. In fact, all of her doctors were wonderful.

Slowly, the lung started to heal up. So, Dean and Mo went home, knowing she was on the mend. Dawn, though, stayed with her mother.

A few nights later Eliza started wheezing a bit.

"We will soon get rid of that," said the nurse, setting up the nebuliser and handing it to her. Eliza had used a nebuliser hundreds of times before, so she knew it was not normal when her heartbeat quickened after the first few puffs. The nurses had monitor panels on their desks, and they came rushing in to her with a machine to test her heart. A few minutes later two doctors rushed in, and two more doctors soon arrived behind them.

"Your heartbeats are out of rhythm so we will have to take you to theatre, stop your heart, and then shock it back into rhythm," said one of the doctors. Have you had anything to eat or drink in the last hour?"

"Yes," replied Eliza. "I had a glass of milk about ten minutes ago."

"We can't do it then," he said. "We will have to put you on a drip and hope that controls it."

When Dawn came in the next morning, she was furious. "Why didn't anyone ring me up? You had my number. You knew I was staying on the premises. I would have come over," she said.

"We did think about it and decided against it, for if Eliza had seen you here in the middle of the night, it could have made the situation more difficult." Actually, in the state Eliza was in, she wouldn't have even noticed if it was day or night.

Eliza hadn't had a poo since her operation, and that was causing some concern. *What next?* She was beginning to think that she would never leave the hospital alive. Everything seemed to be going wrong with her, and now her belly was swelling.

"We asked a surgeon from another hospital who specialises in that department to come and see you," said her doctor, David.

The surgeon examined her. "Your bowel's blocked with gases," he said. "You would never survive an operation of the kind it would take to fix this surgically. You haven't recovered from this one yet, you are far too weak."

Eliza didn't care anymore.

The next ordeal to be faced was when the nurse came in, carrying a tube. "David's coming back to see you in a minute," she said.

"What's the tube for? Are you going to put it up my arse?" asked Eliza.

David walked in with Dean, who sat on the bed with Eliza and held her hand.

Noting that Dean's eyes were red, she asked, "Have you been crying?"

"No. I had something in my eye."

"I have to put this tube up your nose and down into your stomach. We have to try to release the gases in your abdomen," said David.

Eliza gagged as he tried to put the tube up her nose it kept curling round and coming out of her mouth, instead of going down into her stomach. Finally, after several attempts, the tube went down.

"How long does it have to stay in?" she croaked, her throat quite sore by then.

"Until the gases are released," replied David. "You won't be able to eat or drink anything, but we will let you suck a little ice. We have to keep your stomach empty."

"I'm sorry," he said the next morning. "It's not working. We have to get that tube out and put another, thicker one, down."

"Oh, no!" said Eliza, looking at the thickness of the tube. "That will never go down!"

"It has to!"

The doctor eventually managed to get the thicker tube down, and Eliza dozed off, not having had much sleep the night before, or any night since her operation.

As Eliza opened her eyes next morning she was amazed. Her brothers and their wives, Mo, her husband, and all five of her own children surrounded her bed.

How did they all manage to get in the room? Eliza wondered, but she had no idea why they are all there. She didn't know the doctor sent for them because the doctors feared she wouldn't recover from the bowel problem.

"Look at the size of my belly!" laughed Eliza. "It's like a football."

Nobody laughed with her and she was annoyed.

"Why are all looking so blooming miserable? It's me that's ill."

"I'm sorry, there are too many in the room. You can't all stop here at once," said the doctor. So, they took turns.

All of a sudden, Eliza started farting and couldn't stop, and the smell was atrocious!

"Let's get out of here quick," said the visitors.

"What's that terrible smell?" asked the nurse walking in the room.

"It's Eliza breaking wind," replied Dean. "It's killing me and Dawn as well."

"Open the window!" she said. "All the other patients are complaining."

A few minutes later David, the doctor, walked in. "I've heard the good news, the tube is doing the trick. All you want now is a good poo," he said, standing at the bottom of her bed.

"I would move from there," said Eliza, just as she farted again.

"Who's a good girl?" said David.

It was a wonder the noise and smell didn't make them evacuate the whole hospital—even the woman in the next room left.

"I can't stand that, I'm going over to the canteen. Please have someone fetch me when the smell's gone," she said holding her nose.

"Quick! I need a bedpan, I want a poo." Eliza still had drainage tubes on each side of her abdomen with the big bottles attached, so it took ages for them to get her out of bed and help her to the commode. Eliza couldn't sit there alone, but none of the nurses would stay because of the rotten smell.

"I suppose I will have to stay," said Dawn.

After fifteen minutes, Eliza did a poo, then leaned on the bed for Dawn to wipe her bottom.

"Gawd blimey, Mom! What a stink! You must be rotten inside. I never thought the day would come that I would have to wipe your bottom."

"I did it for you when you were a baby," Eliza said, laughing. It was the first time she laughed in weeks—she obviously felt a great deal better.

David came back to see her. "I told you, you were a good girl, didn't I? I will, take the tube out from up your nose, just lie still. You can have some soup for dinner today. I bet you're starving, aren't you?"

"You know the other night when you said it looked as if I had been crying—I had," said Dean, as Eliza was eating her soup. "They told us you would probably die from a blocked bowel"

So, that's why the whole family were here, Eliza thought.

"Who's a good girl," said Mo, mimicking David, as she and John entered the room laughing. That night, as each family member said goodbye, Eliza again felt blessed to be part of her loving family.

Eliza's recovery went smoothly for the rest of her hospital stay. It took another two weeks—a month from when she arrived—before David delivered the best news of all. "You can go home now."

Am I she really going home? Eliza simply couldn't believe she had survived.

The journey back home was horrific! Every little bump sent ripples of pain through her body.

"I never ever thought I would see this place again," she said to Dean as pulled in their driveway. Eliza's face lit up when she spotted her mother, Tilly, standing on the doorstep, waiting for her. Eliza had never been happier to see her mother, and her home, in all her life.

"I will get the kettle on," said Tilly, ignoring the note telling her not to switch the kettle on as they walked inside together. Eliza struggled into the front room and flopped on the settee.

During the first few weeks, the nurse came to check on Eliza frequently. She also took her blood to test the medication levels in her system. Eliza was still having a hard time standing upright, and her back pained her worse than ever.

"I suppose it's because I've hardly done anything for the past year or so," she said to Tilly.

Eliza lay on the settee most days. Her breathing was a lot better, and it was improving by the day. Best of all, she wasn't gasping all the time.

Jill, her childhood friend, phoned. "Dean tells me you are not eating much, so Graham's bringing me tomorrow. I'm going to cook your dinner and tea for you."

~

"I bought some potatoes with me," she said, as she came into Eliza's front room the next day. "What have you got to go with them?"

"I don't have a clue you will have to take a look," so Jill went in the kitchen. Eliza could hear the doors of the cupboards and fridge opening and shutting.

"Tilly, can you come and peel some potatoes for me, please?" asked Jill, as Tilly went into the kitchen to help. "Do enough for Graham and me," said Jill. "We will be having our tea here as well. I might even stay the night I've got to perk Eliza up a bit."

"Don't give me much," said Eliza. "I don't eat a great deal" Despite that, Jill brought her a plate full of creamed potatoes, salmon, peas, and parsley sauce. "What am I supposed to do with all that?"

"Just try your best and eat as much as you can."

"Thanks, Jill, that was delicious," said Eliza, eating the last bit off her plate.

"I thought you were going to eat the plate as well."

"Are you sleeping the night?" asked Dean.

"Yes, I am," replied Jill. Unfortunately, every five minutes, Jill popped outside for a cigarette.

"Why don't you pack that in. You have a terrible smoker's cough," said Eliza.

"I have tried, but I can't!"

"I thought that! But it's better than dying, you can't' smoke when you're dead, can you?"

CHAPTER 20

The next day, Derek and his partner called in. They had just come back from the hospital, where Derek went for his check up.

"Make us a cup of tea, please, Mother,' asked Derek.

"Okay," she replied. "Does anyone else want one?" she called as she walked out of the room.

"Yes please," they all chorused.

"The cancer is still there," Derek informed Eliza once Tilly left the room. He didn't want to burden her with the knowledge that he was fighting cancer. ""I knew it was. The surgeon suggested I had been smoking, but I swear, I haven't had a cigarette since I found ou I havecancer. I think the surgeon believed me in the end."

"So, what's the next step?" asked Eliza.

"I either have a Laryngectomy, which means having my voice box taken out, or gradually choke to death. So I have no alternative but to have the operation," Derek then explained that the surgeon gave him a week to make up his mind. He didn't want to be mute, but he had no other choice.

Eliza thought her operation was bad enough, but she wouldn't want the one her brother was facing. It sounded horrendous.

The next week Derek went in for his operation that took hours to complete. The radium from his earlier treatments burned his throat so much, that the skin didn't hold together once the surgeon removed the cancer and tried to close Derek's throat. The skin was so unstable that the hole kept getting bigger. Finally, they managed to finish the operation, but the hole was not the way they hoped it would be.

Everything seemed to go wrong—Derek had to have many operations over the months that followed. They took skin grafts from his legs and tried that. Next, they tried grafts from his stomach, and later, from his back. They called him the 'Miracle Man,' but the doctor knew the skin around the inside of his throat was fragile.

At last, he went home, but he couldn't eat. He had a tube on the outside of his stomach, going to the inside of his bowel. He had to feed himself every night, putting special liquid food into a drip. He slept all night while the food dripped into him. Eliza couldn't believe what he was going through. He also had a tube up his nose and down into his stomach, with a jar attached to collect bile that came out of his stomach. Derek just lay on the settee all day long. He was like that for months.

Then, one day the surgeon called Derek's girlfriend on the phone, saying he would try one more operation. He would use muscle from Derek's back, and leave the muscle tissue attached to his back while Derek's throat healed. The doctor pulled the muscle over his shoulder and used it to fix his throat—keeping the muscle tissue viable by leaving it attached to try and heal the hole.

The operation was long and tricky, but, at last, Derek could eat again and the tubes came out. His neck was tight because he had a right mass of scar tissue. However, that didn't bother Derek. At least he could eat.

All the time Derek was in and out of hospital, even after he had his voice box removed, he had never written down what he wanted to say—he mouthed words to people and woe betides those who couldn't understand him. He scowled until people knew what he meant.

Twelve months later Derek was still improving. He tottered about his greenhouse, planting seeds. He planted dozens of pots for his garden, and he made a wicked curry on Saturday nights. At long last, he was cleared of cancer, but he was determined to talk again.

"I will talk again one day if it kills me," he mimed.

May was inconsolable when her husband died. As the months went by, though, she started coming to terms with the loss of her beloved husband, and visited Tilly and Eliza again. Every Wednesday May turned up, with her slippers and pinny, had coffee and toast, and began cleaning Eliza's house from top to bottom.

"Nothing's changed, since you used to come to my house all those years ago, has it?" asked Tilly, as the mats went flying out of the back door.

There was no sweeping 'round the mats for May! The house was sparkling clean. May was from told stock, everything had to be done properly. Afterwards, she caught the bus to town to meet her sister Lilly, who was also a widow now.

Thomas and Cher had another baby—a boy, who, just like all the family babies, was round-faced, sweet-smelling and had cherry-coloured spots on his cheeks.

Tilly's son, Joseph, and his son, worked for the same man for years, in the building trade, but now the man was ready to retire, so he asked them if they want to buy his business. Several men worked for him, but he took a shine to Joseph and his son.

In addition to that job, Joseph also worked for himself as well. He and Donna had a lovely house, which was a council house until they bought it. Joseph did it up bit by bit, and it was beautiful. They were, indeed, lucky when they got the house that sat in a lovely position down a country lane. Joseph even built a swimming pool in the giant garden. "So, what do you think, son, about buying that business?" asked Joseph.

"Call him up and ask him round for a drink, we can sit on the patio by the pool to discuss it," said his son.

Joseph got three glasses and three cans of lager, then their gaffer arrived with his books, one with the outgoing accounts, and one with the incoming fees. He did a lot of work for the local council.

"I'm telling you straight, Joseph, if you buy my business off me, you won't look back."

After talking with their wives, they decided to go for it. However, they had to get the money together first. Everyone in the family remembered what happened to Eliza, Dean, Dawn and her husband. In the end, they went for it, and the man who sold it to them offered them plenty of help and guidance. Now, they were well on the way to making their fortune. The two wives did the office work for a few years until they could employ others to help.

Jay decided to convert the bungalow into a four-bedroom house. To do that, he needed to extend the existing house in order to support the addition of an upstairs level.

"Dad, will you come up week ends to help me?" he asked Dean.

"Of course, I will, son."

Jay was dedicated to the project. He worked every spare minute, never seeming to rest at all. At last, the house was finished, and what a transformation it was! The home was absolutely fabulous! What a credit to him—still in his early twenties. He's tripled the value of his property.

When Derek went for his check up, the surgeon said he was "very pleased" with him. More importantly, there was no sign of new cancer.

"Can I have a voice box fitted?" he asked.

"That's not advisable. You've had thirteen operations, all on the same area. You know how lucky you are to still be alive?" the surgeon then explained that Derek didn't have enough muscle tissue to house a voice box.

"I want to talk again," Derek persisted. "I'm prepared for the consequences and I have great faith in you!"

"I will discus it with my colleague."

When Derek received a letter from the hospital, he was overjoyed. They said they would do the operation. "But, they warned, "The risks are very high." The hospital had plenty of blood of Derek's type on hand for all of his surgeries. He had lost so much blood in his past surgeries that they wanted to be sure they were prepared for problems.

The whole family prayed and sent Derek positive thoughts as his operation went ahead.

After it was over, .Derek's son rang up Mo. "It's a success," he screamed in the phone. "Dad's going to talk again!"

Derek's whole life was transformed. He still had the hole in his neck but he could speak again, and he was ecstatic—absolutely over the moon. He was also weak, and he hadn't been to work for a years, even though he still pottered about the green house.

A few months later, he went back to work, but he found it hard. Plastering required a lot of stretching so that work was hard for him since his neck was so tight from all his operations. He had to work because his sick pay stopped. They said he was no longer ill, so the authorities insisted he was fit enough to work!

Although Tilly's memory was getting really bad, she loved playing games with the children. She often sat for hours playing Ludo and Jenga with them,. Eliza had arranged for her mother, to be taken to a club for pensioners once a week. They came to the house about nine thirty in the morning, and then brought her back about three in the afternoon.

One day Eliza was sitting in the swinging hammock, reading the paper, when she heard voices on the side of the house. One voice sounded like her mother's—but Tilly was supposed to be at the club. Eliza looked over the fence into the driveway, and there was her mother with a strange woman.

"I think this is the house," Tilly said.

"Who are you?" Eliza asked the woman.

"I found Tilly at the bus station, and she asked me where she lived. Luckily, I used to see her on the bus a few years ago, and knew she lived here somewhere. I live up at the top end of the estate. What on earth's she doing at the bus station on her own? It's quite clear she's very confused!"

"She's supposed to be looked after at the club."

Tilly went into the house, had a drink of water, and opened the cupboard. Eliza knew that Tilly was after the jam. She loved bread and jam with loads of butter on the bread first. After preparing her bread and jam, she then, went and sat on the settee to eat it. Eliza phoned the club up to give them a piece of her mind. They hadn't even missed her!

"Well, she won't be coming again," said Eliza.

Eliza told her husband about it that night.

"I know you won't like this," Dean replied, "but I think it's time you thought about putting Tilly in a home!" He noted that they had to get someone to sit with her when they went out and that Eliza, herself, wasn't strong enough to care for her. "We have to get someone in to help shower her every day. And I even had to get up in the middle of last night, because Tilly was trying to unlock the back door."

"Not on your life! My mother's never going in a home as long as I live!"

Tilly had a terrible cough, so Eliza made an appointment for her with the doctor, and she asked Ann to take her.

"How did she get on?" she asked when they got home.

"The doctor said there's nothing wrong with Tilly's chest."

"You're joking, you can hear her wheezing, and she's coughing up loads of rubbish." Eliza made Tilly another appointment, only this time she asked Dawn to take her.

Dawn came back and said the doctors had said the same thing. Eliza was annoyed and worried about her mother's health since she had kept them awake half the night coughing. Finally, Eliza phoned her sister Mo.

"Do me a favour and take Mother to the doctor, will you," explaining what had been going on. She knew Mo would get to the bottom of the problem.

On Friday, Tilly went off with Mo. "This is the third time this week we brought Tilly to see a doctor," said Mo to the doctor. "You can hear her coughing right now."

"I think she has asthma," he replied, sitting back down after examining Tilly's chest. "Give her one of these tablets before she goes to bed, and one in the morning when she gets up" he said, handing her a prescription.

Eliza gave Tilly the tablet that night, along with the Zantac tablet that she has every night, because of her ulcer.

That night two of Eliza's granddaughters came to the house, as usual, to sit with Tilly and to stay the night. Dean and Eliza were going out for a meal with Sam, his wife, Thomas, Jay and their wives. They went out every Saturday night, usually for a Balty, a type of curry.

Sometimes other members of the family came as well. There were usually eight to twelve of them—sometimes more. They always had brilliant laughs, and if Mark went with them, they cried laughing. He was wonderful to go out with—able to tell funny stories, to mimic and get a joke right—unless he had too much to drink, then he would just go to sleep.

Tilly was already in bed when Dean and Eliza got home

"Nanny, Tilly's been saying her leg hurts in the groin area. She had a job to get upstairs," said one of the children.

"I know the feeling," replied Eliza.

She and Dean looked in on Tilly in the bedroom. She was snoring away, but they could still hear her chest rattling.

"She looks all right," said Dean, "but I don't like the sound of her chest."

The next morning Eliza heard Tilly coming downstairs, sliding on her bottom, the same as Eliza did—it was easier.

"How are you this morning, Mother? The children said you had a pain in your groin last night."

"I did. It's just here, and it still hurts," she replied, touching the spot on her groin

"Well, if it gets any worse, I will get someone to take you to the hospital. The doctor's are shut today, it's Bank Holiday Sunday."

Tilly didn't mention the pain anymore, so Eliza and Dean assumed it was gone.

The next day, Mo came to Eliza's house to make hanging baskets with her. It was Bank Holiday Monday. Dean was mowing the lawn and Tilly' was sitting outside in the brilliant sunshine, scraping potatoes. Mo showed Eliza how she made the baskets.

Tilly mentioned her leg a couple of times.

"Do you want me to take you to the hospital?" asked Mo.

"No, I will see what it's like tomorrow."

"Well, if you are sure. Only you know how bad it is," said Mo.

That night as Dean took Tilly up to bed, he noticed she was limping worse. After helping her to undress and put her nightie on, he came back down for Eliza.

"Someone will have to take Tilly to the hospital in the morning, she was limping quite badly when I took her to bed."

By the time they got up the stairs, Tilly's was fast asleep, snoring.

"It's work for me tomorrow!" said Dean as they got in bed.

Eliza and Dean had just gone to sleep, when they were awakened by a big bump.

"What's that!" asked Dean.

Eliza got out of bed and staggered into Tilly's bedroom. The light was on, and her mother was slumped on the floor with her back against the wall.

"Quick Dean!" she called out. "I think Mom's had a stroke!"

Dean ran in and cradled Tilly's head, trying to stop it from rolling about while Eliza phoned in the emergency.

"Ambulance, please. Come quick, it's my mother I think she's had a stroke."

Then Eliza phoned her sister, Mo.

"I will be there in a jiffy," Mo said.

Dean had propped Tilly up the best he could, and Eliza sat talking to her, but she knew her mother couldn't hear her. Soon she heard the paramedics coming up the stairs.

"In here," she called out.

The paramedic team was made up of a man and a woman.. "What's the problem?" they asked, walking into the bedroom.

"I think my Mum's had a stroke," said Eliza.

"I think you're right," said the female paramedic, popping the oxygen mask over Tilly's mouth and nose.

Just then, Mo ran in. "I will go to the hospital with Mum." She knew Eliza wasn't well enough to go and had to be careful.

The next morning, Mo called Eliza..

"I'm afraid Mother's paralysed," she said.. "She can't move at all, and her throat muscles are paralysed as well so she can't swallow. She won't be able to eat, even if she comes 'round. The doctors say she had a terrible chest infection as well."

"I knew her chest was bad," replied Eliza. "The doctor should have given her antibiotics the first time she went last week. Then, maybe none of this would have happened to her."

"The doctors don't think she will live long."

"I have to go and see her," said Eliza.

"The rest of the family and I don't think you should!" said Mo emphatically.

A few days later Eliza insisted on going to see her mother. Luckily, there was a wheelchair handy just inside the hospital entrance. Eliza sat in it, and Dawn quickly pushed her to Tilly's bedside.

The window was open the sunlight shone through, dancing on Tilly's silver hair—the hair that used to be jet black when she was younger.

Eliza was shocked to see how thin her mother had become in the few days since she last saw her. She wet her mother's lips.

"It's me, Mom," she whispered to her, stroking Tilly's arm.

Her eyes fluttered!

"Did you see that?" she asked Dawn.

The nurse came to the bed.

"What treatment is my mother on? She has lost so much weight in a few days."

"None," replied the nurse. "It's kinder to just let her go."

"You mean, starve her to death! My mother has brought nine children up, and worked all her life to feed them. I'm not going to let her starve to death. I can't."

"I will make arrangements for you to speak to the doctor in charge of Tilly."

"The only way we can feed your mother is to put a peg in her stomach," said the doctor, "and that's not advisable. We don't think Tilly knows what's going on. Her brain's damaged beyond repair, and we think she's very near death."

"I know what a peg is, my brother had one in for a couple of years, and we want you to do it. We can't just let her starve to death. And, I'm sure she can hear me. Her eyes flickered as I was speaking to her."

"You will have to sign the form for the anaesthetic and then we will do it at the earliest moment we can."

When they visited Tilly next day, the tube was in place, and Tilly was being fed through it. She looked a lot better she had a tinge of pink in her cheeks. Tilly started moving her arms and legs a few days later, and the nurses sat her in the armchair at the side of her bed for a couple of hours at a time.

Tilly had been deaf for the last few years and wore a hearing aid, so Eliza took it in for her. It was no good talking to her if she had no chance of hearing them, but now they couldn't find it.

"Where's her hearing aid?" she asked Dawn.

"It was probably lost in the sheets that were sent to the laundry."

A few days later Tilly still didn't have her hearing aid, so Mo went to the nurses' office. "How do you expect us to communicate with our mother without her hearing aid? Can you arrange for a new one today, please?"

Tilly started improving even more with her new hearing aid.

Eventually, she was doing well enough to be transferred to another hospital where she could get better physio-therapy. It was in the town where Jim used to sing, and whistle and play the accordion fifty years ago.

"We will soon have her walking again, but she must have good strong shoes, so if you leave the money, someone will come and measure her feet."

They knew what sort of shoe to get, and Tilly slowly started to walk again, although she was still being fed by the tube, but her mind was worse than it was before she had the stroke.

One of the other patients complained, saying Tilly had eaten her banana.

"She can't swallow," replied the nurse.

"Well, she swallowed that."

When Mo went to visit the next day, a nurse called her into the office. "We are going to put Tilly in another ward tomorrow."

"Please don't do that!" pleaded Mo. "She's just settled in here. Why do you want to move her?"

"She pinched someone's banana and ate it."

"That's brilliant," replied Mo. "That means her swallow came back."

When Dawn pushed Eliza in a wheelchair into the ward the next day to see her mother, they discovered that Tilly was gone. They had moved her into the next ward, so Dawn pushed her to the next ward, into the sitting room where they thought Tilly would be, but she wasn't there.

"Where's Tilly?" they asked a nurse.

"She's in that room over there," she replied, pointing to a little side room. What a shock they had! Tilly was lying flat out in the bed, and they couldn't wake her up, she was in a terrible state.

"What's' going on, Nurse?" asked Eliza.

"She's under sedation by orders."

"Whose orders!" exploded Dawn? "You have just undone months of care and work that the other ward gave her."

Eliza and Dawn complained that they want her put back in the other ward. Later that day Tilly was put back in the first ward, but the day before had been such a big trauma for her that she started having seizures. The doctor told them not to expect Tilly to last much longer.

Dawn and Eliza were sitting in the side room with Tilly.

"We are going to sit Tilly in this armchair, now she has come 'round. She's a tough one, your mother," said the nurse.

"She has to be," they replied as the nurses left the room.

Five minutes later Tilly started to have another seizure, so Dawn ran to tell the nurse as Eliza held her mother's head in her arms so she didn't fall out of the chair.

The doctor came running in.

"Can you go outside, please," he asked Eliza.

"Sorry, I'm staying with my mother!" she replied.

He glared at her, and then injected Tilly to try to stop the seizure. Afterwards, she was put into the bed. Both Eliza and Dawn were sure the seizure was brought on by whatever they had given her in the other ward to sedate her.

Despite this, Tilly recovered again, and a few weeks later, she was on her feet again.

"We think this is as good as she's going to get. It's time to think about where she's going to live." Despite the peg still feeding Tilly, she was eating the odd snack as well. "You have to think about putting Tilly in a nursing home. There are only three that take people with the problems Tilly has."

This was the moment, Eliza had been dreading. She had always hoped to be able to take care of her mother, but she knew now that she could not. Eliza couldn't' even look after herself, let alone anyone else.

Mo and Eliza looked at three homes, and they decided on the one nearest to Eliza's house, only a half-mile away. There was space to park right outside the room where Tilly would spend her days with the other residents.

Eliza went every day to see her mother, sitting for hours with her, as did Mo and others in the family. One day, Tilly smiled, her whole face lit up. She held her arms out to Eliza as she came through the open doorway. She grabbed Eliza by the hand, looking straight at her.

"Please take me home," Tilly pleaded, tears welling up in her eyes.

Eliza turned her head the other way as tears trickled down her cheeks. She was gutted. *Has mother's memory returned? Does she have her speech back?* When Eliza was able to look again, her mother's eyes were blank.

There was no way Eliza could look after her mother. And, no way could they afford to hire anyone twenty-four hours a day to look after her.

"I promise I will come back after tea to see you."

When Dean arrived home from work that evening, he found Eliza sobbing.

"What's happened?"

"Mom asked if she could come home today."

"You know that's impossible," he replied, putting his arms 'round her.

"I know, but for that moment, she seemed to have her full faculties, she was looking straight at me."

Later that night the matron phoned Eliza.

"Can you bring Tilly's handbag in. She keeps pinching the bag from the lady in the next chair."

Dawn and Eliza took the handbag in to her. Tilly was sitting, nursing a doll, and she was calling the doll "Mother." Another woman wanted the doll back since it belongs to her.

"Will you nip up town and get Mother a soft toy to hold, see if you can get a nice fluffy dog. She would love that."

Dawn came back with a fluffy lassie dog and puts it on Tilly's lap. Tilly stroked the dog, and then pointed to the doll the other woman was holding and said, "Mother."

Has Tilly's mind gone back to when she was a girl aged ten again? Was she thinking about her mother dying and her baby sister being born?

One day Tilly pulled the tube out of her stomach.

"We are sending her to hospital to put it back in," said one of the nurses at the home.

The doctor there decided Tilly was eating enough without the tube in, so they left it out.

Another day Mo went to visit her mother at dinnertime and was appalled to see her mother sitting in the chair, with the dinner and pudding on the table in front of her. It had gone cold, and Tilly didn't know it was there.

Mo took it into the kitchen and asked for it to be heated up in the microwave, then took it and fed Tilly

Then, as soon as Tilly had enough, Mo went straight to the office and complained. "You must know my mother's not capable of feeding herself."

After that episode, the family made sure someone was there at every feeding time, though Tilly never ate much. Tilly seemed to be going downhill so rapidly, that Eliza got to the point of wishing her mother would go to sleep and not wake up. She hated seeing her like this. Her mother had no quality of life left.

One day, as Mo and Eliza went 'round to the home to visit their mother, a nurse met them at the door. "Your mother isn't very well today, so we left her in bed."

Mo helped Eliza to the lift, and up they went to Tilly's bedroom. Quietly opening the door, they went inside.

Tilly looked awful.

"I never realised Mother had gone that thin," said Eliza.

They tried talking to her, but got no response, so Mo called for a nurse to come in, saying, "We think our mother's in a coma."

The nurse looked at Tilly. "I think she's in a deep sleep."

Mo and Eliza sat there for two hours, damping their mother's lips. Then, later that night, the nurse phoned Eliza. "I think someone should come and sit with your mother, she is poorly."

Biron said he would sit with her that night.

At six o' clock next morning, Eliza's phone rang again—it was the matron. "I think you should come round, Tilly's very ill."

Dean took Eliza 'round to the home on his way to work. "I will take you up to sit with your mother," he said. They walked into the bedroom, where a member of staff was sitting with Tilly.

"I told your brother to go home at two o'clock this morning, to get some sleep," she said. "I have been sitting here all night looking after your mother.".

As Dean left, Mo came in. The nurse, who was at the end of her shift, stood up to leave, put her hand gently on Tilly's arm and whispered, "Goodbye, Tilly, it's been a pleasure to meet you." She stroked Tilly's arm, with tears in her eyes.

Mo and Eliza thanked her. Tilly's other children and the elder grandchildren came to visit her at different times during the day.

At four forty five—tea time—Tilly passed away, with Eliza, Mo, Dawn, and Michael's wife at her side. Tilly was eighty-five years old.

Mo asked if she could use the phone to call her husband.

"You are free to call whoever you like, we will leave you in the office."

Mo then phoned the rest of the family, and her husband called the funeral people up. This time they decided to use a different firm than the one the family had always had before.

"I thought we would give them a try," said Mo. "I have heard they are very good."

"The funeral director's coming to see you tomorrow, Eliza. I have left the rest for you to sort out."

The next day Dean answered the door. "Come in, my wife's in here," he said, showing the young man in.

"My name's Simon," he said. "Can you tell me all about your mother and family?"

"I hope you have all week!" Eliza replied.

Simon at last stood up to go, saying, "I feel like I knew Tilly myself—I will see that Tilly has the funeral fitting for a lady like her."

Tilly had always said she didn't want to be buried, so they decided she would have a service at the village church where she and Jim first met and where they were married. Then there would also be a short service at the crematorium. Eliza's family ordered loads of gladioli, to mingle with the other flowers all over her coffin.

The hearse waited outside Eliza's house. As they climbed in the cars behind their mother, someone whispered, "Tilly's last journey."

It was only a few yards to the end of the road. Simon got out of the hearse, stopped the traffic, and saluted Tilly's coffin as it passed him. Then they all stopped for him to catch up with with the others.

"What a wonderful gesture," said Ken. They then carried on up to the village and the top of the drive where The Tin House had been. The beginning of the drive was still there, but the fields and the gardens were long gone. A new road and housing estate ran through the land where The Tin House proudly stood those years before.

Simon stopped the hearse at the top of the drive, saluting it and Tilly again. They entered the church as the organ softly played 'Waltzing Matilda' as a tribute to their wonderful mother. Doll and Rene were in the church, and so were lots of the kids who had played down at The Tin House. Of course they weren't kids any more. They were grown-ups with their own children—even grandchildren—of their own, and all of them remembered Tilly.

After the service, they followed Tilly to the crematorium. The mourners then met at The Rose and where the family had arranged a buffet, and people were packed in.

"I have an announcement to make," said Mo's daughter. "I wasn't going to say anything yet, but under the circumstances I think I will. I'm two months pregnant!"

There were congratulations all 'round that news certainly cheered everybody up a bit.

Eliza and Dean had to be up early next morning, as it was time for her three-year check up. They had a long day ahead tomorrow.

Was it really three years since my transplant? Eliza thought. The time flew by, probably because she had been visiting her brother and mother for the last three years and hadn't spent much time thinking about her own problems.

CHAPTER 21

A year passed by, and it was time for Derek's check up.

"Christ!" he said, after having his routine biopsy. "I felt that! It seemed as if the needle went straight through to my back."

That night he complained about the pain again, but Derek thought it would be better by tomorrow. It was Saturday night and he had prepared a barbeque, marinating the steak all day, for his stepson's birthday.

As Derek bent down to take the can out of the fridge in the garage, he felt something burst, and blood started pouring out of his neck. He staggered into the house, where his horrified partner called the emergency team.

"Quick, we need an ambulance before he bleeds to death," she said.

Meanwhile, several family members—Joseph, Donna, Dean, Eliza, Sam, his wife, Thomas, Cher, Jay and his wife—were all sitting outside a pub in the evening sunshine, enjoying a drink before they went inside for a meal.

One of the barmen walked towards them. "Is one of you Eliza? There's a phone call for you. The caller says she's your sister."

Eliza wondered how Mo knew where she was.

Donna went to answer the phone. "How did you know we were here?" she asked.

"I rang Dawn she told me," replied Mo. "It's Derek. He's losing a lot of blood. They have taken him to Q.E. Hospital. One of his sons will call me back after they see the doctor, and I will ring back when I know more."

No one felt like eating then, but the meal had been ordered. Twenty minutes later Mo rang back. "Stop panicking, they stopped the bleeding. Derek's having a blood transfusion and he's in good spirits."

The next morning Mo phoned Eliza. "I'm at the hospital. Derek's bleeding again," she said. "They have blood going into both arms." She explained that they were trying to find the surgeon that saved him on so many other occasions. However, they learned that the doctor was on holiday and they couldn't reach him.

According to Mo, a nurse sat next to Derek putting pressure on his veins to stem the flow of blood. She reported that the nurse said he would die if the bleeding didn't stop soon. That night Derek passed away.

God rest his soul.

EPILOGUE

Derek had been cleared of cancer, but all the operations had taken their toll on the veins in his neck, weakening them. He deserved a medal for what he went through.

There are over a hundred in the family now, several quite wealthy, employing a hundred or more people. Tilly and Jim would have been so pleased they had done so well. Eliza's friends, Jill and Janice, have both died. All, Tilly's sons live in big houses and are prospering. Eliza and Dean live in the beautiful cottage that Thomas had lived in. He and his family have moved on to a bigger place. Jay and Thomas have bought 'The Star,' where the family had shared so many happy times together, knocked it down and built twenty-four apartments on the ground where it had stood.

Eliza will be eternally grateful to the people who donated their loved one's lung. That goes equally for the staff at the hospitals, for without them, she wouldn't be here. Last but not least, Eliza would like to thank all her friends and family who supported her through her ordeal.

ABOUT THE AUTHOR

Elizabeth Owen, one of nine children, wrote *The Tin House* to pay tribute to her wonderful parents Tilly and Jim. This is Elizabeth's first book, but it upholds the values she lived with all her life: family, love, loyalty, and helping one another. She was exposed to asbestos for ten years at her job, and also smoked heavily, which started her of on a path that eventually led to a lung transplant. Elizabeth's family included two dearly loved brothers who valiantly battled cancer. Elizabeth, with the help of her family, cared for her mother Tilly, until the last few months of her life. Tilly died at age 86.

Elizabeth and Dean have 5 children, 12 grandchildren, and 3 great granddaughters. The story in this book ends in 1999. In 2004, Jay and Thomas, her sons, bought The Star and Garter where the family shared so many happy times.

There are a lot of people Elizabeth would like to thank for their help with this book: Richard Lanz, for putting her computer right so many times, Melvyn Williams the proofreader, her editor, Kathy Brown, and her publishers, Pam Marin-Kingsley and Coralie Hughes Jensen, for all their hard work on this project.

Printed in the United Kingdom
by Lightning Source UK Ltd.
127486UK00002B/163-192/P